# The Dance of Durga

**Kanika Dhillon** is a screenwriter and author of the bestselling novel *Bombay Duck is a Fish* (2011). An alumnus of the London School of Economics and St Stephens College, Kanika divides her time between writing films and books. She currently resides in Mumbai and is on a quest to live stories and capture them in words. You can connect with her on Facebook and at https://twitter.com/KanikaDhillon

# THE DANCE OF DURGA

Kanika Dhillon

HarperCollins *Publishers* India

First published in India in 2016 by
HarperCollins *Publishers* India

Building 10, Tower A, 4th Floor, DLF Cyber City, Phase II,
Gurugram Haryana – 122002, India
www.harpercollins.co.in

1 2 3 4 5 6 7 8 9 10



P-ISBN: 978-93-5177-710-6
E-ISBN: 978-93-5177-711-3



Typeset in 11/13.4 Adobe Garamond Pro Regular at
MicroPrints India, New Delhi

*For my Father*
*I lost you last winter, on the eve of a new year.*
*I wonder if there is any way, to talk to you one more day*
*And get a chance to say good bye.*
*To you I am forever grateful. I miss you.*
*Love you, Papa.*

'What you seek is seeking you'

– Rumi

# RAJJO

# 1

## August 1971, Gurdaspur, Punjab

JASWINDER, pot-bellied, balding and in his mid-thirties, cursed his luck as he frowned at the old lady sitting on the lone wooden bench in the corner of his shop and muttering to herself. She was eating jalebis from a paper cup. It was a busy day. Jaswinder was swamped with work and rushed customers filed in and out of his cramped shop. Furthermore, he had a headache, the stocks of oil and sugar were running low and he suspected his wife was sleeping with one of the boys who worked in the shop.

With all these worries hovering over him, he was in no mood to babysit the old grouch. She sat grunting in one corner with a narrow cinnamon-coloured face sheathed in wrinkles. Contours crisscrossed her skin, etched with the relentless needle of time. Watery eyes peeped out at the world wearily with a tinge of blue. She had cataract. Her lips were no more than a surly dash that moved while she muttered.

'You rascal, don't you dare tell them where I am hiding. I have seen you grow up naked on our streets.'

Jaswinder shook his head for the hundredth time, ignoring her ramble and went back to attend to an impatient customer. He barked at his teenage employee, 'Gappi, pack a kilo of barfi.'

*Perhaps he could ask Gappi if he knew which one of these boys was fucking his wife on the sly!*

The old woman's hair was covered with a white cotton dupatta, rumpled with time and age. A few wispy white strands fell rebelliously on the brown face. There was some white hair on her chin. Perhaps that was her licence to be senile.

'Why don't you go home, Mata-ji, your son must be worried about you!' Jaswinder hoped she would scoot soon.

'Let the rascals worry, they won't listen to me, they won't believe me, they won't let me name my granddaughter! Here, give me some more!' She stretched out her cup assertively to be refilled with the sugary sweet.

Jaswinder feared the old lady, easily ninety-plus, if not more, would die in his shop from a sugar high, but what he feared more than her dying in his shop was that she would create a scene in front of the customers. He better refill her cup. He was going to whack Gappi for allowing her to sit here in the first place.

'I told you not to entertain her,' he told Gappi.

'She said she was dying of thirst, so I gave her water and she wanted to sit and drink it. Now you are serving her sweets!' Gappi's accusatory tone irked him.

Jaswinder gave the insolent boy a stare. Gappi was getting too big for his boots!

*Rascal!*

The old woman's nasal voice rose. 'The idiots don't get it! I saw Goddess Durga in my dream a week ago! She said I was going to have a granddaughter soon, name her after me!'

Jaswinder rolled his eyes, 'Next time she pays you a visit, just ask her what colour should I paint my shop walls so that it will turn out to be auspicious and increase my sales!'

Gappi and a few patrons tittered and that enraged the old woman.

'You rascal!' the old woman spouted in anger and turned her beady eyes to the customers in the shop. Wagging her index finger she warned them, 'Don't take his sweets, he reuses the oil and the houseflies have nested on his ingredients.' Saying this and muttering profanities, she slunk out of his shop.

A patron, almost ready to bite into a succulent creamy pedha, stopped midway.

'You will see, she will be Durga, and she is meant for great things!'

The customer eyed the old woman as she dawdled away. With a jaundiced eye he studied his sweet. A radio played a Punjabi song somewhere inside the shop.

Jaswinder cleared his throat, 'Don't mind her, she is senile. So you were saying, three-kilo barfi, and two-kilo jalebi? Should I get them packed?'

'No, actually, I am not sure, I will just confirm with my wife and get back.' The patron scurried out, not wanting to look at Jaswinder but clearly a little put off by the old lady's insinuations.

Jaswinder abused the old lady under his breath. 'Next time that old hag saunters into the shop, just shoo her away!' He ordered the lanky teen, Gappi, who was least bothered with what was going on between the master, the old lady and the patrons. He wanted to get it over with and go fuck the boss's wife whilst he was ostensibly helping her with chores. She gave him nice food after the sex. Bliss!

The old lady continued her jabbering all the way to the end of the lane, annoying Jaswinder no end. It made the boy smirk. Thankfully for Jaswinder, she turned the corner and he could breathe a sigh of relief.

Just then a worried-looking man, Kartar, in his early thirties, robust and well-built, wearing a white crumpled kurta over his lungi, entered the shop. His turban was half done and beads of sweat glistened on his face.

'Sorry, have you seen my mother, Veerji, she has run away again!'

'Yes! She has gone that way! And why don't you keep her chained! She is a menace!' Yelled Jaswinder as the son, Kartar Singh Kahlon, sprinted out of the shop, hoping to find his absconding mother in the bustling market.

The two men searched for the old women in all the places she usually ran away to. Kartar hoped he would find his mother in one of the small shop units around Hanuman Chowk, or on one of the benches in a dingy sweet shop in Kabootri Darwaza. Streaks of worry and anger marred his face. His wife, Saroj, was due to deliver any time and the constant bickering between her and his mother over the past week about naming the unborn child had left him in a thunderous mood. And there were bikes and cycles piled up in his repair shop to fix. He also needed to make another trip and drive a delivery truck to Himachal and back that would cover the extra cost expected to be incurred during the baby's delivery. He knew his wife was barely managing. He needed to hire another puncture repair boy. Perhaps he could ask one of his friends. If only he had a son, instead of two daughters, he could have him do the odd jobs here and there.

Kartar focused his tired eyes on the busy, narrow streets. Wares from shops encroached upon the already narrow lane, making it difficult to walk down. Fabrics in bright yellow, apricot, indigo and sapphire hung along the street. Ladies in colourful suits milled about as men towed cartons on handcarts and rickshaws. There was no sign of his mother.

'Why has she run away now?' asked Moga, his friend and neighbour, who was an electrician by profession and worked in the fields for additional income. Moga was fair with green eyes. People always wondered where the lightness came from, given both his parents were on the darker side with eyes as black as soot. Moga tried to hide his lightness with an ample beard that was also brown in colour. He was referred as 'Bhoora' (the one with light eyes and light beard) by the villagers mockingly.

'She and Saroj are bickering again! I want to kill myself! She had a bloody dream where some goddess came and told her Saroj will have a daughter and to name her Durga. Saroj insists she wants to name her Rajjo or something!'

'Durga!' Moga rolled the name around his tongue, testing it. 'Strange.'

'Is that the only thing you find strange in all this?' Kartar rolled his eyes, sweltering in the heat, looking up at the sky hoping for some mercy and rain. The crops and grounds were parched and dry. The rains were delayed and the unease was growing.

'Can she ask the goddess next time she meets her if I am going to have another boy next time around?! Or are we getting any rain sometime soon. I am worried!'

But Kartar was gone in a jiffy, running after an old woman and almost picking her up from behind, screaming. 'Biji!

What the hell is wrong with you?'

The old woman turned and whacked Kartar repeatedly. She was clearly not his absconding old mother.

'Don't you have mothers and sisters at home! Outraging my modesty on the road!'

Kartar, slightly taken aback by the response, cleared his throat and added sheepishly,'I thought you were my mother. Sorry!'

The old woman squinted at him 'Is that the line these days!'

He could hear Moga laughing behind him all the way to the rickety bike.

Biji was sitting by the side of a busy freeway at a lone dhaba, overlooking a carpet of green fields. Her nose twitched. Armed with a dismal face and a woeful expression, she hoped the gaunt sweaty man frantically baking rotis in the round tandoor would pass her some.

*The bloody fool useless son of mine hasn't been able to find me yet!*

She was hoping Kartar would look for her here, as the last two times she was found sitting on this road. She was tired and hungry now. Their house was another twenty-minute walk away and Biji was in no mood to do the trek. They lived in a small village near Dhaliwal. Biji usually escaped to Gurdaspur city if she got bored or wanted to hide from the family. She went back to ogling the man baking rotis in the tandoor.

*Perhaps the sweaty bugger hasn't seen me.*

The old woman crawled closer to the guy. She could smell the freshly baked tandoori rotis. The man did not even pause to glance at her. He wore a singlet, his clammy shirt discarded. One hand crudely tied in reams of cloth was acting as a baking glove. He was feverishly taking out hot, crispy breads that a helper was plating and rushing to the main kitchen inside.

Biji coughed to announce her presence.

*Asshole, look up once at the old woman dying here!*

She moved closer. Biji could almost peep into the tandoor, a circular mud structure with bread stuck to the sides turning light hazel and fluffy with the heat.

'Go away!'

The man muttered without looking up.

'You dog! One loaf of bread is not going to kill you! I had a dream that my granddaughter will be born tomorrow. She will be named after Goddess Durga and all of you will be chanting her name! Better still, I will come as a ghost in your dreams when I die, and scare the living day lights out of you!'

The man, unperturbed, continued slapping fresh flattened dough inside the tandoor walls and removing the round, baked, brown ones.

Biji tried a fainting spell, and immediately the man flung a fresh piece of roti her way.

'I am not carrying you to the hospital.'

'Why must you make me faint then … and only one! You miser!' Biji straightened up.

While Biji was wondering if she could wheedle a couple more for her two little granddaughters at home, and perhaps one for that surly daughter-in-law Saroj, she saw her son with that fair neighbour Moga trailing behind.

*These buggers with light eyes can never be trusted! Bloody Bhoora!*

Biji had to do the fainting spell again, so they would put her in the rickshaw and take her home. She hid her roti in the little cloth bag hanging on her thin gnarled hand and with a move perfected over two decades, fainted.

Kartar and Moga rushed over just in time to catch her.

'What now?' Moga wondered

'At least she will not be eating our head on the way back!' muttered Kartar as he collected his mother in his arms, cradling her like a child.

'She has taken a roti from here, you wanna pay up?' The cheeky man baking the bread commented.

'Bastard! You can count your rotis when God takes you to hell!' Biji erupted like a volcano shaking Kartar who almost dropped the terror from his hands. Biji directed her wrath towards the surprised son.

'You better hold on properly to me! Tomorrow Durga is coming, I want to die after I see her face… You hear me! And that's what you name her Durga, else I am not coming back home with you!'

At home, Saroj was hoping they would not find her mother-in-law until she had delivered her baby. She was a ravishing, tall woman with pale skin and amber eyes. Biji constantly remarked over her pale complexion, wondering where it came from and insinuated Saroj's grandmother had taken a lover. She was sure it was the handsome foreign student who had come down to complete some project in the village. He smiled at everyone in the village and offered the pretty girls sweets. Biji had her eyes on him but Saroj's grandmother had swooped in on him.

Saroj was convinced Biji was the devil incarnate, sent on earth to torment her. She sat on a high stool with a swollen belly. The sweat trickled down her back and her little hand fan didn't do much to help. Kartar had also put a small table fan in the open kitchen where Saroj cooked the meals and everyone sat around to eat in a corner of the courtyard. The kitchen enclosure had a raised muddy platform with a stove. Steel utensils, blackened with heat over time, piled up on each other and struggled for space. The entire house was a mix of brick and mud.

A pot simmered on the stove as she tinkered with the wood and burnt cowdung used as fuel to cook with. She went back to chopping the vegetables but it was uncomfortable to even sit on the stool. The smoke was becoming unbearable for her. She stirred the broth one last time and covered the pot to simmer. Her two little girls – Rano, aged four and Reet, aged five, sat giggling next to her, lost in their own world, playing with the tea set made from mud that she had bought at a fair last year. Half the set was broken.

As Saroj shifted her weight again, she hoped the old fusspot was wrong and it was a boy. Even if it was a girl there was no way in hell she was going to name her Durga.

The heat stifled her, perhaps she should pour herself a cool glass of buttermilk. *If only the bloody rains would grace them!* An earthen pot placed on a wooden frame to girdle the curd and make buttermilk sat ready, but Saroj had no energy left in her to lift a finger. Her gaze went to the jumble of green feathers and a cherry-coloured beak – their parrot Totu – who was unusually quiet today.

A couple of chickens ran around the courtyard as Saroj sharply ordered the girls, 'Make sure the doors are latched, I don't have the strength to run after these two now!'

Just then the doors opened, the girls squealed in delight, and the parrot howled at the disruption. It was her husband carrying her crafty, raw-boned mother-in-law back into the house.

*God help me! I hope she dies soon! Or at least before the baby comes.*

*Is she dead already?*

*No, I haven't said goodbye to her yet!*

A frightened look crossed her face.

'Don't worry, she just fainted!'

*Ah! She is back to her drama!*

Saroj would never admit the relief she felt.

They sprinkled some water over the old lady's face as the girls huddled around her.

'Durga, her name is Durga and she will rule the world, you see. She is destined for greatness! She is God's child! The world will know her! You all will know I was right!' She turned to plead to her son, 'You have to promise me you will name her Durga! And not Rajjo! This Saroj is just acting difficult! On cue her head swivelled accusingly in Saroj's direction. 'You will also be a grandmother one day, you see how your daughter-in-law treats you. I will be laughing at you from up there!' Her index finger pointed to the heavens above.

Saroj rolled her eyes, going back to chopping her vegetables.

# 2

RANO wore her special red frock as she stood in the Jaggery makers' compound, waiting for him to pack their stuff. Crushed, dry sugarcane piled up in the compound. A machine that chewed and ate up fleshy sugarcanes to collect the sweet juice that trickled from them was placed in the centre of the entire operation.

A wooden cot stood on its last legs, a few blackened drums dotted the area, a baby cooed, tied in a scarf hanging like a hammock between two poles. A woman rested on the cot next to the baby, her face and hair covered with an orange scarf.

A middle-aged man stirred the simmering copper coloured mixture in a giant pot, a cloud of smoke filling up his lungs. The sugarcane juice was directly fed into this giant iron vessel with fire smouldering below it. Rano knew the man needed to stir the mix continuously for three hours or so, till the gleaming liquid became semi-solid.

Long spoons were used to stir the mix. Next to the black kadhai, there was a big wooden crate lying on the ground where the hot, thickened sugarcane mix was poured in. Rano could bet the entire moon could fit in here. The mold held a semi-solid batter, thick and dark yellow in colour. A dirty cloth was placed next to the mold, with uneven balls of jaggery laid out to dry like cakes of cowdung, only glittery and golden in colour.

In this corner, where they stood, an old man was collecting hardened balls of the thickened mixture that must have been left overnight to dry. Most of the compound was covered with limp sugarcane leftovers.

Rano loved the smell of burning sugarcane and sweetness, mingled with mud and the fields. She could barely stop smiling, careful not to let her sister Reet notice her happiness.

Rano knew it was a momentous occasion. This frock she wore was carefully wrapped in the trunk and her mother had laid it out for her a day before she had been rushed from the house, crying, in the middle of the night. There was a special yellow dress for Reet too, which she had refused to wear and Reet was in her normal crumpled clothes.

Rano was worried for her mother last night, as she was being taken from the house, crying and grunting in pain, till Reet told her they usually cry and are swollen like a buffalo before a baby arrives.

Rano had woken up early, at the crack of dawn and worn this frock (she had only worn it thrice before, on happy occasions or when someone important was coming home!). It even had an old limp bow on it. Someone had given it to her mother, and her mother had mended the hemline to Rano's size.

Rano's heart was beating rapidly as she remembered her grandmother's words. Lying on her cot in the courtyard, her grandmother had whispered to Rano through the night that she was going to get a sister who was going to change their lives. She was going to take them away from this village to beautiful unknown lands; the world would bow to her! Most importantly, the grandmother had told her that Rano was in charge of taking care of her, not Reet.

She said Reet was jealous.

Rano beamed with excitement and Reet stood with a surly expression on her face. Reet resented her mother's preoccupation with the new baby on the way.

The old grandmother had dragged the little girls to the sweet-maker, to get some gud (sugar made from sugarcane juice) packed. She was going to get Moga's wife to make sweet brown rice, to welcome her granddaughter in the neighbourhood.

Suddenly there was a squeal of delight. The man stirring the mixture, the woman resting on the cot and the grandmother all looked up at the sky with relief and excitement. The nebulous clouds hung low.

'I can smell the rain,' muttered the grandmother triumphantly.

'Move your hands faster old man, Durga is not going to wait for you to finish packing our gud.' She badgered the old man.

Rano wanted the man to quickly hand over their stuff so they could get back home to welcome this wonderful baby.

The man wore a dirty brown shirt and pants, squatting on the floor with a toothless grin. He was in no hurry.

Rano eyed the basket next to the old man, from where he fished out round, almost crooked cakes of solidified gud (jaggery), and packed them for the impatient customers. He placed the gud in an old newspaper as the grandmother mumbled in excitement. 'We have been sweltering in the heat and see what day the clouds chose to grace us! When Durga is getting home!' As if on cue, the wind picked up. The tang of mud and water and rain made Rano heady and she wanted to dance with excitement.

The green fields glistened in the sun. A gust of wind kissed the fields playfully, making the leaves sway delicately. Rano was going to remember this day forever.

The trio reached their house, and stopped short when they heard the cry of a baby.

'She is here!'

The grandmother screeched happily and ran inside.

Rano stood, awestruck at the scene. Her tired looking mother and father were holding the baby.

'It's a girl.' Kartar announced to the mother. Patting the baby's head. And added almost immediately.

'I have to leave tonight. I am taking up the Himachal delivery.'

'Stay tonight. It's Rajjo's first day at home,' Saroj whispered.

'Rajjo! You mean Durga!' The old woman screamed. She kissed the baby five times, gazing at it like it was a treasure. Saroj weary and tired, wanted to whack the old woman and go to sleep.

She was gobbling up the gud in her excitement at seeing the baby.

The baby was crying.

The thunder hit the skies and sweet rain drenched the entire village.

The old woman screamed. 'Don't you see, the heavens are welcoming her! She has come and the drought has gone!'

'Yes! I can hear the bugles all the way from heaven!' Saroj muttered, annoyed.

The old woman, unperturbed by the jibe, danced with Rano like a child as the rain spattered into their courtyard.

Saroj cursed the woman as she picked the baby girl and went to sit under a shade, worried about her clothes hanging on the clothesline getting soaked in the rain.

'Girls clear everything from the courtyard! Now!' Saroj asked in a tired voice.

'Durga Durga Durga!' The old woman screamed. Making the girls giggle at their grandmother's outburst.

And that was when it happened. The rain kept falling but the old woman stopped shrieking and fell dead.

A silence followed, only to be broken by the gurgling laugh of a baby who seemed amused. Saroj looked at the strange scene unfold in front of her.

'Let's name her Durga,' said Kartar, closing his mother's dead eyes gently. She looked happy. That was a relief. Tears streamed down his face.

Saroj just left the gurgling baby on the cot and went inside. She needed to breathe. The baby started crying again, till Rano took her in her tiny arms and cradled her to sleep.

It rained the entire night. The girls cried for their grandmother and so did Saroj. The baby girl slept peacefully through the night and the morning after, a few villagers came to pay their last respects to Biji.

Saroj quietly collected Biji's things and put them in a box. She was not ready to let it go just yet so she shoved the box under the bed. Her hand lingered a minute longer to touch the cold steel of the case. A tear escaped her eye till her newborn baby claimed her attention with its shrieking.

Durga a.k.a. Rajjo had announced her arrival into the world.

# 3

RAJJO, all of five now, was sitting with Rano, now nine, and their surly beautiful sister Reet, who was ten. They held on to their books half-heartedly as they sat watching the fields. They watched their neighbours, uncles and aunts work. They could smell the ripened, golden wheat cut and placed in tiny mounds, dotting the shaved fields.

They were still wearing their school uniforms; limp orange shirts and blue salwars. Threadbare red ribbons trailed down their braids. Reet's was perfectly woven into her plait but Rajjo's was all over the place. Her luscious, thick, curly hair glistened in the evening light. Her face looked radiant and untouched. She was dusky in colour with striking tan eyes that made you stare at her for a second longer. Her mouth was a perfect bow. She had a heart-shaped face, tawny eyes, she was willowy and sported a defiant chin. Reet knew she had serious competition in Rajjo. Rano was pretty, but Rajjo was fiercely beautiful. Her hair, unlike the other sisters', fell in ringlets of curls, a curtain of velvety satin.

She hated that most about Rajjo. Her beauty. Otherwise she did not mind her rebellious sister's escapades.

Their fourth sister Rikki, who was three, was playing with the broken tea-set. The older sisters were supposed to mind the younger one but they were unmindful that she was chewing mud.

The girls looked on as their mother prepared dinner and monitored the evening fodder for the cows, and their father drove a truck to some place south. He travelled a lot lately. However, he never came back emptyhanded from any of his trips. He always got them little tokens, whether it was needed or not, like Rajjo got a plastic toy bus that she could not think of anything to do with. Reet had already dismissed her gift, knowing her father had absentmindedly picked up something on the way. Rano on the other hand, collected hers and everyone else's and hoarded them in her special trunk that she had festooned with ornaments and trims. Her mother would fondly call her the 'hoarder'. She had an inquisitive nature and collected things to put them to some good use, be it-discarded clothes, toys, bedsheets.

Rano loved toying with numbers. She knew their mother was proud of her financial acumen and the thought made her belly swell with a warm, secure feeling.

Rajjo inhaled the smell of freshly cut wheat. Her neighbour Karam worked alongside his father and mother in the field. Karam was striking with his pale colouring and light eyes like his father. His mother had a pale leaf coloured dupatta tied around her head covering her nose and mouth like a dacoit. She had a sickle in her hand that moved deftly in bold, confident strokes. Moga also wore a dark cloth covering his eyes and face. Except Karam, everyone had covered their faces. Karam had removed it when he had seen Rajjo and party looking on.

Rajjo smiled at Karam and looked up at the beautiful cantaloupe-coloured sky. The sun wove golden civvies in the horizon. An old man wearing a loongi and a kurta thrashed bales of wheat on a round circular drum.

Just then Rajjo noticed a swanky tractor pass, followed closely by a lofty gleaming car with tinted windows. A proud beast gliding on the roads arrogantly. People wearing flashy sunglasses stepped out to take pictures with their cameras. They looked affluent, like they'd descended from another world, fascinated by the peasants who were gathering wheat in the fields with their faces covered. Their cameras clicked away, like they'd spotted exotic animals.

Something rose inside Rajjo, she wanted to run up and snatch the camera and see for herself how they saw them through their own lens.

Having taken a few shots, the travellers went on their way.

'Mom says they wear new clothes everyday, shop, eat at restaurants, and have rooms each to themselves, with separate bathrooms,' Rano muttered enviously. A tinge of wonderment glimmered in her eye. Her cheeks had turned a delicate shade of pink.

'We too shall have all that and more,' Rajjo stated quietly with an impenetrable resolve.

'Huh! Your prince charming will descend here in his big swanky car and take you away from all this? As if! Dream on!' mocked Reet.

Rajjo ignored the barb and got busy looking at the blades of ripe wheat glistening in the last ray of sunlight. 'It's going to rain tomorrow, they won't be able to finish storing the wheat if they don't work through the night!'

A woman working in the field close to the sisters stopped her work and glared at Rajjo.

Reet sprinted to the house and came back with their angry mother in tow, who immediately whacked Rajjo across the face twice.

'How many times have I told you not to speak ill! You have a kaali zubaan, what you say happens! Don't talk rubbish!'

'It's not rubbish, it's going to rain tomorrow!' Rajjo looked at her mother with defiant eyes. She was sure in her knowledge, and baffled that her mother would not make good use of it.

Saroj dragged the little girl by the ear towards the house.

Tears streamed down little Rajjo's eyes from the pain of having her ear pulled by her mother. But Rajjo was damned if she was going to whimper or apologize. She had done nothing wrong.

'If you are sure you are not in the wrong and stating the truth, you should not be afraid to say it!' Rajjo muttered.

'The teacher told her this in the school!' Rano quickly muttered trying to shield her sister from more thrashing.

'No, I read it myself!' Rajjo countered haughtily.

Rano rolled her eyes.

'They will burn you like a witch! How many times have I told you to keep your mouth shut in public! You should have gone with your senile grandmother!'

Saroj, hassled, screamed at the girl as they reached her compound.

'And stop reading those godforsaken books the whole day and getting stupid ideas. I am going to burn them!' Saroj screamed.

'Truth is like a vast tree which yields more and more fruit – the more you nurture it.' Saroj paused seeing the defiance in the girl. 'Mahatma Gandhi said this, burn him too!' said the cantankerous Rajjo.

Saroj impulsively slapped her daughter again. Rajjo had a quick tongue that angered her, and it did not help that the little scoundrel had an elephant's memory. Everything she saw, read, glanced was stored away in her camera eye. Nothing escaped her keen gaze.

Rajjo's face was streaked with red angry marks.

Guilt attacked Saroj immediately at the beautiful tear-stricken face and red ears, the eyes still defiant. She was her most beautiful born out of the four sisters and one brother. All the girls were pretty in a conventional way, but this one had a fierceness that made her stand out. The other girls had pale milky skin and straight silky hair, but not Rajjo.

She wanted to reach out and hug this stubborn, obstinate kid who baffled her.

'I will go, I will fall in love and elope with a man who will take me away from this all!' Rajjo stuck her nose up in the air and sniffled with resolve.

Totu, on cue, screamed from the cage as if underlining the prophecy.

Saroj just sat looking at the girl straighten her limp shirt, wipe her tears and walk out of the room like a princess adjourning her meeting. She walked with her back straight, head held high, regal demeanor. She was a princess in a village of paupers, all right.

*What if that old hag was right about Rajjo?*

*Can you stop screaming, Totu!*

Saroj was convinced Totu carried the dead mother-in-law's soul, always excited when Rajjo was around.

With that thought Saroj marched out to gather the rest of her kids, slinging Sheru, her one-year-old son over her shoulder. Sheru gurgled and giggled as Totu screamed, and Saroj looked at the dusky sky and wished the impending rain away. It looked unlikely, but Saroj had learnt not to undermine the girl's prophecies. She would light a lamp with a special prayer tonight for rains and clouds to pass them by.

Saroj and her little girls were busy making sure plastic sheets covered everything in the courtyard, in case it rained again.

As predicted by Rajjo, the untimely rain arrived with the approaching dawn in sudden savage showers. It had damaged the standing crops that were waiting to be stored and sold. After a whole morning of deluge, the rain slowed down to a drizzle and the household was bustling as Saroj and her daughters put their house in order.

Saroj warned the girls not to tell their father that Rajjo had predicted something and it had turned out to be right yet again.

She counted the little girls scurrying around and as usual Rajjo was missing.

'Where is she?'

'She went to throw the trash out and is stuck there, standing by the bridge. She has been there for an hour now, useless oaf! I bet she is going to get us in trouble by just standing there!' Reet muttered as she herded the cows back into the courtyard from where they had been sheltered.

Rano was constantly on the lookout for Rajjo. Now she could see her huddled in the corner staring at the bridge of the village. Her pale green frock was billowing in the wind. The rickety bridge made of dry bamboo logs put together with iron nails was the focus of her attention. It was built over a canal where kids bathed with the cows and buffalos in hot summer months.

Only today the canal was overflowing. The current was really strong. Across the bridge were fields followed by the railway tracks. They could hear the shrieking trains and hooting engines come and go and knew the timings by heart as well.

Rano saw her mother glaring at her and quickly finished wiping the floor. 'Can I go and call her? It's drizzling now, it may start to pour later,' Rano enquired.

'Asslicker,' Reet goaded Rano with disdain.

Ignoring Reet's sarcasm, Saroj nodded and Rano bounded out of the house, gathering a plastic sheet for protection over her head, calling out to her favourite sister.

'Rajjjjjjooooooo!'

Of course, Rano was in no hurry to come back. She had gone to call her sister, but obviously she was hooked on to something Rajjo was telling her. Saroj knew eventually she would herself have to go to fetch the girls.

Reet marched off to do the needful, and then so did Rikki as she did not want to be left behind when her sisters were getting into trouble. It was always fun to watch! While Saroj washed the utensils and finished some household chores, she could hear some hubbub outside. She peeped through the open door and could see from a distance that a few people had gathered around the little girls and there seemed to be a commotion.

Saroj gathered Sheru, deftly placing him on her right hip like a piece of luggage, and ran towards her girls.

She could hear Rajjo's voice trailing towards her. 'I am telling you I have been sitting here all day to tell people that the bridge will collapse, don't get on it!'

Saroj knew this time Rajjo had crossed the line. She was going to thrash the girl.

'She is just talking nonsense.' Saroj butted in.

'She says these weird things,' a neighbour muttered.

'She comments on the rain and it happens.' Karam's mother looked at Rajjo accusingly.

'No, it wasn't her!' Karam immediately defended her, lowering his eyes, stared down by his mother.

A few villagers stepped on the bridge as Rajjo was being dragged back by Reet and her mother.

'No! They are going to fall!'

And as soon as the words were uttered, there was a deafening sound and the rickety bridge crumbled into the gurgling angry water.

There was a brief shocked silence before Karam and a few boys plunged into the water to catch the ladies screaming and waving their hands in panic.

Rajjo felt a slash across her face. Saroj had slapped her. Her cheeks were red and for a minute she could not see clearly.

She was just trying to help, and could not understand why was she being punished yet again.

The ripened wheat fields, now soiled and laden with stacks of wet wheat, stood towards the west, the rows of green vegetable fields spread far and beyond, glistened in the aftermath of rain, like they were scrubbed and spruced up nicely. The wind picked up, the rain fell, women cried for help as Rajjo was being dragged away.

'Fine, I will let everyone die and never open my mouth, can you let go of my hair now?'

Saroj could see that the girl's face had almost swollen, her lips trembled and her eyes were moist, her chin defiant. Saroj let go of her in a moment of weakness.

Rajjo simply marched inside the house. She crossed the woven manjis which had become soddy because of the rain water and remembered that if their father got back tonight, he would scream at them for not covering them from the sleet.

*But if he heard about the bridge…well nevermind, I am going to run away any way.*

Totu yelled with excitement as Rajjo passed by with tired feet and burning face.

The girls were dressed in their Sunday best. Reet was now fifteen, Rano fourteen, Rajjo ten, Rikki six, and Sheru three. Their mother had come to visit her sister in a nearby village after a year.

The kids were asked to sit on a wooden charpoy with their books they had carried, and study.

Saroj threatened them with dire consequences on the way if anyone of them misbehaved or moved about.

They were all to behave like dogs, thought Rajjo.

'We should be on a leash when she comes to visit her sister!'

'Shut up and don't get us into trouble' Reet commented, running her hand through her hair and pulling at her chest, trying to make it look bigger. She pulled her dupatta lower and looked coyly at the boy standing next to a tea shop.

The shop was small, with four cardboard walls; sweets and eateries were crammed inside. Packets of colourful potato chips were strung on one wall and biscuits had been put up for sale on the shelves. Two wooden tables faced each other where patrons sat and enjoyed the tea served with the savouries that were for sale.

'Oh! Now they are going to look at each other all the time,' muttered Rano, noticing Reet blush as the boy checked her out.

Rajjo giggled.

She took in the open area she was sitting in. This was outside their aunt's house. It had an open porch overlooking mustard fields. Rajjo liked the place. They had six or seven cows and buffalos tied to the logs.

On one side they had the toku machine where a helper was cutting fodder for the cattle. The wheel whirred incessantly, as the machine sprouted out minced and chopped leaves. The dark sunburned arms of the man who worked the machine were chiselled and his torso was bathed in sweat.

The tinkling of bells caught her eye again. An old man was extracting mustard oil in the corner. The cow had a bell on her neck and a lot of paraphernalia with ropes that attached her to a wooden apparatus, that moved in loops as the cow moved in circles. A straight rope from her neck was linked to an arm that moved inside a circular pot where the old man was putting the mustard seeds.

'She must be cursing him…the cow,' muttered Rano.

'No, she is hoping she is working hard enough to feed the old man!' Rajjo explained.

Rano thought about it. 'Can you really tell what the cow is thinking?' Rano asked in disbelief.

'What do you think?' Rajjo smiled mysteriously. She loved the fact that Rano was almost deferential with Rajjo's knowledge and prophecies.

'Rajjo, move to your left. I need to sit that side!' Reet commanded.

Rajjo could see the boy had moved his position and Reet wanted to be in his line of vision.

Just then their little brother tugged at Reet's arm and pointed to a sweet longingly, as a woman was buying it from the teashop. They were little circles of orange batter sprinkled with sugar syrup. *Jalebis.*

'Sheru, I don't have the money and stop pointing at the lady.'

A miffed Reet muttered.

'He is hungry, we haven't eaten for four hours, go in and tell mother…' Rajjo turned to Rano.

'We are guests here, they will offer us food, mom just about has the bus fare…don't embarrass her,' Reet grunted.

Rajjo was staring at the fat lady feeding her son and enjoying the eateries.

Sheru made a puppy face and looked at Rajjo.

'I am going in to get something for him.'

'Don't be stupid! She is going to get mad at us and take us back home right away!'

Reet obviously wanted to be admired a little more and she was in no mood of changing the scenario and getting her screaming mother to make a scene in front of her potential Romeo.

'Don't you think he has seen enough of you?' Rano blurted.

A whack followed.

'Rajjo stay here, I am warning you. Why don't you use your special skills and smile at the tea shop guy? And tell him we are from the neighbouring village and give him our address…so he can deliver some sweets perhaps, if need be?'

'Why don't I call that boy with long hair and just whisper it in his ear so he can come and ogle at you some more and father can break his legs as well?'

'Go to hell!' Reet butted in.

Rajjo marched to the tea shop and looked at the lady.

The fat lady looked at her weirdly. And then her expression changed from amusement to disdain as soon as Rajjo made this request.

'Can I have a piece for my brother?'

'Get lost and don't look at my son's food, he will have a stomach ache.'

Rajjo had a sudden flash as her face paled.

'Don't make him sleep on the terrace tonight. There is a snake in your house, you have a room on the terrace… he will come from there and bite him.'

The woman stared at the girl for a minute. Shocked that she knew the layout of her house and that they slept on the terrace, she just picked up her son and left without paying for the sweets, leaving the hapless shopkeeper screaming at her to come back.

The tinkling of bells from the cow and the sniffling of her brother were the only things she heard before she closed her eyes. She was going to have a tough night.

'They are calling her a witch…' Rikki whispered to Rano.

'She is special,' Rano countered.

'Please! She pretends.' Reet snarled.

'The bridge?'

'Any idiot could tell it was collapsing. She had been watching it for hours!' Reet muttered.

'The rain!'

'She can smell it… half the village can! I can tell now too!' Reet continued haughtily.

'This boy and the snake?'

'She scared them out of their wits for amusement. Wait till I tell mother – she is going to get it!' Saying that, Reet sauntered in as the bells tinkled and the cow moved in circles hoping the old man would make enough money to feed his family before the droughts hit them.

Rajjo and Rano sat at the railway tracks waiting for Reet to finish with the boy. Rajjo looked at Rano with a naughty conspiring glance, and with mutual consent, they simultaneously ran behind the large mountain of wheat stack to take a peek. Reet and the boy were in the middle of the field, cocooned by foliage. A small bambi sprouted a thick stream of water into a circular pond a little distance away on their left. The young boys and girls dived into the pool on hot sultry days.

Rajjo craned her neck to take a better look at the couple. The boy was from the tea stall. He was struggling to get a hold on Reet's breasts from under her blouse. He moved feverishly like a man possessed.

Rajjo and Rano stifled a giggle.

'That's what the whole hulla-hoo is about?' muttered Rano, almost disappointed. Rajjo noticed the tell-tale flush on her pale cheeks.

'I am sure it feels great to be in love,' Rajjo sighed.

'Do you think this is love?' Rano enquired with a disappointed look on her face.

'Could be,' Rajjo said.

Just then the guy moaned from the fields, and so did Reet.

'It's gross!' muttered Rano as they ran back to watch a train go by with the wind kissing their faces, arms outstretched like they were flying.

'When I grow up I want to be a fairy!' shouted Rano.

'When I grow up I want to fall in love!' screamed Rajjo. 'And run away!'

They could hear Reet and the boy making the tall stems in the fields sway again, oblivious to the world. The grunts and the moans continued.

'How long are they going to be like that?' wondered Rano.

'Till one of them wants to pee, I guess?' muttered Rajjo, looking up at the beautiful blue sky chasing a cloud.

'Where will you run away to?' Rano enquired, chewing a blade of grass, hoping that she would take her along when she decided.

'That doesn't matter, I haven't decided yet, but running away is the point!'

They both squealed in delight as a blob of rain fell on their faces.

'Can I come along?' Rano asked hopefully.

Rajjo's answer was drowned in the noise of a shrieking oncoming train.

# 4

KARAM, tall, handsome and light-eyed, invited shy glances from the ladies who had gathered in the courtyard in their finest silks. It was just after five and the festivities added a sweet caramel flavour to the evening. Rajjo's house sparkled with flowers and smell of the feasts being prepared in the back of the house. The cows and the calves ignored the mingling crowd and stood in their corner. In the milieu of merry-making, Karam's eyes searched for Rajjo. She had turned nineteen last week and had fought with Karam because he had not got any gift for her. While his eyes searched for her, the ladies in the courtyard devoured the handsome man. The younger lot looked on, hopeful for his restless gaze to settle on them even briefly.

Groups of ladies sat around a woman working with a henna cone, drawing intricate designs on their outstretched palms. Reet, the bride, had covered her arms and feet in henna motifs as a mark of festivity and celebration. She was getting ready to meet her husband soon, and hoped for a dark tinge when she scraped off the dried henna from her body. It was believed darker the colour, deeper the bonding with the mother-in-law.

To the family's pride and relief, Reet was marrying well. The groom's family had come in their own tractor and they owned a white Omni van as well. Everything seemed to flow smoothly but Reet was acting like a crazed bride, with her entire focus on the cameraman who had taped the event. She wanted him to capture her from every angle.

Her errant podgy brother, regardless of the camera or the taping, ran helter-skelter, inviting Reet's wrath, and their mother was having a tough time controlling her daughter and gently reminding her to act like a bride.

As Karam made his way through the festivities and deluge of women folk, he wondered when Rajjo would get married to him. Will her henna have any colour at all, given his own mother's obvious dislike for Rajjo? Karam shrugged the unpleasant feeling away and hunted for her.

'She will be your undoing! She will ruin your life, mark my words... if you keep running after her like a love-crazed lunatic when she doesn't even look at you!' He could hear his mother's shrill voice ringing in his ear. Karam silently swallowed the insults partially because it was true.

It seemed to Karam that the entire village was privy to his personal life and unrequited love for Rajjo. For them it was an ongoing saga that continued even when the electricity went off for hours together and the rickety TV sets remained shut. They sat in the fields, looking up at the sky passing time, worrying about the violence and terror that had gripped the state lately, wondering if life was going to be as uncertain and then worrying some more about the bills and the groceries, the rain and the fields, the government subsidies and life. Perhaps latching on to the local gossip and having a laugh or two about Karam and Rajjo's situation gave them some welcome relief.

But where would he find her? He could not wait to meet her and give her the gift! It was carefully wrapped in an old newspaper, tucked safely under his arm. He looked at it once more just to see that the gift was securely tied in when he saw the newspaper headlines. V.P. Singh had taken oath to form the government with the National Front on 6 December 1989 and Rajiv Gandhi had lost the elections.

The paper looked almost three-to-four months old. Whatever political games they were playing up there, Karam hoped the whole terror threat would subside soon. He wanted to get out of the village and look for a city job but with the violent situation in the state, youth like him had to stay holed up in their villages. Extremists recruited the unemployed Sikh youth to form the backbone of the militancy, to create an independent state, Khalistan. He shrugged the pall away and focused on the few ladies sitting in a circle; singing folk songs, clapping and dancing in the courtyard. A mosaic of red, blues and greens moved around. Their voices echoed through the lanes of the village. The folk poetry and songs they sang had been etched in their hearts since they all were little girls watching their mothers perform the dance. They mouthed the folk poetry handed down by generations.

Usually the festive atmosphere would lift Karam's spirit but not today. By now the ladies had brought Rajjo's mother and sisters into the circle too. Rikki was here but where was Rano! She would know where Rajjo was!

He had to find Rano. He bumped into Rajjo's overweight brother Sheru, eyeing a tray of sweets and helping himself to some. His younger sister Rikki was trying to shoo him away telling him the sweets were counted as per the guests attending the function. Their mother would force them out of his stomach if they fell short for the guests. Sheru was least bothered and continued with his quest to fill his ample belly.

'It's our sister's wedding, the guests hog and go, we get to eat nothing? What's the point?'

Karam hesitantly approached the squabbling siblings.

Both of them ignored Karam's urgent question regarding Rajjo's whereabouts. A glacial foreboding rose in his gut.

*Was she with him?* The boy she was talking about? The one she had met with Reet's husband? Was he the groom's cousin or something? No, it can't be! But given Rajjo's captivating beauty only a blind man would not fall in love with her at first glance. He had to find Rajjo and find her now!

He turned around to spot Rano walking with Reet's mother-in-law, carrying a few Phulkari dupattas in hand as gifts for the bride and her sisters. Karam glanced at his own little offering, also a phulkari dupatta. Green and orange needlework done in a spectacular style, considered auspicious. It had a verduous green cotton as a base, with floral embroidering in contrasting silk threads of orange and fiery fuchsia. He'd bought it after making a special trip to the city and haggled with the shopkeeper till his throat was parched and sore. Rajjo was going to love it! If only he could find her.

Rano caught Karam's eye and a tell-tale flush crept up her cheeks.

Karam knew Rano would not deny him any thing, not even his beloved Rajjo's secrets. Rano looked pretty in a blue outfit, and Karam complimented her on her look. Her face lit up only to drop glumly as the compliment was hurriedly followed by an enquiry about Rajjo.

'Do you know where Rajjo is?'

'Why do you think I have nothing better to do but keep track of her?' Rano spat back.

'I am just asking…'

'Is there anything else you ever think of asking?'

'Like what?'

'Screw you!'

Karam was used to Rano's outbursts and ignored them.

'Fine, but do you know where she is?'

'Yes!'

Rano deliberately did not elaborate.

'And…' Karam waited for a response.

'And…?'

'Come on, please, Rano, I have some work with her…'

'You will be old and withered and she won't look at you. Your teeth will fall from your gums and your paunch will touch the floor! She still won't look at you!' Rano hissed. Her face contorted with sheer wrath.

'In that state even you won't!' Karam quipped.

Rano looked at him nonplussed. 'I mean look at my face when my teeth fall of, etc.'

There was a pause as Rano grunted.

'Get lost…and drown in the village river.'

'We don't have a river in this village, Rano, it's merely a canal and if I stand in it, the water is up till my waist. I will have to try hard.'

'Then try till you die!'

Rano was about to leave and then she stopped.

With a strange expression she readily offered him the information.

'I promised not to say anything, so I will just say that she is where she goes when she wants to get away…'

Karam knew exactly where that meant, but paused at Rano's expression. Like she had punished him, by telling him about Rajjo's whereabouts. Shaking the thought away and tucking the soft velvety dupatta under his arm, Karam was on his way to find Rajjo.

'Yes, run like a mad dog and hope you break your knee caps on the way!'

Karam turned around only to blow a kiss.

In an instant Rano's heart flipped and melted, she called out to him. She had to warn him.

'Karam! Wait...!' She ran across and whispered in Karam's ear, staying close to him for a second too long and inhaling his desperate wanting. His sweat mingled with the fragrance of the soil he worked hard with.

'Kashi is here...Kashmir Singh...' whispered Rano.

'Who?' Karam enquired, a bit clueless about Rano's insinuating tone.

'Kashi – Kashmir Singh, Reet's groom's friend, that boy, he is here.'

Before Rano could feel Karam's pain and feel the hurt at her dismissal of his affections, Karam sprinted out.

Karam ran like crazy, trying to beat the dusk. He wanted Rajjo to see the colours of the silk thread sparkle when the sun was still up in the sky.

His heart hammered in his chest, reminding him that perhaps Rano had heard wrong. He crossed a man sitting next to a pile of brinjals he had just plucked from the fields. He was sipping water, waiting for sundown so he could call it a day and head home. Karam marched on, fervently hoping for a miracle. He had prayed all these years to be with her. It wasn't going to go in vain.

Usually Karam would stop to exchange a greeting with the old man, but today he just wanted to run till his legs would buckle. He wanted to run beyond the fields today. He wanted to run to a place where the sun and the moon disappeared from the wild blue yonder. He wanted to meet Rajjo somewhere beyond time and space.

He tasted his own sweat as he ran and crossed a row of goats greedily drinking water. He ran and ran until he reached an open field.

A few yards from where he stood, there was a dried up bambi with a small brick enclosure erected next to it. Lack of use, overgrown shrubs and hedges had almost circled the brick enclosure making it a private haven for lost souls or those looking for a secret rendezvous.

He sat on the circular ledge of the dried up tubewell filled with leaves. He could hear the birds chirping as they headed home. The sky was streaked with the red of a setting sun. His gift tucked firmly under his arm, he heard her giggle. Rajjo was definitely in there and then he heard her moan. She wasn't in there alone. He sat there waiting for her. The sun disappeared and dusk enveloped the fields. The weight of his gift; the silken threads mocked him. Just then she emerged looking like a vision in a yellow suit. Her ferocious curls let loose – disheveled. A rosy tint and twinkling eyes enhanced her beauty as she stepped out and stopped short, stifling a scream as she discovered Karam sitting there.

'I was just passing by…' Karam added hastily.

'Have they asked for me back home?' she asked, almost panicking.

Karam could not answer. He just shook his head in a negative gesture.

'Good! There is so much to tell you. Let's walk back and I will fill you in.'

Rajjo fell in step with Karam as they crossed the fields together. Karam was quiet while Rajjo chatted on and Karam wondered where to drown the silken threads or where to burn the vibrant colours till they turned ashen like his heart. Just then he heard her say, 'He wants to marry me. We will elope as I have told him my father won't agree to an alliance that I have found myself! It's all planned. I am in love, Karam, and I am going to elope! Finally!'

He stopped breathing for a minute and then slowly got his breath back. He was alive. That was good news. Almost instantly Karam decided he was going to keep the silken threads as a penance. A penance for what, he was sure to find out in the years to come.

Just then Rajjo paused, she could sense the quiet that had settled around her friend since they had started the walk back. Rajjo's tentative enquiry about why he was so quiet did not elicit any response.

They continued the walk side by side in silence, each lost in their own thoughts when they crossed a queue with three or four villagers standing and waiting for their turn patiently. Each one of them carried some oil in a container. An old man, the caretaker of the little temple, sat at a little distance away from the devotees and the deity. The temple was not bigger than a little kiosk. On a muddy raised platform sat the god of Saturn, all black, known for granting boons and accused of making life tough if not pleased enough. The Shani god gave results of one's deeds in one's life through appropriate punishments and rewards. The villagers, like the rest of the Indian community, worshipped him every Saturday and paid the old man one rupee to pour oil over the deity in the hope that all impediments in their life would be removed.

Rajjo laughed out loud as they crossed the queue.

'It all boils down to Shani – work not going well? Shani is unhappy, Shani is in a bad house. Love life screwed? Shani must be sleeping. Not getting married? Shani is slow! Poor thing gets blamed for everything, I almost feel bad for him and every Saturday they drown him in oil and leaves. Including me! But I am praying to him for Kashi and me. I am sure all will be well!'

Rajjo looked at the dark black deity sitting in the tiny mud enclosure. It held a sword, arrows and two daggers mounted on a crow.

'I come here every Saturday,' Karam muttered, not telling Rajjo that he came here every Saturday to ask Shani to give him Rajjo. Perhaps something would happen and she would be his. He fervently wished to the God he so believed in.

'Oh my-my! I never took you for a believer!' Rajjo laughed. 'But that's OK, I come here too. Father says, when Shani opened his eyes as a baby for the very first time, the sun went into an eclipse. It affects the astrological charts! He is the giver of boons!'

'So what has he given you so far…,' Karam enquired.

'Everything. He has given me Kashi!' Rajjo was flying.

'I can't wait to meet him again. We are going to live in Tarn-Taaran, he is going to take me away! He will speak to his parents so they can come and talk to mine, and if that does not work I am eloping.'

Karam noticed that the brinjal man was no longer there. The evening prayers blared suddenly from the temple down the road. He heard what Rajjo had said.

'Rajiv Gandhi lost the elections.' He found his voice again, not knowing why he told her that.

'That was ages ago, you fool, months back! He will be back soon though.' Rajjo continued skipping ahead, sure and happy in planning her future.

Karam admired this about Rajjo, she was well appraised of the world around. She read everything that came her way. With her fearless take on politics she always kept her father on tenterhooks, but to Karam that was the most desirable trait about Rajjo – her fearlessness. Rajjo, his warrior, she was the sharpest person he had met in his entire life. Maybe that's why she was not going to be with him, because he was not smart. Now how the hell could he get smarter? How smart was this asshole she was planning to elope with? And how smart was it of her to plan to elope with a man she had just met?

He knew the woman he loved was counting the hours until she was going to elope with a man named Kashmir Singh! Well, perhaps Rano was right after all – he should stand in the village canal and try to drown himself!

Rajjo's wait had begun. The hot summer months ended in June. A whiff of monsoon was in the air now. Time crawled with a heavy heart. She was supposed to be on her way back after collecting some groceries her mother had asked for, but here she sat in the open fields, thinking about her beloved Kashmir Singh, fondly called Kashi, remembering his broad shoulders, his twinkling eyes and hungry mouth.

She tried to distract herself by watching a noisy scooter chugging on the road that cut through the fields. She could see a faded poster of the movie *Dil* plastered on the back of the scooter. The hero reminded her of Kashi again! It was supposed to be a good movie and Rajjo wished she could get the videotape and watch it with Kashi.

She had been visiting the Shani temple every day instead of just Saturdays, offering oil and flowers. She was sure Kashi was going to call her soon and take her away. Her faith in the black diety was unyielding.

She closed her eyes to drive out thoughts of Kashi and opened them again to watch an aged man milking his buffalo in the fields. The buffaloes were tied to an old dilapidated cart that had not moved from the fields for decades. One of the buffalo stared directly at Rajjo. The silver bucket placed under the udders was almost full with pristine white milk. Not only her, the other four buffaloes standing next to this one, who were chomping on the fodder till a minute ago, looked up and gawked at Rajjo. As if they knew what she was thinking. Rajjo could swear they were sneering at her. Only what she could not tell was whether the feeling was a good or bad one. A wave of nausea hit her as she ignored it and started walking towards her house.

It had been almost three weeks now; Kashi had not called her. But Rajjo was sure he was fixing everything at his end. She could still smell him on her body and a shy smile sat on her lips as she slept under the stars on her charpoy, thinking of him.

As she crossed the fields with Rano to visit the temple yet again, she saw her father sitting with a few men, sharing a hukka, deep in conversation.

She knew the conversations these days were morose and hopeless, limited to the violent terror outfits, the government's ineffectiveness. Rajjo, however, felt removed from all the turmoil in the world. The men discussed it passionately, but at the end of their discussion they would worry about feeding their families or a sick cow. Why would they agonize over the current situation so long and hard? Predict and take sides. Analyse and comment? Perhaps they felt more involved if they were discussing it. Felt less helpless? But why would they need to be involved in the first place. Rajjo knew she was mulling over random things endlessly to avoid thinking about Kashi.

The monsoon gales brought in romance and longing. She was pining for the call from Kashi. Usually Rajjo was able to distract herself by drowning in the second-hand books her teacher would provide her with. It was a vast collection she read, depending on the charity of the donor. However, she had not picked up a book in the last month now. And then she heard her sister Rano speak.

'Do you think he will call? It's been two weeks?' Rano muttered, half happily and half with worry. She did not want Rajjo to go away after all! She secretly hoped that Kashi would not turn up but knowing how badly Rajjo wanted to be with him, Rano squashed her thoughts.

'Father should not be sitting with him!' Rajjo changed the topic pointing towards her father who sat amidst friends, chatting and smoking in the middle of the fields.

'They are discussing the news… it's harmless.' Rano defended them.

'No, Mother was saying he is offering father a business deal… he is going to betray our father!' Rajjo muttered.

'Oh come on! That's Karam's father!' Rano added defensively.

'Yes, but it is not a good feeling…'

'Now don't go about opening your mouth in front of father…' warned Rano.

Rano trailed behind as Rajjo sauntered towards the men who sat in a circle surrounded by stacks of wheat, hukkas, and with their tiffin boxes strewn around.

Having spotted his girls in the fields, their father tightened his turban and took his leave from the little assemblage. Rajjo was surprised to notice he had aged overnight. His body not as agile, his shoulders not as broad. A lump rose in her throat as she remembered the tall towering man of her childhood. There was something painful in seeing things wither.

He met Rano and Rajjo with a not-so-happy glint and gestured them to return to the house.

Rajjo casually added, 'Dealing with Karam's father may not be so fruitful, I am not getting a good feeling about it!'

Their father laughed with an empty sarcasm. 'My Shani is sitting in the wrong house, even if I deal with a saint it won't fall correctly. Let's just hope the bad period will pass soon…'

Her father bowed reverently as they crossed the black deity on the muddy roadside. Since it was a Friday only a few dry garlands graced the deity and it was not slick with oil. Saturday would be a different story. Rajjo looked at the deity and quickly said her prayers, promising to come back and make her offerings later.

'If it was all up to Shani, then why is he making things difficult for you, father! You are a devout!' asked Rano aloud.

'Why do you think Reet got married in such a good house without any glitch? He's going to make sure all of you get married in good houses and that my son conquers the world… just my business needs to pick up! He will show mercy, I am sure. He has his ways.'

Rano rolled her eyes at such obstinate faith. Rajjo whacked her.

'He is right!' Just then a wave of nausea and something else hit her. She ran a few steps across to throw up on the side of the road.

The father stood their worried, watching his daughter anxiously. As the bile rose in her mouth Rajjo knew she was in trouble. Fear glided in, freezing her bones.

The black deity looked on.

Sheru sat in the corner of his house, near the blackened stove, eating his mini snack, looking at his beautiful sister. Her lustrous curls piled up in a rough bun. Her sparkling brown eyes were dry and arid, her lips slightly parched, her face pale. Their mother watched her like a hawk and Totu howled whenever she crossed him, like he was angry she had not offered him water in the past week or so, or whistled at him. Totu's sulked and caused havoc in the house, screeching. Sheru in turn ate more to cope with the tense atmosphere around him.

Moreover, he had his own issues to resolve. He looked forward to going and watching the Test cricket being played between India and England on their neighbour's rickety TV set.

The new second-hand TV their father got after haggling till his voice ran dry was just metal scrap. It did not work. As soon as it arrived, their mother had reverently wrapped it in a bed cover lest it got scratches before they used it and shoved it under the bed.

Could anyone tell her it was second-hand? wondered Sheru.

It needed to be opened and fixed!

Sheru wanted to get the TV fixed; his friend's father could open it and fix it, but Saroj rejected the idea outright. According to her no one was allowed to touch the TV till his father got some expert to look at it.

Rajjo was too lost to get involved in the fight, Rikki was happy to let Sheru do the bickering with the parents and Rano was too worried for Rajjo to intervene in the TV battle.

However, it was clear he could not broach the subject with all the simmering tension in the house. Their mother was in a bad mood. She would forbid him to go and watch the match at their neighbour's house. All she did these days was open her prayer books and read out aloud, after she finished her cooking.

Sheru willed his elder sister to feel better and hoped things would sort themselves out till the cricket match. Lying listlessly on the cot, he looked at the cows tied in the courtyard and it seems even they were sulking. The weather was hot and humid.

Just then their mother muttered there was no milk in the house. Sheru groaned. Was she going to send him marching to get it just when he wanted to take a nap? Thankfully, his elder sister Rajjo sprang up from the corner with eager buoyancy like she was waiting for an excuse to get out. Before anyone could react, she was out of the main door.

Saroj had learnt about Rajjo's affair a week ago and she suspected something was amiss. Rajjo had assured her that Kashi would come and speak to the family. But the wait seemed endless. Rajjo found it difficult to be around Saroj and took every opportunity to escape.

Following her mother's quick glance, Rikki ran behind her sister to accompany her, since Rano was in the bathroom.

'You never move from your throne King of Persia… Couldn't you go and get the milk.'

Saroj admonished her lazy son who was still eating his snack as he lay on the cot.

'I was about to but Rajjo went…' Sheru mumbled.

'And couldn't you accompany her?'

'I was about to but Rikki went…'

'About to…. about to… Were you climbing down the Himalayas? All you had to do was get up and get going.'

Saroj continued to mutter as Totu started screeching.

Rikki ran behind her sister, and fervently hoped things at home would get sorted soon, or else their plans to watch the movie the following Sunday would go for a toss. The videotape was available only for a day and everyone in the village was gathering at the big house down the road to watch it.

But one look at her sister's face and Rikki again felt a pang of guilt. She wanted to make her sister feel better, but sensed that she was in no mood to talk. They reached the milkman's house down the road. Rajjo called out to him and left the empty utensil at his door. They sat waiting in his courtyard. Rikki stole a worried glance at her pale sister.

Rajjo sat quietly staring ahead at the dry and arid courtyard and a rusted motorcycle parked in the middle.

Washed pots hung on a dried shriveled tree, like the tree had grown multiple heads made of steel. An old rickety table had a few utensils turned upside down so the water could drip out nicely. A few rags and cloths, washed and rinsed, hung around the utensils.

To pass the time, Rikki started to count the clouds passing over her head. They were turning grey and black. When she reached seventeen that's when she heard the guttural sounds. To her horror, her sister retched inches away from the milkman's washed and dried pots. When Rikki ran up to her to pat her back Rajjo shoved her hand away.

She wiped her face with a dried cloth and hurriedly hid it in a bundle under her shirt lest the milkman on his return would find it soiled.

'Don't tell mother about this.' Rajjo looked at her sister with her deeply haunting eyes. Rikki simply nodded.

Just then the milkman returned with their utensil filled with milk. He sniffed around at the weird odour, and before he could ask the girls, both of them scooted away. Rikki was petrified that he was going to call after them and scream. Her legs moving fast; her little hands holding her sister's, both to comfort her and be comforted. The snowy fresh milk dripping as they walked on unsteady legs.

Just then the angry black clouds came rushing in and covered the green fields, followed by thunder. Rikki wanted to rush home, but Rajjo took the longer route home. Rikki knew she was going to the little Shani Temple. These days she visited the temple three times a day, sometimes four. Sheru had whispered to Rikki that their sister was losing it or perhaps a ghost had possessed her.

As she watched her elder sister light a lamp, she could see a tear trickle down her face. Just then the heavy black clouds burst on the fields, drenching one and all, including Rajjo's little lamp that could not bear the torrent of rain. Rikki stood there, watching her sister pray to the little black deity as rainwater mingled in the white pristine milk and made it salty.

Rajjo lay on her back in the middle of the fields. She could smell the earth. She could see the sky. She could feel something crawl up her hands. She could smell the milk of the grass blades. She thought of the black deity across the road, which she had been worshipping since she was a child. He was not going to let her down.

She sat day in and day out outside the tea shop, waiting for some news about Kashi's call. She worshipped the black deity, spoke to him, cajoled him, challenged him, showered him with her love, declared her devotion – anything for him to have mercy and forgive her. She asked God to reveal himself if he was anywhere around, and then vowed to never bow to him if he did not pay heed to her prayers this time. She hoped he was listening, but that was all she could do.

Saroj, worried for her daughter, had been reading prayers from the little prayer books sold outside the temple in the house. She would take a bath, cleanse a corner of the house and call Rajjo to sit next to her as she recited the prayers loudly. Usually she did it once a day, but the past week it had increased to three or four times a day. Saroj did it when she was overwrought and Rajjo felt guilty that she was in a state. Her hair where streaked with white, her beauty fading with time and her eyes filled with worry.

Lying in the fields Rajjo struggled to drive her mother's troubled face out of her head. She took in long deep breaths. She knew they were looking for her at the house.

Her mother had known when she had heard and seen Rajjo throw up in the backyard as she took off the laundry from the clothesline. Immediately she had enquired about her period and Rajjo had turned her panic-stricken eyes away. Before her mother had reacted, Rajjo had taken off. She was having trouble breathing as she ran. They knew!

It had been a month and a half and Kashi had not called. She could hear Rano calling out to her. Rajjo did not move. She did not have the strength left in her to do anything.

Rano screamed yet again, 'Kashi has left a message! He is going to call back in an hour!' Slowly, the words seeped into Rajjo's paralysed brain. Breathing quickly, Rajjo got up and shot away towards the local tea shop. He was going to call her in an hour! It was going to be all right!

A slow smile spread across her face. Jubilation she could barely contain. She had a weird taste in her mouth; it tasted like metal. It was relief perhaps. She knew it was going to be all right!

She waved at her podgy brother running after an overloaded tractor carrying bright green fodder. The tractor was loaded to maximum capacity and it looked like it was heaving under the weight of the bundles. It was a surprise that it could move at all.

Sheru stopped in his tracks wondering why Rajjo was laughing and so happy all of a sudden. Either she had lost it completely, or things were going to be normal at home and they could get the TV repaired!

Happiness surged again and Sheru was hungry to celebrate with a feast already. He had to tell his mother how happy Rajjo had been, and maybe that would earn him a snack! He hurried home with the good news while Rajjo ran all the way to her black deity.

She hurriedly offered a prayer of thanksgiving, promising to devote her life to him for this favour. She promised to be his ardent devotee and then she ran like the wind.

While Sheru reached home with dreams of earning a snack, he found his mother screaming at Rikki and completely out of sorts. Her eyes were red and puffy from a bout of crying. She spotted Sheru and screamed that she wanted Rajjo brought home right away. Sheru ran out of the house before anyone else could. Forget the snack, he doubted he was getting any dinner tonight. He went as fast as his podgy legs would carry him to find his sister sitting outside the tea shop, her hands and legs twitching.

'Mother is wailing and screaming like a hyena! Go home!' Sheru apprised her of the impending calamity.

'You go. I am right behind you.'

Sheru eyed the sweets and eateries hanging in the shop and quietly started on his way back to convey the message.

Rajjo did not know what to do with her limbs as she waited excitedly by the tea shop. She hugged herself and ordered a cup of sweet tea so she could sit and wait there. Her eyes were fixed on an old black and white clock that ticked away mercilessly.

Rano stood at a safe distance hoping and praying that he would call. However, she was petrified that Rajjo would not go away. She was not going to let her leave! She hated Kashi!

To Rajjo's delight the phone rang. Rajjo lunged at the receiver and spoke hurriedly into the mouthpiece, half-relieved, half-angry, half-crying and half-laughing.

Rano stood a little away, watching her sister, but could barely make anything of the conversation. Rano tried to console herself that once Rajjo was gone, Karam would at least turn his affection towards her. She would give him a shoulder to cry on. Just then she saw Rajjo's face turn pale with shock. She inched closer as she heard Rajjo informing Kashi that she was carrying his baby. Rano assumed after hearing that the line had gone dead because Rajjo just held the phone silently, without moving.

Eventually Rajjo let the phone go from her lifeless fingers. And she walked away. Rano walked at a safe distance. She had suspected there was a pregnancy. Her heart bled for Rajjo. They crossed the dirty muddy road, where people rushed with little oil offerings since it was a Saturday.

'Let's go and offer a prayer. All will be well, Rajjo!' Rano placed her hand on her sister's shoulder. Rajjo stared at the deity for a long time. The oil poured and spilled on the muddy road.

Feeling an intense betrayal, Rajjo spat out. 'God is hogwash! There is none! I wish I never have to hear that word again in my life…'

Spitting in disgust at the black deity, Rajjo marched towards her house. She knew it was time to face the music, and this time she was ready for it. She had given up God from her life with a vengeance.

# 5

THEIR father had not returned home for two days since the news of Rajjo's pregnancy broke. Her mother had wailed and cried and was now running a fever. Reet was brought back home from her in-laws' house to take care of their mother. Rano felt bad for Rajjo, as Reet gave her incriminating looks.

Sheru was gobbling down food, lying on his cot, wondering what the fuss was all about.

The next day Reet had given a powder to Rajjo that she got from a city doctor, along with some pills. Rajjo took them quietly and sat in the corner, waiting. Rano saw her sitting in the room overlooking the backyard. She stared at the sky and watched the day pass. Rajjo bled a river. Rano was there to nurse her. She was worried that Rajjo would pass out with all the pain, so she stayed awake holding her sister's hand through the night. Rajjo had not spoken to anyone for two days.

The next day she had more pills that gave her cramps and made her throw up. The bleeding continued along with the cramps. Rano's heart went out to her sister.

A tough night later, Rajjo knew her body and her soul had bled Kashi out of her life forever. She was cleansed and sterile to the emotion of love. She was never going to hope for it! All she could hear was the rain pelting outside and her mother reading out from the prayer book aloud as all the siblings sat around listening to her voice, drawing comfort.

*'By Guru's grace, dry woods blossom forth again in lush greenery. Why are you so afraid O mind! The flamingoes fly hundreds of miles leaving their*

*young ones behind. Who feeds them? Who teaches them to feed themselves? Why is the mind in a state of unrest when for each and every person our lord provides sustenance?'.*

Rajjo wanted to shut out the prayers and focus on the rain beating down on the roof. She wanted to obliterate the vision of flamingoes flying away leaving their young ones behind to fend for themselves. She wanted to stop a flamingo with flaming pink feathers and ask him, where did the faith come from when there was no Lord around?

It was the end of monsoon, the clouds were retreating and the fields were lush and satiated after the pearly showers.

Rajjo sat quietly as they put some henna on her hands. It was going to be a very quiet affair. She was going to be married to a man who lived in a small town somewhere near Ludhiana. He was fifty years old and his wife had died in childbirth. He had taken one look at Rajjo and agreed to marry her. He ran a printing press and Rajjo's mother was relieved that at least she would not want for material things.

Saroj had not spoken to Rajjo ever since the episode and neither had her father. Rajjo had not made the attempt either. Only Rano and her other siblings spoke to her. Karam hovered around the house only to be shooed away by Rano.

However, on the wedding day Karam had managed to slip inside the house and whispered to Rajjo desperately. 'Don't worry, I won't let you marry the old man. I will marry you! I am just going to talk to my mother again else we will elope!'

'I dropped Kashi's baby, tell your mother that…' Rajjo muttered to Karam in a waterish tone. Karam froze as soon as the words were uttered.

As Karam walked out in a daze Rano assaulted him, 'Happy! I told you to stay away but you had to buzz around her like a fly. Stay away now, please!'

'Why didn't you tell me?'

'You think we should have given it in the papers? Use your brains! She is going away, getting married, so stop coming over!' Her voice cracked, and Rano slammed the door shut on Karam's shocked face.

As he walked down the road, he saw a motley crowd sitting in a bus arrive at the main road. It was the groom's party.

Rajjo was going today. It dawned on him that they were taking her away. He just sat there and watched the wedding party enter Rajjo's house.

The phulkari dupatta still hidden under his mattress made him feel nauseous. He wanted to give it to her so that she would remember him. He ran all the way without stopping and fetched it, running all the way back, just in time to see her standing on the steps of the bus, waving at her family.

Sheru and the younger siblings watched the whole thing play out, sad that another member of their family would be gone.

Although he would miss Rajjo, Sheru was excited that the second-hand TV would be unwrapped and fixed now! Perhaps he could broach the topic tomorrow.

Now that Rajjo was gone, Sheru knew the third in line, Rano, was going to be a tantrum queen. He glanced at her. She stood at a distance from every one else. Like she was singled out by her immense grief at the turn of events.

Rano was numb. She stood alone at a distance – aloof – and refused to bid Rajjo goodbye. She knew that once the bus went out of the village there would be a distance between her and Rajjo. Grandmother was wrong on two accounts; Rajjo was not going to be all that she had promised, and Rano was not going to be a part of her sister's life. Rano wanted to scream at her grandmother up there for being a fraud.

Just then she saw Karam running towards the bus as the bus driver had started the ignition.

*Oh come on… that fool was going to get under the bus now! Perfect!'*

As the others sprang into action to stop Karam from obstructing the bus, Karam simply ran up to the bus door.

*'Well, looks like he is going to climb in and go with her… this just gets better*, thought Rano.

Karam climbed the two steps and reached towards Rajjo who sat there looking at him. He simply handed her the parcel. This time Rajjo accepted it with a smile. 'Look after Rano,' she mouthed.

Karam stepped out of the bus just as the driver started to drive, leaving behind a cloud of dust and sad people.

Long after the bus had moved away and the family had moved inside the house, Karam stood there smiling to himself. Perhaps this is where Rajjo's story was going to end. Perhaps this is where he was supposed to say goodbye.

But he also remembered the last look she had given him before the bus had turned a corner. She'd looked out and stared at Karam. She'd looked directly into his eyes.

Perhaps this was not how it was going to end, and they would meet again. The question was for how long was he ready to wait.

Just then he heard his mother's acidic voice attacking him.

'Are you going to move from here ever, or should we build a mausoleum in your memory while you stand and wait for your beloved to leave her rich old husband and jump out of the bus?'

Karam cleared his throat and responded.

'I will be in the fields in ten minutes…'

The mother shrugged and continued to babble. How she hated the overrated emotion called love. She wanted to boil it in a pan of tea and drain it off. It was of no use to anyone; it did not plough the fields, nor did it put food on the table.

And then she heard Karam shout.

'I will be there in ten minutes, just leave…'

Thankfully, this time she did.

There was no sign of Rajjo, no sign of the bus. The workers had gone back to working in the fields. His mother continued her day-to-day chores; Rajjo's father was heading to his shop accompanied by the reluctant Sheru.

Rajjo was gone and everything was already moving in to fill in the void. This would continue, till Rajjo was a distant memory. With that thought, Karam headed to the fields. His mind was numb. He was never going to fill the void. He was going to keep her alive.

Rajjo took in her pot-bellied, bearded groom. He had a fake tooth capped in gold as he smiled at the onlookers.

She turned one last time to look at her house and the people she was leaving behind.

Through the cloud of dust, she saw Karam smiling and waving at her. He was the only one waving as her mother and sisters stood in various stages of disapproval and pain. Sheru was the only one who followed Karam's action and chased the bus while waving.

But then Sheru was like a dog; he liked chasing moving vehicles despite his increasing weight. Rajjo smiled involuntary at her brother and felt a searing pain. When would be the next time she would see him? Would he still be this innocent child, or someone singed with time and desire?

And with one final look at her mother, father and sisters, she turned away to look at the road in front of her. It stretched on endlessly. Empty.

The wedding party in the bus surrounded the couple as the bus driver had stopped outside a highway eatery. Rajjo just stared at her lap. The smell of henna rose up Rajjo's nostrils. She felt and nauseous. The intricate pattern drawn on her hands was beautiful. She wanted to wash it all away with soapy water, rub it, tear it and wipe it clean. Remove it with a knife. Bleed the skin and colours dry.

The driver climbed back into his seat and the bus started moving again. Her husband instructed him to make another stop at the temple on the outskirts of the town. The driver nodded. 'Okay, Seth-ji.'

Everyone called her husband 'Seth-ji'.

A sharp pain rose from inside her body. She could feel something excruciating pass through. Was she bleeding again? A wave of nausea hit her as she looked out of the little window of the bus. Bidding adieu to the village that had once been her home.

They passed the serpentine queue outside the little Shani temple. They passed the marigold fields, the mustard fields, the carpets of wheat and paddy fields. They passed the milkman on the dirt road with his pots.

They passed the old men who smoked in the fields; women who worked with their scarves, sickles and babies; cattle ploughed the mud, with bells tinkling around their necks.

She bid her village adieu. 'She is Durga, she is meant for great things!' her mother's often told story about her grandmother, and the prediction she'd had about her future rang in her head.

'She is God's child…'

Rajjo wanted to laugh out loud. She refused to cry. The bus stopped outside the temple. To everyone's surprise, the young bride refused to alight from the bus and pay homage to the deity in the temple. After a minute of consultation it was decided that perhaps it wasn't the correct time of the month, and Seth-ji went by himself to seek the blessings of the deity.

An old lady approached the beautiful girl staring out of the window.

'That time of the month, you can't go to the temple?'

'No, I just don't want to go …'

'Why?'

'There is nothing for me in there…'

The woman wondered why they named her 'Durga' in the first place. What a shame!

Rajjo could smell the rain approaching her village and she was glad this was the last of it that she was going to see.

The wet road and the water-filled manholes indicated they'd just missed a rain shower. The street was crammed with houses. It was one of the crowded residential areas in the sleepy town of Dholakpura.

As soon as Rajjo stepped out of the bus, she could see a large black gate, rusted in parts, engraved with intricate circular design. Beyond the gate stood the multistoried bungalow. The paint, a dirty pale pink, peeled in places and grey patches of cement peeked through. Wooden window frames on tinted dark glass gave a gloomy sad look to the house. She had never seen a house this big in size.

The cemented driveway lay bare. Water dripped from the leaves of the mango tree that grew in a corner, with a patch of garden left around it. The tree grew into the wall and spread across the neighbour's house as well. It was old and gnarled, with anchor roots hanging down. It looked tired and sad, despite the fresh gleam of moisture on the leaves. But Rajjo liked it.

As she walked through the gate, the smell of grey concrete filled her lungs mingled with the smell of the old mango tree. The pale pink house looked foreboding. A few neighbours stood in their balconies, curiously observing the old man and his new bride.

After a few hurried rituals done by the great old aunt at the main gate, who Rajjo feared could die any minute, the little party escorted the new bride in.

The first thing Rajjo noticed was the dark and damp interior. Feeble lamps lit up the large rooms. The floors with yellowed marble, the walls painted a muddy cream. The house smelt of stale bread and moths. Despite its size the house was claustrophobic, with a maze of rooms and scattered furniture.

'The house belonged to a professor. His wife was murdered, and then he went senile and left. Kullu bought it then.' The great aunt made conversation with Rajjo. Rajjo wasn't sure she had heard correctly. 'He is a very sharp boy, my Kullu.'

Rajjo suspected the boy being referred to was her fifty-five-year old husband.

A servant walked in barefoot to take her bags. Rajjo followed him. The suitcases were kept in one of the larger rooms with a big bed occupying most of the room. A few pictures of Guru Nanak and other Hindu gods, along with a calendar sponsored by a gas agency, hung by the iron nails hammered inside the wall.

'Oh why has she gone inside, that's the wrong room and anyway she has to be outside, then you girls have to take her in, once Kullu comes! Bring her back, you idiots.' Rajjo could hear the senile aunt. All this while her husband 'Kullu' was settling accounts outside with the bus driver and other vendors.

The ladies from the neighbourhood streamed into the house to glance at the new bride, just as they would when a neighbour got a new car, or electronics. It was a neighbour's birthright in a small town to inspect anything new that was acquired by anyone on the street. Rajjo felt the intense scrutiny. Some hid back a smile or two, given the odd couple; a man old enough to be the beautiful bride's father.

The great old aunt sat down with a sigh, asking the help to make sure a glass of milk was kept in the bedroom and for a bowl with water to be brought to her immediately. To Rajjo's horror, she took off her dentures in the drawing room, placed them in a bowl held out by the servant and settled in comfortably. 'What a menace, I feel like carrying a whole platoon of missiles in my mouth!' And she continued in the same tone without pausing for breath.

'Has someone kept the milk in the bedroom, where is that rascal boy, Kesar…'

A little boy emerged from the gathering. Kesar wore blue shorts and a pale yellow worn out bush shirt, silky floppy hair covered his forehead and kind eyes peeped out from behind. His face had a perpetual smile that warmed the heart.

A wave of nervous laughter followed. Rajjo's face was flushed with anxiety as she sat in the living room with its sofa sets, lamps and stale smell. She could hear her husband walking in the main door, talking to someone.

'Have you kept the milk as I asked?' asked the great aunt again. A bout of coughing followed.

'Yes, but usually he does not drink milk at night. It gives him diaorrhea.' The little boy's comment elicited a few smirks.

'Today he wants to bathe in it, so shut that little trap and keep it here…'

The aunt clearly had a temper. She sat in the room like a queen and ordered everyone about, complaining of knee pain at regular intervals. Through her incessant rambling Rajjo learnt that she lived in the house with her nephew, and occasionally travelled to another city to visit her daughter and sons.

'Kesar, now get me a cup of tea. I have just attended a hectic wedding. But I am happy Kullu is settled with a nice bride. Now the lord can call me up there! I will go happily!' The aunt looked up with a divine expression. Her thinning white hair, wrinkled face, toothless grin and sharp tongue made her more fearsome than likeable.

'When will he call you up there, you think?' asked the little boy, Kesar. 'You had promised to buy me a new school bag for my evening classes. Now where will I chase you once he calls you up there…?'

The other ladies bit back a smirk as Kesar's mother, who helped around the house with the chores, took him by the arm to give him an earful. Kesar seemed like a happy boy around her. The old aunt continued to mutter as she slurped on the tea. 'Rascal!'

Just then Seth-ji passed the living room and disappeared in the bedroom, not exchanging any pleasantries with the gathering of ladies and neighbours.

The aunt swung into action again.

'What are you girls standing there and giggling for? Now I have to move my ancient legs and take the bride in the room? Move it and take her in there!'

Promptly, a few cousins escorted Rajjo shyly to the master bedroom.

'I want a great grand nephew soon, I am telling you right now,' hollered the old woman. Rajjo's face burnt with humiliation as she heard giggles erupting at the comment.

Thankfully, she escaped the living room only to be ushered into a bedroom.

Rajjo skimmed the room painted in a pista green colour. Patches of cement on the roof spoke of harsh seasons. Muddy yellow and white curtains hung on the window listlessly, and she could glimpse the mango tree through them. A double bed and a steel Godrej cupboard took up most of the room. A mirror attached to one of the cupboard walls reflected Rajjo. She looked resplendent in her red outfit.

The cousins fled the room as they saw Seth-ji come out of the bathroom. With a hungry look on his face, Seth-ji inspected his new bride, ignoring the shy giggles. He lay down on the bed with a loud sigh staring at Rajjo expectantly. He made an odd sight, sprawled on the colourful printed bed-sheet, his belly falling towards his right and his eyes devouring Rajjo. This was not the vision Rajjo had of her husband.

She saw him smile at her. He patted the bed for Rajjo to join in.

With a calm that rose from deep inside, Rajjo knew she had to step forward and embrace the pain. If she had to survive, she had to be the first to move. She quietly turned round to shut the door, only to see a sweet smiling face standing by the door with a glass of milk.

'I put the milk in the other room by mistake, and I am Kesar. I studied till class one and if I had continued I would have been in class three. Now I study in the evenings.'

His twinkling eyes smiled with affection. He reminded her of her sister Rano back home. A lump formed in her throat as she took the hot glass and turned around to keep it on the table. With a deadpan expression she shut the door on the face of the sweet little boy.

'If you need anything just let me know…'

Could she ask for two spoons of death from a little boy in blue shorts and rubber slippers. Perhaps not yet!

# 6

## November 1990

THE year was coming to an end. It was November already. A lot was happening in the world, but Rajjo's life could be best described as indeterminate. She filled in the hours and lived the daily journey from sunrise to sunset.

She tried to remind herself that living with Seth-ji had its own advantages. For instance, she had her own TV and unlike in her village she had access to news 24X7. She watched a special report on the state-run channel, Doordarshan, where a news presenter reported the resignation of V.P. Singh and the anointment of Chandra Shekhar as the eighth prime minister of the country.

Lately, Seth-ji was also talking about getting a cable TV connection. One of his enterprising friends had started a cable TV business. Rajjo had not understood what exactly it was but there was more to watch on TV than just Doordarshan. She learnt from Seth-ji that his friend Gulmoher had wisely invested in videocassette recorders and had set up a unit in his garage. Cable TV offered to show two to three Bollywood films a day. No running to the video library anymore! Apart from Bollywood movies, they also had a menu of English movies, pirated Western comedies, music and game shows. It was a matter of time when it would be available in their town as well. Rajjo had grunted at regular intervals as Seth-ji shared his excitement. He wanted to start his own cable TV business. He was convinced it was a gold mine. He had already started making plans.

As the sharp knife grazed her finger, she came out of her reverie. The news reporter continued in the background as Rajjo resumed chopping cabbage in her living room alone, trying to react to something she had learnt on TV. Somehow, it did not affect her at all. She continued with her chopping. Perhaps it was the cold and musty weather that had dulled her instincts. Back home, she had heated political debates with her father and siblings. Her mother frowned upon Rajjo for having extreme political opinions and constantly schooled her to tone down her outbursts.

The reporter moved on to a piece about the Gulf war and the bombing of Kuwait by Saddam Hussain. Rajjo did not want to hear anymore of the morose news so she muted the sound and let the visuals play.

As she continued to chop the cabbage in her living room, suddenly and unannounced came a violent rage at all the months she had spent in the house, feeling bottled in a jar that was ready to topple over any minute. The feeling hit her like a blizzard. She'd tried hard to keep at bay. It was dreadful to lie in bed next to her husband till he was satiated and fell asleep. Rajjo curbed the desire to run off from the bed and scrub herself clean, with a bar of soap and a bucket of water night after night.

The loud snores that followed instantly would keep her awake as she stared at the mango tree through her window, and spotted a star or two between the leaves and the shadows. Sometimes, when the snores got loud and unbearable like a screeching train getting derailed, she would kick him hard out of frustration.

The next morning he would wonder about the tender spot and a bruise, but never dared ask Rajjo that he suspected she kicked him in the night. Once when Seth-ji mentioned his recurring dream of being kicked, Rajjo would just look down, pretending to focus on her kitchen chores. It was her little secret.

Rajjo had found ways to pass the time, and the most important discovery in the last few months had been the red diary in the cobwebbed attic.

She'd discovered an abandoned steel trunk full of musty books eaten by moths and time. It was a collection by some imminent philosophers.

The covers had peeled off, the binding had come undone. The musty smell made her cough. And as she was going through the books she found a red leather diary, scribbled with notes. Someone had penned down thoughts and verses by well-known philosophers. Painfully jotted down with an ink pen, a patient nib and a calm soul. Rajjo thought of the professor who lost his wife and then his mind. She was sure all this belonged to him. In time, the professor's diary became her most prized possession.

The diary had seen her through the monsoon to the harsh winter.

One crisp winter morning, Rajjo and Kesar stepped out for their weekly vegetable shopping, clad in warm sweater and stole, with Kesar wearing a woollen monkey cap. They were supposed to cross the local temple to offer a garland and some oil to appease Lord Shani, so that he would grant a boon and profits in Seth-ji's dwindling business and bless his plans for starting his own cable TV business. The local priest had suggested the remedy. Rajjo wondered if all the priests got commissions for subscribing all and sundry to appease Lord Shani!

Apart from running a printing press, her husband was a worker in a local political party and specialized in organizing crowds for political rallies. She had seen him through three of those and Seth-ji went ballistic when he was in the thick of organizing a political rally. Rajjo dreaded another rally soon.

She knew Seth-ji was nervous about his upcoming political rally for two young politicians; pulling the crowds in for young politicians was going to be tougher. The local astrologer had warned him that as Shani in his charts was not favourable there could be problems.

They arrived at the vegetable market as Rajjo took in the familiar sights. The entire area was covered in green, purple and reds. Beans, brinjals and tomatoes. She moved further ahead to see piles of potatoes. Since dusk had already set in, each seller had a bulb hanging above his stock of vegetables.

Rajjo had a sudden urge to throw everything away and scream. She wanted to cut herself and see the blood spill on the tomatoes she carried in the white plastic bags.

On their way back it was time to finish the chores and offer the oil in the Shani temple to remove any impediments in Seth-ji's work. Kesar quietly slipped off his slippers and ran in with the oil to hand over to the temple priest. Rajjo waited outside, staring at her shopping bags and thinking about going home and starting to cook for dinner. And then she saw a little chemist shop around the corner. She simply walked over and bought a blade. Sharp enough to slice a wrist.

She waited outside the temple, with the metal blade tucked safely in her brassiere. The temple bells started ringing in a giant roar indicating the evening prayers had begun. The sound reminded her of her recent life experiences. It rose like a wave of nausea and threatened to drown her. Rajjo tried to break away as she focused on a field ahead of her. She wanted to use the metal blade and end it all.

'Apples, bananas, cabbage, capsicum, cauliflower,' she muttered the names of the fruits and vegetables in her bag to quell this fearsome urge. However, in the middle of it all, she could taste Seth-ji's tobacco on her mouth and skin. She wanted to throw up and wash it away. She wanted to drown in the smells of the vegetable market.

'Corn, cucumber, ginger, curry leaves, garlic, green mustard, green peas…' The ringing of the bells stopped as abruptly as it had begun. Thankfully it passed. She saw Kesar bobbing down the temple steps carrying some sweets to share with Rajjo.

Rajjo knew she was drowning. She had to find a way to keep her head up. Her only solace was during the times she spent reading her red diary. One particular thought had completely engulfed her mind lately. 'Aristotle said the faculty of desire was responsible for all motion.'

Why was she standing outside this temple? Why was she frying onions in the kitchen? Why was she here at all? Nothing made sense, because she was bereft of any desire stirring her soul, because she was living from sunrise to sunset without any desire to exist.

The question plagued her the next morning as well as she worked in the kitchen. Finally Rajjo switched off the gas. The bubbling of the sizzling oil subsided as she stood there, watching her onions turning cold. She had to start directing her life again else there was no way out of the black hole.

She went to the living room and sat down to regain her balance. She could see some brochures of the upcoming rally left around the room. Her eye caught a face. A very handsome face stared into the camera. Brown eyes, light wavy hair, square jaw line, four-day-old stubble, broad shoulders on a six -foot frame. Rajjo skimmed his name. Harsh Vardhan Singh. He was one of the young political leaders attending the rally. It seemed like he was looking at Rajjo. This picture was taken for Rajjo to discover it.

If Rajjo had not known better, he could be a film star. There was something about him that held her gaze for a long, long time. Finally her eyes dropped. The unexpected thunder outside made her step out on the concrete cement to pick up the clothes that were hung out to dry earlier in the evening, while her mind fervently debated whether to ask Seth-ji to let her work with him.

The mango tree looked older than the last time she saw it. Torn and unable to decide on a course of action. Rajjo sighed at the irony. Sometimes she could tell if other people were about to suffer, or have a good fortune, but in her case, the only thing Rajjo could tell was that she had to take the clothes off the clothesline as it was going to rain. And that was enough.

She was going to ask Seth-ji to let her work with him. Otherwise the vegetable market would eat her up. The gods and goddesses that hung on every wall of the room were going to eat her up. The temple bells down the road were going to drown her.

She heard it before the drops fell. The approaching thunder storm. Her freshly washed laundry still in her hand, she just stood there as the raindrops drenched her soul. She shivered under the December rain shower. Her tears mingled with the water raining down. She stood there on the grey concrete and cried endlessly till the rain stopped. There was no more water to hide in. She had to go back in.

She served him a breakfast of paranthas. The smoke in the kitchen smothered Rajjo even though she cooked on gas unlike her mother who toiled on a stove. Seth-ji screamed into the phone while sitting on the table. Rajjo thought he was going to die any minute. If only he would die after eating the parantha she had made, burning her fingers, kneading the dough, boiling the potatoes while he slept.

He wanted sex in the morning too, but thanks to the excruciating pain he felt in his stomach he had refrained. It was some sort of food poisoning, the doctor on the home visit had said. Complete bedrest given his age was mandatory, and that had not pleased her husband one bit. He had ordered her to make a parantha, to defy the doctor.

Rajjo simply walked into the kitchen and did as instructed. She wondered how he was still getting the energy to have sex every other night. She hoped he would age faster, she hoped he would slip and fall. A tear escaped her eye as she hoped for various calamities to fall on her husband.

'Why don't you let Mukesh handle everything…' she placed the parantha in front of him and suggested hesitantly.

Seth-ji grunted, stuffing a bite in his mouth, 'So that he can make points with the higher-ups and they give him all the charge? Once they see he has done a good job, I am out of work. All political links and clout gone. Most printing press jobs come from these rallies, and once Mukesh takes charge who is to know where the wind will blow and where will he face? If he turns away from me, my business is gone. He needs to stay in his place and just manage the printing. He has ambition. I don't like him. In fact I will kick him out soon! Get me another one of this, and too much salt, cut down on the salt for heavens!'

While she heated the next parantha, she mulled over her complex husband. Seth-ji was nice to her, never abusive, always polite. He tried to reach out to her whenever he could find the time from his work and his friends who were usually his party coworkers. Rajjo turned the parantha over and over on the hot black plate with her bare hands. She poured generous oil all over it and made it sizzle over the heat. Steam rose to her face, in her nostrils, in her hair till she could breathe no more. She plated the parantha, scooped two spoons full of yoghurt and walked towards the dining table.

She put the hot meal on the table, and Seth-ji eyed his beautiful wife.

'Can I come work with you? Help you out?'

He eyed her for a good two minutes. Rajjo waited with bated breath.

'What will you do? There is so much work to be done, Durga. Get the required crowd; get the tents done, speakers done, ferry the villagers into the venue, distribute food and liquor so they come, distribute pamphlets, keep them entertained? What aspect will you take care of?'

Rajjo stood there, with her beautiful black curls falling below her shoulder, smoldering amber eyes firm and steely, pink lips fuelled with determination.

'Everything. I will take care of everything…for you.'

Seth-ji thought for a second, moved a bit and winced. He knew he needed a handyman. Since he was not going to move about a lot in the approaching days, he might as well take her up on the offer and make her happy. He had noticed the sad moping look on her face. He had tried to be the husband she wanted. He had dyed his hair black. He was on medication for his performance. He even made sure he was gentle with her in bed. He indulged her. He wanted her happy, but the sad faraway look in her eyes sometimes angered him.

But Seth-ji was obsessed with his new toy. Even though it was lifeless, it was his. And now that she had asked something of him, how could he refuse? Especially if it suited him just fine!

He grunted in an odd fashion and asked for some more curd.

She immediately scooped some in a bowl.

'Don't forget to go to the Shani mandir and offer some oil. If he is happy it will all be smooth. That bastard has told me my Shani is sitting in the wrong house, no wonder such calamities are befalling me… I also need funding and permission for the cable TV unit.'

Rajjo realized Sethi-ji had not answered her plea of wanting to work with him. Dejected she walked back to the kitchen wondering what to do next as Seth-ji hollered, 'Now come my lovely and understand what you need to do for today. The rally is not happening in my kitchen! My dearest, its freaking set-up in the market square and a minimum gathering of seven hundred people is required…where will they come from? I hope I don't have to sire them!' He looked at Rajjo with twinkling eyes and laughed at his own joke.

Rajjo smiled feebly, still not believing that he had agreed for her to work. 'They have no idea what requirements they give from those offices up there! The village dogs won't come to see what these good-for-nothing young leaders have to say! If it was up to me, I would kick them all the way back to where they came from.'

He saw his young bride looking at the pamphlet with the faces of the young handsome leaders. She looked at one of them long enough for a burning sensation to crawl on him. While her husband burned in his possessiveness, a thought struck Rajjo. He was going to be there, the man with deep brown eyes and the stubble. The man she saw last night. A wave of hope and happiness flared as she sat next to Seth-ji with a pen and a paper.

## December 1991

The cold seeped in everywhere. It was difficult to move around in the thick smog after five in the evenings. Rajjo's hands were frozen as she sorted huge cartons of water and other goodies for the rally lined up in the living room and bedrooms. It was just a week to go before the rally and Rajjo was in the middle of it all, helping Seth-ji who was glued to his phone with the long-winding wire.

Rajjo had boiled down the entire exercise to numbers. How they could maximize the numbers?

She had heard the table over and over as Seth-ji had made her count, 'Aslam gets hundred, Kulwinder gets twenty-five, bastard good-for-nothing pig, Shailendra gets fifty-five, the amount he has eaten from me he should be getting me a country full of people, I also helped his bloody son-in-law escape arrest! Then they all come grovelling for favours.'

Seth-ji had repeated this sentence many times with his nostrils flaring and cheeks turning red.

It was clear that the Aslams and Kulwinders had to be fed and their pockets lined over a period of time to ensure the number of people they would bring to the rally. It was a long-drawn-out game that Seth-ji played. Rajjo could see new worry lines etched over his wrinkles.

As she sat numbering the parcels and boxes, she felt the hair on her neck stand up as she heard a familiar voice. Kesar led someone in through the main door. Rajjo turned around to see Rano and Karam standing in her living room.

Rano was clad in a green sweater and green shawl embroidered with yellow and pink silken threads. Rajjo had fought over it with Rano, as it was their mother's and the sisters had decided to wear it turn by turn. With a few parcels in hand, Rano just came forward and hugged Rajjo. Rajjo wanted to hug her and run away and hide at the same time. She was not ready to meet them yet. She was not ready to meet anyone from her village. Rano was looking pretty and happy. Karam looked handsome in a white kurta. His hair was shorter, his face thinner. Something came rushing back to Rajjo. Nostalgia tasted strange. She could taste the days and nights spent in the village fleetingly. She could smell the wheat fields turn ripe as many afternoons were spent with Rano lying in the belly of the soil.

It brought back sweet lazy days, gulping down the sweet sugarcane juice, drinking the last drop and racing to the house to feed the fodder to the cows. They smelt of home.

Kesar was happy to see someone from Rajjo's house had come to see her. He took the little gifts they brought with them and offered them water. Seth-ji acknowledged them and asked a few distracted questions. It was clear they were a hindrance to his hectic schedule. He went back to making some notes, but Rajjo had learnt from this brief awkward exchange that Karam had started working in a shop just on the outskirts of the city but now he was heading back to the village for a while. Shortly after the tea was served, Seth-ji made an excuse and moved to the bedroom leaving the trio alone.

The three of them together had never known silence before this. The teacups rattled, the spoons clinked, the heater in the corner of the room under the table blared. Every tug, every sigh and every thought was magnified till Rano made some generic comments. Rajjo responded in monosyllables in response to Rano's hesitant questions as she sat slurping the sweet hot tea.

Karam did not speak at all. Rano filled her in about the village and tales from back home, 'Totu is unwell. Father is frailer than ever. They found an alliance for me, I refused last minute so now Rikki is finalized for the boy.'

She paused but Rajjo looked on with a stony expression. 'We welcomed another calf this winter and Sheru named it Sanjay after the actor Sanjay Dutt! Reet is ready to deliver her second child the following spring and Sheru failed his classes again. He also ran away from the house and was hauled back by the local villagers and father. He got a sound beating. Mother blamed grandmother's genes because she would run away from the house just like Sheru did!'

Rajjo smiled hearing about Sheru, as Rano paused to catch her breath.

'These days he is on a trip that he wants to be a truck driver...some days he wants to be a tailor and those are the good days,' Rano smiled.

Another slurp and some more silence. Rano noticed Rajjo had dark circles under her beautiful brown eyes.

'Mother really misses you and sometimes she cries too, she wanted to come and see you and invite you for the wedding, but father told her not to go, since he was travelling and someone needed to be home... so I've come with Karam.' Her voice faltered just a bit towards the end.

Kesar sat there looking at the beautiful mistress staring into her teacup like it held some fascinating mysteries. Refusing to speak to her guests.

'Father also could not come as he is travelling...'

Rajjo got up and went back to packing the stuff away. She clearly wanted them to leave. It felt like they were all leaving her behind – all of them back home in the village. The seasons were passing by, along with her fugacious youth, while she was sitting here trapped in cardboard boxes. She wanted Rano to leave and go far far away, where she would not remind her of the wheat fields or the lazy afternoons they spent stealing guavas from the guava orchards. Ripe and sweet.

Rano quietly unwrapped something from her shawl and handed her to her sister. It was an idol of Goddess Durga. 'She will protect you, she will give you strength...' whispered Rano in Rajjo's ear and then she was gone.

Karam took one last look at Rajjo and his heart flipped over again. The hauntingly beautiful face ravaged by tragedy had only grown more mesmerizing. And then he was gone too.

Kesar looked up at Rajjo agitatedly slotting the boxes, counting packets and neatly arranging the food parcels. As Rajjo's hands moved of their own accord to the feverish rhythm, her mind wondered what to do with the deity, as she sorted the cartons one by one. Perhaps she was going to keep it. Her namesake.

*'For Protection and for strength...'* her sister had whispered.

Perhaps she was going to need it. She could sense it, she could smell it, as pungent as the first shower of monsoon soaked in by the parched soil; that the next few days were going to define her destiny.

Rajjo realized pulling a rally together was a mammoth task but she loved the part she played in it. The permits for the rally had come. Seth-ji was screaming at anyone and everyone.

'I have told those idiots not to keep rallies on any festival days or concerts or something that is entertaining the crowds somewhere else. Now they realize Maan Singh is performing in a nearby city! Idiots. That cuts my crowd further! Now how can a singer sing in this freezing weather? Why would people drag their arses out to hear him sing, why can't they hear his audio tapes instead?'

Rajjo by now had understood the basic thing. They were supposed to fill in the seats by hook or by crook. Realizing her husband was a smart man with ample experience, Rajjo readily soaked in all that he had to offer.

Rajjo felt vibrant and alive for the first time in days. Last night, after Seth-ji was satiated and fallen asleep, Rajjo sat by the window staring at the mango tree and the red diary sitting in her lap. She thought of the lunatic professor who once lived here and wished she could meet him.

She smiled at her foolishness as Seth-ji caught her expression. 'What are you so happy about today, my aunt is still alive!' He cackled at his own joke.

'You know I have read, a thing will continue to grow if it has an inherent pattern. All life forms have it. All plant life grows in patterns – an oak tree always grows taller and drops acorns and a baby will eventually grow taller and become a full person. I want to be an oak tree, grow taller – I don't want to be a shrub...' Rajjo had decided last night, that she was an oak tree, being a shrub was not how her story was going to end. She was going to learn and grow.

Just then Seth-ji's nasal acrid voice cut in her thoughts. 'Burn that red book you keep reading. That mad professor wrote in it. What happened? He went ballistic. I am going ballistic with the rally, and we can't have three ballistic people in the same house, it will affect my real estate on the house…no one will buy it at a good rate!'

Rajjo just stared with an odd expression at the incoherent blabber Seth-ji spouted. He wearily sat on the dining table, rubbing his hand on his almost bald head. Just then the phone rang and Seth-ji barked into it impatiently.

'How do we fill in the numbers? The villagers are not going to rain down from the skies, they ask for food, money, clothes! Madhuri Dixit is not descending upon the city that truckloads will throng the rally!'

Seth-ji, annoyed, slammed the phone yet again.

Rajjo placed a hot cup of tea on the table and muttered.

'Offer them something they can't resist'.

'I am offering them something already, some money and free food. Now do I have to offer them my house and my head?'

'Depends on whom are you offering all this to?'

Seth-ji turned to look up at his beautiful young bride.

'Get the school children to fill up the seats. Offer them sweets and something cheap. Talk to the teachers. Where else are there numbers and big crowds? They will come for half the price of the villagers and fill up the crowds…'

Seth-ji took his time sipping his hot tea. The only other thing he hated apart from running out of his tobacco was someone who seemed smarter than him. He really hated that.

Rajjo continued as she sipped her own tea.

'Shopkeepers in the mandi – offer them something they would want and in return each one of them sends two of their family members… count them in.'

'What do you think I could offer them in the mandi that they send their families?'

'Those food packets your party is sponsoring, you pick something from them for whoever participates. Get the food and the people…you give them business, they get you the crowds…'

Seth-ji looked at his wife with pride and anger… He smiled lovingly at her.

He had no appetite all of a sudden. It was a good idea and the bitch had beaten him to it.

Rajjo smiled at her husband. He was encouraging. She really wanted to see the rally come together. She was doing something worthwhile. For the last few days she didn't have time to dwell on her thoughts. She looked at the little deity she had placed on top of the fridge after Rano had left. She quietly picked it up and kept it on her bedside. Not that she was going to start worshipping it, but because it was a gift from Rano after all.

She was an oak all right. And that gave her the will and strength to get by.

The day of the rally was here. It was dark and grey. Clouds and smog painted a dark hue across the horizon.

Green carpets were strewn all around, and a crowd of almost five hundred people was preparing to settle down. People were huddled under thick winter clothes.

A few media people and cameras hovered around. The stage was set.

The podium and the speakers were tuned in, but the crowd was getting restless.

Seth-ji had made it out of the house and was sitting on a chair in the corner, issuing orders. His stomach pain had flared up again.

He was furious since the comedian who was supposed to keep the crowds entertained had not turned up. The average out-of-tune singer was belting out popular Bollywood numbers on stage but he was being booed by the restless crowd. They were enjoying the uncomfortable position the organizers had found themselves in, and the crowd found its own way of entertainment. Booing everyone off the stage.

It was going to be easily another ten minutes before those politicians arrived. Seth-ji was well aware if they were not going to engage the crowd they would not be able to hold it and welcoming the guest with an unruly crowd was a nightmare.

'How will it look if those idiots walk in wearing fancy clothes and are booed?! Seth-ji hollered to no one in particular, wondering how they could salvage the escalating situation.

Thankfully, the comedian made it in time and was hurriedly deposited on stage but unfortunately his jokes did not cut it. At one point someone from the crowd threw a potato.

Alarm bells rang in Seth-ji's head. *No, someone was carrying potatoes! Not a good sign!*

'What the fuck is the security doing? I haven't called them to ogle at the girls. Tell them to move their butts and see if there are any troublemakers in the crowd and someone remove that blasted potato and get that guy off the stage!' hollered Seth-ji and everyone around him swung into action.

Rajjo scrambled onto the stage, as no one else wanted to be booed whilst they cleaned it up. She picked up the potatoes and some empty bottles with a smile. Slowly the boos from the crowd turned into appreciative whistles. As Rajjo was about to leave, she sensed that the crowd was looking at her. They were observing her. Standing here in front of a crowd felt familiar. She was not scared. She confidently moved towards the mike to set it in position and did a hesitant mike check.

'Are you singing a song for us!' Someone hollered from the crowd.

'Would you like me to…?' Rajjo impulsively retorted.

'Yes…' A few young men howled. Seth-ji, furious with the turn of events, muttered to Mukesh, 'Who sent her up there?'

'Sorry, actually I sent her to set the mike up. She was standing there so I gave her a chore.' Mukesh blurted.

'Why don't I give you a hole in your sorry head? Get her off the stage.' He gestured the singer and the comedian to take over the stage.

Rajjo was going to pay for it, but for now Seth-ji had to move and welcome those young foolish politicians, as he could hear their chopper in the distance already. And someone had whispered that Jaswant, the local politician, was here already.

As Rajjo stood facing the crowd she had gathered over the past one week, it seemed like she had personally invited each one of them. No, they were not strangers to her. They had come because she had made sure they were here to warm the carpet and fill the seats. Afterwards, the singer and comedian claimed the floor and Rajjo once again stood in the crowd observing the whole thing unravel. She looked up to observe the strings of banners converging in the centre, crisscrossing the skies, announcing the arrival of these two faces that were going to descend from the chopper. Seth-ji had mentioned that they would be landing in a field nearby and then be ferried by white official cars with red blaring sirens. As the pamphlets fluttered in the sudden wind, Rajjo had an urge to run across and witness them descend from the skies.

She sprinted across the field, following the welcome party and went towards the crowd that had gathered at a little distance. By the time she reached the gathering, a sandstorm had taken over the entire area. Dust devils rose in a mad swirl and consumed everything with a vengeance. Amidst that descended a metal bird, gleaming blue and white in colour. It settled on the ground with its blades whirring menacingly.

She saw him then. He was the first one to get out, and wore a white kurta over jeans and boots. He was devastatingly handsome and Rajjo knew him by name.

Harsh Vardhan Singh.

The crowd stirred into action, some moving forward with garlands. A haphazard welcome followed. Organizers and party workers jostled with each other to get closer to the guests, including her husband who was trying to move through the crowd to make his presence felt. The other man, slightly older than Harsh Vardhan, with a moustache and a serious expression, was the senior political leader who was going to give the speech. Harsh Vardhan Singh was being groomed to take over the reigns of his political dynasty.

Rajjo could feel something pass through her body. Did he look at her? Suddenly self conscious of how she looked and what she wore, she tucked a stray strand of hair covering her face. Little did she know she made a vision standing in the clear daylight, wearing a flowing blue salwaar kameez as clear as the wild blue yonder, her curls dancing around her heart-shaped face in excitement. Her blazing amber eyes captivating one and all.

He had spotted her in the crowd and walked straight up to her with a smile. He took the garland she held on to and thanked her, looking into her eyes with an arrested expression on his face.

'Thanks...'

'That's not for you... actually it is for the other gentleman, I was told,' blurted Rajjo.

Harsh Vardhan froze for a second and threw his head back and laughed. Rajjo, slightly self-conscious, her cheeks burning, tried to get the garland back lest he refused to return it. Harsh gently offered it to her and walked ahead. Rajjo's eyes followed him. He turned one last time to look straight at her and then he was gone. Swallowed by the crowd.

She heard someone call out her name. It was Seth-ji. He was stewing with rage. But never did he raise his voice at his beloved wife. With a benign smile he asked her to let go of the garland as he wanted to use it to welcome the other idiot politician.

Rajjo quickly handed over the garland to Seth-ji. She was sure he had seen the exchange with Harsh Vardhan. There was a look on his face like he was going to make her pay for this. She could sense it in the smell of the gutter that rose to engulf her.

Running all the way back, her cheeks burning, Rajjo didn't know why the interaction with Harsh had affected her so deeply. Why should she bother? They were strangers, ships passing in the sea, and the sea was so vast that they were not going to converge in this lifetime. With a heavy heart she lay down in the dark room with printed bed sheets, staring at the ceiling. She could feel the frosty blade against her breast; she had tucked it in her brassiere so she could feel its presence at all times.

An urge rose in her to use it and soak the printed sheets red and end it all.

No. It was not time yet. She stared at the mango tree and noticed some sparrows fluttering in the branches. It was late afternoon. Tired and exhausted from the last few days, Rajjo fell into a deep, disturbing and exhausted sleep. Thankfully her husband was still out in the market square managing the rally. As she fell asleep, a thought repeated in her head that gave her hope to wake up from the afternoon nap.

*She was going to be an oak.*

Rajjo was woken up frantically Kesar. 'Seth-ji is very angry and he is asking for you! There is chaos out there, because there is a sudden shortage of food packets and food packets and everything is chaotic, they need more hands...'

Rajjo grabbed her dupatta and ran out. She came back in and grabbed the deity from her bedside.

She felt bad for leaving a job assigned to her midway.

Dusk had settled, and she could hear the receding noise of the chopper. Her heart sank. How could someone she did not know affect her to this extent? How could he make her feel these emotions when he did not even know her name?

It was strange.

She was not going to think about the stranger who had disappeared in the skies. She started handing out packets to the disgruntled villagers who wanted more food. Some complained they were promised liquor and that next time no one from their village would turn up if they did not live up to their word!

The little plastic packs contained some bread and a few vegetables from the mandi. The villagers were also handed water to drink, along with a threadbare blanket. People were sitting back in the vehicles assigned to them; tractors, buses, cars and were heading off in various directions.

Rajjo was glad the day was ending.

She caught sight of her husband looking at her, sitting in a chair with a smile on his face as he gestured to her.

'We have the local MLA coming over to our house in the night for dinner tomorrow. Prepare something nice – we have to entertain him. He is impressed with your work. He saw you on stage! And he will help me set up the cable TV business. So be ready for tomorrow.'

Seth-ji smiled at her. Rajjo knew she was supposed to be the perfect host and she rushed back home to start the preparations for the following night.

Seth-ji came home shortly afterwards. He simply hugged her and slept. In the early morning, he reached out for her and this time, Rajjo willingly gave herself to him.

As he lay spent he looked at her lovingly and muttered, 'Be good tonight.' Rajjo nodded as he turned over to sleep some more and dream about the handsome Harsh Vardhan.

## December 1991: New Year's Eve

It was a cold day Rajjo woke up to. Grey and dull with the temperature dropping to 12 degrees outside, Rajjo shivered inside the house. The puny heaters plugged next to the bed and layered clothing were the only solace against the biting cold.

The overcast sky loomed as she collected the damp clothes from the terrace. She would have to put the fan on in one of the rooms to dry them and get rid of the musty smell. But how could she get rid of the sense of foreboding she was feeling within? It had been there from the moment she had woken up today. Rajjo had pushed it far behind in her brain, so that the warm scent of the handsome man would take over. Thinking about him made the chores and the sense of unease bearable. It amused Rajjo that she drew comfort from this stranger on a cold grey winter morning.

As she glanced at the calendar she also realized it was the last day of the year. She removed the calendar and shoved it in a drawer. The passage of time irked her.

With a sigh she focused on preparing for the dinner tonight. Out of curiosity she had found out more about the minister visiting them. She had learnt he was a powerful man, a promising candidate, looking after an important portfolio in the party. He was associated with important issues like women's rights and health care. Seth-ji had proudly informed Rajjo how Jasbir Singh had been known to him for a long time and was going to help him with his political ambition and cable TV business.

Rajjo sneezed again. She could feel a headache creeping up.

She was feeling under the weather with the chilly winds, or perhaps something else. She found some time to dig into her trunk and visit her red diary before she had to prepare everything.

Just then the old grandfather's clock tinkled. Another hour had gone by, it was almost six and time for Rajjo to be ready for the evening. Her dinner party was arriving at eight-thirty.

She could hear the birds flying homeward, reminding her of walking back home along the little canal that ran through their village after sunset with her siblings. She shrugged the thought away and lit up the gas with a matchstick, hoping Seth-ji would be satisfied with her efforts for the evening.

Strains of a classical song could be heard from somewhere inside the house along with the smell of Rajjo's cooking. The dinner guest had arrived and was happily devouring the snacks prepared by Rajjo while she served them drinks. She had mastered the art of fixing a glass of whisky just the way her old husband liked it. She hated the pungent smell of whisky but sometimes she gulped it down when Seth-ji was not looking. The burning sensation warmed her from head to toe. As she stood on the kitchen counter making another round of drinks for the men, she gulped down yet another neat little peg of whisky. Kesar, who was chopping onions for the salad, chuckled. It was their little secret.

They could hear the important guest and Seth-ji discussing politics. While Rajjo waited for the fried potatoes to heat before she could serve them, she stole a moment to think about him. Harsh Vardhan. Her mind wandered around the man who had come down from the skies in the chopper. There was something about the way he'd held her gaze. It was the same feeling she had when she had guzzled her first glass of alcohol in the cold winter.

Rajjo peeked at the guest again through the green curtain.

As she made a trip to the drawing room once again, she sensed an odd stench that hovered around their guest like an old wet blanket. The minister was a burly bearded man with glasses, more fit to be a wrestler than a politician. Rajjo caught him leering at her lustfully as he sipped his drink.

Rajjo went inside again to serve another round of fried snacks and she could feel the guest's insolent gaze all over her.

Jasbir initiated some conversation with Rajjo about her village and the weather, but she deliberately kept her head down and the conversation to a minimum as she served some paneer.

Somehow her heartbeat had picked up pace and she could feel herself sweating in the cold dead night. The hair on the back of her neck stood up. She could smell a foul wound festering – but could not understand her discomfort. She was aware of the tension in the room as Seth-ji watched them. And then as she passed Jasbir his hand accidentally brushed her back and went lower. Rajjo looked at her husband who merrily ignored the act, nursing his drink and swaying to a classical Punjabi number that belted out from a giant stereo covered with a white embroidered scarf.

Rajjo hurriedly retired into the kitchen. Relieved to find Kesar, wrapped in reams of warm clothing, guzzling down the dinner Rajjo had given him to eat.

It was time for the main course to be laid out.

Seething from Jasbir's impudence, Rajjo reached for the jar of fiery ground red chillies, took a spoonful and sprinkled it in one of the main dishes. Kesar watched with his mouth agape, and his hand frozen midway. Rajjo winked at him as she took the food out to serve.

She came back inside the kitchen where Kesar waited for her with a worried look. Just then a bout of coughing followed. Rajjo did not move as Kesar hurriedly wiped his hands on a rag and ran out with a jug of water and a few glasses.

From what Rajjo could hear it seemed they both were coughing their lungs out. Rajjo bit her lower lip to stop the urge to chuckle. It felt good. The high of the drink made consequence seem like a fuzzy detail.

Kesar came back with a worried look. Rajjo wanted to share a hearty laugh. She turned to peek from the jaded green curtains through the haze of cigarette smoke and crooning of the old song. She could see Jasbir wiping his mouth with the handkerchief. His eyes were watering and his nose was an angry shade of red.

Clearing her face of any telltale mischievous expression, Rajjo stepped in the room to clear the plates as Seth-ji cleared his throat deliberately.

'Jasbir, you were always a disciplinarian, and my young wife here gets into trouble just about too often!'

Rajjo's hand froze midway as she picked up the dishes. The feeling was back again. Perhaps she had misheard the comment. Seth-ji stood up and instructed Kesar to clear everything. He gestured to Rajjo to follow him into the bedroom and made her sit on the bed. Rajjo did as instructed and her old drunk husband collected his favourite pillow from the bed. The sense of dread and panic began to set in. Rajjo sat immobile. She clutched the Durga deity that was on her bedside tightly to quell the sense of foreboding. A fleeting hope clung on, refusing to leave. Maybe she had misunderstood.

While Seth-ji changed into his nightclothes, displaying his old sagging skin as he removed his formal attire to don his nightwear, he turned to Rajjo.

'He is an important man…' Seth-ji explained calmly, as if he was talking to a little child.

'I will be sending him in.' He patted her head gently. There was no expression on his face. No pity, no guilt, no apology. It was like he was sending her to do a chore in the market.

Through her shock and numbness she heard him call out to Kesar who was washing the dishes in the kitchen to come out and press his feet. Minutes later the tall and heavyset Jasbir walked in reeking of alcohol. Something deep and guttural raged. He towered in the room. She heard the door being locked from the outside. Should she run, should she scream, should she just sit?

Rajjo was not going to move, she was not going to give in. She was going to fight. But her resistance was no match for the lust carried by the man. She could hear the strains of a beautiful song sung by a classical singer permeate the room as Seth-ji had increased the volume. She knew the porous house walls could not contain the noises.

It was going to be a long dark night. As if on cue, a flurry of fireworks went off. She remembered it was New Year's Eve. The dark black sky outside exploded with firecrackers as the man assaulted Rajjo. She could see the beautiful lit sky through the window as she was pinned down on her bed. It was a spectacle to watch the dusky black sky erupt with firecrackers and illuminate the firmament.

As she heard the firecrackers ushering in the new year, she could almost feel the warmth of the stove her siblings and she sat around. She could almost taste the customary sweets her mother cooked for them at New Year as they watched the firecrackers go up in the sky from their courtyard.

As she lay unmoving underneath Jasbir, her face changed to horror when she saw him removing his leather belt and looking at Rajjo with lust. As Rajjo lunged away in panic, her cries were drowned in the crackers of the night and the classical song striking high notes in the room next door. The crackers continued for an hour, but her ordeal much longer.

In the morning, Rajjo was blue and black in most places, dried and curdled blood marked her entire body. Vicious bite marks marred her satiny skin. She was barely in a state to walk. Her mouth was swollen parched and dry. Her desperate thirst was killing her more than the wounds. A loud blaring siren in her would suddenly go quiet and blare again. She could feel her blood stuck to the sheets – she could smell last night all around her. A thick sticky liquid oozed and swirled in her right ear.

She had an urgent need to get out of the bed. The first thing she did as she collected her clothes and painfully dressed, was to hunt for the Goddess who was supposed to be sitting in the room looking over her. She could not move without wincing, she could not feel her legs. Her fingers seemed crushed. A voice was streaming into her ear. Someone was calling out her name. It was her mother perhaps. She had come to take her away from it all. It was a bad dream. No… it was her husband.

Seth-ji was knocking at the door. 'Durgaaa!' his voice came from a distance. The minister snored and slept next to her. At some point he must have locked the door from the inside.

Rajjo slowly and painfully found the Goddess and walked towards the bathroom like her feet were chained with a thick metal rope, half scared that the monster would get up and attack her. She wanted to reach the door and lock it from inside. As soon as she reached the washroom and locked the door behind her she opened the window.

Another dull grey and cold morning greeted her, the beginning of a new year. Her mother used to encourage the family to pray at the temple first thing in the morning to bring them happiness through the year. Rajjo looked at the deity and threw it as far away as she could with disgust, using up all the strength she had in her bruised body. She fell into a heap. The knocking had stopped. The tap water trickled behind her, the sound came from a distance yet again. Her world did not sound right. The whistle of an engine and a long howl of a shrieking train were the last things she registered before she passed out in a deep sleep.

She could hear the thundering again. Was it raining outside? She felt the hard cold floor. The images returned. She was in the bathroom.

Someone was knocking on the door gently. She took the metal blade carefully from the sink cabinet where she'd hidden it and sat staring at it. Her right ear seemed numb as the knock could be only heard in her left. She turned her right ear towards the noise. There was only a deadly silence.

She could smell freshly cut wheat. She could smell the fodder. She could smell the rain, the old man preparing fresh balls of jaggery and laying them out to dry back home. Strains of prayers blaring from the loudspeakers jutting out from the gurdwara bordering their village every morning and evening.

Was this tiny glinting blade the end? Was this her destiny, to end it all in a dingy bathroom with two old men looking over her body? Someone hammered at the door.

'Durga! Durga come out!'

She wanted to scream at them telling them not to call her Durga.

She just sat, locked in the bathroom for hours. She could not tell what time it was. The water was cold, her body was cold, the blade was cold and no one called her out. No one called her name anymore. She had heard Kesar call out once or twice but then he had also stopped.

Finally when the silence was utter and complete, she stepped out.

Kesar sprang up, huddled in the corner of the bedroom, waiting for her to emerge. He had almost dozed off as he waited for her to come out. He saw her standing at the door. His face wore a shocked expression. A cry escaped his lips. He could barely recognize her face. The bed sheets lay rumpled and soiled from the night before.

The man was not there.

However, Seth-ji limped in. Smiling at her. Stopping short for a second at the sight of his wife's bruised face and then recovering from his shock as he limped towards Rajjo. 'Bastard. Next time he'll pay for this, I will make him pay. He is not getting away with this. Kesar make her some hot milk.'

Kesar did not move from the spot, frozen, still staring at Rajjo's face. Seth-ji shot a warning look at the boy who scuttled out of the room.

He turned to look at his wife, her eyes blazing. He could see the glint in her eyes. He also noticed the blade in her hand. She was holding it close to her wrist and in a minute it was pressed next to his throat.

Shocked and scared at the sudden turn of events Seth-ji held his breath. Wise enough not to talk or placate her. He let her decide how she wanted to proceed for that was his best chance of survival.

Rajjo was inches away from cutting the veins on his neck. She was going to do it. She could sense his fear, she knew she had his life in her hands. A small cut was all it would take for the warm fresh blood to soothe her wounds, to flow out and stain the room dark red.

Kesar came back with a glass of milk in his hand and stood frozen to the spot. He looked on. Watching the scene play out. And then to his relief, she put the blade away. Then she walked out of the room.

Seth-ji collapsed on the bed. Kesar realized she was leaving. He hoped her husband would stop her. But Seth-ji did not call out to her, he did not scream, he did not want her back. He just slumped into a ball and coughed a bit.

Kesar sprang into action and ran after her, he tried to stop her. Held on to her hand as she reached the main gate. The cold hit them both. His warm salty tears mingled with the blast of cold on his face as he pleaded her to stay. He knew she was going to leave him and go far away.

Before she left, she turned once more to look at the little boy in a cream shirt, a threadbare yellow sweater barely keeping the cold away, and blue shorts. She wanted to remember his sweet smile and his soulful eyes. She wanted to carry him with her.

Kesar could not help but wince as he saw her looking at him. Tears spilled down his face. She stood there with a swollen face, the black eye, broken jaw, the fresh cuts angry and red. She looked wounded and broken. She could barely walk.

Kesar called out to her one last time. He wanted her to wait. He rushed inside to fetch the red diary from under her bed. Kesar had often seen her smile as she read it over and over. He held it out to her. With great effort she grabbed the diary, and then she turned away. It was difficult to see if a tear had escaped through her bruised swollen face.

Kesar stared at her departing figure. He had to tell someone. He knew the shop of the man who had come to see her from the village. Maybe he would help out. Wearing his little rubber slippers he ran all the way to the busy market plaza. While he ran, Rajjo limped through the busy marketplace, getting curious, sympathetic and horrified reactions from onlookers. A little further she passed out, only to wake up in a small government clinic.

They had put her on a drip and questioned her repeatedly, but apart from her name and her husband's name Rajjo did not say a word. The clinic was called Satnam Charitable Centre. The woman in charge spoke to Rajjo calmly and explained to her that they were going to take pictures of her bruises. She had been assaulted and a police complaint had to be lodged. Rajjo went through it all, trying to hear what was said with her left ear. There was complete silence in the right one.

She sat listlessly and the camera clicked. She was taken for a medical examination as Rajjo sat through it all. The doctor gave her a pitiful glance shaking her head. They had prepared her report. They suspected rape and torture.

'One of your ear drums is severly damaged.' The doctor informed Rajjo.

'But these days you can get machines and advance procedures to help you.' The doctor then turned to a nurse who wanted to take her away to attend to another patient.

It began to drizzle as the dark clouds ushered in the dusk. Rajjo gulped some cold air and passed out again, only to wake up in the dead of the night on a strange narrow bed with the smell of sterile hospital spirit flooding her senses. Suffocated and scared, Rajjo quietly left the clinic. As she walked the deserted streets, watching the fires lit on the sidewalks gently warming the huddled souls in blankets around them, she went back to the professor and the red diary one last time. If life were a story, the plot of tragedy was its soul.

Was it pre-written that she would walk the streets half dead?

Her mother's voice filled her ears as she sat reading from the holy book next to the blackened stove. She could feel the heat from the cooling stove as her mother's voice emboldened with faith spread across the house.

*Nights, days, weeks and seasons, wind water fire and nether regions, in the midst of this he established the earth as a home for Dharma, upon it he placed the various species of being. By their deeds and their actions they shall be judged. God himself is true and true is his court. The good and the bad, the ripe and the unripe shall there be judged.*

Rajjo damned it all and continued to walk. She rejected the court of God as she passed out outside a small temple on the roadside with a dry chuckle. She was convinced this was her last breath and all she wanted was to go back home and lie in the expanse of the sea green fields under the turquoise blue sky.

# 7

## January 1991

RAJJO woke up in a stark room. There were four walls painted white and there was a narrow bed in one corner. A steel jug of water covered with a plate had been placed on a narrow side table along with an apple and a few bananas. She could hear light strains of a religious prayer floating in the background.

The room was cold as the evening mist drifted through the open window. Her body ached and her stomach rumbled like she had not eaten in ages. Without thinking Rajjo reached out for the fruit, peeled the banana and chewed on it. Immediately she winced in pain. She paused and looked around once more, wondering where she was. Was she back at the clinic?

Her mind threw up a hazy visual of her sitting on the highway on a cold winter morning, watching the cars whir by in a haze as the kind owner of an eatery had pitifully offered her water since she was bleeding. She could not recollect how she had reached the highway either.

And then her mind turned soft and feathery like a cloud, it was numbing down the aches and the biting cold, a liquid streamed across her body, a sharp horn hooted, a giant truck sped through the highway and then there was bliss again.

She'd woken up in this narrow bed. She took a cursory look at her surroundings again, when she read a sign through a window.

The board said Shradha Swami Foundation. Living in the grace of God.

Rajjo just stared at it. She was in some sort of hermitage.

From the open window, she could see colourful twinkling lights hung over a big and imposing black metal gate. Her foggy mind reminded her about this religious group, Shradha Swami Foundation. It was a huge spiritual establishment and they had organized a blood donation camp in her village along with a free dental check-up. The participants were also given a packet of biscuit as a bonus. She remembered her brother had gone three times for the extra packet of biscuits till he was shooed away.

Her lips felt parched and her throat burned. With an effort Rajjo reached for the jug of fresh cold water and gulped it down thirstily. As she put the jug down, she noticed the picture of the man who was the founder of this spiritual organization. A Godman. He wore a white robe, an orange turban and an affected smile. His hands were raised in a gesture of blessing. Rajjo smirked at the pose.

An unexplained anger formed in the pit of her stomach towards the man of God in the photo hanging on the wall. Rajjo looked around the place and hunted through the drawers awkwardly, finally chancing upon a lead pencil. She limped up to the calendar only to draw a moustache, dragon teeth, bushy eyebrows and disfigured nose with a vengeance. Every stroke of the pencil made her feel better till the lead was spent.

A soft chuckle made her look around.

It was a woman wearing a white salwar–kameez. Her hair was tied up in a black turban-style cloth. Her freshly washed face beamed at Rajjo. She wore a military green sweater buttoned all the way up and her feet were clad in wornout sneakers. Rajjo sized her up as someone in her late thirties. As the woman moved forward one could see a slight limp in her gait.

'Your medicines are here…' the woman said in a matter-of-fact way.

Rajjo did not respond. Her voice had authority and so did her posture.

The woman scraped a chair and sat down with a sigh.

'What happened with you?'

Rajjo stared at her visitor, defiant. It was clear no answers were forthcoming form her side. The woman after a long pause continued.

'So I am guessing you know where you are? This is a hermitage, an ashram – we call it the Ashram from the Shradha Swami Foundation. We have more than fifty million followers who believe in walking the path of God with us. His Holiness Amrik Singh-ji Maharaj was the founder and now the ashram has been taken over by his third descendent, Her Holiness, Ranjot Kaur Mattewal, also known as Rani Maa to most. Her grace and presence wash away the sins of her devotees. I am Kuljeet and I am here to welcome you on behalf of the ashram.'

Rajjo stared on with a blank expression. The woman could sense her disinterest and slight animosity. She continued in a sharper tone. 'This place was a barren land infested with snakes. With his belief, Maharaj-ji made it into a haven. The orchards and the gardens you will see around this ashram were created by him for his followers to stay in peace and follow the path of God. A devout truck driver brought you in half dead. It is for a reason. This path of God has chosen you.'

As soon as Kuljeet had finished talking, Rajjo managed a sarcastic grunt. Her swollen face barely moved with the effort. A small mirror with a dirty pink plastic frame hung on the wall opposite to her. A disheveled face and hair stared back at her. She turned away from the image in disgust. Kuljeet observed Rajjo's behaviour and continued as if there was nothing amiss.

'The ashram regularly organizes relief for people from cyclone and quake-affected areas, disease, vaccination and education camps, apart from dedicating itself to the service of God and taking his message to his people.'

Rajjo smirked again. As if in response to the smirk, Kuljeet added...

'...and beaten up, spent people like you also seek shelter here, which we give freely...'

There it was said out aloud in the room. The woman continued in the same unaffected tone.

'I am Kuljeet. In case you need anything ask for me. You can stay here till you recover, and then we shall see how you want to continue. When you feel better you can help around with the chores if you feel like. The medication, if you choose to take it, is on the table.'

As she limped out of the room Rajjo spat out.

'I don't want to be here.'

Kuljeet turned around, her face clear of any emotion; surprise or disappointment. Unruffled.

'Then don't. That's the gate. You are free to walk away. Just fold the bed-sheet and the quilt before you leave.'

Kuljeet turned to leave, their eyes locked for a brief moment and then she added for good measure, '*As is pre-ordained people speak their words. As it is pre-ordained they consume their food. As it is pre-ordained, they walk along the way. As it is pre-ordained, they see or hear. As it is pre-ordained, they draw their breath. It's all the will of God.*'

Rajjo stood defiant, holding her limbs. Not waiting for a response Kuljeet added in the same breath. 'Also a pair of fresh clothes, a sweater and a bar of soap is provided for you, it's on that chair – you can take it with you if you want.'

Saying this the woman limped out of the small dark room.

Rajjo sat on the cot. Numb. And then she started putting the quilt away. Rajjo was not going to stay a minute. She was going to go far far away. She had not figured where, but somewhere. As she reached out for the clothes, she saw a booklet sitting on top of the pile. The charismatic face of a woman stared back. Rajjo wanted to know more. She read the label on the booklet. Shradha Swami Foundation – An Insight.

Despite herself Rajjo opened the booklet and there she was, Rani Maa, staring at Rajjo in her full glory. Wearing a red sari, a huge bindi sat on her forehead. Her glistening hair added to her royal stature, her piercing gaze looked through the camera. She was devoid of any adornments. She seemed like a royal rather than a Godwoman. A hint of a smile played on her lips. A paragraph about Rani Maa extolled her virtues, and Rajjo gathered she travelled the world and visited the ashrams and gatherings, meeting her devotees. Ostensibly, this Godwoman was spreading the grace of God and bringing her devotees closer to the almighty.

A picture of Rani Maa standing on a podium and addressing a gathering of thousands who bowed in reverence stared back at Rajjo. She gazed at the picture for a long time.

The twinkling of the lights outside lit up the deep dark orchards around, the chill coming in from the window intensified. Rajjo found herself shivering. The chorus of the prayers increased to a crescendo, they were going to wrap up for the night. She zoned out the chants, her mind still in turmoil. Should she choose to stay on, where would this path lead? Why was she compelled to stay? Was she really free to choose? She wished she could cut her brain out and put it in a jar and place it by the windowsill and let something else decide. However, the more she looked at the picture of the Godwoman and her devotees, the more the desire to stay tugged at her heart. Was the choice she made right now her own?

Rajjo took an instant decision to stay. Somehow this Godwoman pulled her. Slowly Rajjo sat down, opened the bedsheet and spread it back on her little cot. The chanting outside stopped. The prayers were silent. As she sat alone by her little window, welcoming the cold mist on her face, she heard the crickets and the silence. She wondered about that picture which drew her to the Godwoman? Perhaps she should wait around and see if the answer presented itself.

## March 1991

March was here already, chasing the winter away and gradually leading the skies into the bright summer months. The crops would be ready to harvest soon. It had been over a month since Rajjo had arrived at the ashram.

Just as the winter was fading away, so were the marks on her face and her wounds. She moved around in the familiar compound, spending a lot of time in the courtyard built around a patch of garden with two fruit-laden guava trees. One bore pink guavas and the other white. They seemed like siblings.

For the past month she had lived in the hermitage and been provided with clothes and other basic necessities. No one stared at her healing face or asked questions. She liked being here as no one bothered her when she sat for hours, not moving or twitching. It was bliss. This place had its own rhythm.

Unlike Kuljeet and the other people in the ashram, Rajjo did not pray three to four times a day or read the holy books. She just sat endlessly under the guava trees. However, she had been gently reminded a week ago to decide if she wanted to take on the duties of a sewadar (devotee dedicated to working in the commune) or if she wanted to leave. She was still indecisive. A fly buzzed around her and sat on Rajjo's nose. Rajjo wanted to swat it, but she did not move. Inaction had been her state of being for the last few weeks. Unexpected and sudden anger flared up inside her that she had allowed herself to sit here, her life suspended and trapped between two beautiful guava trees. Having made up her mind, she straightened herself as she shooed the offending fly away from her nose.

She had to look for Kuljeet. She was the one who gave orders around here. People were not too fond of her, but they didn't hate her either. They were just indifferent.

Rajjo went around the ashram looking for the familiar limping figure wearing her trademark woollen scarf in blue or military green colour over her white sewadar uniform. She could smell the food being cooked in the huge kitchen for the community lunch. It was a familiar, comforting smell.

As Rajjo walked the length and breadth of the ashram looking for Kuljeet, she once again stopped at the big black gate with a board that announced to the outside world, Shradha Swami Foundation! Rajjo walked through the corridors, peeping into the rooms alongside. The beds were occupied with people who were unwell. Rajjo had been on one of the beds till a couple of months ago. Some rooms were allotted to sewadars who stayed in the ashram. There were others, mostly volunteers, who visited from the nearby villages to pray and partake of the community meals.

Rajjo had also seen a few young armed men welcomed in the compound, given food and rest, only to slip out in the middle of the night like phantoms. Rajjo had not given it much thought. One moment she wondered what was happening in the world outside and then she did not want to bother.

She checked for Kuljeet in the administration wing, a large hall that had a cheap wooden table with some plastic chairs strewn around. A handsome man, all of thirty, sat behind the desk immersed in some papers. He wore a long blue robe. He was Arjan Singh, someone important. He had the kindest eyes and, like Kuljeet, he religiously read the holy book and offered his prayers. He had fair skin and a gentle voice. He towered over most people in the ashram and Rajjo often wondered how was he so contained and nimble even with such a huge frame. The day-to-day running of the ashram took place between Kuljeet and Arjan Singh.

Arjan smiled fondly at Rajjo, but despite making an effort Rajjo could not smile back.

'I am looking for Kuljeet…' She muttered.

'She is in the langar ghar…,' he spoke kindly as if he was talking to a scared child.

Rajjo was touched at the way he spoke. This handsome man with melting brown eyes, he was going to be in Rajjo's life. She felt a warm breeze envelop her. It seemed as if there was a connect between him and the places she had known and liked while growing up, places familiar. Yes, he was going to be by her side. Rajjo shrugged the thought away, staying a second longer, examining that feeling. And then she left, securing her faded red shawl tighter.

Rajjo rushed to the langar ghar where food was being served to people sitting in rows on long red carpets on the floor next to each other. Rajjo could see used plates stacked up in one corner, indicating that the lunch service had ended.

Rajjo glanced at a few empty chairs in the yard under the guava trees. A few patrons were leaving post the community lunch, some were mingling with the sewadars, enquiring about Rani Maa's next visit. The only place left for her to check was the kitchen.

As Rajjo walked across, her heart started to beat faster. Would she let her stay and work? What if she refused, given Rajjo had not lifted a finger in the past few weeks. Even her disinterest in God was quite clear.

The large kitchen crammed with workstations, giant utensils, washing areas, buckets to chop vegetables and food stores welcomed her. Kuljeet was in the middle of it all, ordering around two sewadars who were taking stock of the pulses, oil, wheat and rice. She saw Rajjo entering the kitchen but ignored her. Rajjo stood in one corner waiting for her to finish. Then suddenly, in between her hectic instructions and ordering groceries, she paused and addressed Rajjo. 'You will need to wear the white salwaar-kameez, like the other sewadars and take on their duties if you want to stay on…' Kuljeet stated in a matter-of-fact tone.

Rajjo, shocked that she did not have to ask, nodded.

'You will be fine in the kitchen.' Rajjo nodded again, with a lump forming in her throat.

Kuljeet's act was neither out of kindness, nor fondness nor curiosity. Yet it was the most significant thing she had done for Rajjo. She'd officially allowed her to join them as a sewadar and stay on in the ashram. And then she heard Kuljeet add, 'Wisdom, honour and wealth are within the grasp of those whose hearts remain with the Lord.'

Rajjo stole her gaze away like a thief. She was not here to be one with the lord. Thankfully, Kuljeet continued, 'Anyway, we are short-staffed in the kitchen. Three of my women have moved to other ashrams! Rahat here will give you the overview.' Rajjo strained to hear every word with her left ear and then she turned towards the boy Kuljeet had pointed at.

Rahat was a teenager, barely five feet in height, with an adolescent stubble and acne on his face. A mop of dry curly hair sat on his head. His eyes were glazed. As if he was high on some drug. He stammered while speaking as he showed Rajjo around the kitchen while Kuljeet and the others moved away to inspect the little storehouse situated in the back of the property.

As she followed Rahat, Rajjo almost chuckled aloud. She was going to be serving people in the name of God!

For the next few weeks the kitchen was her solace. Rajjo would wake up at the crack of dawn to get ready for the chores that awaited her. The others would say their prayers before commencing, but Rajjo would resolutely stare out of her window, taking in the sunrise. The religious readings would start in the prayer room in the compound, the sermons could be heard all the way to the kitchen where Rajjo sat chopping vegetables, filling buckets and buckets of cabbage and cauliflowers each day. From absolute inaction she had gone to a continual state of action.

It was cathartic to cut and chop without stopping, without thinking. Her knife was her weapon and she wielded it with urgency. Rajjo emerged as a worker to reckon with, given her speed, dedication and desperation to work until she was exhausted enough to fall into her bed at night as if she was dead. She welcomed the tiredness. It was a race between her mind and body.

All that she allowed herself to think about was the way forward as she chopped stacks of pale green cauliflowers and red carrots that filled up the pink and white buckets. She liked the warm kitchen with its familiar vegetables and her fellow workers who were all connected in their devotion to God. Some women sang and repeated prayers and hymns as they worked in the kitchen, but Rajjo never joined in. Amidst the giant utensils, pots and pans with blackened bottoms, simmering oil and boiling pulses, Rajjo knew she was going to find the answer to why had she stayed back to live under the very name she hated. She could feel her answer was just round the corner, she would find it in a bucket of vegetables or under an onion. It was just a matter of time.

It was Rajjo's third week in the kitchen. She picked up her favoured apron from the dozens or so hanging in the quiet kitchen. Switched on the lights, opened the windows, upturned her little stool, washed her hands, and decided she was going to try another chore today. The chopping of vegetables had taught her focus. And now she wanted to learn some perseverance.

She decided on kneading the dough this week. She had seen many heavyset women heaving and panting with the effort to knead, since it was done for a hundred or more rotis that were cooked for the lunch gathering.

She scooped a box inside the giant drum brimming with ground wheat and poured the wheat in a large circular steel dish, followed by a jug of water. The pungent smell of water mixing in the fresh ground wheat took her back to her village. As she started kneading the dough, a pain shot up reminding her that her wounds were still healing. She welcomed the reminder and worked her body harder. She felt the pain rise and bubble and finally die out as it flowed all the way to the dough through her fingers.

The others started filtering in the kitchen after finishing their morning prayers, not surprised to see Rajjo as the first one there.

While Rajjo mechanically worked her hands, her mind wandered off to things she had assimilated lately. She had heard some whispers. Rahat, the thin lanky boy who secretly smuggled cigarettes and cheap drugs in the compound for one or two junkies, was her self-proclaimed friend and companion. The God house was beginning to show its true colours and Rajjo was glad to learn everything and more.

After her chores, she liked to sit on the edge of the property facing the orchards to watch the sun go down, while the others offered evening prayers from the holy book.

Rahat often joined her as he rolled up a beedi to smoke and watched the sunset. He empathized with Rajjo, perhaps because she was brought in half dead, with a busted ear and she spoke very little. Yesterday he had boasted about his hero Mehtaab Sarkari, a revered Godman who ran the entire place. It was the first of him Rajjo had heard and she was sure she was going to hear much more of him. She was surprised to learn from Rahat's not so subtle insinuations that Mehtaab had close links with important leaders of the extremist Sikh outfits that had the state terrorized since the mid-eighties. Apparently, Mehtaab had flourished through this period of turmoil and now he was the policy man in the ashram.

Rajjo wondered if Rahat knew the amount of trouble he could get into if he was caught saying all this to other people. Despite herself she advised him sharply, 'You should watch your words, be careful with them.' Rajjo cut short his accounts of Mehtaab and his association with the Khalsa movement.

Rahat shrugged.

'I think it's good, what they are doing, the extremists. I want to be with them…fighting for our rights and religion.'

'Then why are you not with them? Fighting? What are you doing here?'

'I am a bastard. I am scared, I am lazy, I am a cunt…one day I want to fight with them and the other days I just want to tell them to go to hell.'

And then he went back to smoking his joint.

Rajjo looked at the strange boy. He had complete clarity of his own character that was rare to find. But she knew the chinks in this God haven were beginning to show.

The next morning, in the kitchen, Rajjo shoved the conversations with Rahat aside as she worked the rolling pin, flattening the little balls of dough before they were put on a black pan to bake. The lady passing her the round balls of dough spoke to Rajjo in a friendly voice, 'Heard there is a visitor from a newspaper. Kuljeet will be bringing the visitor in here…'

Rajjo worked on the rolling pin non-stop, flattening the dough balls to a perfectly round shape and placing them on the hot griddle. Sweat rose and engulfed her. She could feel it running over her body as the heat from the hot griddle seeped into her clothes and pores. There was a slight flutter in the kitchen as the visitor finally arrived with Kuljeet, wearing pants and holding a notepad. He seemed to be some sort of journalist. Kuljeet was giving him a tour as he stopped by to peep in the kitchen. Kuljeet informed him how food was cooked for hundreds here to feed the villagers and other devotees.

'Wow, in the name of god Rani Maa is moving thousands for a good cause. More power to you…'

Rajjo stopped the rolling pin as she heard the awe in his voice.

'It's a hoax!' Rajjo wanted to scream. But she continued to look on, till she felt a sharp nudge from the lady as she waited for Rajjo to put a fresh batch on the piping hot griddle to bake. Rajjo's hands started moving again.

As she entered the kitchen the next morning she moved on to a new chore. Her favourite chore in the kitchen strangely proved to be chopping and piling up mountains of onions in coloured buckets. She could cry her soul out, she could cry in public and no one was going to be any wiser. It was liberating. However, she felt the guy in the long beard and black turban knew. The tall quiet and handsome Arjan toured the kitchen twice or thrice a day. Every time his eyes lingered a moment longer on the beautiful Rajjo. His kind eyes watched her closely.

As the week passed by, the onions got harder on her. The tears were drying up; her eyes were hurting. While she peeled the onions conversation steered to the history of the ashram. Rajjo's ears pricked up.

The heavy old lady who was a regular volunteer from the village knew everything about everything. She wore gold bangles, gold hoops and gold chains. She knew about recipes, she knew about wars and she knew about piles and other diseases. They called her Mai – a term used to address the elderly. She slurped on her sugary tea and continued her rant as she took a break from her chores.

'They say some dust fell on his pious feet from the top of the mound, when Amrik Singh-ji walked by. He sensed that some old souls were lying buried in the mound crying for salvation. The underground water was known to be very salty but the handpump pointed by the holy Amrik-ji yielded sweet water. First a gufa or tunnel was constructed and a diggie for water was dug. Canal water was arranged for water supply and the whole village drank for twenty-five years from that.'

Immediately after finishing her story she folded her soiled hands and prayed to the divine force. On cue the others in the kitchen did the same. Rajjo wanted to laugh. Suddenly it dawned on Rajjo that she was done with the onions and the chopping, it was time to move on to a new chore.

As she washed the sink full of utensils, the month spent in the kitchen raced in her head. It had been fruitful. Her obvious wounds almost healed, her body had become tougher. The soapy water swirled around, the tap gushed water on the mound of utensils piled up on the sink. A round water bubble floated up to her deaf ear and screamed, 'You need a sidekick to sell and a miracle to tell.'

As nights chased away the days, Rajjo found herself on the sewadar duty roster to serve langar in the main hall. She used a long spoon to serve the food to the people who had queued up in front of the tables. The others repeated the name of God as they served. Arjan Singh came and whispered, 'Without embracing Him you won't find any peace.'

'I am not looking for peace.' She continued to serve the food. Arjan smiled to himself as he observed the beautiful determined woman, standing behind the table, with a wooden ladle, pouring curry into the patrons' plates. Her lips were tightly pursed. Given the choice, she would probably have shut her ears as well. Arjan smiled, she was definitely the child of God and blessed at that.

It was her fourth week in the kitchen and Rajjo had befriended almost everyone in the kitchen routine with her shy smile. But only up to exchanging a greeting, or a nod as they passed each other. She usually sat aloof, but today she sat next to a new batch of young girls brought in by Mai, her guests visiting her from out of town. Rajjo and the others learned from Mai that the girls were over from the city to celebrate the festival of Lohri in the village and learnt about the ashram. And now they have returned to visit the ashram.

Lohri the harvest festival, marked both celebration and sharing. Wheat sown in winter was ready to yield fruit, and the ripe golden crops were ready to harvest. The bonfires in the night warmed her heart. Sisters danced around it to the beats of the dhols. Little balls of fire lit up their happy faces. They lay awake in the night, counting the stars, waiting for daybreak so the sisters could go from house to house singing folk songs, and neighbours would give them money and food as festival offerings. The songs she sang with her sisters wept in her belly, she dare not bring them out now.

She wondered if these city girls had ever waited for daybreak to go around the neighbourhood singing songs and dancing? The cacophony of young voices broke her reverie.

The girls gossiped as they worked in the kitchen, reminding Rajjo that young girls with curious minds could sometimes be a curse. The giggling got louder as they huddled in the little corner ostensibly peeling the cucumbers.

As the peeling continued, Rajjo heard the girls discussing Rani Maa's brochure announcing her next darshan programme in hushed tones. Rani Maa stared back like a queen from the glossy brochure, clad in a silk saree, an orange mark adorning her forehead. The girls flipped the pages to see other pictures on the brochure that announced various month-long activities that the patrons and followers could participate in.

Recently, Rajjo had discovered another key player in the ashram, a middle-aged woman who was the second-in-command, called Sukhmani, or 'Chhoti Ma.' She was usually in a salwaar kameez, and covered her head with a dupatta. She wore no make-up.

Rani Maa in her mid-forties usually wore a mark on her forehead. With luminous skin and slightly tinted lips, she looked radiant. And then there was the tall and broad Mehtaab Sarkaria who always wore a white turban and white kurta-pyjama. He made a formidable figure and his eyes drowned you. He commanded attention even in the picture in the brochure.

Rajjo lapped up the brochure the moment it had arrived the night before and she was amused to see the giggling girls poring over it in the kitchen. The girl with furious acne and thick-rimmed black glasses muttered, 'I heard Mai fighting with my dad who was teasing her for being a follower here. Mai told him off. And then my father and my mother had an argument where he said that he had friends who followed and worked in the organization closely. Some associated with them for business purposes too, and they said it was a crazy fest in there... that Sarkaria is sleeping with your demi-goddess. They are all flesh and blood! And they are making pots of money selling God!'

The other girls gasped. They were hurriedly shooed out of the kitchen by Mai who suspected trouble from the bunch of girls giggling together.

The giggly cackle soothed Rajjo's soul and stirred something deep within her. She followed the girls to the community eating area where people sat in rows on the ground. Sewadars walked up and down between the rows to serve people and distribute langar. Rajjo picked up a steel bucket filled with piping hot vegetables and started working the line, her mind abuzz with what she had just learnt. A germ of an idea started forming. A sliver of excitement gently unfurled in her limbs. A desire was born again.

Without showing any sign of her excitement, Rajjo quietly carried on, working the line, as she hurriedly wanted to reach the coterie of teenage girls who had sat down to eat with the rest of the patrons. Rajjo found them strangely liberated. Just like Rahat.

Rajjo poured extra vegetables for them and smiled. On impulse, before moving to serve the next person, she leaned forward and whispered to the young girl, 'Celebrate your sister's beauty, envy won't get you much. Open your heart to her, and your skin will clear up.' The girl in glasses almost dropped what she was eating from her hand. Like she had been caught harbouring a bad secret.

Later in the evening as Rajjo poured gallons of milk into the bubbling tea, she knew this was the last time she was going to be in this kitchen.

It was time to move on. She was going to get close to both Mehtaab Sarkaria and Rani Maa. Her work in the kitchen was done for now.

She stepped out with a tray laden with teacups as the bonfire was being set up in the courtyard. She passed the tea-laden tray around and sat in a quiet corner and remembered the festivities. The village kids came in various groups, singing folk songs and collecting their offerings from the ashram. Sewadars were distributing packets of food and sweets. As the sky darkened completely, the bonfire was lit and it roared as high as the guava trees, the warmth reaching all the way to the corridor near which Rajjo sat. The cold winter was far behind and the month of harvest was here.

## June 1991

The day had finally arrived when Rajjo would get to see the revered Rani Maa. She woke up earlier than usual and got on with her various chores for the day. The ashram was spruced up like a bride to welcome Rani Maa. An elaborate stage was set up in the big hall, and carpets were laid out for the devotees to sit on. Fresh flowers and incense adorned the compound.

A huge cutout of Rani Maa had been placed in front of the black gate. Since the month of harvest, Kuljeet and Arjan had made various trips to the other ashrams where they were needed but had returned two days ago to plan Rani Maa's arrival and to organize her sermon.

As Rajjo swept the corridors, beads of sweat trickled down her back. The heat wave from April had continued and Rajjo hoped that with the advent of June the clouds would come as well.

The humid summer months tested her patience as she watched and understood the spaces around. Finally, she was going to see the Godwoman within a few hours.

As her chores finished and the hot afternoon gave way to a heavy warm evening, she heard from a visibly excited Rahat that Rani Maa had arrived through the back entrance and was resting in her room before the sermon. People from nearby villages had started filtering in for the evening sermon.

Rajjo was assigned to look after the seating arrangements as well. While she went about making sure everything was sorted, the huge crowd who had gathered to hear Rani Maa's sermon settled themselves in. She lost track of time and was surprised to see the object of her interest approaching the stage.

Everyone stood up to greet her.

Rani Maa chose her colours for the day according to her astrological chart. So she was in green today. People bowed out of love and affection for this woman. The place was bustling with activity. Rajjo's gaze followed Rani Maa to the stage. Was she truly divine? What was it about her that brought all these people to their knees?

The stage had been ornamented with flowers and Rani Maa sat on a seat adorned with intricate gold patterns. Her eyes were closed in divine bliss. There were three to four mikes in front of the table set on the stage. The crowd waited with baited breath.

Rajjo had heard that Rani Maa's sermons were like unpredictable monsoon spells. Sometimes she talked about God, faith, politics, drugs, family, whatever caught her fancy and people found their answers in her discourse. Rajjo was keen to know what today's sermon was all about.

The mike crackled and her strong commanding voice took over. 'Today I want to talk to you. Really talk to you. Usually I talk about life, suffering, happiness, peace. Today I will talk about myself. For many of you will find yourself in me. I want to tell you my story of faith. I was brought up by my elder brother and married off to a man who was more interested in the gold jewels I carried with me in the house from my father's. I had no children, God did not want me to have any, but they wanted me out of the house, my husband's family. They tried to murder me in different ways, but I survived.'

Just then Chhoti Maa interrupted Rani Maa on the stage. Sukhmani whispered something in her ear briefly and an exchange of words took place.

Rajjo could see the crowd was mesmerized. They did not mind the interruption. Rani Maa turned towards the crowd and picked up from where she had left off. Her voice washed over the crowd, her honeyed notes drowning them. Soothing sitar played in the background, which added to the ambience of divine submission. Rani Maa continued to connect with her audience. Her gaze roamed to every corner of the room. She connected with each and every person in the hall.

'My husband's family performed witchcraft, sacrificed hens. I was bedridden and almost dying for two years. But with the grace of God, I was saved. Finally, unable to take my condition I ingested a poisonous fruit and vomited as my husband looked on. But the will of God was something else. I was taken to the nearby hospital by some kind neighbours where the learned doctors declared I would be dead by 8 p.m. My death was certain. To everyone's astonishment, most of all the doctors, I opened my eyes and walked back home.'

There was a pause. The audience responded. It was a performance where instead of applause, the audience bowed in reverence. Rajjo wanted to laugh hysterically as she muttered to herself, *she is poison proof, she is doctor proof, and she is witchery proof!*

Someone coughed softly. Rajjo turned to find Arjan Singh standing right behind her. There was an odd look on his face like he was trying not to laugh at Rajjo's assessment. But out of all the people, Rajjo thought him to be a true believer – why would he then tolerate any voice of dissent?

They stood listening to the Godwoman on stage. There were a few others dressed in saffron robes who sat on stage chanting verses in between her pauses. The smoke from the incense sticks turned the room into a hazy smoke box, an effective time warp that would carry you into a trance-like world, where Rani Maa performed gloriously. Arjan cleared his throat and whispered.

'I believe in God and giving, not the mediums…'

'Why are you here…?' Rajjo looked him in the eye.

'I have my reasons, you have yours, and the people here have their own, and each one of them is correct and worthy…'

Rani Maa's enigmatic voice sucked in her audience again. Minutes later, Rajjo saw a lot of activity going on back stage. A car had just arrived. Sewadars were gravitating towards the new arrival.

Arjan Singh moved away as well after Rahat whispered something urgently and ran off. Rajjo stood there intrigued with all the sudden activity till Rani Maa's voice filtered in.

'Life continued to be unbearable and I decided to end it by jumping into a well. I am not proud of it, and anyone who thinks of doing it should be condemned.'

Rajjo started walking backstage wanting to see what the whole brouhaha was all about.

She saw him then, Mehtaab Sarkaria, talking to a local politician who Rajjo recognized. But her gaze went back to Mehtaab Sarkaria. He was a tall charismatic man wearing white, in his early forties. He wore a white turban. His beard went all the way to his chest and added to his majestic demeanour. A heavy metal bangle on his right hand accentuated his thick arms.

'I want to leave in a rush. I have a meeting in an hour.' She heard Mehtaab instruct Sukhmani.

Chhoti Maa muttered hurriedly, 'She will just be finishing, she will wrap up in fifteen minutes, I have informed her.'

The divine discourse was to be wrapped up as the man wanted to leave early.

Workers scurried to serve food and drinks to Mehtaab as they retreated into a room. Rajjo joined in to help them fetch eateries from the kitchen. Rani Maa's voice washed over them while they moved about.

'As I jumped in the well, it was about 10 p.m. Some power descended like lightening and a voice called out to me. "Who are you?" I asked the voice… "I am your Lord. You shall not weep from now on. As you shall lay your hands on the sick, they shall recover. Second, you shall speak words out of my wisdom. Third, you shall prophesize. Fourth, my grace and power shall never depart you. Fifth, you shall preach."'

Rajjo was laughing inside as she put some sweet orange balls on a tray. Her brother Sheru could eat five in one go. She shook her head disbelievingly as she set the tray. This bull, people were buying it!

Just when she had mentally written the woman off, and started walking with the sweet-laden tray towards Mehtaab's room, the speakers blared again. Rani Maa's voice rose to engulf one and all, high and passionate.

'And I thought to myself what a useless story. I changed my mind about jumping, dismissing it all like a bad dream. For it was nothing more to me than that. It could not be. I went back to a life, earning money by weaving cane baskets, till my fingers bled.'

Rajjo stopped in the compound. She wanted to hear her finish. Her voice washed over her.

'Day in and day out, hundreds of baskets I wove for the next year. My eyes were weak, my soul defeated. Till one day I stopped weaving the baskets. I chose to believe in the dream he had given me. I chose to believe God had spoken. I chose to believe I was meant for more than weaving baskets and living a paltry life. I chose to believe I was gifted. The boons he gave me were not the boons of prophecy, but that of belief! I am not gifted, I don't have powers… All I have is my unshakable belief in him. And you have your unshakable belief in me!'

Rajjo could feel the applause in the air. Hell! She wanted to!

Attagirl!

The harmonium notes took over, as prayer committee members sang shlokas and religious songs to finish the discourse. Rani Maa walked off the stage, surrounded by sewadars. She passed Rajjo who stood with the tray of sweets, and someone moved her aside roughly so she would not be in Rani Maa's way.

Her deaf ear protested. Loud piercing noises could be heard. Was it coming alive?

Rajjo was stopped from taking the plate of sweets inside and told that Rani Maa, Mehtaab and the minister were having a private meeting. She took the tray back into the kitchen and started putting the sweets back in the box. Rahat followed her inside, his eyes glazed like he was high. Rajjo gave him a few pieces as he sat on the slab eating.

Just then they heard the sirens of the cars blare. They both lunged out to see the minister leaving. Mehtaab and Rani Maa also sat in their big gleaming white cars and drove away.

The thousand-odd people sat immersed in the faith and belief Rani Maa had left behind.

Rajjo and Rahat stood side by side looking at the dust settling after the cars had zoomed away.

'She is something, isn't she?' commented Raahat.

Rajjo was quiet.

'What do you think of her?'

The night was young and dark, the prayers reverberated in the compound and despite herself she heard her hoarse voice.

*'There is a golden saying; the reason why I lost my lamp was that the thief was superior to me in vigilance. He paid, however, this price for the lamp; that in exchange for it he consented to become the thief; in exchange for it to become faithless.'*

Rahat looked at her puzzled.

'Who is the thief?'

'Rani Maa…'

Rahat laughed and offered Rajjo a cigarette.

'So what do you think about the thief?'

'That the thief was superior in vigilance.'

Rajjo took a long drag and let the smoke leave her lungs bit by bit as she savoured the words she'd said aloud.

'I want the lamp, I am willing to be the thief as well, I am willing to pay the price for that…'

## JULY 1991

Rajjo swept the floors of the compound whilst her mind assessed and conflated different scenarios with every sweep. Rajjo now knew why she had stayed behind that cold January night in the hermitage. Her dalliance with a desire had become something deeper. It had crept up and consumed her lately.

Kuljeet and a few others were leaving for another ashram where a lot of activity was planned and Rajjo had to go along if she wanted to get closer to Rani Maa.

The heat wave added to the langour, with no sign of monsoon. For the past few days Rajjo had been waiting for an opportune time to talk to Kuljeet. She had tried a couple of times, but always found her in the middle of her prayers. To Kuljeet, her godliness and devotion was her panacea.

Kuljeet, always the soft-spoken one; with kind eyes, prayed five times a day, followed all the religious conventions and had wise things to preach when she spoke to people. Yet Rajjo could not trust her.

Her godly murmurings made Rajjo uneasy. As she mulled over Kuljeet while sweeping the compound she came across a few cigarette butts and hurriedly swept them away, lest a devout sewadar discovered them. Smoking and drinking was strictly prohibited on the compound. She was going to whack Rahat for being so careless with them. He could get thrown out.

As the day drew to an end, Rajjo could see a morose Rahat moping around the compound. She joined him after finishing her evening chores at the ledge. As they sat side by side in the darkness, Rajjo looked up at the skies. The atmosphere was stifling, with no sign of clouds. Rajjo's first thought was for the farmers back home, her people would be ready and waiting to sow the Kharif crops with the onset of monsoon.

Raahat broke her train of thought with his morose news.

'Militants killed eighty people travelling in two trains near Ludhiana. It is not safe to travel. They attacked the trains about a kilometer from the station, pulled their emergency cords and opened fired inside. Some people have said that Hindu passengers were identified before being shot. It was all because they had announced the elections in April next year.'

Rajjo could sense Raahat's fear and panic.

'How will people travel safely then?' Rajjo wondered aloud. She could see men moving suitcases and cartons across the compound. Grains, food and clothes were being loaded for the move to the next ashram. Again she felt that strange pull as she saw the suitcases being loaded onto a van. Rajjo did not want to be left behind, she wanted to go with them and move to another ashram. She had to request Kuljeet to take her. The echo in her deaf ear confirmed her plan.

'That's why the people of the ashram are never threatened by the militants. I told you, Mehtaab Sarkari is friends with them. They believe the ashram is promoting religious values. Travelling with the ashram folks is the safest. The number of people wanting to travel has thus been growing and it is for security reasons as well!'

'I want to leave with them for another ashram…' Raahat was surprised at Rajjo's admission.

'You are leaving? But why? I thought you liked it here.'

Rajjo averted her gaze. 'And stop throwing your stupid cigarette butts around and stop telling Mehtaab's stories to people. You will get into trouble! Get out of here and make something of your life. You are smart.'

Leaving a perturbed Raahat sitting alone in the dark, Rajjo retired to her room. She tossed and turned the whole night wondering how to convince Kuljeet to take her along. Only senior sewadars with a few years of service travelled from ashram to ashram.

Rajjo woke up with the same worry the following day, noticing the clear skies and unrelenting heat. As she entered the kitchen she wondered if she should make some tea and offer it to Kuljeet to sweeten the request? Rajjo thought of a smile, a cup of tea, a tear. Finally she settled on a dream. She switched off the gas and decided to talk to Kuljeet right away.

Mustering up some courage and clearing her throat she knocked on Kuljeet's room. Kuljeet and Arjan Singh both had the biggest rooms in the compound. She knocked on Kuljeet's door again and then stepped through the door. Thankfully Kuljeet had just finished a round of prayers, the prayer book still in her hand. She looked at Rajjo questioningly as Rajjo launched into her speech.

'I had a dream, I was with you, you were travelling to places far and wide, and I was following you around.' Even to her own ears it sounded corny, not one of the best ideas she had come up with.

Kuljeet just stared at her. Rajjo wondered if hard abuses were coming her way.

Without waiting for a response, Rajjo added hurriedly. 'I want to accompany you and the sewadars to the next ashram.'

Her declaration was followed by an uncomfortable silence in the room.

'I want to know more about the organization, I want to be an inherent part, I want to serve like you…'

One look at Kuljeet's face and Rajjo knew she was doomed. Kuljeet was not buying a word. Short of breaking into song, Rajjo had no idea how to get to Kuljeet. Kuljeet finally wrapped her prayer book quietly and deliberately in a muslin cloth.

'Taking away and giving back, God does not delay.'

Rajjo waited with bated breath. She knew there was more to come.

'We leave at 6 a.m., if there is any space in our van, come along…' The smirk on Kuljeet's face warned Rajjo that it was not going to be an easy ride, if there was a ride at all.

As Rajjo left the room, she felt a moment of relief; she was not going to wait around to be near Rani Maa, she was going to this other ashram tomorrow to seek her out.

Rajjo made a mental note to whisper into her pillow at night before retiring for the day to be up by 5.30. It worked better than a clock for her. But before she could retire, Raahat's gloomy face pulled her back to the courtyard. She saw him sitting on the ledge all hunched up. His thin frame curled up. Sadness hung around his frame. Despite her weariness she joined him.

'I thought you had slept.' He was clearly happy to see Rajjo.

'I almost did… how old are you?'

'Almost fifteen! They will leave at 5, just before day-break, you need to be up at 4, you should get some sleep.'

Kuljeet was teasing her and playing a game. She had deliberately given her the wrong departure time. Rajjo felt Kuljeet's pernicious intent. Lighting up a cigarette, Raahat added, 'Why are you in such a hurry to leave?'

'I have things to do...,' Rajjo muttered to him as he passed the cigarette to her.

'I don't have anything urgent to do, anytime of the day month or year…' Raahat sighed.

'Look for a desire and you will find your passion, your reason to be.'

'I don't desire anything.' Raahat looked up at the dark sky beleaguered with life.

'Then you are just a piece of useless meat, floating around, smoking up, littering the place with cigarette butts, farting gossip and adding to the weight of this earth.'

There was a pause. Rajjo passed him the cigarette after taking a long drag.

Raahat began to laugh. Rajjo laughed too.

They shared a last cigarette and it was time to say goodbye. She hoped Raahat would find his way as she walked away from him till the dark night swallowed her.

Once in her room, Rajjo feverishly finished packing and sat on the narrow cot. Her leg twitched restlessly. The disfigured picture of the Godman still hung on her wall. A tired air hung around the pink plastic-rimmed mirror on the wall. Not once did it spar with Rajjo's quartz-coloured gaze to assure her of her lissome beauty. The steel jug with R written on it sat quietly. It was time to move on. Rajjo knew she was not going to sleep tonight. She was going to wait up for 4 a.m. As soon as the clock struck three, she went to the gate and beyond that into the fields. Not trusting her destiny or Kuljeet's machinations.

Her sleepy tired body threatened to doze off, but she fought it. Kuljeet had no intention of taking Rajjo along. Rajjo stared into the deep dark sky, waiting for dawn to break.

In the bucolic setting sat Rajjo, worried once again that she could not smell the rain. Folks in the village would be looking at the skies everyday, waiting to sow for the next harvest. She hoped the long wait would end soon.

Dawn ushered in a bright crisp day. The sky was clear and cloudless, an endless blue drowning any hope of the monsoons. The sultry day began to take shape as the orange sun gradually climbed the sky. Prayers and chants offered at dawn pervaded through the walls.

The waiting bus was loaded with villagers. Some were local people looking for a ride to their desired destination if the bus was heading in the same direction. Some had decided to coordinate their travel with the group of sewadars for safety reasons.

Kuljeet, Arjan Singh and the others were travelling separately in a van. The luggage and other passengers were to follow in the rickety bus.

Kuljeet was surprised to see Rajjo waiting at the gate with her accoutrements, all set to go. Kuljeet calmly instructed her to stand aside while they loaded the essentials and she figured out the arrangements of her travel. The van, as Rajjo had suspected, was full. Puzzled, Arjan looked at Rajjo who stood in a corner with a hopeful expression on her face, as beautiful as a rain, or a child's curiosity.

Just then Rajjo heard someone running across the compound, a sleepy Raahat was bounding up to see her off. Worried that he had missed her departure already, he was glad to see she was very much here and the bus was running late. He saw her patiently waiting in a corner with her bags packed, all ready to leave and understood the situation. Raahat crossed his fingers behind his back, hoping for Rajjo to get on to the van.

Finally, Kuljeet limped towards Rajjo with a sigh and informed her gently that there was not enough space for her in the van. Rajjo knew Kuljeet was going to make it difficult. But it hurt just the same. Rajjo did not make a move to turn back and stood there waiting for some miracle.

Raahat looked at her crestfallen face and wanted to shake Kuljeet till she agreed to take Rajjo along. He uncrossed his fingers.

Almost as an afterthought, Kuljeet shrugged and looked at the overloaded bus laden with food and other amenities required in the ashram for the event, along with the sewadars and villagers. Many of them were still climbing on top of each other till people were hanging out of windows and doors like a cluster of overgrown bushes bursting through wired fences. The driver revved up the engine. The top of the bus was already crammed with fifty-odd people. Kuljeet paused with a triumphant smile at Rajjo as the bus driver hooted that he was ready to pull away.

'If you really want to come, get onto that bus. Or else help run the kitchen of the ashram here. It's a fulfilling job.' Rajjo stood there numb. Kuljeet leaned closer to Rajjo and murmured in a placatory manner, 'Whatever pleases God's will, comes to pass.'

Confident that Rajjo was staying put, Kuljeet gave her a benevolent smile, and sat in the white van. The van whizzed past Raahat and Rajjo as they stood in a cloud of dust, left behind as an aftermath.

The bus horn tooted with finality. Through the haze of dusty cloud, Rajjo saw the bus crawling away. She looked at Raahat. Raahat's eyes widened, for he knew exactly what she was thinking. Both of them ran towards the bus that was pulling away.

Rajjo ran ahead and stood in front of the bus waving like mad as Raahat whistled loudly, slamming his hands on the metal to get the driver's attention. The driver nodded that he had seen them and they could hop on, and slowed the bus. Rajjo flung her bag at Raahat and ran towards the bus doors with Raahat following close on her heels. Their hearts sank as they saw people crammed in the narrow door like sardines, blocking the bus doors. There was no way Rajjo could get inside the bus. The only hope was to join the cluster of people the top. Well, she was going to be damned if she was going to be left behind.

She ran to the back of the bus and grabbed on to the ladder, as Raahat egged her on. The bus gained speed, the driver unaware. Just in time Rajjo reached out her hand and Raahat handed over her bag.

He waved at her as she hung on to the rear of the bus. They had done it! Raahat was elated that she was finally on her way to where she wanted to be.

She was going to miss him. Just like she missed Kesar, Rano, Karam, her family, her village. The list was endless. Raahat dabbed at a tear and walked back inside the compound, hoping she would find a place to sit on that goddamned bus.

Meanwhile, Rajjo hung on to the bus ladder and her dear life for thirty minutes till someone tapped on her shoulder. Her arm was becoming numb with effort and she was going to lose her grip anytime soon. She turned up to look at the person who had tapped her. It was an old toothless lady with reams of wrinkles and kind eyes. She gestured for her to come up. A few men made way. The bus stopped, two people got off from the roof. Rajjo found a way to squeeze in. She finally had a little space to sit on the roof of the bus.

The bus gained speed again and they were off. This was heaven. She was flying, the wind running through her hair. She could touch the sky, talk to the white fluffy clouds.

She had risked the dangerous climb because she would've regretted her inaction more than anything else.

'You need to get somewhere urgently?' asked the old woman who had given Rajjo a hand.

Rajjo nodded.

'Where are you going?'

'I am not sure but I need to get there fast.' Rajjo replied over the roar of the wind.

The old woman chuckled.

'You are riding on the wind, I am sure you will get there fast enough!'

The woman smiled a toothless smile and turned around to breathe in the scenery bathed by dawn. The slight nip in the air due to the blast of wind made them all huddle closer, an argent-coloured desperation brought them even closer.

Rajjo passed many villages towns and cities. Colourful Bollywood posters adorned the busy market streets like baubles on a Christmas tree. Sitting on the bus, midway through the journey, her heart raced. She could smell the oncoming clouds. Monsoon was finally here!

As they travelled for a couple more hours, Rajjo could not feel her legs anymore, but she dared not get off lest she lost her seat or missed the bus. She did not trust God, providence or fate. She was going to stay put. The pain in her limbs and the bilious attack left her queasy. As her eyes teared up, she felt the first droplet of water trickle down her face…and then some more.

The smell of the first rain shower engulfed her. Rajjo was drunk on it. She hungrily devoured the raindrops and welcomed them on her parched lips. Some of her fellow passengers huddled to cover themselves with cloths and plastic sheets, a colourful botryoidal cluster covering the top of the bus. But Rajjo just turned her face to the skies. It was a sign, the wait had ended and they could sow the fields again. The cycle had begun.

The unexpected rain unleashed another torrent to carry her through the last leg of the journey. Finally they arrived at the destination. Tired, cantankerous passengers alighted from the bus. Some were deep in consultation with the bus driver and conductor, figuring out their onward journeys. Some just sat on the sidewalk catching their breath. Some stretched after the long ride. Rajjo walked through them all, deliberate and confident, towards the gate of the new ashram. It was a black metal gate just like the one in the previous ashram. The board had Shradha Swami printed on it. She shivered because of the wet clothes sticking to her body. Triumphant, she stood outside the gate. Gingerly she opened the gate and entered the compound. It was even bigger than her previous ashram and a different set of sewadars walked about. This one, like all the other ashrams, had a beautiful mango orchard surrounding the walls.

Rajjo walked to the middle of the compound and stood there for two minutes before she spotted Kuljeet and Arjan in a conversation, the same time they turned to catch her looking at them. Arjan was surprised and happy to see Rajjo, whereas Kuljeet threw her a censorious look as Rajjo walked up to them smiling.

'Whatever pleases God's will, comes to pass.' Rajjo mocked Kuljeet, savouring her velvety moment of victory.

Kuljeet recovered soon enough from Rajjo's unexpected arrival, curtly instructing her to help the others cart the luggage, and also informing her that she would be sharing a room with another sewadar as they had not expected her here. Arjan could sense something between them as he gave Rajjo a warm welcoming smile, noticing her shivering through her wet clothes.

Before he could offer her to use his room to change, Rajjo was already helping the others lug the suitcases and other luggage from the van and the bus.

Both Kuljeet and Arjan could not help but stare at the petite woman, driven by an unknown dark passion, her face carved in granite working around the compound; a wounded cygnet one would want to embrace.

'There is something about her that worries me.' Kuljeet said to Arjan.

'Her quiet determination...,' sighed Arjan.

Kuljeet did not know how to respond to this stubborn girl.

Rajjo moved without thinking. Her mind was numb to wetness or the unease, cramps or hunger. She was consumed by passion. All her movements were in tune with a desire and there was no deeper truth to what she had discovered for herself. Desire was the seed and cause of all movement. Desire was the starting and end point of action.

Rajjo was going to take her desire, seed it in a flower pot, nurture it and make it grow until she reached the end point.

Her ambition was written in gossamer prophecies: to become another Rani Maa.

## August 1991

The rain pelted down. Monsoon currents from the Bay of Bengal were coming in hard and fast. People would be busy working in the paddy fields at this time. But even the thought of her village and home did not lift Rajjo's sagging spirits. Rajjo had been here a month but she was still struggling to get past her kitchen chores and move on to something more mainstream. Moreover, Kuljeet had made her share a room with a girl called Asha. She was fair, in her early thirties, plump and surly. She prayed to God almost twenty times a day and had memorized every word of the holy book. She despised Rajjo as she had never seen her pray.

Once or twice Asha had broached the subject of God and divinity, only to hastily retreat as she sensed Rajjo's stance. Since then Asha had written her off. One night as they slept, Asha curtly announced, lying in her little cot, that she would pray to God for Rajjo so he could forgive her impudence.

Rajjo had stuffed the bedsheet in her mouth to avoid a retort. If she was to stay on in the room and the ashram she had to keep her mouth shut and pretend to tolerate Godliness. But God was not the only reason for discord in the little room they shared. Asha snored loud enough for the whole village to hear. She had warned Rajjo about her sinus problem but now it was killing Rajjo. It was clear as daylight that Rajjo and Asha would never find friendship.

God and sinuses were not the only problems. Rajjo had taken a liking to a beautiful little flower pot gifted by a follower from Singapore. It was an exotic plant, and the devout had called it a fairy slipper. Rajjo loved the name as much as she loved the delicate pink flower with a white lip, dark purple spottings, and yellow beard. It was a dainty exquisite creation sprouting from the little pot and Rajjo had begged Arjan to let her keep it. But Asha was convinced the plant would kill her, as she was allergic to flowers and pollens.

Rajjo lived in fear that Asha would accidently break the pot and constantly protected it from Asha's careless nudges. Her globulous dislike was turning Rajjo's plant into a deeper purple.

Apart from God, sinuses and the safety of her flower pot, Rajjo found herself stuck in the kitchen once more, struggling with her debilitated hope.

The dark tea boiled over with a hiss, its fuliginous smoke hung around Rajjo. Rajjo stared at it. She had identified one man who could help her move ahead and out of the kitchen, but he was in a shell, completely withdrawn. Rajjo had no idea how to reach out to him, despite her innumerable efforts over the weeks.

She looked from the kitchen window once again and spotted the skinny man, working non-stop. He was coordinating with vendors and pointing out areas where the tents were going to be put up for the main event, even as it rained hard. He was responsible for the entire organization of the sermons and was considered very close to Mehtaab Sarkaria. The thin man rarely spoke. His real name was Gurbaksh Singh. He was the head of the organization unit for a cluster of ashrams around this village and had been with the commune for over five years. A feral energy emanated from him.

She could see him gesticulating to explain the size of the stage and the dimensions needed for the workers. The sermon was going to be conducted in the big ground outside the ashram. As the tea boiled, the angry showers slowed down to a drizzle. His thin kurta stuck to his back. Sporadic bursts of rain announced the presence of August monsoon. Rajjo sighed and went back to stirring the simmering tea. It was dark brown in colour, thick and succulent.

Determined not to stay in the kitchen forever, Rajjo sweetened the tea with some extra sugar, thinking about the quiet Gurbaksh. Why was he unwilling to talk? Rajjo had tried to interact with him on several occasions but he always averted his gaze. Rajjo wanted to be in his team and she had no idea how to ask him. She observed him from a distance. He did his work quietly and sat by himself. He was a well-liked and admired leader of the other sewadars. His refusal to speak weighed heavily on Rajjo.

Everything, from the decoration, seating, stage, coordination was arranged by him. He only spoke to give quiet but firm instructions. Even when people joked or made fun, trying to be friendly, Gurbaksh did not respond.

All her attempts at getting through to him were coming to a dead end and the only good thing that happened in the last month was when Raahat arrived. Rajjo had squealed in delight. Arjan had called for him to help out with the event, and he had to carry some important papers that Mehtaab needed from that ashram. Also, orders had come from the higher offices that Raahat was to be sent to Mata-ji's ashram shortly. Rajjo teased Raahat on his princely treatment and wondered who 'Mata-ji' was. Raahat deftly avoided the conversation, but Rajjo and Raahat had a happy reunion and soon found another quiet corner in the mango orchards to smoke in.

Rajjo finally learnt from Raahat that Gurbaksh's wife had died in an accident and he was somehow responsible. After the tragedy he had joined the commune.

With a deep sigh and a firm resolve, Rajjo walked up to him with the cup of tea. The thin boyish man turned to look at Rajjo. Rajjo realized his skin was roughened and wrinkled if you looked closely, like he had aged a decade in a matter of months. Rajjo used the unpredictable weather as an excuse to strike up a conversation, but his dark black eyes gave nothing away. A dark ichor ran in his brain that reached her deaf ear. He had screened himself from the rest of the world. She had never seen him smile in one month. He only worked or prayed.

As he took the steaming cup of tea from Rajjo, she could not sense anything except a mild recognition in his eyes, even though she had been serving him tea for the last three weeks at regular intervals.

Rajjo hesitantly added after giving the tea, 'I would like to help out as well, with the decoration or something if you need. I have done that before.'

Rajjo's request met his impervious gaze. Without saying a word, Gurbaksh turned away, to attend to a query from a worker.

Raahat smiled at Rajjo from the verandah where he lounged, pretending to read some religious booklets, 'Didi, how much sugar are you wasting sweetening him? It's all in vain… and next time you prepare some tea for him, don't forget your darling brother… me!' His dogged nosiness annoyed her further.

Rajjo picked up her dupatta and decided to take a walk around the village to get some clean air. Thankfully Kuljeet was out for two days and so the kitchen duties were not as daunting lately. Rajjo knew she had to get into the organization committee to move ahead, to be closer to the powers that be. Gurbaksha was the key to her funnel-shaped desire. It was painful and excruciating to wait.

As they sat smoking in their corner in the dead of night, surrounded by pungent smell of fruit trees, Raahat quipped Rajjo.

'Why are you chasing him like a flea-ridden dog? That Gurbaksh?'

'Because I need something from him…I want to work in his team'

'Why?'

Rajjo did not answer as she took in a long puff of smoke.

'You think by serving him tea you will get there?'

'No … I think I will wait and figure it out.'

'He is a tough nut to crack. No one really gets him, Rajjo didi! And if he doesn't like you, forget about ever getting into the organization committee!'

'That's why I will wait…'

'You have been waiting for a month now!'

'You know, someone said, all of humanity's problems stem from Man's inability to sit quietly in a room alone, and that is exactly what I am going to do!'

'Where do you meet such people who talk such bull crap?' Raahat crinkled his nose in disapproval.

'Don't you doubt, I will find the key to Gurbaksha.'

Raahat chuckled at Rajjo's departing figure.

Rajjo retired into her room as she wanted to wake up early and take a walk around the village. Thankfully, Asha was not there and her flower pot was still intact. The beautiful exotic flower reminded her of her irridescent desire. She wanted to see it flourish and grow. With a sigh Rajjo slipped into a deep sleep.

The next morning, at the crack of dawn, Rajjo was out and about. Asha was still not back. Rajjo wondered where she had disappeared? But she dare not ask in case she offended her and she seemed close to Kuljeet. It was better to maintain a polite distance.

Rajjo walked through the village. This particular ashram was in Fatehpur Sahib district. The nearest town was Kheri Naud Singh and they hoped to attract an assemblage of believers from Khanna and other nearby towns. The village had an elementary school. Rajjo could see kids running around the compound as a distracted teacher read an old magazine. Rajjo smiled.

The question of how to get through to Gurbaksha kept bothering her. She crossed a large volleyball ground located near a gurdwara. A few metres ahead she spotted a cluster of droopy oldies sitting under a giant tree playing cards. Wild hooting at a distance caught her attention. It was the village kids involved in a game of cricket with makeshift wickets and bales. A few oldies were engrossed in the game as they squinted to look at the next ball. Just then she spotted Gurbaksha and a few other sewadars amongst them. Rajjo stood in the shadows of a peepul tree to mull over how to approach her object of interest. They were all rooting for a boy to hit a six as the team needed only five runs to win. The others were animated but Gurbaksha sat there with a straight face. There was tension on his face as he gripped the leaning tree bark he sat on.

A six was hit. The others rushed forward in jubilation. Gurbaksha gave out a happy shout, and then, as if guilty, retreated.

The others had run forward so no one noticed his outburst. And Gurbaksha started walking back towards the ashram, Rajjo followed him only to find him lifting heavy chairs from the truck and unloading them under the tent. He wanted to do some physical work till he was exhausted, like he was apologizing for having spent a mellifluous moment with the children.

A light afternoon breeze was blowing. Some sparrows chirped around and pecked at grains and leftover food scattered in the yard for them. Rajjo went into the kitchen to boil her tea. The brown liquid gurgled and bubbled over. She focused on Gurbaksha's face in the pan – the vapours turned noxious, it was his pain that she would focus on. She knew the words he needed.

Rajjo walked up to Gurbaksha who was still moving non-stop, lifting heavy sacks, his face carved in stone, instructing the workers where to place the chairs on the stage. Rajjo quietly offered him a cup of tea. He continued to work as Rajjo stood there, willing him to look her in the eye and take the tea she offered to him.

Finally he reached out for the glass. Rajjo whispered, 'It's OK to just sit and breathe sometimes. It's OK. Rumi says, "The sum of my entire life is no more than these three words. I was raw, I got cooked, I got burnt."'

There was a look in his eye, like Rajjo had reached out to an old wound and eased the throbbing pain with a whiff of cool air. Gurbaksha went back to doing his work.

Before she could stop herself she blurted, 'They are going to place the chairs on the stage. I was thinking if they did it in a semicircle it would be better, given the width of the stage here. It would look more aesthetic.'

Gurbaksha looked at her and nodded. Like it was the most natural thing in the world for him to follow Rajjo's suggestions.

Rajjo walked towards the wooden platform and started helping the workers to figure out the right placement for the carpet.

Dusk was upon her as she worked away happily on the stage when she heard an appreciative whistle. It was Raahat, winking at Rajjo, raising the glass of tea as a toast!

Rajjo screamed at him, 'Fuck you, Raahat. Get your ass here and do some work!'

He just chuckled.

Rajjo smiled as the sweet scent of victory clung to her. Gurbaksha had accepted her. His self-odious armour had been chipped.

Before she could rejoice a bit more, she spotted Kuljeet standing behind them. Her mouth readying for the next sting. She and a group of others, including the surly Asha and Arjan, had heard this exchange.

'This is a religious commune; we serve in God's name. If you live here you speak with dignity and responsibility…'

Kuljeet marched off with her army of followers. Rajjo and Raahat exchanged an amused look shared by Arjan. Rajjo was happy. She had escaped the oubliette of Kuljeet's kitchen and she was never going back!

## August 1991

The entire compound was alive with movement as they were hosting a two-day celebration event in the ashram for Rani Maa's birthday, ending with her sermon. A special kirtan and snacks had been organized throughout the day. A chilled sweetened drink made of milk, sugar, rose essence and water was being distributed in the compound, and various kiosks had been especially built to offer food served on leaf plates.

Huge blocks of ice were being lugged around to keep the drink cool. Giant vessels brimmed with the milky liquid. It seemed to Rajjo that she and her sisters could easily dive in the huge containers and swim around in the icy cool fluid, the colour of pale pink butterflies that smelt of a rose garden.

Sewadars stood on raised platform under the blue tents, their heads covered with cloth as a mark of reverence, their hands holding colourful, big jugs with the milky drink. Rows of glasses were poured and consumed as mobs of people, primarily hungry and thirsty villagers, flocked to the compound.

The rose essence coming from the sweetened drinks intoxicated Rajjo. She could see Raahat handing out shiny steel glasses with the delicious pink drink to the patrons. She wanted to join him. But her mind was in turmoil. The constant screaming and chattering along with the stifling heat and unusual stillness bothered her.

In the middle of it all, a man drove a rickety blue scooter through the main gate. Riding pillion was a scrawny brown boy, bathed in sweat with just a dirty white singlet sticking to his wiry frame. Hunched in an awkward position he carried a bouquet of loudspeakers, his tiny limbs barely holding on to the four pieces of giant metal. The boy sat with his back to the driver, his shrivelled-up body resting against the man's broad frame. One could barely see the face of the boy hidden behind the cluster of loudspeakers with green letters – Raj – Jalandhar.

Rajjo stood staring at the duo as they unloaded the loudspeakers. Most of the work was done by the little boy who looked barely eight. The man stood there as the little boy lugged the speakers before one of the workers thankfully relieved him of his burden.

The boy wore patched up pants, three sizes too big, rolled up towards the end. His shoes were two sizes big as his tiny feet clung on to the straps to move forward with every step, lest the shoes be left behind in a hasty step.

The workers got busy fitting the speakers on the giant poles. The thick-bellied man waited for the workers to approve the equipment.

The little boy moved his thin arms and shook them, like he was getting rid of some ants crawling under his skin. Then he looked at the crowd eating and drinking in the compound. Unsure whether he would be allowed to stand in the line, despite many villagers waiting their turn, the boy quietly sat across the road to catch his breath. He stared at his dirt-ridden black leather sandals and started wiping the mud off of them like they were some kind of prized possession.

Rajjo, drawn to the silent soul, crossed the road and stood next to where the lone small figure sat hunched up on the ground, now drawing circles in the mud with his index finger. They were just endless circles, all around him. This little being in oversized clothes was trapped and wanted to escape.

They seemed ominous to Rajjo as she finally cleared her throat and asked the boy, 'You go to school?'

The boy shook his head and went back to adding more circles in the mud. Each one of them was in perfect shape, as if drawn with a compass.

'Would you like to?'

He shook his head again, not looking up this time. Rajjo could see his bones sticking out from his tiny hands.

'You like working with this loudspeaker guy?'

The boy shook his head and looked at Rajjo in the eye.

'Would you like to do something else?'

The boy shook his head again and looked away.

Rajjo sighed and stood next to him.

'There is good food in the lunch service, you must eat and go. Snacks and the sweet drink are also being served today. You can take them. It's for free.'

The boy did not respond. And suddenly his rusty voice spoke hesitantly.

'You are sewadar?'

Rajjo shook her head.

'Would you like to become one?'

Rajjo shook her head again.

'You like being here?'

Rajjo smiled at the boy and shook her head.

The boy smiled back.

They were one.

'They are planning to throw me out.'

Rajjo uttered before she could stop herself. She wondered why she had said it. Almost like a burp bothering her somewhere in the system.

The boy stopped smiling, realizing he may not get his food if he was seen being pally with an outcast. Rajjo realized his discomfort and moved away, but she turned once more to smile at the boy and pointed him towards a queue. Thinking about her situation yet again, she felt a wave of nervousness creep up, a shiver in the hot dry afternoon. This was Kuljeet's first direct move to get rid of her.

Kuljeet had informed Rajjo in the morning itself that the head of the women's welfare wing of the organization, Sarika, would be having a word with her. She'd also added in an advisory tone that they offered women a lot of choices once they chose to step out of the commune and live in the real world, so she was free to take help and did not have to stay on in the ashram, spending her life as a devout. Her incarnadine coloured intention of ousting Rajjo whispered a crimson warning in Rajjo's deaf ear.

'Go out in the real world and explore. You have a life to make. The lord almighty, the one who created 8.4 million species of beings, gives sustenance to all.' As Kuljeet whispered those words to Rajjo, a strange odour emanated from Kuljeet. An odour that had crossed innumerable fields and seasons; it smelt of baked mud with unsightly cracks for worms and water to seep through. Rajjo knew this was just the beginning. There were going to be more attempts to get Rajjo out of the commune.

Kuljeet resented that Rajjo was not relegated to the kitchen anymore and was working in the organization committee without her approval. What irked her more was, despite her disapproval, Rajjo had used the good favours of Arjan and Gurbaksha to stay on in the organization committee. Kuljeet's furtive desire to remove Rajjo from the ashram was no longer cloaked by her prayer beads.

Rajjo had to think fast if she was to stay on. She shrugged her worries away as she climbed the makeshift platform where Raahat stood under a blue tent, handing out drinks to the people. Rajjo glanced across the road and was glad to see the little boy had queued up as well, braving the harsh afternoon sun. His empty eyes stared ahead as he waited for his turn to get the sweetened drink and bread.

Raahat's curly hair flopped across his acne-scarred face. While he served, he eyed young girls his age and offered them an extra glass of the sweet drink. Rajjo shook her head at his feeble attempts at flirtation.

'You are looking like a hooligan, chop your tresses off. You can offer them a bucketful of sweet and they won't smile back. You are a cross between a man and a monkey right now!' murmured Rajjo.

Raahat threw her an impish look. 'I am in the service of God, can you find some other time for this sermon... If God wills, I shall cut my hair! He shall whisper in my ear tonight, Raahat, go have a hair cut and on your way back, dig under the papaya tree to find a pot of gold!'

Rajjo chuckled as she handed out a few glasses to an old couple,

'Actually, I was thinking I will spruce up nice and proper to say bye to you when Kuljeet sends you packing…She has called Sarika Tai for your induction.' Raahat's attempt at a joke masked his worry.

Rajjo deliberately ignored Raahat as she continued to serve the thirsty, hungry people in shabby clothes and with blisters on their hands. The ones who had been served already were gulping the pink liquid like it was God's nectar. They could be from her village back home.

Just then she heard the rickety scooter sputter back to life. The little boy who still awaited his turn to get the pink drink turned around. The urgent tooting of the horn and the impatient man on the scooter was signal enough for him to run.

'He did not have his food, neither his drink.'

Rajjo almost ran after him, but the little boy's legs carried him too fast. The need to obey was instant. He had already hopped on to the scooter.

Rajjo's heart sank, as the scooter pulled away. The little boy was seated with his back to the driver and faced Rajjo, and then gingerly lifted his hand and waved at her. Rajjo waved back and he was gone, an innocent who stayed in her heart reminding her of sweet orisons curled up in rosy air.

She wondered if they would ever meet again, for he had captured a bit of her in the little circles of mud. Choked, she took deep breaths to let the emotion pass. The little boy had come to the people serving God, and none of them could assuage his thirst or hunger.

'Now what are you going to do about Kuljeet? Wait and watch…' Raahat interrupted her train of thought.

Rajjo held her tongue as she pondered over Kuljeet's pending plot. A large group of weary travellers consumed their attention, as they were offered drinks and snacks.

'You know, Sarika Tai and the women's welfare wing has its own skeletons.' As soon as the crowd dispersed, Raahat whispered again. He wanted to tell this to Rajjo but did not know how. He was filled with dread every time he thought of Rajjo leaving.

'As in?' Rajjo turned towards him as she stirred the fresh batch of pink sweetened drink poured into the giant tub.

'They are all at Mehtaab's disposal. He uses them for favours with politicians, businessmen and important people. They take good care of the women though.'

Raahat averted his eyes. He did not want to look Rajjo in the face as her mind registered his insinuations.

'Prostitution?' Rajjo asked aloud.

Raahat looked back at her with a straight face and folded his hands in a gesture of divine gratitude. 'No, service of God.'

Rajjo mulled over what she had just learnt.

'In my expert opinion, I think you should just go to another ashram till Kuljeet calms down.' Raahat suggested sounding wise and important.

Rajjo shut her eyes, neon coloured imagery playingin her mind as she tried to digest the information and deal with Raahat.

'Can you just stop speaking? I need to think. And you better clean up, I don't want to be seen hanging with a hooligan.'

'Why don't I get my head and face replaced, may be that will make you feel better?' muttered Raahat, still worried if Kuljeet and Sarika Tai would take Rajjo away.

The truth was, the very thought of Rajjo being removed made Raahat panic. It was like all those years ago, as he ran in the long dark streets to reach his uncle and cousins sitting in a white van, with their arms stretched out, willing him to run faster. Noises and shrieks, mobs and violence could be heard in the near distance. As they neared, a deep fear took over. The mob reaching them was a matter of seconds.

His uncle's family were running away from the back lane of the house, all thrust in a van. All he had to do was jump in with them.

His cousins called out to him, he ran faster, however, the mob appeared before he could reach the van. The driver, Billa uncle, who his family met with on holidays, festivals, marriages, births and deaths, and who had shared his life, had left him behind. His uncle had raced the van and his family to safety.

In those thirty seconds when he ran in the dark lane towards the waiting van, he experienced the true nature of panic. It was dark, it was brutal and it smelt of a graveyard. When the van did pull away, and he turned to face the mob, panic fled only to be replaced by a passive acceptance of death.

But here he was, a decade or more later, still reliving the dreadful horror he vowed never to go back to. It visited him night after night, but he dealt with it, reasoned with it, pleaded, cursed, tried a truce with his nightmare and so far had survived.

With Rajjo, he had bonded like a sibling. He would never let her leave at any cost. He was going to make sure she stayed. Raahat immediately caught himself going down the slippery road of teary emotion and his cool drawl was back in place. He called out to the others for some blocks of ice.

Rajjo's brain throbbed with activity, as she thought over the problem at hand. How was she going to stay on when Kuljeet wanted her out? In her absent-mindedness, Rajjo accidentally scraped her finger against a protruding nail not hammered in properly. Hurriedly she found a newspaper to wrap around her finger. The yellowed paper's headline screamed. '*Rajiv Gandhi Assassinated*'. Rajjo wondered how she had missed that. Reet her sister had kept cutouts of the PM like he was her prospective groom. She liked that he was fair and spoke well when they saw him on TV. Rajjo checked the date – it was from a few months ago. It seemed the world had passed her by in the compound and she felt so removed from the happenings outside.

She shrugged, focusing on the preparations around. The stage was almost ready as it stood in the middle of the giant ground opposite the ashram. The tents were being put up. All the loudspeakers were mounted on poles ready to blare as soon as someone took to the mike.

The life-size cutout of Rani Maa was being brought out from the godown that was situated in the back near the orchards. While four people deferentially carried the cutouts, others turned to fold their hands and pay their respects to the wooden board. The cutouts with Rani Maa's smiling face were placed at regular intervals on the stage and the entrance.

Amused, her gaze stopped on a well-dressed man with neatly combed hair, striped shirt and brown pants, fixing small bulbs around the giant cutout, in order to make Rani Maa sparkle. Raahat muttered in her ear, 'He is the owner of the lights, Akash Studios. He personally comes here for events, to set up stuff as a mark of his devotion. I think he is infatuated with her. So how are we going to stop Kuljeet? Let's talk to Arjan. He seems to have a thing for you or something.'

'Do you know everything about everybody? How big is your gossip tank? And Arjan is not like that!'

'It's as vast and as huge as the Lord's belly!' Raahat folded his hands sanctimoniously and sauntered off as someone called out his name urgently. But his parting shot had Rajjo worried yet again, 'We have to think of something, you can't let Kuljeet make you leave.'

Rajjo went back to observing Akash work with reverence and quiet devotion. He had first removed his shoes, washed his hands and said his prayers before he had started work on the cutout.

Did he know they had stashed so many of these discarded cutouts in the tacky godown and the birds were shitting on them?

However, Rajjo walked up to the man, who was sweating profusely in the sun. He smelled of expensive soap. He kneeled in front of Rani Maa, as if he was worshipping a deity. It was clear to Rajjo that if the cutout asked him to jump into a well, he would do so happily.

Rajjo was dying to know how and why a feeling this intense could be aroused and sustained. She hesitantly asked about his devotion to the spiritual commune. The man immediately went into a stupor of emotion and gratitude. 'She changed my life. She gave me hope. I gave up drugs and took over my father's business – I am forever indebted to her.'

Rajjo was taken aback by his earnestness. She felt something rise up in her throat like a serpent. The fact that Rani Maa aroused such divine devotion plagued her. Rajjo moved away, wanting to clear away the bad taste in her mouth. Her scurf of indecisiveness had fallen away. Her desire had taken seed, the roots curled in her heart. Rani Maa's throne beckoned. All she needed was to find a way.

Dark clouds started gathering and people started whispering as the day progressed. Raahat came and squealed in Rajjo's ear, 'The deal for the ashram is done with the local panchayat in a neighbouring village. Rani Maa's actual birthday gift is half a village from Mehtaab!' Raahat winked as he carried a giant slab of ice back to his kiosk to keep the sweetened drinks chilled.

Rajjo followed Raahat and pressed him for more information. She was shocked to learn that according to some villagers, the ashram's deals were unfair and illegal usurping of land, encouraged by the local politicians and businessmen. Raahat continued in the same tone as he broke the ice into smaller pieces with a hammer. 'However, now the land belongs to the ashram or Rani Maa. Ostensibly, it was partly donated and partly subsidized using various legal clauses. Now they will formalize it by making an official request to Rani Maa to bless the village with an ashram. After some time, workers will go there, take the land and build an ashram in the middle of it. You can go there. So Kuljeet won't send you away!'

With a loud thud a giant block of ice broke into half as Rajjo yelped. Thin slivers of ice landed on her face and neck.

Rajjo looked at the young Raahat accusingly, rubbing her face.

'Tell me one thing...you believe Rani Maa can change destinies?' The ramble of the devout fixing tiny fairy lights on Rani Maa plagued her.

'I believe believing in her gets me food and clothing.'

'Prostitution, land-grabbing included?'

'Camps, schools, hospitals, prostitution, land-grabbing, me being clothed and fed included...

Raahat took another crack at the muddy block of ice as Rajjo moved her face away to avoid the onslaught. After hammering the ice to a crunchy cluster, Raahat sat back in the corner of the tent, hidden by the table from plain view and retrieved a joint.

'Where do you get this stuff from?' Rajjo asked disapprovingly.

'I have a nose for finding dealers. They supply to the foreign guests also!'

'That is nothing to be proud of...'

'Here comes your party...' Raahat hurriedly hid the joint. Behind his talk, you could see his worry about Rajjo leaving the commune was eating him up.

Rajjo observed the van that arrived at the main door. The focus shifted to the stream of women walking in, most pleasant and good-looking. They all seemed happy, wore the white salwar-kameez like the sewadars and were shepherded by a woman wearing a green cotton sari and dark kohl-lined eyes, with shoulder-length silky hair that glistened in the sun. The others addressed her as Sarika Tai. She was in her late forties, and Rajjo loved the way she was dressed. Her cotton sari creased all over. She had a thin Titan watch across her wrist and she smelt of jasmine.

Sarika Tai looked in Rajjo's direction as she and Kuljeet quietly shared a word. With an encouraging smile, Sarika Tai came across and sat down on a stool next to Rajjo.

Rajjo by now had taken the hammer and was replicating Raahat's move to thrash another block of ice.

It somehow felt nice to thrash something as she spoke to Sarika Tai.

She introduced herself and told Rajjo about the women in her care. Rajjo smiled politely, and paused to take a breath.

'You are beautiful,' said Sarika Tai, assessing her amber eyes, lustrous curls falling below the waist, pink lips and dusky diaphanous skin, beauty difficult to hide even behind the dowdy attire of the sewadars. A connossieur admiring a delicacy from the glass window, she asked, 'Do you have any questions for me?'

Rajjo stared at her and asked with a straight face.

'A boy came here, hot and sweaty, thin and hungry, emaciated. Stood in the queue but did not get a drop of milk or a morsel of food. You think God was watching?' Anger sluiced through her.

Tai stared back. Rajjo smiled at her and turned away to hammer the block of ice into a crushed white pulp. She was not ready to have this chat yet.

Sensing her mood, Sarika walked away from Rajjo without any further questions.

As darkness cloaked the ashram, Rajjo looked up at the sky, worried she could not see the stars. She dreaded it would rain in the night, soiling the stage and the tents. They would have to redo a lot of work. As an extra measure, plastic sheets had been drawn over the lights and the cutouts. Rajjo knew these feeble efforts seldom stopped the whims of a downpour if it wanted to destroy.

As the darkness ate up the last ray of light, Rajjo went into the hall, where mattresses were laid next to each other for the fifteen girls to stay together. The atmosphere was charged with jokes and giggles. Rajjo learned a lot while fixing their bedding. Some were pursuing college education, some had enrolled in vocational subjects and a few were the independent ones who were doing well in life. The ashram initially supported them in return for a few duties they were entrusted with. Some continued their association with the ashram and some were mere followers.

She interacted with them and realized, like her, most of them were battered and orphaned. Fate much worse than Rajjo's had descended on many of them. Damaged beauties marked by cruelties, deftly hidden under makeup. They were all given food and shelter by the ashram, just like Rajjo.

Just then Sarika Tai walked in and stood next to Rajjo. Shortly afterwards she pointed out the three most beautiful women in the group. They wore jewellery and expensive perfume with their white uniform. Their skin and hair glistened as if they had been taken care of by the best salons. 'They have their own properties now. They chose their path. They chose to give company to some important men. I will not mince words Rajjo, you are beautiful and you can earn much more than Ranjita there. She is planning on buying her own house next year.'

Rajjo smiled at Sarika Tai. 'They are a part of this religious commune? They do this in the name of God?'

'Because of their choices should they be thrown out? Everyone is equal in the eyes of God and is equally entitled to be showered by his grace.' Sarika Tai smiled back.

Rajjo laughed. 'That's how you sell this package?'

Sarika Tai was not laughing anymore. Neither was Rajjo. Her egregious offer hung between them.

'Don't judge me. Nobody is forced. You have other options too… If you want to enroll in a vocational college, do a beauty course, sewing, cooking, I will help you. Many of these girls do that'.

'I want to be here…in the ashram.'

'But young girls like you need to make a life, marry, have a family. Why do you want to devote your life to the service of God at this age? You are barely twenty-two, I hear.'

'Who says I want to devote myself to the service of God? I don't!'

Sarika Tai looked at her, confused.

'But you will always be dependent on the organization if you stay here. You can learn some hands-on work and make a living. Decide what you want to do and let me know tomorrow. Moreover, Kuljeet wants you to relocate now.'

Rajjo stared at Sarika in the eye. 'So it's about Kuljeet wanting me to leave?'

'It's also about you making a life of your choice…' Sarika Tai countered.

'I am not ready to move yet. I want to serve here in the ashram. I am not ready to leave.'

Sarika Tai smiled at Rajjo.

'You are ready when you are ready. It's fine by me. I will let Kuljeet know.'

'What do you think would happen if I say yes and go with you right now?'

' What is destined will happen … it's all in the hands of God, your staying or leaving is predecided by his will.' Tai smiled benevolently.

Rajjo could hear the pedestal fans whirring in the hall. The lyrical chit-chat of the girls billowed around them, a laugh here, a shriek there. Rajjo heard her voice added to the milieu of sounds. 'A philosopher argues if God is omniscient he knows not only what people will freely do in the future, but what each possible free creature would have freely done in each set of possible circumstances. If God has knowledge of future actions, then he knows what he is going to do to his followers. Despite praying to him, he looks on, letting them fall and bruise. So if God is the positive force that one looks to for salvation, then he does not exist. He lets you get into a mess, despite knowing all the possible outcomes you would have met with from the choices you make. He does not guide you, he does not come to help you, he does not warn you… He does nothing much. He lets a little boy burn under the sun, get lost in circles of dirt, and go by hungry. God is a sham. This is my choice and mine alone. God has not helped me choose this. I just wanted to say that.'

Sarika admired her eburnine beauty and looked at the soft brown eyes of the girl, with a hint of steel lurking underneath. Her front tooth was slightly chipped, strangely adding to her beauty. There were some scars on her face, near her brow and her chin, which accentuated her flawless skin and cheekbones. She'd heard her one ear was busted and she noticed she favoured her left ear when she was being spoken to. She was one of the most beautiful women Sarika had seen. And she also knew this one wanted the entire sky, not just a piece of it. There was no point trying with her. In her outburst she had revealed an ambition. And it ran deep enough to shape her destiny.

'She wants you to leave.' Sarika Tai sighed.

'I need some time. Please tell Kuljeet I said I want to stay on for Rani Maa's darshan and then I will be ready to move.' Sarika Tai nodded.

As Rajjo walked towards her little room the skies broke into a downpour. She could see some men scurrying out to salvage what was left of the stage and the arrangements. Rajjo knew there was no point. The rain would destroy everything. She was going to worry about it tomorrow.

As she entered her narrow room, she realized Asha was not in there. One thing was certain; she had a lover in this compound. The question was who?

The next morning, the hustle and bustle was immense. Kuljeet was not too happy with Rajjo's decision and it was obvious time was running out for Rajjo. She spent most of her day with Gurbaksha and his team, making sure the last-minute arrangements were perfect for Rani Maa's visit. However, there was something peculiar in the arrangements made this time around. She was intrigued that a few rooms were being prepared for a VIP visit and there was some scotch smuggled in as well. Treats were kept separately for the VIP guests and the back entrance had been spruced up to welcome them. Some of the sewadars were put on security duty to man the crowd and make sure VIP areas were out of bounds. All these covert arrangements were being done under the close supervision of Gurbaksha, Arjan and Kuljeet, ironically the most devout sewadars in the ashram. Rajjo smothered a chuckle that threatened to spill over in a hysterical laugh.

Men of God, reading scriptures, smuggling scotch, serving food to the poor. There were multiple narratives in these godly stories but Rajjo struggled to find divinity in anything she saw and witnessed around her.

Intrigued by the secrecy, driven by the need to peel back another layer, Rajjo deliberately started working closely with the people appointed to cater to the VIP section. Arjan had earmarked a room with five chairs. Rajjo wondered what was going to happen in there. As the evening drew near, the excitement in the air spiralled.

The girls had all dressed up in saffron saris and were seated on stage singing verses. The crowds had started to filter in. The music and the chants had taken over. A group of three priests sang shabads, with their beards flowing, their eyes shut in divine bliss, their hands moving in time with the harmonium and the musical notes.

Only there was no sign of Rani Maa as Rajjo and everyone else waited endlessly. Just then a car stopped outside the back entrance, followed by much movement in the compound amongst the workers. Rajjo ran out to greet the guest and it turned out that it was Sukhmani, Chhoti Ma. She alighted from the car alone. She had a beautiful face, with a flawless milky skin and waif-like features.

A worried look was exchanged between Arjan Singh, Kuljeet and Sarika Tai. An unsaid fear was conveyed between them as Chhoti Maa walked up to the stage. Shortly after, another car arrived. A thunderous looking Mehtaab alighted and headed straight into the VIP room without exchanging a word with anyone.

Sukhmani started the sermon on stage and hundreds of devotees looked on with reverence. Rajjo witnessed another drama unfold behind the scenes. The key players scurried in different directions and it seemed like Rani Maa was not going to turn up for the sermon after all.

Finding the whole thing odd, Rajjo sought Raahat out to fill her in on the situation, only to find him high as a kite. All he could coherently tell her was, she had to find a way to stay back!

Rajjo wanted to whack him and hug him at the same time. Worried for him to be discovered in his inebriated state, Rajjo dragged him away to the kitchen and insisted he guzzle a glass of milk lest Kuljeet or someone else caught him. Raahat laughed at her concerns and said, 'With so much action happening on the compound even if naked women dance in the premises, no one would know!'

Rajjo whacked him and enquired about the situation outside. Rani Maa had not turned up, Sukhmani was on stage and Mehtaab was furious. Raahat made a face like a surgeon pondering over various theories of medicine to arrive at his important conclusion.

Just when Rajjo was convinced nothing was going to come out of his drugged brain, Raahat spilled the beans. 'Sometimes when Rani Maa does not turn up,' and he laughed, followed by a strange hiccup, 'it makes him mad like he has ants in his pants, that Mehtaab.' And he laughed again. Rajjo wanted to shake him from his stupor, but she restrained herself. 'Especially if he has organized meet and greet and meet and greet and meet and greet.' Rajjo nudged him hard, willing him to complete the sentence. 'I like saying meet and greet, it rhymes!'

Rajjo slapped her palm on her head. And then on cue, he started his blabber again.

'Meet and greet with some businessmen and politicians. Not to mention the land deal he had finalized in the neighbouring village.'

Just then the loudspeakers crackled to life and strains of Sukhmani's sermon could be heard. Rajjo deposited Raahat in his room and went to the main stage to have a look.

Sukhmani sat next to the big cutout of Rani Maa. Rajjo almost laughed at the thought of a cardboard Rani Maa blessing people. The patrons touched Sukhmani's feet and then the cutout's feet and dropped some money in a box next to Chhoti Ma.

Rajjo shook her head at the cardboard divinity as she walked around the compound towards the VIP rooms. Shocked to spot a tottering Raahat carrying some snacks towards the room, ostensibly given to him by Asha, she pounced on him, ordering him to get right back into his room. Rajjo headed towards the VIP room with the tray of food, to find the room full of smoke.

The men were in deep conversation, unaware and unmindful of the quiet sewadar setting the tray on the table. Rajjo gathered the local businessman seemed disappointed that Rani Maa could not make it. Mehtaab assured him that next time she would be here. He was also assured a fifty per cent partnership in running this particular ashram and partnership in the meditative cassettes Rani Maa was coming out with the following winter.

Just then he abruptly turned to look at Rajjo, surprised to see a new face as she was quietly making her exit.

'Where is the boy, Raahat? Usually he is around for these chores.'

'He is unwell,' mumbled Rajjo, surprised that Mehtaab knew about Raahat and a bit nervous she was caught eavesdropping. Instead of scurrying out she confidently turned and served the guests some eateries. Both Mehtaab and the businessman had taken a moment to notice the beautiful girl serving them.

Once Rajjo stepped out of the room, their discussion resumed.

But Rajjo stood by the door, pretending to wipe the tray and eavesdropped. She turned her left ear closer to the door and wished she had not busted her right one. Like a funambulist walking a tightrope she stood there. Just as she inched a step closer to the door to be able to hear better, she was discovered by Arjan. They stood facing each other. Sweat trickled under her armpits and snaked down her back.

'You should not be hanging around here. You should be in the main hall.' He spoke gently with a hint of warning. 'Mehtaab would be upset if he found you lurking around'.

Rajjo nodded.

Before she moved away Arjan gave her an odd look and simply said, 'You are playing with fire…'

Rajjo just stared back, wondering whether to feign ignorance or face it head on. With honesty in her voice she muttered, 'I know.'

Rajjo went and sat outside the main tent in the middle of the fields as Chhoti Maa's voice washed over the lanes and streets through the loudspeakers.

She heard the birds chirping as they flocked back home. She drew circles in the mud thinking of the dark little boy. A circle for Rani Maa, a circle for Chhoti Maa, a circle for Mehtaab, Arjan, Gurbaksha, the ashram, the devotees.

She was trapped somewhere in between these circles, and it was only a matter of time she found her way up.

## August 1991

On a sleepy hot afternoon, green donation boxes, usually kept on stage, along with sacks filled with cash, were being unloaded from a rickety tempo. The boxes and sacks were deposited in a room, where a security guard with a rifle manned the door.

It was clear that money from the donation boxes went into the pockets of the patrons of the commune. A few elderly men had gone into the room with the boxes, holding on to some official-looking notebooks, followed by Arjan in his blue robe, carrying a prayer book.

Rajjo and Raahat hovered in the compound outside, pretending to read some literature on the ashram, but their eyes followed the movements closely. At Rajjo's behest, they trailed the men and hovered outside the cash room.

'Why are we standing here, they are not going to be throwing the loose change out of the doors or the windows. It's going to be counted for, every penny, and then unaccounted for,' muttered Raahat, wanting to head right back into his room and catch a nap under the fan, his shirt stuck to him due to the heat and humidity.

'Shut up, I am not here to catch the pennies!' Rajjo rolled her eyes, fanning herself with her dupatta.

Raahat was puzzled with Rajjo's interest in the room. 'It is clear what they were doing inside, opening the donation boxes, counting the cash, making a record that would never be declared and the sack of cash would disperse from here. Unless you want to grab a sack and shove it under your bed?'

'Do I look like a thief to you, you idiot?'

'But you are behaving like one! Lurking outside the cash room!'

'I am just curious... What do they do with all the money?' whispered Rajjo.

'Run the ashram, live like kings…feed us.'

Raahat made a pathetic face at the last statement.

'Now they are partnering with a businessman who makes sugar. Rani Maa will use that sugar and tell her followers it is pure and they will buy it.'

'Mehtaab is a genius…' muttered Rajjo.

'Some people are sceptical it may not work…' Raahat added.

Rajjo smirked.

'That's the future of Godliness. It will be bought and sold in the market. Packaged and spruced up for all pockets, according to the demand and supply!' The inchoate vision of her future was deepening with a colour that shone on the blush of her cheek.

Arjan cleared his throat. He had obviously heard their dismissive comments. Both Raahat and Rajjo stood outside the cash room with a telltale flush on their faces.

'The mind and bodies of humans are filled with darkness. They find no shelter, no place of rest. Through countless incarnations they wander lost, like crows in a deserted house. Only through Guru's teachings is the name of the lord received. Instead of snooping around and questioning everything, you both should start reading the prayer books. You will find many of your answers there.'

Raahat nodded many times over, eager to please and display his idoneous obedience. He looked like he was going to run away and learn all the prayer books in the ashram by heart rightaway!

Rajjo, however, did not aim to please. She was not worried or scared.

'I just wanted to see if they needed any help?' So the cash is collected from all the ashrams regularly. Is it taxed?' With a deliberate pause, Arjan glared at her. Raahat coughed nervously, wanting the impervious Rajjo to stop.

Rajjo waited for an answer as she stared back at Arjan. Despite his admonishing words Arjan brought a strange sense of serenity whenever he was around Rajjo. His indefatigable calm filled her with ease. She may not have spent years knowing him, but with the intuitive knowledge that assures a bright day follows the darkest night, she knew she could trust this man with her secrets, her dreams, her desires and her distrust.

Another box was hauled in by an old man with a thin frame, skin as dark as black leather, wrinkled face, tired old eyes, a dirty cloth around his neck and body bathed in sweat. Raahat and Rajjo watched as the man manoeuvered the box of cash inside the door, his veins bulging with the effort as he disappeared inside the room. As Arjan was about to follow him inside, Rajjo mocked him again.

'Do you think that poor man, wearing a mere loincloth, lugging the box of cash is muttering the name of God? If he gets half of what is in it, he can live decently for a few months,' said Rajjo. Arjan didn't answer. Rajjo continued, 'If I was God, I would definitely let him have some…'

Arjan sighed and added under his breath. 'They need it to run such a big organization. They need the money, and a lot of it goes to charitable causes.'

Rajjo leaned forward, thrusting her left ear forward. There was a strange look of pride and a telltale flush of vulnerability. She had not heard him clearly, but she did not want to ask him again.

Arjan repeated what he had said, a little louder this time.

'I heard that…' muttered Rajjo, swallowing a lump. The silence in her ear sometimes ate her up.

Raahat mumbled, 'I need to finish my prayers,' and disappeared, sensing the tumultuous mood. Rajjo was an unpredictable hurricane ready to erupt unannounced anywhere. As Raahat moved away, he heard Rajjo say to Arjan, 'I want to be transferred to the ashram Rani Maa is visiting next.'

Instead of answering or responding to her request, Arjan surprised her with a question. 'Do you want a machine for your right ear? Do you want to consult an ear specialist?' Arjan asked. Rajjo was taken aback with the sudden question as she shook her head and shrugged her slim shoulders.

There was something about this girl that got to him. She reminded him of a brutally bruised doe, the doe now fighting alone in the night, with her shadows, with the tree barks, with the leaves, with the forest. For everything around her was a predator. The only thing he could extend was comfort and support.

An invisible fibril connected them.

Rajjo's request was odd. But he could not deny it outright. Maybe Rani Maa would be able to engage her and bring her back to embrace faith. 'Let me check Rani Maa's schedule and see if something can be done.'

Rajjo nodded with relief. At least he was going to consider her request. The weight of the warm afternoon burnt her neck and shoulders. Half of her world registered the harmonium strains permeating the stillness across the compound and the priests reading out the holy shabads on the loudspeaker.

However, the other half of her world was dark and silent. Neither a flap of a bird wing, the trickle of water, the patter of rain, nor her mother's melodious voice reading prayers out loud for her little daughters and son could shatter that ultimate silence.

She ached to hear a tune in her deaf ear, the one she heard from the fluteseller's flute who crossed their village every summer, reminding her of a maudlin story of doleful lovers in her village.

The day went by, the cash was counted and then stuffed in rice sacks, piled into a white car and sent away like a precious bride.

Rajjo spotted Arjan going towards the prayer room and intercepted him. It was imperative that he made an official commitment to her about the date of Rani Maa's visit and the name of the ashram. She wanted to leave as soon as possible. Rajjo thought of little else the day. She knew she had to maintain a calm front, but the question was out before she could reign it in.

'Please let me know what her schedule is? I want to be there for the next sermon.'

Arjan looked at her, trying to understand her restlessness and urge to be close to Rani Maa. Perhaps it was more than what he thought. The hungry look in her eyes and the desperate tenor of her voice indicated she was not chasing Rani Maa to find a path.

'You who runs away from the name of God, wants to be a part of Rani Maa's sermons?' he probed gently.

'Yes, I feel I need to be around her. Closer to her.'

Rajjo averted her gaze again, unable to look him in the eye. They saw too much.

'I am not going to ask you why. But I do want to remind you…it's written. The day dawns and then it ends, the night passes away. Man's life is diminishing and he is unaware that each day the mouse of death gnaws at the rope of life. Just pause and think now and then, what is it that you are chasing?'

Rajjo took in the words and exhaled deeply.

'I have been in a paused state long enough, Arjan. I have given it a thought. Day dawns and night passes away. In between this passage I sit and think about what I want, and my answer is still the same, I want to be in her service. Perhaps I will discover how to deal with God and how he has dealt with me…'

Arjan coughed slightly. Like he knew she was lying through her teeth. Rajjo stood there like an errant child. He understood her ambition then, intuitively. It was clear as daylight. The doe wanted to dig a tunnel all the way to the heavens, wanting to wage a war with Gods.

There was little he could do to dissuade her and his resistance would only make her desperate.

He mumbled, 'I'll see what I can do.'

Rajjo was careful not to smile too much.

As he walked away, Rajjo twirled in the air, triumphant. She heard a mellifluous melody in her deaf ear. She failed to notice the thin lanky boy and his odd expression. It was Raahat. He had witnessed the entire exchange.

'Has what my acne-ridden brain understood from all this mumbo jumbo correct? Am I right to think what I am thinking?'

Rajjo looked at Raahat and nodded.

'Why do you want to be in Rani Maa's service? Since when has the divine tree taken roots in your toxic heart?'

Rajjo laughed at his rambling.

They both quietly walked back to their smoking place in the middle of the gardens surrounding the compounds. Crickets and frogs croaked and chirped. They sat side by side, sharing a cigarette like old comrades.

After a few puffs, Rajjo broke the pleasant silence.

'I want to be in her service, to learn how to be a Rani Maa!'

There, it was out. Her yearning floated in the orchards.

The trees, the shrubs, the flowers, the crickets, the owls, the wind, the sky – they heard her. Not to mention Raahat who sat there with a stricken face.

Raahat almost swallowed his tongue, followed by a bout of coughing.

'What! Are you freaking out of your mind?'

Rajjo nodded again.

There was a silence.

Rajjo smiled at him as she said, 'All the time I waste assessing and rethinking, I'm not getting where I want to be.'

'You are crazy…' Raahat said after a long pause. Like he was toying with the notion that Rajjo had partially lost her senses with her hearing, but then arrived at the conclusion that she must have lost her brain entirely.

Having made the grand announcement, Rajjo was lost in her thoughts, savouring the smell of trees in the dark night. She smiled and ruffled his hair with affection.

'Uff, what's all that stuff in your hair?'

She snatched her hand out of his unruly hair and sniffed her palm. It smelt awful and she could see the grease stuck on her hand.

'It's desi ghee. I got it from the kitchen. I heard the girls say that ghee will make the hair shinier, and I am sick of my messy curls. You also keep screaming at me!'

'You mooncalf! People fry vegetables in that and you have dipped your head! No wonder you smell odd!'

Raahat resettled his hair just the way he liked it.

'Stop spoiling my hair anyway.'

As Raahat worked his hair, it reminded Rajjo of her brother back home and wished she could know what he was like. Did he have a curly mop of hair? Or had he cut them really short? Was he still fat? What were those annoying habits? Had he fallen in love yet?

'Rajjo Maa, I think it's time for you to go home! I can come with you, if you want,' muttered Raahat and chuckled, shaking his head. Rajjo focused on a picture hidden in a warm place somewhere inside. A shrivelled-up old tree with freshly washed pots and pans hung on the branches to dry out. A lump caught in her throat as she remembered her village, the smells, the sights, the mud, Totu; her screechy parrot, her sisters. The memory of her podgy brother running after a tractor carrying green fodder made her smile. No, she was not ready to go home yet.

With a sigh Rajjo shut her eyes. Old memories enveloped her in the dark night. She wanted to escape the past and run into the future, but for nows he had to bear the present.

## September 1991

Rajjo stood in the large airy kitchen, with the smell of tea brewing. It was September already, the monsoon was retreating and winter was almost upon them. The days were generally dry and fair. Rajjo knew back home they would be waiting. They would have burnt the weeds and the debris of the last crop and ploughed the lands before the advent of monsoon so the soil soaked in maximum moisture.

Come September they would sow the lentils and sugarcanes. Their father insisted they should grow both on their tracts as they both complemented each other.

Just as back home they were preparing to sow a new crop, it was the right moment for Rajjo to burn the weeds and surge ahead, it was time. The only thought consuming Rajjo now was, how to get into the core committee. Arjan had shifted Rajjo to the ashram where Rani Maa's sermons were scheduled, but just being around Rani Maa was not enough, she needed to get closer if she was to move forward. She had to be on Rani Maa's service. Otherwise she was just another one in the sea of workers hovering around the Godwoman.

Rani Maa's last sermon was hurriedly wrapped up as she had to leave for the airport to fly to Europe. Just the thought of it made Rajjo dreamy-eyed.

That night she'd got Raahat to get her a world map, and both of them had together travelled the world marking Rani Maa's trips, sitting on a narrow bed in a tiny dark room. The lizard stuck on the ceiling peeped over too, as the excited duo marked the places Rani Maa had visited on her latest trip and all the other trips that Raahat remembered.

Now Rani Maa was returning to the ashram, and Rajjo needed to make peace with Kuljeet. Arjan could not help her here anymore. She had to soothe Kuljeet's ruffled feathers, as she needed an introduction and Kuljeet's blessings to be able to get on to Rani Maa's personal service. However, it was not going to be easy as Kuljeet, already annoyed with Rajjo, had made her displeasure public. She'd mentioned it to Arjan that she was unhappy with Rajjo's insubordination as she had left the last ashram without her permission.

Rajjo shrugged the web of fears and problems away and concentrated on brewing a hot cup of tea for Kuljeet. It was time to make peace, over a steaming cup of tea. She hoped the differences Kuljeet had with Rajjo would be carried away in a ball of steam that rose from the cup, through the little window, up, up and away, perhaps to settle on a passing crow's head.

She poured the hot tea in a mug, walked through the sleepy corridor and knocked on Kuljeet's door. A few religious symbols hung on a thread.

Kuljeet looked up from her prayer book like she was expecting her. Her knowing look made Rajjo uneasy but she continued anyhow.

'I came here without permission because I wanted to meet Rani Maa, I wanted to be in her grace, feel her divinity. Sorry, I did not consult with you, please forgive me as your younger sister…'

While Rajjo spoke, Kuljeet's mind ticked. Rajjo could almost hear it in her dead ear. Kuljeet did not trust Rajjo, perhaps rightly so because Rajjo had never given her any reason to. Like wary enemies, wedged in a room, they sized each other up. Rajjo could feel her distrust and wariness filling up the room so much so that it was difficult to breathe. Finally Kuljeet cleared her throat and added dismissively, 'I thought you did not believe in anything, you were an atheist and suddenly you want to follow the path of God with Rani Maa?'

Rajjo lowered her eyes; she'd not expected this direct confrontation.

Choosing her words carefully, knowing fully well Kuljeet could send her packing at any minute, Rajjo replied, 'I may not believe in one God, but I believe that the human mind relies on some kind of special supernatural assistance in order to complete its ordinary cognitive activity.' Rajjo peered up to see if Kuljeet was confused enough or amused enough at her text-book answer.

Kuljeet in turn was reminded of a performer on stage, under the spotlight, hiding under reams of makeup, carrying a bloody secret in her heart. She had something dreadful to hide. Perhaps it was a wound from a violent past. However, she could not be trusted.

Rajjo cleared her throat as Kuljeet simply stared on. Rajjo wanted to put her hand in her head, and cut out her thoughts. Her expression, however, clearly indicated that Rajjo would have to do more to convince Kuljeet. She was a woman who drew her individuality from prayer books, teachings and religious symbols. A whisper in her dead ear erupted, behind all this was the shadow of her woebegone past.

'Why can't you read the scriptures and gain some true knowledge, and then think of learning more from Rani Maa?'

Kuljeet saw a scintilla of something burning in her beautiful tiger eyes. Kuljeet almost shivered with the intensity as the waif-like girl with a fierce gaze looked on.

Rajjo was going to let this conversation play out. A long endless silence stretched out in the room. Rajjo noticed the neatly laid-out bed, folded sheets, not a paper out of place. She felt the walls were scrubbed clean by Kuljeet as well. The tiny mirror sparkled on the wall as if Kuljeet cleaned it every hour. A few books were stacked on the table. Empty frames with no pictures made for odd decorative pieces. As the silence stretched, Rajjo wanted to scream. Kuljeet wanted a declaration that she would be devoted to the cause of God.

Who made this Kuljeet his crusader in the first place? Rajjo cleared her throat lest she said it aloud. She continued meekly, 'That voice that tells me not to do something bad gently is divinity. I want to nurture it, and being in Rani Maa's grace will allow me to do that. I don't know if that is God, but I do know I want to get closer to it.'

There was another long pause. Rajjo had run out of spiritual conversation.

Kuljeet had to grudgingly accept that Rajjo made a compelling argument and it was evident her heart was set on it. Kuljeet usually considered herself a righteous woman, but something about this stubborn girl brought out a side of her she would rather not meet often. It was a Kuljeet similar in features but different. Her Kuljeet always tied her hair in a headband, this Kuljeet flipped it in wild abandon and with rage in her eyes. This Kuljeet wanted to burn the prayer books, for she was wounded. She wanted revenge. It was the part of herself Kuljeet doused in kerosene every day and lit a match to, while she read out of her prayer books.

Kuljeet gave in to the urge and sweetly added, 'She is coming tomorrow. She likes well-dressed bright young things. Spruce up. Look nice, and I will do an introduction tomorrow and suggest your name for her personal service.'

Rajjo could barely breathe. Just when she thought Kuljeet would never consent, she had surprised her. Rajjo nodded and silently slipped out of the room. She could not wait for the day to pass.

Kuljeet stood staring at the steaming cup of tea. The steam entered her pores and her soul, burning it ever so lightly. Was she doing the correct thing by playing her? Then she heard a shriek. 'She deserves it. An atheist, with devious plans.' Only the voice was hoarse and it dripped with vengeance. Kuljeet tasted her pyrrhic victory in the sweet tea she sipped.

The next morning was bright and clear with a slight nip in the air. Rajjo took care of her appearance. She bathed, oiled her body, she ironed her clothes, she made her hair, the glistening curls carefully arranged around her face. She put kohl in her eyes, a tinge of rose on her lips.

She had requested Raahat to pinch a few things from Asha given Rajjo had none of her own.

Rajjo's lissome looks and gossamer beauty attracted admiring glances from all and sundry at the ashram. She crossed Arjan outside the admin. hall, a worried expression flitted his face like a passing cloud. He was about to say something but then he changed his mind.

Just then the sound of honking and the screeching of tyres made everyone in the compound swing into action. A wave of excitement and anticipation rose in Rajjo.

Rani Maa and Mehtaab had arrived. A small welcome party including Sarika Tai, Kuljeet, Arjan and Gurbaksha were at the gate to receive them. Sarika Tai had arrived two nights ago, However, she had not interacted much with Rajjo apart from a few pleasantries. It was evident anyone who wanted to be in the good books of Kuljeet maintained a safe distance from Rajjo.

Rajjo moved towards the gleaming white car. She had rehearsed and practised her introductory chat over and over again.

Mehtaab alighted first followed by Rani Maa.

Kuljeet stepped forward and introduced Rajjo to Mehtaab.

'Rajjo, Durga Kahlon. New at the ashram but is showing keen interest in events and some in God, thankfully.'

Her barb had not gone unnoticed. Rajjo could sense the meeting going sour from that very second. A flock of crows cawed overhead and flew ominously towards the south. She knew she was in a deep ditch, deep enough for the earthy taste to douse the smell of the leaves and the skies. Kuljeet had pushed her in there and this was not going to turn out well.

Rajjo came back to the conversation as she noticed Mehtaab nodding at her appreciatively. At the same time Rani Maa joined them and Kuljeet added, 'Now she desires to be in Rani Maa's personal service'.

Mehtaab looked at her, with a man's eye appreciating a woman's body. Rani Maa was swift enough to catch that glint and Kuljeet was fast enough to heave a sigh of relief. It had worked out all right.

'She has been eager to meet Mehtaab-ji and you,' added Kuljeet for good measure, she knew Rani Maa well. Amongst other things, she knew her joint aches, she knew her medicines, the sugar in her tea, the wounds she festered, the salt she avoided, the heartache she carried within. And she knew exactly how this meeting was going to turn out.

A stinging glance and Rani Maa left without a word to Rajjo. The words Kuljeet said hung in the air for a while only to be dispersed by a dry gust of wind. Rajjo just stood there as the little gathering moved on.

It would take her some time to get out of the ditch Kuljeet had shoved her into. Instead of coming closer to Rani Maa, Kuljeet had made sure Rani Maa dismissed her. To add to Rajjo's woes, on her way Rani Maa whispered something in Sukhmani's ear, like the wind. Rani Maa continued meeting key people and sewadars standing in a line to greet her, blessing them with a divine expression pasted on her face. Rajjo wondered bitterly if she maintained that while she ate and farted.

Sukhmani came and whispered something to Kuljeet. Kuljeet nodded her head and approached Rajjo, 'You are not to accompany Rani Maa. She does not want you there on stage, she feels you need to meditate more before you can join her service.' The lagoon she wanted to cross was now an ocean!

A victorious gleam was evident in Kuljeet's eyes, which was followed by a flash of remorse. Despite herself, she head her voice telling Rajjo, 'You need to embrace the name of God more. You need to be one with him. For in the third watch of night, the swans, the white hairs will come and land upon the pools of your head. Youth will wear itself out and old age triumph. And when the messenger of death carries you away, all things you keep close are left behind. Your intellect, wisdom departed and what is left is penance. All that is left to do is repent on your evil deeds…'

Kuljeet felt a sense of emptiness. She needed to read her prayers. She turned and left. However, Rajjo understood the biggest lesson of all, that she should trust her instinct. She was right about the unease, the nagging voice, the scowl. Kuljeet was never going to extend a helping hand.

Rajjo stood in the compound. Numb. Kuljeet had played her very well, knowing Mehtaab would notice her as a woman, and so Rani Maa would too. The age old vice of jealousy had come to Kuljeet's aid. It dawned on Rajjo that Kuljeet had used her knowledge that Rani Maa was in love with Mehtaab to get her thrown out. Sukhmani passed Rajjo in the compound and whispered politely, 'We at the ashram believe in simplicity, humility, service… You should devote yourself to the service of god, that would be devotion to Rani Maa's service.' Sukhmani threw a censorious look for good measure.

The place was swarming with bigots, thought Rajjo as she nodded meekly and retreated to her room, to sit on the narrow cot. She'd had a strange sensation as Chhoti Maa Sukhmani had whispered to her; a flash of a womb and a baby's cry had rung out. As always she'd heard it in her right ear. The one that had been silent for so long. Rajjo was unsure she'd heard the wail in her right ear and so clapped, just to make sure if it was still dead. It was.

But she was also sure the wail heard in her dead ear had been followed by the cackle of girls. It seemed familiar. It was the sound of sisters sitting and playing together. Disturbed and restless with noxious thoughts, Rajjo collected herself and went towards the kitchen.

She cooked till midnight and packed some lunch boxes and put them aside. All the while her face was carved in stone. With the lunch of potatoes, chapatis and some pulses and rice, she was going to pass on the bad news.

As the night crept up, it dawned on Rajjo why the silence in her ear was broken now and then. It had started listening to its own language, it refused to be dead. There was a message to be conveyed.

As frost was the harbinger of winter, the whispers in her ear were for the village.

The next morning, as Rani Maa's coterie was ready to leave, Rajjo went to Sukhmani with packed food she had prepared the night before. Sukhmani smiled and blessed Rajjo for her thoughtful gesture. Rajjo leaned forward and whispered in her ear, 'Tell your sister to be careful in the next two months. She might lose the baby she carries.' Her gentle warning startled Sukhmani, who almost dropped the packet from her hand. Her face mirrored an incredulous expression, 'How did you know she is pregnant.'

'I didn't… I just had this message for you.'

Sukhmani moved away from Rajjo with an uncomfortable look, clearly baffled about the conversation they had exchanged.

Sukhmani sought out Kuljeet and harangued her about Rajjo. Rajjo noticed Mehtaab leave his room. Mehtaab furtively glanced at her as he walked towards the main gate. Hope and something else cold and clingy inched its way up from the pit of her stomach. Quelling the uneasy feeling, Rajjo approached him with a smile and immediately bent down to reach his feet.

Mehtaab's eyes hungrily took in Rajjo's voluptuous cleavage. His lecherous gaze ate her up. Rajjo with her head down whispered to him, 'I look forward to meeting you next, Mehtaab-ji. I really look forward to being on Rani Maa's service and being blessed in the process.' Her scarf billowed around her coquettishly.

Rajjo, unsure of his reaction, was testing the waters. She was beyond caring as her defeat had left her with little to lose. She was at Kuljeet's mercy and could be asked to leave anytime. She saw Mehtaab's lecherous response. His eyes taking in her curves carried a carnal glint. His pulse had quickened. Shedding the brief hesitancy, she pushed herself a little more towards him. She had crossed a line with him. The air crackled between them. Her full breast clad in a muslin fabric almost brushed his tightened chest.

*But for the land to be ready to receive the rainfall, and suck it in, it had to be mercilessly ploughed. It had to nurture a crop. Rajjo had to nurture a dream.*

Mehtaab nodded with a smile. He breathed heavily. The air was pregnant with promise. She stood close enough for him to smell her skin. Her breast almost grazed his chest again and Mehtaab checked his urge to grab her and undress her. Her slim waist and full hips already stirred a deep guttural desire. However, Mehtaab also knew it was not accidental. She deliberately tempted him in broad daylight. Rajjo stepped even closer to him. The swell of her breast brushed his chest yet again. A yearning and lust suspended him for a few minutes. He was going to have her. She bowed her head in reverence.

She dared indulge in this tap dance out in the courtyard for the world to see. That excited Mehtaab no end. She did not cower as he held her gaze. The reprehensible glances glided off her swan-like back. She was a creature to keep in the stable! He would keep her close.

Arjan broke the moment as he approached them carrying a briefcase for Mehtaab. Mehtaab smiled at Arjan and patted his back.

'Do bring her along when we have a Sangat next time.'

There, he had said the magic words. Rajjo could leverage that to extend her stay with Kuljeet. A flood of relief ran through her body. Kuljeet would have to wait to throw her out as Mehtaab had asked for her. However, the cold clingy veil that crawled up her throat was hurriedly growing into a poisonous weed that covered her neck and face as well. She stood like a plaintiff in the courtyard of her mind. She strangled the guilt and moved out. There was still time for retribution.

As soon as Mehtaab, Rani Maa and her coterie had left, Arjan turned to Rajjo and whispered. 'You have made a promise and you will have to deliver...'

Rajjo's face was white with fear for a moment. And then, shaking off her hesitation, she muttered with her chin thrust forward.

'I am prepared for it.'

Arjan read her delicate features and quivering lips. She was a child woman, hurt and scared. She was fighting the forest – banging her head on the tree bark. Not realizing the forest would never bleed red.

'I don't think so…' he whispered into her ear and walked away into the dark night.

Rajjo resolutely pushed her tears away.

She had taken the first step into the blazing fire and was ready to risk being burnt.

The passing wind whispered in her ear, the monsoons were retreating. Winter frost was going to enshroud the sapling of the monsoon in an alabaster grave.

## October 1991

October was back and so were the dry winds. Rajjo was at another ashram in a sleepy village called Himmatpura. As Rajjo wandered the muddy streets of the village, she realized she was happy to be there.

Rajjo had been here a month and this ashram had grown on her. Like the ephemeral joys of childhood, she knew it was a short respite, but she enjoyed it. It was one of the big ones, with a huge darbar for the spiritual meetings, land worth fifteen acres, nine big halls, thirty rooms. A beautiful garden of fruit trees encircled the compound. The tangy smell of mango trees wafted in and out of her little window overlooking the orchards.

Arjan had joined them a week ago along with Raahat, and until then Rajjo had been handling the ashram with the old woman who everyone referred to as Mata-ji. Rajjo had been standing in for Asha, who had fallen ill with jaundice which had only worsened her disposition. Mata-ji was only too happy to let Rajjo take over the workings of the ashram under her astute eye.

Now and then the events of the fateful day flitted across her memory, leaving a sliver of dread in its wake. Almost immediately after Mehtaab's departure that day, Arjan and Kuljeet had a quiet consultation. The winds in the room passed through cracks in the walls and whispers spread. Kuljeet was livid that Rajjo had tried to act the tease with Mehtaab, and had witnessed it. Arjan was adamant Rajjo would not leave, as Mehtaab wanted to see her in the next congregation. Finally Kuljeet acquiesced and agreed to send her away to another ashram for a while.

Rajjo knew she had plummeted down and often the way up from a ditch was arduous, but she was willing to wait and climb up one step at a time. Moreover, she was glad to be away from Kuljeet.

The night before she left that ashram, she'd sought Arjan out and whispered her gratitude and hesitantly asked him the question that she often wondered, why he fought for her so hard. Why did he help her always?

Her question shook Arjan's imperturbability for a moment. After composing himself once more, staring into the deep dark night, he whispered, 'I was in love with a girl called Rajjo.'

And then he was quiet for a long time as they sat in the courtyard looking at the lights of the glowworms. It was a beautiful spectacle, dazzling lights lit up unexpected dark corners, as if a magician had ordered them to twinkle now and then.

Rajjo could feel his heart break. He struggled with a long-held memory.

'My mother used to say glowworms burnt themselves to attract their mates.' She heard herself saying to fill in the silence.

Arjan simply laughed, 'Some do it to attract their prey and some to warn the other they can't be eaten. Whatever the cause, they burn. And we rejoice in the beauty, little stars crossing us in the dark night, now and then.'

Rajjo hugged him before leaving and wondered what happened to his beloved. She was going to find out from Arjan soon enough.

A smile crossed her face as she thought of Arjan. Almost twisting her ankle on a protruding root of a tree, Rajjo jerked back to the present.

It was time to head back to the ashram, and perhaps it was time to start thinking again. How was she going to make any headway? Was she ever going to find her way out of this? As the stygian gloom descended, Rajjo focused on the happy parts of her life in the ashram over the last one month.

Although she was always bitter with everyone, the diaphanous and old Mata-ji had taken an instant liking to Rajjo. Having heard stories about her own grandmother, from her mother, somehow Rajjo knew if her grandmother were alive, she would be like Mata-ji.

Mata-ji constantly jibed Rajjo about her youth, her age, her romantic interests. She was the most non-spiritual person Rajjo had known in the spiritual commune. Her volubility impressed Rajjo. Mata-ji wanted to know about Bollywood gossip and conspiracy theories. She cheated on her religious books, consumed alcohol, smoked, all in the name of old age.

She touted God's disinterest as the reason for her behaviour. He was busy watching the younger ones so it didn't matter if she behaved or not. Rajjo found her increasingly endearing as days went by and learnt about the frail lady's indirect control over the commune.

Raahat constantly riled Rajjo over the old woman's fondness, 'The old woman likes you, else she would have torn you apart and not let you enter, let alone run things around here…She may just be thinking of you as her daughter-in-law... And guess who the son is? Mehtaab!'

Rajjo laughed at Raahat's blandishments but saw the truth that lurked in his banter.

When the good weather and clear stars beckoned, Mata-ji and Rajjo would sleep in the courtyard sometimes, with their cots laid out side by side. They would look up at the stars in the cold October nights, huddling under the quilts. Not talking just looking, listening to the winds of night and incessant gurgling of Mata-ji's hookah.

Then one clear starlit night Mata-ji spoke in hushed whispers, her voice doused in nostalgia, transporting Rajjo to another world.' I had a lover. He was strong and young. Ten years younger than me. He came to my village as a migrant from Pakistan, before the bloody horrors had begun. He was a boor, I tell you, but looked like a prince. He had left his wife and children behind, who were going to join him shortly once he settled here. But that one year we spent together is what I think about. The day we met to the day we parted. For the last twenty years, that one year was enough. I can still smell him in the air and feel his big and strong arms around me. And then he was butchered on the train on his way back home.'

Their love story spread in the courtyard. It was all around them. It conjured up an era of great romance and destruction.

Rajjo just stared into the dark night with the old woman's voice washing over.

'There is someone meant for you too, you will meet him soon. But it's going to be a rough path.'

That statement made Rajjo smirk. 'I am unlucky in love…'

'It's your salvation…' The old lady nodded wisely as if she knew all the mysteries of the world and smoked them from her hookah pipe.

'He will come from the skies; the earth will rise up to meet him and one look! It'll all spin out of control, yet the moment will last beyond the blue moon…'

The prevision sent shivers up Rajjo's spine.

*That's it! The oldie was on drugs!*

Rajjo turned around in her cot to shut out the old woman's raspy predictions. She did not want her feeding her brain with stupid tales.

But the imagery the old woman drew instantly reminded her of Harsh Vardhan. She cleared her head of any thought of him.

'These two love birds, Rani and Mehtaab, I have seen them grow under my eyes. Idiots, they should marry and be together!'

That got Rajjo turning her side again. She was listening. She was truly listening to what the old woman had to say. But after that Mata-ji decided to say nothing at all. Rajjo did not want to push her and decided to wait another day to pick up the conversation.

The next afternoon, as they sat side by side, Rajjo oiled her arms under the sheesham trees, the old lady breathed in deeply.

'Sheesham… worship this. I used to cure an entire village with pieces of its leaves. It's so powerful, mix it in honey and use it for pain in the eyes, its godsent for indigestion and heartburn, a tincture of the bark will lighten any stubborn dark marks on your skin, paste from the bark also takes care of boils and pimples. That stupid Raahat, that mad boy, he needs it. I'll have it ready for him. The leaf and root can also be used as astringent or stimulants. It cures leprosy and many diseases of the private parts too … It is a work of God.'

Rajjo grunted.

'But I don't know which sheesham to find to cure your burns and diseases…'

Rajjo stopped midway. And then she resumed oiling her limbs again cautiously. Mata-ji had caught her off guard.

'That boy was always bright, that Mehtaab.' Rajjo sighed with relief that she had picked up her favourite topic. And then the old lady chuckled, remembering something. 'First made merry by being a child baba, squeezed all the women he could, went to jail, studied there. He finished reading the bible, the Quran and many other religious scriptures; he became a learned man.'

'So he came out of the prison a learned man?' Rajjo interjected.

'Ya, he came out learned enough to hoodwink the world twice over, and then created Rani Maa!' Mata-ji cackled again. Her asthmatic laughter took its own sweet time to recede.

'He understood that the oldest and most foolproof business in the world is the god business. You see the entire world is in it! From the church to the mosques, to the ashrams, they run the world! It's the best business ever… He and Rani got all the rich and famous people in the area, the MLAs also, to come here and lift some muck. Lift some bricks and mud.'

And then she paused abruptly, like she was bored already with this conversation. A few minutes of silence later she turned to Rajjo.

'What is the hoopla between you and Arjan? He is a good guy. I will break your neck if you hurt him, although I know nothing is going on between you two…'

The cackle was back again.

Since dusk was upon them and the echo of the crickets could be heard far and wide, Rajjo wanted to escort Mata-ji to the yard outside her room. But Mata-ji would have none of it. She wanted to soak in the night, she said. Rajjo marvelled that Mata-ji saw everything with her cataract-ridden eyes. She was no comic, she was no senile. She was a shrewd old lady who had figured it all out.

Rajjo, scared that her heartbeat would give away her deepest desire, wanted to collect her mattress lying in the yard and hide inside her room.

'I'll be taking my mattress inside tonight, it's a bit chilly here.'

The old lady chuckled at Rajjo's sudden decision to retreat for the night.

'Why are you here? Why don't you go out and live in the real world? What are you looking for? It's not God for sure. What is it? Food, shelter, happiness?'

Rajjo was caught unawares and a little nervous that the shrewd old lady could peep into her soul. Fumblingly she repeated something from her red diary to cover up her unease.

'If happiness makes life desirable and complete, it cannot be exceeded, and is therefore the end of action… So no, I don't want happiness because I don't want to stop moving.'

The old woman laughed, looking up at the Sheesham tree as she shook her head in resignation and disapproval.

'Things we say and do to hide …'

The old lady turned to nurse her hookah, dismissing Rajjo.

Rajjo walked out of the orchards and reached her room. The door safely shut and latched, she closed her eyes, trying hard to get rid of the screeching laughter and searing gaze of the old lady as she huddled further inside her quilt.

It was going to be Diwali in five days and lights would streak the skies. Rajjo looked forward to it, remembering her and her siblings waiting for Diwali night to eat the delicious sweets their mother would prepare for them. They would light up the house, divide the sweets equally amongst themselves, go into the fields and lie down side by side, to see the fireworks. They stayed up most of the night, eating, gossiping, giggling, till the sun climbed up. She would miss the hot stove and the sweets prepared this year. She would miss the voice of her mother's prayers as she gathered her children round her and read from the prayer books. A tear was hurriedly pushed aside, with a resolution to keep the memories at bay. She fell into a deep sleep, as the layers of darkness engulfed her, only to find herself lost in a forest with sheesham trees. A cloud gently unveiled a full moon, the forest bathed in a silvery hue. Through the leaves and flowers, a familiar face took shape – that of her mother, who'd just finished cooking by the stove and fed Totu some milk, and walked into the forest. She drew closer to

Rajjo and smeared a soothing paste on Rajjo's face and neck mumbling her prayers that echoed in the forest. Rajjo's charred and burnt body was miraculously healing. The pain disappeared in a whiff of smoke, as Rajjo was carried away by the wind, only to disappear in the embrace of a sheesham tree, away from it all. She was finally at peace as she inhaled the blissful scent of the wood.

## 9 November 1991

Raahat was still teasing Rajjo about her lover who would descend from the skies. He'd hid somewhere in the orchards to smoke and had ended up eavesdropping on her conversations with Mata-ji. Rajjo admonished him for it, and Raahat appeared remorseful for exactly thirty seconds before he added, 'My favourite part was when she described Mehtaab as a pervert and said they should get married. Mehtaab would bury her in the forest alive if he heard her talk like that!'

He threw his head back and laughed all over again.

Rajjo did not pay attention as she continued sorting out the files she was working on for Arjan.

He broke the silence again by saying, 'Rajjo didi, I have a confession to make. I am in love…'

That got her attention.

'…with Asha'.

Rajjo whacked him with a file and walked out of the room, muttering. 'It's an auspicious day today. Can't you think of happy things? She is old enough to be your great grandmother!'

'I am seventeen years, two hundred and two days old and she is thirty and one day old…' Raahat added with an innocent smile, ignoring Rajjo's minacious look.

Rajjo hurled a utensil at him but Raahat ducked deftly. Rajjo hoped it was a joke just to rile her. Busy with the Diwali preparations, Rajjo had no time for Raahat's idle banter.

Just then, surly Asha, her milky-white face twisted in a scowl, approached them and stared at Raahat accusingly. 'Today is an auspicious day! Don't while it away in nonsense. Say some prayers.

Remember the lord, else you will be hanging here like a ghost on that mulberry tree, with no God, no religion and no faith to tide you by!'

Jaundice or something else had inured Asha. Perhaps Rajjo's closeness with Mata-ji and her increasing fondness?

'She knows about our smoking?' Rajjo gave Raahat a pointed look as Asha walked away fuming. Raahat, with a cute apologetic face, assured Rajjo, 'I like her feisty spirit. Don't worry, she is harmless.'

Hopeful that the next phase was just around the corner, the festivities of the day perked up her mood. Specially prepared sweets were being distributed as prasad all around. Rajjo wandered into Arjan's neatly organized office to give him some sweets and finish the filing he had requested her to do.

He smiled at her, as Rajjo hesitantly broached the topic. 'You think if this upcoming event goes well, they will induct me in the core team? Despite Kuljeet?'

Arjan continued to pore over his file without looking up. And then he finally muttered, 'Focus on doing a good job. Mehtaab already knows you. It is a matter of time.' His reply had a mild reproach not lost on Rajjo, but the fact that he would be watching her back was a given.

Rajjo felt a sense of relief. Arjan was an ally and he was going to help her get where she wanted. Just when she was leaving the room, a magazine cover caught her eye. Her body tensed. Her hands were sweating, her heartbeat fluttering. It was Harsh Vardhan Singh, along with his young politician cousin. Rajjo casually went back to the table and picked up the magazine, quietly noted by Arjan.

Rajjo flipped through the pages, happy to learn that the duo was supposed to tour Punjab the following month. Rajjo could feel it in her blood. He was going to meet her.

Rajjo mentally shook her head, reprimanding herself for biting into Mata-ji's crazed rambling. She collected her tray of sweets and headed out.

As she stepped out of the administration wing she could see Mata-ji slowly cross the compound and she hid behind a pillar with a guilty bubble bursting in her chest, for she had been avoiding her for a week since their last chat. Mata-ji said too much and saw too much.

But today being the festival, Rajjo had a feeling she was not going to succeed in avoiding her altogether.

A few hours later, the surly Asha informed her that Mata-ji was asking for her in the gardens. Asha, with her peaches and cream complexion, churlish expression and thick plait wound around her head, seemed to have gained more weight with her surliness lately.

Rajjo liked the idea of going to the orchards. There was a beautiful clearing in the middle of the mulberry trees, with white benches and seats arranged in a circular pattern. It was an idyllic setting.

Rajjo prepared some tea and carried the steaming hot cups into orchard. It was a clear bright day. She wanted to rest her head and sleep under one of the mango trees.

Handing the tea to Mata-ji, she noticed her taking some powder from her 'medicine box'. Perhaps it was the magic powder. As soon as Rajjo took a seat next to her, Mata-ji impugned her actions.

'Asha tells me things about you. She is stupid and petulant. But she is loyal. Kuljeet has been talking to her and she has been parroting to me. You were brought half dead to the ashram, then you became healthy, you backstabbed Kuljeet, you used Gurbaksha, you ensnared Arjan, you befriended and used the young kid Raahat, you were luring Mehtaab till you were almost kicked out and were sent here.'

Rajjo waited for the accusations to sink in. It was a bright clear day with a nip in the air. A group of sparrows pottered around without a care in the world. Time ceased to exist here. Rajjo knew the old lady was keenly looking for her response.

And then she simply nodded with an expressionless face. Adding shortly in a bland voice.

'It's true, in a way…'

The old lady guffawed.

'You scoundrel! I know what you are up to!'

Rajjo did not respond as they both sat there and sipped their tea while the sparrows chirped around their feet in the garden, sharing their secrets.

'What is the hideous red book you carry around? Asha was telling me that instead of the scriptures you follow a Satan's diary.' The old lady chuckled again.

Rajjo spoke about the dead man's trunk. 'My red book belongs to a man I never knew. He disappeared and the diary remained in the cold attic of my husband's house. I carry it now, and it carried me. I read in it once that someone wise had said, '*The reason why I lost my lamp was that the thief was superior to me in vigilance. He paid; however the price of this lamp; that in exchange for he consented to become a thief; in exchange – to become faithless.*'

Whether it was Mata-ji's solicitious expression that made her to bare her soul under the sheesham tree or if she was she under the old woman's spell, she did not know but she continued

*'So to answer your question, I want the lamp. I am the thief…'*

They both sat there as the group of sparrows suddenly took flight. As if the wind had whispered to them about another beautiful garden. Rajjo felt a sense of loss.

Mata-ji coughed and broke the silence, 'You know how this village name changed from Jusampura to Himmatpura? When it became known in Moga district that a visit by Guru Hargobind was imminent, people gathered from far and wide to seek his blessings. Amongst them were villagers from a place named Jusampura who asked the Guru to bless their village. Guru-ji said he could not accept their invitation immediately, but he would visit their village later. Before the Guru departed, one of the villagers stole the saddle of Guru-ji's horse. The following day Guru-ji was told of the theft and the day after Guru-ji returned to Jusampura. The village requested forgiveness for the saddle theft, saying the man who had taken the saddle was crazy. After the thief had returned the saddle, Guru-ji was not pleased when he noticed one of the gold rings was missing. Nevertheless when he left the village, Guru-ji bestowed his blessing on the villagers with good wishes for prosperity. He also changed the name from Jusampura to Himmatpura…'

Rajjo looked at the old woman and smiled. Dusk was upon them and it was time to move inside. The woman had told her the story, and stopped. It was up to Rajjo to draw out the thread of meaning that had woven it. Perhaps Mata-ji meant a little bit of cheating is allowed? Or did she mean that the end justifies the means? Or it was the bloody magic powder talking, and there was nothing to understand in the old woman's tales!

Suddenly Mata-ji's body trembled with cold and Rajjo wanted to hurry her inside and put her in a warm place. She was too precious.

While Rajjo slowly walked her back, Mata-ji whispered in a raspy voice, 'Remember, if you are the thief and are aware of your theft and the price you will pay for it, you will be fine. But the day you feel tainted, throw the bloody lamp! It's not worth it!'

Rajjo could smell the jasmine oil she used on her old papery skin. She wanted to protect Mata-ji's frail body in a warm cashmere blanket, where neither the wind, nor the water neither the heat nor the cold could gnaw at her old flesh and bones. She wanted to keep her safe from time, occluding its unforgiving jaws.

On her way back, Mata-ji requested Rajjo to lie on her cot outside, so she could see the firecrackers light up the sky. As they entered the compound, they saw Raahat, Asha and the others had just finished lighting the candles and lanterns. The ashram glittered like a bride.

That evening Rajjo sat on her cot in the courtyard. Winter was here as they huddled in the quilt against the biting wind. Rajjo could smell the firecrackers in the air, the smog descending on them. She could hear Mata-ji smoking her hookah on the cot adjacent to hers.

She went to look for Raahat. She wandered to a quiet corner and was surprised to find Arjan sitting on the ledge alone, enjoying the firecrackers lighting up the sky like a bouquet of stars erupting now and then. She joined him and simply asked. 'What happened to your Rajjo?'

Arjan waited for a firecracker that went surging into the skies with a whistle, only to burst in circles of brilliant stars and fade away into nothingness.

Inhaling a deep breath filled with smoke from the blazing crackers, Arjan spoke in a detached voice.

'It was a terrible time. '84. Complete media and press blackout was forced on the state. Journalists were physically removed. Many were lined up in army buses and asked to leave and the ones left behind were under house arrest. Rail, road and air service was suspended. Foreigners and NRIs were banned from entering. Water and electricity supply was cut off. My Rajjo's brother was arriving from New Delhi in a train. He was her only family. No one knew where he was, just that his train had arrived at the station. He was untraceable. There was no information from anyone. I left her that day and told her that I would find her brother and get him back. She begged me to take her along, but I was firm in my decision that she was safer here. I left her with her uncle. They lived in the inner city, in Amritsar. That was the last day I saw her. Before I could get back, the army had entered the temple. Markets and shops were shut for three days and then more violence erupted after the curfew ended and the main leader was killed. Baleful stories whittled with a butcher's knife surfaced but the bodies did not. I never found her; neither her family, nor her body. And that is the worst part. Not knowing.'

The blood-soaked tale made her toes curl. She could almost hear the agonized cries in her deaf ear.

'So you came here?'

'Till I find somewhere better to go.'

With a loud whistle, the sky lit up with hundreds of sparkling lights as the fire- crackers began again.

Arjan and Rajjo looked on, while Mata-ji's hookah gurgled behind them.

It was a strange feeling thought Rajjo, to not know if someone lived or not. She finally understood his devotion. Arjan was here in the house of God, serving people in the name of God, pleading to him everyday, pleasing him every day, to somehow get his Rajjo back.

If only she could tell him that there was no one up there beyond the milky skies to please. His Rajjo was never returning to him.

## November 1991

Rajjo's time at Mata-ji's ashram was coming to an end. Mata-ji had been taken ill, and Mehtaab and Rani Maa had preponed their trip to seek her blessings. They were to arrive on Mehtaab's birthday.

Rajjo had devoted all her time to caring for the old woman like her own mother. She watched over Mata-ji as the old woman slept, willing her to wake up again, scared that she might slip away naughtily, without saying goodbye. The mischievous old woman was capable of anything. Rajjo just wanted the old lady to be healthy again. The abysmal thought that she might leave engulfed Rajjo with fear.

One night, waking from her stupor, Mata-ji had asked Rajjo in a childlike voice if she could lie under the stars.

Rajjo set it all up and sat next to her, looking up at the inky sky.

'He smelled of cinnamon and tobacco.' Mata-ji smiled to herself. Her eyes twinkled. 'Please get better and stay!' Rajjo heard herself pleading in a hoarse voice; she felt the shadows looming large around her. She hoped her pleading would buy the old woman some more time.

'He wants to feel like a king, that's his weakness, my Mehtaab. If you make him feel like a king, he will make you the queen.' Saying this the old woman had a bout of bronchitis. She coughed and coughed in the night as Rajjo nursed her through it. But her mind had latched on to what Mata-ji had offered her; firstly she'd won her affection and, secondly, she'd shown her the way. Rajjo had to make this celebration into a spectacle and on a scale that Mehtaab had not seen before.

The next morning, as they sat in the garden, soaking in the sun, Mata-ji looked at Rajjo with a strange expression.

'You are friends with that boy Raahat? That scoundrel. He is dear to me.'

She coughed.

Rajjo nodded her head with a smile.

'He is all right… He reminds me of my brother Sheru back home.' A few birds flutterd in the orchards,and took her back to her village with them. She relished the fleeting memory of her siblings; it faded away like an evanescent rainbow as Mata-ji broke her train of thought.

'You know, when Raahat was barely seven, my husband's sister got him here. His family were neighbours with them, living in Delhi. His father was a sweet-maker. A decade ago, when the state was burning, the flames reached Delhi as well. Two Sikhs, her own security personnel, killed Indira Gandhi. Her son was sworn in the next day, as the streets of Delhi burnt. The way the hearts of the people burnt here when they were butchered in the Golden Temple. People turned against the Sikhs on the streets, they burnt their houses, dragged them out, killed them, burnt their beards. His family was killed in that massacre but he escaped with the neighbours and was brought here. He stayed at this ashram for the first three years, and the nightmares from his memories would wake him up. Then he went away. I don't know how he is doing, but look out for him. He has seen fire, so there would be burns inside. I can see you have a bond, so I am asking you in case I am not here to keep an eye out. I make it a point to call him to this ashram twice a year. But he has grown up. He seems all right, but my eyes are too weak to see that well. Just check on him now and then for me.'

Rajjo had a lump in her throat. She squeezed the old woman's hand and muttered, 'Don't worry, that idiot will be just fine! You focus on getting better soon.'

Mata-ji sighed and shut her eyes, gulping in air, as if she was too tired to speak anymore.

It was the week before Mehtaab and Rani Maa's arrival. Rajjo had officially taken over the organization as Gurbaksha had fallen sick and was in the dispensary. He had left everything to Rajjo, and now was the time to surge ahead. There was some news to celebrate in the ashram. In a nearby village, the government had given another eighteen acres to the ashram.

Rajjo had planned everything to the last detail. Raahat and the other sewadars had gladly done her bidding, as she worked round the clock to make the celebrations a success. But each day, she took out an hour to rub some jasmine oil on Mata-ji's old papery skin, sitting under the orchards with the sparrows watching them.

The preparations were geared to be spectacular; a jeep was to ferry Mehtaab into the village as he greeted the sewadars lining the streets to welcome him and Rani Maa. Banners with his face, would be fluttering in the skies, reminding him how he had become the kingmaker and almighty for so many souls. Drummers would be placed at regular intervals to announce his arrival. A feast would be prepared to fill bellies with all kinds of dishes and desserts. She could already see the serpentine queues crawling around the compound, as villagers would be queuing up for the food. Cardboard cutouts of Mehtaab would loom over the ashram. The main gate would be festooned with flowers. And as he entered the gates there would be a stage with a few performers ready to welcome him with a performance fit for a king.

Rajjo's mutterings were interrupted by an acerbic Raahat, 'It's Mehtaab not the Prime Minister. I hope you know that. And everyone is whispering that you are trying to suck up to Mehtaab and Arjan is letting you…'

'Good,' muttered Rajjo, as she went back to pore over her lists. Raahat fidgeted around, and then erupted again.

'You think I can marry Asha one day?'

'Yes, after you get her a denture, because by the time you grow up she would need one..!'

'Such love, such affection, now I know why people become better in a spiritual commune!'

Rajjo dismissively reminded him to make sure the important men from the panchayat and the local singer who had agreed to make an appearance and belt out popular melodies was ferried here to welcome Mehtaab.

'How did you convince the singer?'

'Her husband was being threatened by the extremists and militants as he had cut his hair short and did not support a turban, they came to look for help and I suggested they would get it if she came to greet Mehtaab and belt out a few numbers…'

'Does Mehtaab know about this trade-off…?'

'Depends. I'll figure what best I can do.'

'You are crazy.'

Raahat spotted Asha crossing the hall and sneaked out.

Rajjo hoped he would come back to his senses soon.

As the big day arrived, all Rajjo's worst fears were put to rest. Everyone praised the birthday celebrations.

Rajjo had mentally rehearsed the celebrations for two weeks, to the extent that she'd filled out the colours of the buntings and decorations in her dreams, and heard the beats of the drummers in every step. And on the day they all played out, Mehtaab and Rani Maa were stumped at the preparations.

Shortly afterwards, Rajjo was called into the room with a beaming Mehtaab, tired Mata-ji and amused Rani Maa. Arjan was there too and it was clear that compliments were being duly conveyed. Rajjo was careful not to make eye contact and be demure. Mata-ji called her closer and lovingly patted her back.

That was a gesture enough for others to understand Mata-ji's fondness for Rajjo. Mehtaab, pleased with the fondness his mother displayed, was convinced Rajjo was quite a find.

'Well done…' Mehtaab's gratifying tone gave Rajjo hope.

'Rajjo wants to play a larger role in the events and organization,' volunteered Arjan.

'Of course. She should be in the core committee,' Mehtaab said.

There was no reaction whatsoever from Rani Maa. For her Rajjo did not exist. Rani Maa had dismissed her and forgotten her as well. Or she was wise enough to know she was outnumbered by Arjan, Mata-ji and Mehtaab.

Rajjo walked out with Mata-ji, and they inched their way towards the fruit garden. The old woman chose to sit under a mango tree. Her cataract glinted in the sun. Rajjo sat next to her. Breathing deeply, the old lady continued to smoke her hookah, and Rajjo was happy to see the sparrows were back in the garden again. She had made it to the core committee and there was a lot she had the doddering old lady to thank for.

She knew requital or words of gratitude were not needed. It was all around them. Rajjo'sgratitude was in the deep sigh of relief, the gurgle of Mata-ji's hookah and the chirping of the happy sparrows. There was no need for words.

## April 1992

It had been five months now since Rajjo had left Himmatpura and Mata-ji behind. She'd said her goodbye in the orchard, while she untangled the old lady's silvery hair. Both of them knew Rajjo was leaving, but none spoke about it. After braiding the old woman's hair, Rajjo moved her hookah closer, fed the sparrows and walked out with one last look at Mata-ji.

Seasons and the people around her kept changing. The Congress Party had swept the Punjab Assembly elections in February 1992 and the President's rule was over. Rajjo was elated that she was a key member of the organization, and she'd strengthened her position by efficiently running the events of the ashram. Gurbaksha was moved to another ashram, and they divided the events between the two of them. Currently, Rajjo was in a village called Odhigarh. It was located on the block road that connected Dasuya with Himachal Pradesh via Kamahi Devi. A major rivulet, a seasonal tributary of river Beas, ran through Odhigarh.

Rajjo was mightily impressed that this ashram had a public hospital for the villagers. Twenty-five rooms with a verandah, a langar hall, a diggie for drinking water and a boundary wall all around were part of this ashram. Trees laden with fruits covered the entire area. It also boasted of a TV room and Rajjo was intrigued to see a local cable TV offering a variety of channels, just like Sethi-ji had predicted.

Rajjo realized this was also the village her elder sister was married in. But she deliberately pushed the thought from her head. Her one and only focus was organizing the blood donation campaign. But the one thing that she really looked forward to was that there were going to be a few young politicians.

She hoped the gargantuan preparations for the biggest event she had organized for the ashram so far would bear fruit.

The devotees Sangh was already informed and they were sending five thousand people including doctors, paramedics, electricians and reconstruction workers to start the set-up for the following day.

The next day people erupted in the village as the set-up began. The villagers started queuing up and the welfare force of the ashram was in action. Between Gurbaksha and Rajjo, they had pulled off a herculean task. Raahat had been an infallible support to Rajjo through it all. Asha also had mellowed a little, after seeing the hard work Rajjo had put in.

The blood donation drive was successfully underway, with a huge ground converted into a makeshift camp. Kiosks were set up where different kinds of services were offered. Hundreds of villagers, families, workers, volunteers and doctors milled around going about their business. One booth was dedicated to examining blood pressure and cholesterol testing. The main centre for blood donation was in the covered tents where a few makeshift beds had been placed. Huge hoardings had been put up showing the visiting politicians, Rani Maa alongwith the local peacocky businessman who had donated help.

The villagers had turned out in huge numbers. The event was well organized and Rajjo knew it was a feather in her cap. The local media and press were invited, and Rajjo made it a point to introduce herself to the photojournalist. She was an extremely raw-boned woman, short and petite. Frail, but with the eyes of a war hawk. Rajjo hovered around her but she did not offer one polite smile in response and stood at a disdainful distance swirling a cigarette. However, her bosses had sent her to cover the event so here she was. Her name was Neeta Sahni.

Amidst the well-organized congregation, Rani Maa and Mehtaab arrived together in a big car, with clouds of dust blowing as it came to a standstill. Rani Maa got out with her hands folded, a smile pasted on, and wearing a celestial expression whilst she blessed everyone. She retired into the inner sanctum of the ashram Mehtaab stayed put to have a quiet conference with a few people who had alighted from a car that had followed him.

He was particularly happy with what he saw. He had to give it to the beautiful girl, as he thought of Rajjo, a sliver of desire sliced through. Mehtaab dismissed the feeling. He knew there was time for that later.

A chug of metal wings and the whirring of a motor announced the arrival of the whirly bird. Rajjo knew before it landed; he was in it. The metal bird swirled and sat on the ground, blocking the buttermilk sky with its shadow as the ground rose up to meet it.

Harsh Vardhan alighted. Their eyes met once more as they were introduced. There was a slight hint of recognition which was lost as he was introduced to other people but it was clear that he was riveted by Rajjo. His gaze would seek her every two seconds.

Harsh Vardhan was reluctant to come to the camp. But his father's orders had been strict enough for him to take his seat in the helicopter. Harsh, the rebellious child being groomed into a successful politician, was not at all happy to be shoved in the middle of a hot village, full of tents and dust and a few hoax godmen and godwomen. But the moment he saw Rajjo his disfavour was forgotten.

The dust devils around were a feathery hue, heat rushed through her body and settled on her cheeks like a purple rouge. Her eyes pierced through his heart and soul. The most beautiful eyes, succulent embers, huge with a perfectly arched brow, stared at him. Her milky skin, tenuous body, lustrous curls, perfect pink bow of a mouth; Harsh Vardhan had never seen beauty like this before.

Rajjo could not take her eyes off his capacious frame. He wore a white kurta over a pair of jeans and suede boots. Rajjo was floored, oblivious to the stunning image she made.

Drawn irresistibly, he came towards her. They stood facing each other, Rajjo with a welcome bouquet and him wearing an arrested expression. Her eyes scorched his heart. Harsh Vardhan was smitten.

Rajjo had been called away by Mehtaab, just when she felt Harsh Vardhan coming over to speak to her. But there was time. She hoped they could at least hear each other's voice.

Rajjo watched the photo shoot taking place. The guest politicans smiled like imported Gods, Rani Maa had her hands raised in blessing and some villagers beamed at the camera. She heard Neeta Sahni's nasal voice muttering, 'Now with the pictures if they would only hand over the lands they have usurped and details of other crimes, that would be swell.'

Rajjo offered her a cold drink and Sahni refused, gesturing to her assistant that she was going to cover the stage. The assistant followed.

Everyone stood beaming against a cutout of Rani Maa and the company's logos.

'It's amusing.' She heard a thick, masculine voice right behind her and her insides melted. She knew without looking, it was Harsh.

Rajjo turned around and he stood there, merely inches away. Rajjo could smell some sharp and tangy fragrance. Her gaze skirted his jaw and the well-shaped mouth. Rajjo's throat felt parched. His eyes dawdled on her full lips a bit longer than necessary. Rajjo knew she looked as if she was having trouble breathing. She had to come up with a response. She could not just stand there and gawk.

A drumfire in the sky surprised everyone.

He looked up. Rajjo admired his profile. His honey brown eyes, his aquiline nose and the plush mass of hair was messed up. If he were to ask her to leave everything and walk away with him right now, she would.

Just then she heard someone clear his throat. It was Raahat and he perhaps stood there long enough to have a knowing smirk on his face.

'Once you are done, could you advise what is to be done if it rains. Arjan is saying to start the wrapping up.'

'It won't rain,' she croaked.

His gruff voice interjected again.

'Why, have you read the weather report?'

Rajjo shook her head and blushed.

Then she noticed Raahat still standing there with a characteristic simper, despite Rajjo asking him to scoot with her eyes.

'So I think since I am here I am going to donate some blood.'

Rajjo turned to stare at his face. His voice was making her brain fuzzy.

'Me too…'

*What! No she was not!*

'Oh, you have not done so till now?' He said it like he was pleased to hear that.

They both fell in step and walked towards the little tents.

'You think I should also donate blood since you are heading that way?'

Raahat muttered to Rajjo on the side.

'Go donate your head somewhere…'

Rajjo muttered back.

She could hear Harsh laughing behind as they walked towards the cluster of green tents and white beds.

Rajjo had no intention of giving a drop of blood, lest a bottle, but well, in this case she could bleed her body dry. Two beds lay vacant side by side and they were both asked to lie down.

There was something heightened about them both going through the same process together, with their eyes meeting every few seconds. Rajjo did not feel the prick of the syringe or the surge of blood dropping bit by bit filling up the bottle.

This was by far the most beautiful moment of her life; the flies, the mud, the heat, the smell of antiseptic, the smell of spirit and the smell of Harsh Vardhan. His voice was seeping into her veins. He made a few jokes, which Rajjo was never going to recall, because her mind was stuffed with cotton.

As Rajjo sat up and munched on the drink and the glucose biscuit, she caught his eye yet again roaming over her body. Before this Rajjo had never bothered about her shape or the allure, but right now she wanted to run to a mirror to take a look. What was he looking at? The momentary hungry look in his eyes gave her pleasure beyond words, like she had swallowed a ball of sun.

The bliss abruptly ended when Mehtaab and his cronies sought out Harsh and took him away! Rajjo, suddenly disappointed and having lost all the pride she had felt about organizing the event, went to calm herself inside the four walls of the Ashram.

Before she could make it to the main hall, she heard Raahat's voice screaming in the corridor, 'People give flowers in love; our beauty here gives blood in love! Superb!'

Throwing an admonishing glance at Raahat, Rajjo moved away only to bump into Harsh Vardhan! She floundered and there he was in an instant, his forearm encircling her. His hands were just inches away from the swell of her breast. His breath fanned her cheek. He was a good two feet taller. Rajjo could actually feel an electric field around her, pulling her face and her mouth towards him. She knew them coalescing into each other was imminent. She could feel him leaning down towards her till the surly Asha thrust a packet of glucose biscuit in her direction. 'These'll help you not to faint.'

Embarrassed, Rajjo straightened herself, realizing many eyes had soaked in the spectacle. She started to move away when he called out to her. 'Actually I was looking for someone to show me around the village, a quick round, you think you can take out twenty minutes or so?' Her pulse quickened.

Rajjo smiled at him and bashfully whispered, 'Meet me at the back entrance of the fruit gardens.' And then she was gone.

They walked under the nebulous sky, glinting pearly and ashen. Rajjo showed him the ruins of wells and buildings in the village. Auburn bricks stewed with time.

'In the pre-independence era, the village was inhabited by Sikhs and Muslims. After Partition, Muslims moved to Pakistan and Sikhs remained in the village.'

They visited a beautiful mosque and a temple while walking. A little stream bobbed along the burgeoning fields. It was magical. Rajjo never realized before this village had so much beauty to offer. Or was it Harsh that made her see everything anew?

They sat amongst the ruins next to the stream. A star-shaped desire like a zephyr lili grew between them. They stood watching side by side. And then, just like that, he reached out to her and she held his gaze. He bent down and kissed her, hesitant at first, Rajjo parted her mouth gently, to allow his cinnamon and cigarette-doused tongue to enter her. Their breath mingled, their bodies merged and on that day, overcast with magical clouds, by the gushing water, their souls soldered as one and ran through the stream to unknown lands, filled with love and joy, making the water sweeter than it ever was.

As she reached the compound of the ashram, Rani Maa and Mehtaab descended in the courtyard looking for Harsh Vardhan. Before she could have a last word with him, she was called away by Arjan urgently.

As she moved away from the compound and away from Harsh Vardhan, it seemed like her awning snatched in the middle of a thunderstorm. Was this the end, or a beginning?

She turned to look back only to find him standing in the compound as a part of the group. An allusive look was exchanged between them as he stood in the courtyard under the twilight sky. He wanted to be with her. The orange of the crepuscular light seeped into her skin. She felt him in her pores.

They all moved into the VIP room but he turned to look back again. Rajjo knew, he was saying it was not a good bye. He was going to find her again. She smiled at him and he smiled back.

Rajjo went about her work in a haze, making sure the event ran smoothly, but her senses were tuned to Harsh Vardhan. She had to go over a few shots with the surly photojournalist. Once she had approved the photo shots with Arjan and exited the administrative wing, she realized to her horror that the helicopter had started – the blades were whirring.

He was leaving without saying good bye. She ran on the terrace to take a last look at him. She wasn't sure if he could see her standing on the terrace of the ashram.

She made a vision with her dupatta fluttering in the wind, a hue of red and pink; her face forlorn. Like the water ran in the rivulet to unknown seas, they were supposed to stream ahead too, collecting whatever the banks offered and moving along. Not pausing, not holding on, not looking back. Perhaps that was the nature of what it was with Harsh or would ever be. A rivulet.

As Rajjo stood there numb with something cold inside her heart, like she would not be able to walk again, she heard Raahat mutter, 'First he gave blood, now he gave his number!'

Rajjo swiveled around. Raahat was smiling with a brochure of a political party in his hand. 'That handsome young politician left it for you…or was it for Kuljeet.' He laughed at his own joke.

There was a number scribbled with a pen. It had a code. 'It's a Delhi code,' muttered Raahat triumphantly.

A smile spread across her face. A broad smile. Rajjo ran to the fruit gardens outside and it began to rain. She soaked it in, feeling him all around her, inside her. Enveloping her. Perhaps the sun had snatched the beautiful moment from the running water and was now pouring it on her. Perhaps there was a way to hold on, even if one was a streaming rivulet.

## May 1992

The heat in May was sweltering. The furiously whirring table fans were ineffective. Sweat trickled every now and then as Rajjo splashed buckets of water in the courtyard to cool the air. Relentless heat gave her a headache but a splash of fresh water from her buckets on the parched courtyard gave her some solace. The fragrance of the dry mud and water lifted her spirits. Within minutes, the hungry gravel soaked in the water and was parched again, asking for more. The stubborn sun glared on. Rajjo's eyes watered as she tried to look at the horizon beyond the black gate, hoping for some answer, staring at the fields. There were a lot of questions she battled with. Having made it to the core committee, Rajjo was still waiting to be on Rani Maa's personal service. How she was going to get there was the problem she pondered about day in and day out.

After the success of the blood donation drive, Mehtaab had insisted that Rajjo be put in the service of every big event and no one had argued. Rani Maa had not reacted to the news at all. Rajjo realized she did not exist in Rani Maa's orbit.

That night, as Rajjo walked across the compound, still thinking about Harsh Vardhan, she wondered if she should she call him tomorrow? Would he still remember? Mooning over Harsh was the only thing that kept her sane as she mulled over how to get into the inner circle of the Godwoman. She had a golden opportunity too good to let go, as both Rani Maa and Mehtaab were staying put in the same ashram like Rajjo for a week. There were moments when she wanted to drown and sit in the bottom of a river, to stop the chatter in her head. As she approached her room, a light and some shadows caught her attention. It was coming from the VIP room where Rani Maa was staying.

Rani Maa usually checked into a nearby hotel and travelled back, but sometimes she stayed in the compound. Unable to resist the urge to peep, Rajjo softly approached the room. Rajjo looked in, only to find an English movie playing. Rani Maa watched the white and blonde characters who spoke with a twang whilst sipping on a glass of whisky. She wore a simple long nightgown, her face scrubbed clean of makeup. The characters on the screen seemed to be in love. Rajjo wanted to see more of them, but was aware that hanging around outside the door and watching a movie over Rani Maa's shoulder was not the best thing to do. Just then she heard Rani Maa say, 'Sukhmani, did you get the pills?'

Rajjo understood that Sukhmani must have gone for an errand, which meant she was returning any time now. She tried to slink away, holding her breath and retreated into an aphotic corner just in time. Rani Maa, sensing a presence, turned sharply and moved with winged agility towards the door. She walked around like a cat spotting a mouse and took her time to make sure she'd not missed a retreating figure.

Suddenly, she looked towards the corner where Rajjo hid. Rajjo was going to choke.

Rani Maa simply shut the door. One thing was clear, Rajjo had to take control of her mind and not slip up. The weight of her ambition could crush her, but all she needed to look at was her pot of desire, growing furiously by the windowsill and breathe.

There was a yearning to go and meet her sisters as Rajjo sat in the middle of the night, gazing at the ebony sky and holding the brochure with Harsh Vardhan's face staring back at her. She wanted to show them the brochure, share the number with them, tell them about Harsh, giggle and ask them about their lives.

With a sigh she decided she was going to go to the local market and call Harsh Vardhan tomorrow.

The next morning, streams of devotees trickled in for darshan. The duration they sat for was in accordance with the money they'd paid. It was a very fair and square business. One of the devotees caught Rajjo's eye as he lay prostrate in front of Rani Maa, crying and kissing her feet.

She caught up with the man wearing brown trousers and expensive leather sandals as he gathered his stuff for his journey back home. Rajjo discovered that he was from Bangalore. His son had been diagnosed with cancer and needed a very risky operation that could cost him his life. Having come to a dead end, he'd sought Rani Maa's blessing. She told them their son who was diagnosed of cancer did not have the disease, they needed to get a good second opinion. And she was right! It turned out his son had a rare condition that was not diagnosed by the specialists that had worsened and displayed similar cancerous traits. Ever since, he had been a tenacious devotee. Such devotion brought tears and something else to Rajjo's eyes. She was perplexed. How did Rani Maa do it? Rajjo remembered her lost in a glass of whisky then and a saviour now. Perhaps the endowments of a Godwoman were hidden in the folds of her robes.

'There are many, many stories of her grace!' Beaming, smiling and bowing his head in reverence, the man wiped the sweat off his face with a pristine white handkerchief and left.

Rajjo turned to inspect Rani who wore a pair of glasses and Rajjo knew they were not for her eyesight but the late night and the whisky. She also knew Rani Maa had waited for Mehtaab to join her at night in her room and the night before that, but Mehtaab had not come back to the ashram for almost three nights.

What did Rajjo believe in? A hungover Rani Maa pining for her lover, or the ardent devotee who would give up his life for her? Perhaps there was no difference and it all merged into one.

However, the hum in Rajjo's brain was back again. It was perhaps time to stop chasing the queen and look directly at the queen maker again. She had gone that route before and been burnt, but she still had enough flesh to offer up in the flames. Mehtaab was the key to moving ahead, he had made Rani Maa who she was. Desperation came and sat on her shoulder like a black crow, plucking out her hair, one at a time. It was imperative to find a solution but it was also imperative to keep her sanity.

Rajjo walked towards the little bathroom and sat on the stool. She took half a bucket of water from the leaking tap and poured it on her head. Her clothes soaked with salmon water that permeated her skin and seeped into her soul. The crow cawed and plucked away at her hair as she sat on the little plastic stool, wet and shivering.

Twilight brought a few devotees and representatives from a nearby village. They had come to invite Rani Maa for a darshan during Diwali. Mehtaab had strictly advised the executives working on her appointment diary to keep the festival slot free. He awaited the highest bidder. Hopefully Mehtaab would visit the ashram, to sort out the Diwali booking slot for Rani Ma. The news infused her with calm and hope.

The lights glittered on the stage as the sangat adorned the halls. Mehtaab had extended personal invites to a few important guests along with their families and assured a special audience with Rani Ma. Rajjo could sense an atmosphere of turmoil in the air. Woodpeckers knocked on her deaf ear incessantly. Soon enough it came to the fore. Her dead ear worked in sync with the good one to hear the quarrel that was happening out in the open courtyard. As a reprisal for Mehtaab's truancy, four nights in a row, the green-eyed Rani Maa refused to come out of her room and go on stage. A lover's tiff. Even God had to endure it, chuckled Rajjo.

Amused, Rajjo ambled into the compound with a glass of water and came face to face with an inebriated Rani Ma. Her eyes bloodshot, her face contorted. She gulped down the water and directed Rajjo to lead her back to her room. Rajjo supported the wobbly woman, but before they could reach the room, Sukhmani and Kuljeet ran to her side and shooed Rajjo away. Immediately, as Rani Maa shifted her attention to Sukhmani, she leaned into her face, almost touching her nose and assiduously studied her soul. And then, 'Where were you last night…?' Her voice was full of conjecture.

Kuljeet exchanged a look with Sukhmani. Rajjo could smell the salty allegation in the air. Sukhmani had turned a delicate shade of pink as she stammered, 'I was not well, I took some medicine from Kuljeet and slept.'

Kuljeet maintained a deadpan face, neither confirming nor denying. Rajjo knew there was something to dig.

'What shape was the pill, round or oval? Big or small?'

Taken aback, Sukhmani hesitated and answered, 'Round, like a button.'

'What colour…'

The coral on Sukhmani's cheek incriminated her beyond doubt.

Rani Maa, abruptly pulled her arm away and decided to totter by herself to her room. The woeful whispering of her silky robes and her drunken perfume reached one and all.

The satsang was already underway, when Rani Maa finally arrived. Kuljeet had made up Rani Maa's face and applied kohl and sindoor. Sukhmani apprised the gathered devotees about the shortened sermon owing to Rani Maa's ill health. Rani Maa's performance was interrupted by loud and menacing thunder.

Rani Maa looked at the skies and roared like a lioness, 'Garjega, barsega nahi?' … ('Just scaring us, are you?'). Like she dared the clouds to disobey her. The villagers were happy enough that guru Maa had said that and the rain gods was not going to defy her.

Rajjo sniggered. They made millions out of this? Rajjo walked amongst the enraptured devotees and sat in the last row watching the 'darshan' (greeting) ceremony post the eventful sermon.

Rajjo was brought back to her duties as Arjan hurriedly thrust a few important-looking guests in her direction. 'Just take them back to the enclosed VIP area.'

Arjan hurried back, his mind miles away.

After escorting the guests back to the room, Rajjo took advantage of the opportunity and hovered around long enough to witness the papers of a land deal exchange hands. Mehtaab had just acquired some more land in the nearby area.

Meanwhile, from the loudspeaker one could hear that on the stage Rani Maa was bordering on hysteria.

Mehtaab clearly disturbed, shot a meaningful look at Kuljeet who despite her limp was out of the door like a bullet.

After a quiet word with Sukhmani, Rani Maa was off the stage.

As Mehtaab walked the guests to their expensive cars, Rajjo trailed behind them. The cars sped away and Mehtaab heaved a sigh of relief. He turned and found Rajjo staring at him. Rajjo stepped closer to Mehtaab so he could almost feel the heat from her body. She could feel Mehtaab's desire reach her all the way and she conveyed her acceptance. It was a communication without any words, as old as the holy books. The look of desire between a man and a woman, holy or unholy, right or wrong.

The moment was broken by an ashen-faced Arjan, as he took Mehtaab away on an urgent matter throwing a cautious look towards Rajjo.

Both Rani Maa and Mehtaab were in the compound today, as VIP rooms were occupied. Time ticked on as she burnt a cigarette stick with a vengeance, like she wanted to suck all the smoke out of the stick in one go. She may never get a chance to spend so much time with Mehtaab in one ashram, as the busy season was just around the corner. The thought went on in her head over and over again.

The panicked chatter made her restless. Disappointed and perplexed that Mehtaab had not sought her out after their deliberate exchange, a fear gripped her deep inside. What if she had played it all wrong?

Rajjo, unable to sleep, felt the demons of doubt dance in the dingy corners of her room.

She shrugged the negative thoughts away and walked to the prayer hall. Some of the familiar faces were lost in prayer and meditation as it was an auspicious night. They had organized for an all night paath and most of the sewadars were either attending this or sleeping.

Rani Maa's room was shut and so was Mehtaab's. There was not a squeak from either of the rooms. Rajjo wondered where the two had wandered off to, and walked to her favourite spot in the fruit garden. She slipped from the side gate to inhale the musky smell of the mango trees and hear the soothing crickets croak through the night. She walked deeper into the orchard, familiar with the layout she'd maneuvered many times on a moonless night. And tonight was a full moon. Nimble and sure-footed, she floated around the dark orchard bathed in silvery moonlight, reacquainting herself with the ominous shrubs and trees that seemed only too eager to befriend her in the daylight. Just then she suddenly stopped. A yelp! Had she stepped on a cat? No, it was a moan! A woman moaning in the throes of passion or an animal with his tail stuck in a barbed wire?

Tentatively she walked towards the noise.

She heard the moaning again. A woman. There was definitely no tail and no barbed wire here as she spotted a couple in the age-old dance of rhythm. The woman was in throes of an orgasm as the man was panting alongside, moving as one, thrusting into the woman. The woman's hair swayed in wild abandon as the man caught her by the neck, ready to wring her delicate throat and fulfil his need at the same time. Despite their faces masked in the deep shadows, Rajjo knew it was Rani Maa and Mehtaab. The man muttered in between his grunts.

'If you pull this stunt again, I will get you thrown off from the seat you know…?' He pulled at her hair sharply. Pumping into her harder. Rani Maa moaned in pain and pleasure. In a raggedy loud voice, bordering on another release, she moaned, 'What else will you do…' Rajjo could see them moving in the moonlight as a cloud whispered through the trees and travelled to a distant sky. The burnished light bathed Rani Maa's silhouette: full rounded breasts, naked body and long tresses. Mehtaab's tall and strong body complemented her, his nakedness almost as complete as Rani Ma's. His mouth devoured her full breast as she moaned and he renewed thrusting into her, legs parted invitingly. Rajjo felt a pang of yearning, which surprised and angered her at the same time.

Mehtaab muttered hoarsely, unable to frame his sentence, 'I will destroy you, if you play games with me!' and he whacked her hard.

Like his assault held her absolution, Rani Maa screamed her release and Mehtaab grunted, his eyes shut. Mehtaab lay limp.

Rani Maa lit a cigarette as she put on her clothes and said, ' I want to go to London for the summer.'

Mehtaab zipped up his pants as he muttered, 'No you are staying here for the two weeks I have fixed up meetings.'

'Will you come to see me?'

'I will try, if you are a good girl.' He fondled her breast one last time and their eyes met. An understanding passed between them, hidden in the silence of the grove.

Rajjo quietly retreated from the scene she had just witnessed. She waited in the swarthy shadows as Mehtaab left. Rajjo figured he would leave and go inside and then Rani Maa would follow ten minutes later to avoid arousing suspicion.

Rajjo could smell the cigarette and the post coital moment in the orchard.

Rajjo's brain ticked at breakneck speed, she had to do something. She could feel this particular moment carried the weight of her future. She shut her eyes, taking in the scent of the woods and the burning filter.

Having arrived at a resolute decision, she sat on the ledge, looking up at the sky, sure of the fact that Rani Maa while passing would find her sitting here.

Rajjo sat calmly and counted the stars in the sky and as she counted the twenty-eighth star on her index finger she heard Rani Maa approach the gate.

The footsteps stopped, she knew Rani Maa had spotted her. Rajjo turned around and looked at her straight in the eye, careful not to show any surprise on her face. Making sure Rani Maa understood that she had been sitting here for a while.

Rani Maa schooled her features, puffed on her cigarette a bit more and approached Rajjo.

'What are you doing here?'

'I was planning what to do this summer, should I continue working in the ashram or should I go back and join the world?'

Rani Maa knew the girl had heard and witnessed everything.

She was a beautiful, viperous Ivy, fierce and dangerous.

Rani Maa decided to ignore her and started to walk away.

'He was with Sukhmani the night you were waiting for him. He was not with you. And Kuljeet knew.' Rajjo's barren tone delivered the cannonball.

To give Rani Maa credit, not one expression gave away her emotion.

This was probably one of the few moments Rajjo wanted to sympathize with her. Without uttering a word, Rani Maa turned and left.

Rajjo could hear a bird sing in the dead of the night. Either she was going to be thrown out of the commune tomorrow at the first light of dawn or it was time for the next round of battle.

In the wee hours of morrow the cockcrow would announce her destiny.

Daybreak woke people up to the usual routine. The sewadars were going about their morning chores and the prayer room was filling up. The community tea and breakfast was being served. A special tray, overseen by Sukhmani and Kuljeet, was being prepared to be sent to Rani Maa's room. Mehtaab had left in the early hours of the morning. Rajjo was going to have to wait a bit more to know which way the river would flow, taking her along or mercilessly drowning her.

As she watched the sun travel through the day to the centre of the empyrean and then all the way to the west, she counted the minutes, seconds and hours. But there was no news. The waiting made her numb. It looked like she was carved of stone as she sat expressionless on her narrow cot.

However, in the evening, Kuljeet came up to Rajjo with an urgency.

Here it was, the moment of truth, charging at her with a limp and a prayer book!

'What have you done now? She was asking about you. You were always too big for your boots. It's time to go back in the kitchen and prepare for the evening meal. Because I don't want you on her service for the evening or be seen in the open, in case she reacts.'

Rajjo wanted to hold on a bit longer before giving in to those feelings of despair.

'Did she say that? To remove me from her service, or get back to the kitchen?'

'She didn't need to. I know her.'

'I know the nature of days and nights, and yet I get surprised and am fooled by an eclipse now and then!' Rajjo goaded Kuljeet.

'If nothing else, you sure have learnt to talk,' Kuljeet shot at her with disdain and turned to move away as Rajjo stopped her.

'How well do you know her?'

Kuljeet by now had given up on rolling her prayer beads, and her eyes were fiery.

'*Better than you will ever… Remember the reaper does not look upon any as unripe, half ripe or fully ripe. Picking up and wielding their sickles, the harvesters arrive. When the landlord gives the order they cut and measure the crop*!'

Kuljeet, collected her things, thought better of arguing with this mad girl.

'You are barely twenty-two, find a nice guy and settle down.'

Kuljeet had sealed her fate.

Just then Sukhmani came and whispered something to Kuljeet.

With a pitiful expression she turned to Rajjo, 'Go in, she is calling you…'

'No need, just tell her to be ready, she is in Rani Maa's personal service.' Sukhmani hissed. The shock on Kuljeet's face took over almost immediately as the bowl in Rajjo's hand clattered to the floor. The sound of the vessel echoed along the entire verandah. It was the most beautiful tune Rajjo had heard in eternity, she was not being sent away.

At least not for now!

'Don't be smug, it's your luck, I will make sure it does not last too long.' Sukhmani smiled at Rajjo vindictively, her beauty making her more vicious than an ordinary face.

'*And …. So… what were we saying? Oh! Yes… picking up and wielding their sickles, the harvesters arrive. When the landlord gives the orders, they cut and measure the crop.*'

Rajjo sauntered off as Sukhmani muttered venomously to Kuljeet.

'She is a lunatic. You can't trust her.'

Kuljeet gave Sukhmani a sharp look.

'...and you have a lot to answer for, Sukhmani. This betrayal will cost you. As it should! I will tell her the truth if she asks me again.'

Kuljeet's reprimand about the night Rani Maa questioned her whereabouts left Sukhmani enraged. Kuljeet limped away as it was time for her evening prayers.

She crossed the hot compound to reach the administrative wing, the heat sitting like a heavy block on her shoulders, making her sag and, more importantly, the strange manner in which Rani Maa behaved where this new girl was concerned caused Kuljeet anxiety. She could see Rajjo splashing buckets of water in the courtyard with a delighted expression. Kuljeet limped on to think in peace.

Rajjo got soaked as she splashed water from the buckets. The smell of water seeping into dried-up grass reminded her of the oncoming monsoons. The crude scent of water on soil refreshed her tired brain. It was time to look up at the wild blue yonder with hope, for the heavens would break anytime soon.

## August 1992

Something had angered the monsoon and it was here to extract revenge with ferocious thunderstorms and unrelenting showers.

Rajjo initially welcomed the relief from the heat but now the overflowing drains, dripping walls and roofs, buckets of water filling under punctured pipes was a bane.

Moreover, it was over two months since Rajjo had joined Rani Maa's personal service. She knew everything she needed to, the way she held her teacup, the right foot that rocked when she was agitated, the right eye that twitched when she saw Mehtaab, the things that tickled her, and the onset of mood swings. It was all stored in little wooden boxes in Rajjo's brain. The prayer books she borrowed from, the hunger to read, the way she favoured Marks & Spencer products from London, the passion to better her sermons, the wanderlust to travel far and wide. It was safe to say Rajjo knew the pattern of breath, her personal imprint.

Rajjo had made it her ambition to know her inside out but there was a line she could not cross. Rani Maa had a space where no one else was allowed and despite Rajjo's attempts, she was still on the fringes.

There were seasons of complete silence, when Rani Maa would not communicate with Rajjo at all and then there were bursts of conversations. These days, Rani Maa accepted Rajjo in her immediate environment like it did not matter to her. She could have been the Ivy that grew from a pot on her windowsill.

One day, Rani Maa had suddenly asked, 'What is your real name, Rajjo?'

Rajjo cleared her throat, paved way for the words she had not used on her tongue for a while to roll out, 'Durga Kahlon.'

'Durga. Durga.' She said it twice or thrice as if she was savouring a flavour, deciding whether she liked it or not. Feeling the syllables, the movement of her tongue, as she said Durga. Finally, having arrived at a conclusion, she declared, 'I like it. You should be called by your real name. It's a perfectly good one.' And then she leaned forward and whispered, as if she was sharing a well-protected secret: 'Names can change destinies. I was Sarita before I became Rani and then Rani Maa!'

A full month of ferocious monsoon passed between the last conversations they had over her name. The ivy had grown out of the pot, all around the windowsill, circled the balcony and was worried where else to go from here. Rajjo started looking around for opportunities once again. There was one question that was still a mystery and plagued her now and then.

'What did Rani Maa feel for her?'

Did she hate her? Abhor her? Or worse of all, was she indifferent?

Rani Maa, it seemed, had entirely forgotten the incident in the orchard with Mehtaab, in her interaction with Rajjo there was no recollection, no subtext, no reference, no averting of gaze as Mehtaab was mentioned in the conversation, so much so that Rajjo began to think she had conjured up the whole thing. She had to remind herself that she was here because that incident had happened. The crickets had been loud, the moon shone like a ball of fire in the charcoal sky and she had seen Mehtaab and Rani Maa naked.

But Rani Maa behaved like Rajjo had not witnessed her deepest darkest moment.

Rajjo travelled with her to various ashrams, kept up with her hectic schedules, learnt and suffered innumerable sermons and knew she could give one in her sleep now. However, in this marathon she missed the friends she'd left behind, Raahat and Arjan.

Raahat had been travelling with Gurbaksha's team to take care of chores that Mehtaab needed done.

When Rajjo was feeling a crust of algae and dust settle on her mind and heart, she realized it was time for movement. And it came along one wet morning, as Rani Maa sat smoking in her private garden.

As was the practice in the ashram, a part of the compound or the orchard was dedicated to Rani Maa where she could invite only the people she wanted to share her privacy with. And that day she called for Rajjo to sit next to her. A newspaper was cast aside like she had read through every single daily for the day. A cold teacup sat untouched on the elaborate tray. A cassette player whirred along in the background. Rajjo noticed some English audiotapes lying around the garden. Rajjo was hoping Rani Maa would call for the hugely successful audio tape of Saajan. She had heard the songs on every tea stall. She liked Sanjay Dutt. That reminded her, she was going to try Harsh Vardhan's number again.

The last two times she had tried his number, someone had said he was busy and then he was not available, only to bang the phone down abruptly. On some occasions, they'd asked for a name, twice she had said a hesitant Rajjo, expecting a sneer from the other end, and got the same dismissive response, till the third time she'd confidently screamed her name as 'Madhuri Dixit!'

Raahat's ice-cream cone had spilled from his hand as he heard Rajjo say that into the telephone, not to mention the amused glances she'd drawn from the patrons and the shopkeeper. Raahat had laughed all the way back to the ashram.

Rajjo was sure he would never know it was her who was calling for him. How would he know it was Rajjo or Madhuri, he did not even know her real name? Angry tears of frustration welled up inside as she dabbed at them resolutely sitting in the bus on her way back to the ashram.

And now, a week had gone by and Rajjo itched to go to the marketplace and try the number again. The strains of a soft English song washed over her as the piece of tin cried and cooed. Overcast skies and the musical notes reverberated in the orchards. Rani Maa's silky voice interjected her thoughts. 'You know what my gift is? I can sniff out a person. An intention, and yours I am afraid, is suspect. I get something muddled from you. Why are you here, Rajjo?'

Rajjo stared at her. Numb at being caught unawares, the song crooning behind, filling up Rajjo's shocked silence.

'You are ambitious, ambition is good, but people around you don't like ambition.' Rani Maa continued as she reached out for her cold cup of tea and sipped. Rajjo could not fathom how anyone could relish a cold cup of tea, but that was Rani Maa! Her brain had not come up with a suitable response as Rani Maa looked at her with a pointed question, her burgundy sari pinned to perfection, hair coiffed up, face painted. Rajjo felt like an old country cousin kneeling on the ground, facing her inquisition.

'What are you thinking?' Her silken voice washed over Rajjo's senses again.

'That I want to see that new movie if you will call for that videotape: *Saajan*.'

Rani Maa did not laugh. She observed Rajjo's imperfect yet beautiful face for a full two minutes, and then looked away. Minutes ticked into hours as they sat side by side, looking at the flies. The singers from worlds Rajjo did not know or heard about, poured their hearts out in a fruit orchard where she sat with a Godwoman and an uncomfortable silence.

A particularly heartwrenching song later, there was a welcome pause as the player worked towards playing the next one.

Despite herself, Rajjo blurted, 'Do you believe in God? I mean, really?'

Surprisingly her face broke into a smile.

'He feeds me, literally'. Rani Maa smiled.

'I don't.' I don't believe in him and that's what keeps me going!'

There, Rajjo had said one of the most intimate things about her to a woman she did not particularly like or trust, a woman she wanted to dethrone and betray.

'You are named after a Goddess…' Rani Maa goaded her. Poking to see how deep the waters ran and if the wounds were still fresh.

'Ironic, isn't it? But I am named after a senile old woman's stubborn wish. If that's God, then so be it!' Rani Maa chuckled as if an errant child was sullen and misbehaving.

And then she chuckled yet again as she looked at the beautiful petulant girl sitting by her side. Rani Maa knew their fates were intertwined.

'Would you call yourself a good person?' Rani Maa had finished the cold tea and the cassette ran itself out.

Rajjo shook her head honestly and muttered, 'No.'

Rani Maa gave her a pointed look and asked again.

'Courageous?'

Rajjo wanted to dive inside the tape recorder and hide from Rani Maa's keen gaze.

Rajjo shook her head.

*'It's a habit. Once we become habituated to despise what is terrible, we become courageous. I could become one, but there is time yet'.*

'Well said.' Rani Maa sighed deeply. 'True, there is time indeed'.

They settled into the silence once again only to be interrupted by Sukhmani hurriedly announcing the arrival of a few patrons, special guests of Mehtaab. Sukhmani waited with an expectant smile. Rani Maa waved her hand like a queen and sent Sukhmani scurrying back to bring the patrons through. Rani Maa was ready for her devotees as Rajjo quietly walked away, leaving the queen to her throne with a burning desire to sit under that tree herself.

Rajjo noted it was a thick old mango tree with a gnarled trunk, roots spread out far and wide, leaves and branches spreading endlessly, obliterating the sky. She wanted to be lost in it briefly. Then, without any prior notice or thunder, somewhere a cloud burst open with an angry grunt, soaking everything within minutes.

Rajjo hurriedly gathered her things, ready to scamper off and escape the thunderous shower, but was surprised to see Rani Maa sitting in her chair, her face tilted up towards the sky. Her arms spread out like a bird's wing all set to take flight.

She sat there endlessly as Rajjo scuttled under the tree and waited for her to move, muttering and complaining about the crazy woman.

Finally, when she'd had her fill of the rain, Rani Maa walked away slowly, towards her room with Rajjo in tow, her clothes drenched, soaked and shivering to the core.,

## September 1993

September brought grief, mourning and music as Rani Maa had been quiet and withdrawn. It was common knowledge that lately Sukhmani was Mehtaab's favoured one, travelling more often with him than Rani Maa who filled her hours listening to records of Kishore Kumar and Mohd Rafi. Bob Dylan gave them company intermittently.

However, Rajjo noticed that Rani Maa, with her glass of whisky, always preferred to listen to her old records on her prized antique record player than the mini audiotapes. In Rani Maa's grief, Rajjo discovered various artists and singers. As Rani Maa crooned songs nursing a whisky, sharing anecdotes about the rich and famous artist and their lives, Rajjo lapped them up and wanted to know more about these magical people who lived beautiful lives in fantasy lands. Perhaps their pin codes were closer to where the Gods resided hence they got a 'friendly neighbour' treatment. Who knew! Rajjo voiced her thoughts and Rani Maa chuckled.

Before the grief-filled afternoons, Rajjo had no opinion or interest in music, but thanks to Rani Maa's turmoil, Rajjo had entered a new world. She wanted to understand rhythms that soothed her nerves. Earlier earmarked as unbearable in her head, now the best part of the day for her was sitting in the afternoon with a plate of fruit, enjoying the warm sun greedily while the velvety voices crooned behind her, sparrows pottered about, and the flowers bloomed. Rajjo was in bliss. She hoped she could help ease the pain and heartache Rani Maa was in, and apologized for the pain she was going to cause her.

Rani Maa had aged in the last one week and Rajjo noticed the tell-tale signs of stress and despair around her eyes and face. She had lost her divine charm and there was a dangerous gleam in her eye. Rajjo suspected it was the calm before the storm as Rani Maa had not reacted at all to Sukhmani and Mehtaab's liaisons becoming public knowledge.

In fact, Rajjo had reacted more to this news than Rani Maa as fear, insecurity and rejection had made her stop thinking and plotting for a couple of days.

'I am going to get her thrown from where she came, that Sukhmani. She will not know what hit her…' The sudden savagery in Rani Maa's voice made Rajjo shiver.

And then what came next was something that Rajjo would never forget. Its colour, shape, texture; a thing called opportunity. For she dressed in silvery robes, hopped with a fickle gait, smiled and then she was gone. The lucky ones who grabbed her in time had the silvery ashes whisking their palms leaving fortune lines in their wake. Rani Maa's voice rang in her ear again.

'Are you listening? Next sermon, you take her place! I dismiss her from my service with immediate effect.'

'Me?' Rajjo repeated with a shocked look on her face. Recovering fast enough she added, 'I am speechless and honoured…'

'Don't be, I would have made a donkey sit there as Chhoti Maa, anyone but Sukhmani. I will show her…'

Rani Maa was angry. The red had taken over her brain and the green of envy added another coat – trapping her in a psychedelic prism of emotion.

Rajjo asked hesitantly, 'Why not Kuljeet? I thought she would be your obvious choice.'

'She has a limp'. It was an uncomfortable question, but her answer was simple enough, Rani Maa was clearly annoyed that Rajjo had asked such a question.

'Get ready for the evening sermon, I will introduce you as Chhoti Maa directly on stage.'

'You won't wait for Mehtaab?' Rajjo was surprised at the speed in which things were progressing.

'Does the sun wait for Mehtaab to arrive before it rises or sets?'

Rajjo rolled her eyes as Rani Maa walked away with a song crooning in the background. She had a victorious expression on her face.

In turn, Rajjo saw the silvery waif-like thing, sitting on a tree branch as the phosphoroescent cinders around it lit up the grove like a shimmery bride.

Rajjo felt surreal all dressed up. Rani Maa made her sit in Sukhmani's place on stage, and addressed her as Chhoti Maa Durga. The sermon had begun and she just sat there, floating through time.

The news made jaws drop, from Raahat, to Asha to Arjan to Gurbaksha as they all stared at Rajjo sitting on stage, her head bowed in reverence. Looking at the stunned expression on their faces, Rajjo had an urge to giggle. It was the same feeling she got when she played house with her sisters back home. They pretended to be running a house, then they pretended to be a teacher and now she was pretending to be a Godwoman's associate. She stifled the laughter and shut her eyes tight to maintain the divine expression on her face she had practised over and over in the bathroom mirror.

Rajjo retreated to her room stealthily, post their conversation, not wanting to meet anyone or share her elation with another soul. Rani Maa instructed Rajjo to make her first address to the gathering as Chhoti Maa the following evening. Rajjo had not left her room the entire day in preparation of that.

Kuljeet, standing with the others, watched the petite girl sit in the robes of a Godwoman's associate, and could not help but wonder how she had reached there. What games, what machinations! How could God be kind to those who denounced him? A mild burning sensation spread across her when she had learnt about the new change.

'She is just a stopgap, for the time being we keep her. As long as she can say a line to them she will be fine.' Rani Maa had dismissively shared the information, but the fact was that Kuljeet was the rightful owner of that seat. And it had been handed over to Rajjo on a platter.

That evening, amongst a gathering of two hundred devotees, Rani Maa crowned Rajjo Chhoti Maa Durga in a sermon where a huge congregation was gathered. Rani Maa gestured for Durga to take the mike.

Kuljeet wanted to yell and throw things at the stage. Clutching at the prayer book tightly, muttering a prayer to soothe her rage, Kuljeet headed to the prayer room. Through the mikes and loudspeakers, she could hear Rajjo's voice stream through, it was new and hesitant yet there was an assuredness about it, that it was telling you things you needed to know. Kuljeet retraced her steps and went back to stand in front of the stage. She had to see it for herself.

Rajjo sat in her seat, her palms sweaty, breathing laboured, however, her voice was rock steady. If she showed them she was scared, the crowd would bully and dismiss her. She needed to project faith, draw from it, to make them believe every word she uttered.

She closed her eyes and remembered her mother sitting by the warm stove. She'd gathered her children as dusk set in, and with all her faith in the almighty, Rajjo started her opening speech remembering her mother reciting verses from the prayer book. Her faith mingled in Rajjo's voice, '*Oh Mind, love the lord as the song bird loves the rain. The pools are overflowing with water and the lands are luxuriously green, but what are they to her, if that single drop of rain does not fall in her mouth? By his grace she receives it otherwise, she gives her head.*'

Rani Maa was impressed. She had not expected this from Rajjo. She caught Kuljeet's eye and understood her predicament. Rajjo was not just good; she could be very good as long as she could be contained. Rani Maa knew she had to be careful, but for now it was imperative that Rajjo take Sukhmani's place and be better than her. It was the most important thing Rani Maa wanted. The rest she could deal with later.

After the sermon as Rani Maa retired and Rajjo went to pay her respects. Rani Maa asked Rajjo with a chuckle, 'Do you believe that? What you said to them?'

'Sometimes.' Rajjo smiled and averted her gaze.

'But they need to know if they have nothing in life, they still have honour. Which should be above all things monetary. Else they would never come to terms with the lack of what they don't have. Honour fills in for material want.' Rani Maa added.

Rajjo looked at the wise woman, taking in the odd vignette of her sitting in the robes of a Godwoman and filing her nails. She had started chanting a mantra. Rani Maa confused Rajjo. She shrugged the confusion away to clear her mind for what was to come the next day. Mehtaab and Sukhmani were arriving at daybreak.

As she walked back to her room, she could sense Raahat wanting to have a word with her. She simply went into her room and shut the door, but it was a matter of time when she would have to stop hiding and talk to those around. But for now it was time to pack her things and move into a new room, a new bed, a new windowsill but the same pot of desire – a blooming coral orchid in a small yellow pot.

The next morning, Sukhmani returned with Mehtaab to find Chhoti Maa Durga in her quarters. Mehtaab had a quiet consultation with Rani Maa and pondered over the proposal to send Sukhmani to another ashram.

Rajjo could sense potent anger. She realized it was not just coming from Sukhmani but from Kuljeet as well. Everyone in the commune felt the tension. One of them was going to be sent away, either Sukhmani or Rajjo.

As the minutes ticked on, Rajjo realized she did not have any strong ally. Rani Maa had used her only to make a point to Sukhmani. It was her anger and vengeance, the colour green and red had given her the saffron robes on stage, but they were weak and with one wash they could be stripped to nothingness. Rajjo was on very weak ground, but Sukhmani had Mehtaab's affection and desire. Arjan was her only mild supporter and Kuljeet would oppose every move that would further empower Rajjo. The worst was she couldn't guess which direction Kuljeet's feelings were headed or how potent they were. Rajjo knew she was all set to lose the battle as Mehtaab mulled over his decision. Sukhmani sulked Rajjo sat by the window in her new abode and Rani Maa beamed. In one stroke she'd snubbed both Mehtaab and Sukhmani.

The day wore on. The compound swirled with tension and anticipation. Rajjo was locked inside not wanting to interact with anyone. It was known to all that Mehtaab had stayed the night to take a final decision on the situation the next morning.

Rajjo did not sleep a wink, wondering if it was time to play another card that could change the whole scenario, bring her on the brink of being thrown out or have a secure position in the ashram. As she saw the pink and orange dawn approach, Arjan Singh walked the corridor towards Mehtaab's room. It was clear Mehtaab sought counsel from his trusted aides. Rajjo knew Arjan would try his best to tell Mehtaab that she was harmless.

Shortly afterwards, Kuljeet limped through the corridor. Rajjo knew she would try to convince Mehtaab that she was a worm of the worst kind who they should get rid of.

It was time to play the card. But was it too late already, waiting for dawn perhaps was going to prove too long a wait.

Mehtaab joined Rajjo and Rani Maa sitting in the fruit garden after the morning prayers and breakfast. Rajjo made a vision in the pink sari she wore. She'd dressed up carefully. If she was going to be thrown out, she might as well be in her Sunday best!

Mehtaab admired her curves and the glossy curls she had left open. Rani Maa caught his look and ordered Rajjo to get her some tea with a curt note.

As if on cue, there was a gust of breeze and her bosom was uncovered. She looked up at Mehtaab daring him to look away. There was a flood of excitement and awareness in Mehtaab. Rani Maa felt the exchange between them. She was not sure if Rajjo had been the solution to her problem or was another problem in the making. Asha arrived with a fresh plate of fruits as Rajjo departed with a deliberate swing to her hips, leaving Mehtaab with Rani Ma.

'She is going and Sukhmani is staying,' muttered Mehtaab. Rani Maa nodded her acceptance. His statement travelled all the way from the fruit garden to the kitchen through Asha, and then travelled from the kitchen to the attic to Raahat where Asha relayed it to him as they lit a cigarette after a quick lovemaking session. From the attic it reached Rajjo. But the sun had raced ahead of the news, travelled the sky and was ready to retire by the time Rajjo heard. Darkness took over.

That night, as Mehtaab packed his suitcase, Rajjo entered. She bent down to place a glass of tea. Her naked back, her breast clad in a tight tempting blouse, displaying enough cleavage for Mehtaab to stop and stare, her slim waist almost made his hands itch. She stood like a temptress in full glory. Mehtaab knew he was only to reach out and have her. She stepped closer and his index finger moved of its own accord. It traced the line of her throat, down to her breast, outlining it, down to her waist and before he could lose his control his hand abruptly stopped.

He was not going to fall for any of it. He knew she offered her to him, he desired her but perhaps this time around he was going to let it pass. His libido was not going to dictate his decision-making.

Having made up his mind. He turned away from her, and continued to pack. The message was loud and clear. He had tasted, was tempted and had dismissed her.

Expecting to hear a weepy apology or a pleading tone, he was surprised to hear her chuckle. He turned to face the fiery woman, who looked him in the eye and with each passing second, he feared his resolve dissolved into a wisp of smoke as his desire for her raged and pounded in his head.

'Rani Maa is planning to meet your rival Deependra Kumar. He is going to form his own commune. All her followers will go there blindly. Keep her happy or this is over…'

She adjusted her sari provocatively, making sure he understood what he passed by. With her head held high, heart hammering, unsure whether this would fall the way she wanted Rajjo walked out.

Mehtaab just stood there, turned to stone.

Rani Maa's impending treachery left him dumbfounded.

Chhoti Maa Durga was here to stay.

## October 1993

With the warm sun in the cold October afternoon soothing her back, Rajjo sat in the courtyard feeding the pigeons. It was therapeutic to see the birds move about pecking at the grain of wheat, without a thought, a care, or a worry. Could she be like them? These pigeons? Her reverie was broken as she heard noises. They were hushed immediately after an outburst. Her deafened ear screamed, it was Rani Maa and Mehtaab sparring. She stared at the poster cutout of a smiling Rani Maa, blessing the world while she could hear her anguish.

It seemed many a moon passed by in a span of just over a month. A lot had happened in Rajjo's life. Sukhmani was sent away, Rajjo was the new Chhoti Maa, Mehtaab lusted after her and Rajjo was prudent enough to tease and stay away. However, she could not scuttle any longer, she would have to give herself to him, for he was going to claim his pound of flesh. Mehtaab was staying at the ashram, and Rani Maa and him were constantly fighting. Rani Maa's mood swings were intensifying. Rajjo suspected menopause was the reason.

That evening a car arrived and took Rani Maa away. Mehtaab stayed on in the ashram, albeit in a bad mood. The time was here, and she prepared herself through the day. In the evening she was called in to serve the meal and have a chat. Raahat waited for Rajjo to come to the ledge, but Rajjo did not leave the room till the early hours of the morning.

She had spent every night with Mehtaab since then, slinking out just before dawn to avoid the eyes on the compound. However, she made sure she had a shower before she slept and she spared a thought for her Harsh Vardhan. She was sure in her belief that she was in love with a figment of her imagination, and that was the only thing holding her together.

Arjan smiled at Rajjo, on one of the nights she walked towards Mehtaab's room with a cup of tea in her hand. It had been a week already. Rajjo knew Mehtaab was besotted with her. She also knew Kuljeet was getting increasingly annoyed and suspected something between her and Mehtaab. She would be the first one to go and speak her mind to Rani Maa if her suspicions were proved correct. Rajjo had to get closer to Mehtaab, share her dream and desire, or she was going to be ousted just like Sukhmani.

Arjan and Rajjo stood facing each other in the cold corridor. Rajjo could hear an owl hoot and flutter away in the darkness. Arjan with a knowing look smiled at her and whispered softly, 'Dangerous games have dangerous outcomes… may God be with you.'

If anyone knew her well, it was this man. He never judged her. But he was a man of God and she could not understand him. However, it mattered to her what he thought of her. She stopped him and turned him around to face her in the eye.

'You think I am a bad person?'

'There is no definition of a bad person… ask yourself how you feel?'

'Pure. Driven. Pure. Like when you have been in so much muck, that you believe you have gone beyond the dirt. That pure.'

'Then you are fine...'

Rajjo felt relieved.

'But Kuljeet holds you guilty and responsible. She is a good soul. She is fighting hard to do the right thing. Reach out to her. You may be surprised.'

Rajjo smiled at him, and went into Mehtaab's room.

She did not return that night and spent the night with Mehtaab. In the middle of the night as they lay in bed naked and Mehtaab lit a cigarette, Rajjo asked him casually.

'So why only one Rani Ma?'

Mehtaab was puzzled with the question as he let out a puff of smoke.

'As in?'

'Isn't there safety in numbers? Why do you have two cars? Multiple houses, multiple bank accounts, multiple friends, but only one Rani Ma?'

Mehtaab laughed out loud.

He knew what she was hinting at but Mehtaab was not ready to say anything yet. He continued to smoke his cigarette as Rajjo watched the white stick disappear as puffs of smoke. It clung to her hair and seeped inside the sheets. She wanted to scrub herself clean but she knew she had to take it. Rajjo gingerly picked up her clothes and wore them as Mehtaab began to snore. She had worn them inside out. Ideally she would have left an hour later when she was sure no one was out and about, but she had an overwhelming urge for to wash the smoke from her hair.

She gingerly opened the door and stepped out in the cold corridor. Her slippers in hand, she shivered as the cold marble floor hit the soles of her naked feet. She bumped into a figure. It was Kuljeet who stared at Rajjo accusingly. Two red spots formed on her cheeks.

Through gritted teeth she muttered, 'I want you out of here by the end of the week... Else Rani Maa will be meting out her own justice that won't be pretty. Get out!'

'You didn't snitch on Mehtaab. You kept quiet about Sukhmani and him.'

'Don't test my patience. I have my ways, I want you out of the ashram by the end of the week!'

Kuljeet limped away and Rajjo followed her barefoot with a pleading tone.

'Please hear me out before you do anything or say anything…'

Kuljeet entered her room and shut the door in Rajjo's face.

Rajjo trembled with cold and fear. Just when she thought things were finally falling in place, down it went like a house of cards. She felt helpless. She could see the fog closing in the dark stinging night.

She went to her room, had a quick bath and changed her clothes. Wrapping herself in warm layers she stepped out to look for Arjan. She found him coming out after his morning prayers from the prayer room.

She repeated what had happened and asked for help.

'I need to reach out to Kuljeet; she cannot go and tell Rani Maa the truth about Mehtaab and me.'

Arjan shook his head and turned away from Rajjo.

Rajjo called out to him once again. 'Please help me.'

'You don't know what you are doing.'

'I am fully aware, I know what I am doing, Arjan!'

'*The men asleep, mad or drunk may have knowledge, and not use it and that is the condition of men under the influence of passion!*'

'Who is not using the knowledge and who is under the influence of passion and who is asleep, mad or drunk?'

'You are. All of the above.'

Arjan turned away, a trail of red anger staining his face.

Panicking, Rajjo finally cornered Raahat. Raahat turned beetroot red as soon as Rajjo asked to know more about Kuljeet. Rajjo knew there was something there to uncover.

'I am not sure if Asha will let me touch the her again if she finds out I shared with you what she shared with me what she shared with her in bed…I mean we were all together at different times. Me and Asha and then Asha and Kuljeet. So indirectly I may have made out with Kuljeet! Gawwd!'

Rajjo's deaf ear erupted with the sound of bugles and drums. Raahat came through for her. She had to be sure of what she heard. .

'Raahat, what the heck are you saying?'

'Ok. It's a sad story though and it should not come back to me...'

Rajjo dragged him outside by the arm into the vast farmlands as dawn broke and morning prayers began in the ashram. Raahat narrated the story of a woman named Kuljeet.

Rajjo gently knocked on Kuljeet's door to seek her compassion and grace. Not waiting for a response she pushed through the door and stood there as Kuljeet looked at her with a rigid expression. Before she could ask her to leave Rajjo launched into a tirade.

'I am sorry. In the name of God that you so trust, do you think you can forgive me? I misunderstood you... And then I went about looking for something to blackmail you with. And then I realized it would be fine if you want me to go, because I think you are a brave woman. You live by your choices and your faith. I respect you. Please forgive me... I'll go if you want me to.'

Whatever Kuljeet was about to tell her died in her throat.

'What did you learn about me...?'

Kuljeet had a wary look on her face. She was vulnerable, waiting to be hurled a blow. Taking a defensive position against the approaching squall, she repeated the question softly.

'What did you learn about me?'

Rajjo in a sincere tone uttered aloud,'Just the truth. That you were brutally banished by your in-laws. They beat you with hockey sticks, broke your leg, called you a witch. You braved all that. They found out about your true love from your impotent husband.'

Kuljeet's legs buckled as she sat on the cot with a loud thump. Rajjo continued with compassion, 'I learnt about the bare-skinned truth in the fields, no one else knows or heard. Don't ask me how it travelled there. What's important is for you to know that you should not be ashamed. It's a personal choice and you don't need anyone's permission, not even God's, to exercise it.'

Kuljeet was silent. She had stopped breathing.

Rajjo continued.

'I want to share something before I go. The day you found me half dead, I had travelled a long path and reached here...'

Rajjo relived the horrors of her life. Kuljeet was on a journey with Rajjo, forgetting her misfortunes for a moment as she was unwillingly drawn to her fears and pains. She wept at the death of her unborn child, she cowered under the whiplash of the minister's leather belt, she curled her toes in rage as Rajjo's body was plundered and violated, she tasted blood as Rajjo relived her horrors. Involuntarily her hand moved towards Rajjo's in a comforting gesture. Kuljeet sat next to her, turned her face towards Rajjo's and kissed her on the lips.

Rajjo did not shrink or cower back. She did not kiss her back either. She just let it pass, like a wave washing over, waiting for it to retreat. It was the most natural thing in the world, as natural as the green of the grass or blue of the sky. She conveyed that to Kuljeet without flinching or shirking away from her. Kuljeet relaxed and sat next to Rajjo with her shoulders slumped. Her face was as calm as a pearly winter morning after a tempestuous night.

As forenoon wove into afternoon and dusk crept in through the little window in Kuljeet's room, Rajjo spoke to Kuljeet about her village, her sisters, her mother, Karam, her Totu, her husband, her resolve, her fight with God and then Harsh Vardhan. She moved her hand and showed Kuljeet the bumps she had to prove that even Harsh's name made her shiver with passion. Rajjo sat disrobed and defenseless in Kuljeet's room. Her fears and her passions spilt on the cemented tiles – dark mulberry emotion oozing onto the grey parquet. Kuljeet could not decide what to do next. However, she was suddenly in no tearing hurry to see Rajjo leave. Rajjo had drawn Kuljeet in her life and now she was tangled in it.

'I will leave if you want me to. Quietly.'

Rajjo the beautiful fickle girl with winged feet reminded her of the unpredictable showers in winter. Some days she was the uninvited thunderstorm on others a gentle breeze passing by. Just when Kuljeet felt she had heard it all, Rajjo turned around and spoke the words aloud. 'I want to be a Godwoman. I want to be like Rani Ma. I want to have a following. My own following.'

Kuljeet sat befuddled again.

'Why? Do you believe in God, despite your obvious disregard?'

'No, I don't believe in him, I despise him. That is why I will sell him and become rich.'

Kuljeet laughed out loud at the mad girl and her plans. But she could see the steely glint in her beautiful amber eyes. A wave of protectiveness washed over Kuljeet towards this frail wounded girl who had a hundred flaws but a soul that was still intact.

'It's not easy,' advised Kuljeet.

'She has done it… Rani Ma.'

'Rome wasn't built in a day, Rajjo.'

'The thought took a second to form.'

'Let's talk in your language, what will you sell?' Kuljeet posed a direct question.

'What?'

'When you go about selling your wares in the market, you tell people why you should buy them. You are going to sell God's name. Why should they buy it from you, when there are other sellers?'

'Some offer salvation, some a way of life.' Rajjo shrugged, thinking as she spoke along.

'What God's service do you offer?' Kuljeet pressed her point.

'Something that is attainable yet godly, practical yet divine.' Rajjo spouted, thinking aloud.

'Find it and then dream. It's not easy, you foolish girl. Go back to sleep. But make arrangements to move soon. Rani Maa has supported me. She would find out sooner or later and if she asks me, I will not lie. '

'You betrayed her with Sukhmani.'

'I was protecting her feelings…and I did not lie. I didn't speak the truth.'

Rajjo smiled at Kuljeet. She could see Kuljeet plagued with the karma sword. Guilt tinged her with a blinding phosphorous colour.

'You think he is sitting up there with a paper and pencil counting how many you got right and how many you got wrong?'

'Yes he is… he is, Rajjo. Get your numbers in order before it is too late.' Rajjo laughed heartily at Kuljeet's faith.

'I need to pray, and I will pray for your forgiveness.' Kuljeet stood up. Rajjo left the room with a smile. Rajjo hoped they could become good friends in time. At the door she stopped suddenly. Her deaf ear erupted with a tune.

'And Kuljeet, your mother has forgiven you, she says to visit her'.

A shocked look sat on Kuljeet's pale face; the question evident. Rajjo whispered softly, spilling her secret from one ear to another.

'Sometimes when I connect deeply with a person, my mute ear starts talking. It's an urge, like an urge to itch or sneeze. It happens very rarely though.'

Kuljeet looked up at the ceiling thanking God for his grace.

'He has his eye on you; don't disappoint him! You are in his grace.'

With a disbelieving smile, Rajjo walked out. Kuljeet's words followed her to the darkened corridors.

*'Which is a swan and which is the crane? It is only by his glance of grace. Whoever is pleasing to him, is transformed from a crow into a swan…'*

Kuljeet stood in the dark room for a long long time, breathing over the words Rajjo had said to her. Her mother had forgiven her. A place long forgotten was coming alive with warm colours. From this moment, she had a lot of grace towards this tempest called Rajjo.

# 6

## End November, 1992

A couple of weeks had now passed since Rajjo's talk with Kuljeet. Time was running out but Rajjo was still waiting for an opportune time to talk to Mehtaab further. After that night, Mehtaab had not spoken about it. Rajjo was getting restless. Fear of failure, the black-headed demon, was eating her heart again.

Driving her thoughts away, Rajjo focused on the telephone as she stood at the dirty roadside PCO booth. The dusty phone receiver stuck to her ear. Then she could hear the phone ringing for eternity while she waited on the other side. This was her thirteenth phone call and she knew if she did not speak to Harsh Vardhan this time, she would not make the effort again.

She wanted it to ring and then quietly die out, like the last vestige of hope in her heart. Then in the last minute, a voice picked up, and her heart sank again. She recognized the hushed, hurried hello. Despite having never met the man Rajjo knew she disliked him. When she heard his voice, she had a vision of a disgruntled man with odd hair and pockmarked face. Like he was upset with the world for waking him up.

'Sir is not in, who is this?'

'Sridevi!'

'I will pass on the message'.

Rajjo hung up, annoyed. Because of this man she had started giving out names of Bollywood heroines to annoy him further. Wondering if he ever passed on her messages to Harsh Vardhan.

And he always said in the haughty voice 'I will pass on the message that Sridevi had called.'

'I will pass on the message that Madhuri Dixit had called.'

'I will pass on the message Juhi Chawla had called.'

'I will pass on the message that Bhagyashree had called, Neelam, Amrita Singh, Kimi Katkar, Meenakshi Sheshadri.' She ran out of names, however, he always hung up as if he could not wait to rush off and do the other important things awaiting him.

The woman waiting her turn to use the phone gave Rajjo an odd look. Rajjo put the receiver down and moved away to join Kuljeet waiting at a distance.

Rajjo had accompanied Kuljeet to buy some wares for the ashram and she had taken a chance with the phone. Kuljeet had been the same with Rajjo, aloof and reserved as if that night had not happened. But Rajjo could now feel an ease and comfort around Kuljeet

Rajjo's face had a deep sadness and Kuljeet sensed that her efforts had been futile.

'Leave it to God, he shall find a way.'

'Then it's doomed,' was Rajjo's quick response.

'Don't talk like this…you have so much to learn.'

'And you have so much to unlearn!'

Kuljeet shrugged her shoulders like it was futile trying to convince Rajjo. They passed the bustling market areas taking in the hawkers sitting on the roadside, some selling woven baskets, cane furniture, fruits, and bright painted clay-pots. Each one was calling out to the passing customer and trying to convince them to buy their fare.

Both Rajjo and Kuljeet watched the mayhem as they strolled along refusing most of the hurried pitches. Suddenly, inspired by the hawker's intensity to sell, Rajjo turned towards Kuljeet and enquired. 'If I tell them my unique selling point as a Godwoman is that I can predict the future…then…?'

Kuljeet looked at Rajjo and pointed at the cane basket.

'You see that old man convincing the lady that a heavy man will sit on it and it will not break? Before believing him she will sit on it and test it, and then she will buy it, and if it breaks she won't come back, if it holds she will…'

'And the point being?'

'Can you predict the future? If not then don't advertise it. Do you believe in God, if not then don't claim to, do you have faith, if not then don't sell it to others!'

Rajjo turned her face away, wanting to block Kuljeet's voice.

'You think I won't be able to do it?'

'You may, but you won't be happy in the long run, but if that is your path that he has charted for you then so be it…'

'Are you happy? Is Rani Maa happy?

'No…'

'Then I'd rather be unhappy and be a Rani Maa than be unhappy and be a Rajjo.'

Kuljeet laughed. Rajjo joined in.

'So how did Rani Maa start off? They come to Rani Maa for what?'

Kuljeet sighed as if trying to jog a distant memory.

'For multiple things. You have to diversify what you offer, but start with one thing. She now gives life lessons, meditation, teaches a way of life, peace and happiness. But she started with one thing; when people came to Rani Maa, they were assured if there was any bad thing destined for them it would pass them by. It started with a minuscule idea, that if you were a victim of some black magic, she would cure you of that. She specialized in curing that for one two years, then it gradually became bigger…'

Rajjo laughed.

'It started like that?' Kuljeet stared at her.

'She is very good, she knows what she is doing and she helps a lot of people. She has faith.'

Rajjo sobered down and started thinking seriously as to what she could offer people in the service of God.

'Can I take away their sins?'

'Even the son of god paid a price for it and you want to try?' Kuljeet laughed and limped ahead.

They walked a little further to the grain market as Kuljeet placed her order with her regular trader. Within minutes, sacks of wheat, pulses, and rice were being loaded in a rickshaw for the ashram. The man was surprised that Kuljeet herself had made the trip. Kuljeet smiled and cited the weather that tempted her to step out.

'Infertility?' Rajjo suggested out of the blue. 'Cure infertility!' The shopkeeper gave them a weird look.

'Can you?'

'So something that cannot be quantified?' muttered Rajjo making a mental note.

'I am not going to be a sinner in your fabricated hoax.' Kuljeet turned away.

'You already sinned, you told me what not to do.' smiled Rajjo.

Kuljeet gave her an odd look.

'No, I am joking, I already knew that.' Kuljeet sighed with relief.

Rajjo muttered a few more suggestions as they completed their round of the market and all the items were bought and loaded in the rickshaw.

They decided to walk back and it began to drizzle. It was strange to be sprayed with rain in November. The sky was warm and sunny, the wind was cold and biting and yet there was a light spray.

They treaded through the green fields, merrily swaying on both sides of the narrow path, and both Rajjo and Kuljeet were intoxicated by the weather. Suddenly the drizzle stopped.

And there it was, emerging from somewhere behind the lush patch of fruit gardens, a half rainbow.

It made Rajjo and Kuljeet stop midway.

'I see God in this rainbow…'

'I see colours,' Rajjo muttered.

Kuljeet turned towards her and added gently. 'Find it within you. The answer. Don't look for it around you.'

Kuljeet started limping forward as Rajjo stood there watching the half-rainbow melting away, retreating into the fruit gardens. As the last of it melted away, Rajjo knew she had her answer, and the first person she wanted to share it with was Kuljeet. She ran all the way back to the ashram, racing against the wind. She knew the right answer sat gently in her bosom. It was a little afraid, like a newborn calf with trembling legs feeling the ground for the first time. She carried it, gingerly, all the way to the ashram.

Rajjo entered the ashram in an excited state. The rickshaw puller and Raahat were unloading the wares at the entrance. As soon as Rajjo spotted Raahat she screamed in excitement, 'Kuljeet is a genius! I love her!'

'Be careful with that,' chaffed Raahat.

Rajjo chided him and went looking for Kuljeet.

She barged into Kuljeet who was overseeing the unloading of *gadda* (mattresses) and sheets in the storeroom for the events to be held in the evening. A musty smell caught Rajjo's nose as soon as she was through the door. Somehow it did not seem to bother Kuljeet. Rajjo had to cover her nose with her dupatta, and through that she mumbled.

'I have found it, the answer, it's Shani! The lord of wealth, power, happiness! Half the problems in the lives of people astrologically are based on Shani being unhappy. I would cure that!'

Rajjo waited for Kuljeet's reaction, almost breathless.

Kuljeet did not react as she chewed over what Rajjo's enthusiastic bulletin.

Rajjo continued with the same fervour, 'My father used to tell me this story all the time, that there is a very powerful Shani temple he always wanted to visit. Shani Shignapur! He said it was a live temple, where the presence of Lord Shani is so strong that he punishes anyone committing theft instantly. No house has doors, only door frames!'

'I know, it's somewhere near Ahmednagar city. I know a shepherd discovered the statue of the lord, offered to construct a temple, the lord said the whole sky was his roof. He also granted the village a boon, that there would be no theft or burglary in the village. Ever since then there have been no doors in any of the house! Kuljeet repeated, her mind still working through Rajjo's proposed idea.

Rajjo laughed.

'Exactly! People are foolish in their faith. Lord Shani is a popular God, they fear his wrath. I can be the one to temper it down, get his boons, control his bad effects. They buy the hogwash of that temple to this day and don't have doors! Post-offices, houses, temples have no locks! Due to the fear of Lord Shani. It's hilarious! And that's what I will use.' Rajjo cackled in delight, for finding the elusive cure to her problems but Kuljeet was not laughing.

'I also hope you know that despite there being no doors, no theft or burglary ever occurred in this place called Shani Shignapur. Some who have tried to steal have died vomiting blood within minutes of their act and before they could cross the boundary. Many others who attempted a theft were punished with long sickness and mental imbalance.'

Rajjo shook her head.

'I don't believe that. It's the same how these people believe Rani Maa can cure them and do miracles. So what do you think?'

Kuljeet sighed and after a brief interlude she cautiously added, 'I am sorry I did not hear your plans, because if I did I would have to tell Rani Ma.'

Dismissing Rajjo, Kuljeet turned around to give another set of instructions to the men who had just walked into the storeroom.

Rajjo wanted to dance with Joy. Kuljeet liked it! She was on the right track. Just when Rajjo was leaving the dark musty room, Kuljeet asked the men to leave with the quilts in a sharp voice.

'Your time is running out soon. Rani Maa will know, it's a matter of time. Give yourself a month or so before she finds it and parcels you off to nowhere land. Don't underestimate her, Rajjo. She still wields a heavy wand here. '

A surprising lump climbed up Rajjo's throat at Kuljeet's concern. 'Someone wise has said no great thing is created suddenly, anymore than a bunch of grapes or a fig. If you tell me you desire a fig, I'll tell you that there is a time for everything, let it first blossom, then bear fruit, then ripen. Says Epictetus, in the red diary of the man that wasn't!' Rajjo declared in a prudent tone.

Kuljeet bunched up her nose in irritation.

'You and your man and that Epictetus have a month to ripen your fig or there won't be any fruit left for you! Or any teeth to eat it with!'

Kuljeet limped away, worried for Rajjo.

Rajjo was now set against time. But she was ready for the battle. She could feel the trumpets of victory stirring in her stony ear. Or then, they could be the cries of the ghouls in a wasted graveyard.

## December 1992

Rajjo and Raahat had taken leave from the ashram on the pretext of visiting their families. Arjan had allowed them a week off. That's all they had between them, along with some money, some cigarettes and a red diary.

They were in the city of Ludhiana. Rajjo knew her husband's town was nearby, and she could seek him out when the time came.

December carried an extra chill as they ambled throughthe streets of Chaura Bazaar. Rajjo wanted to hand-deliver the posters announcing a sermon of the new Godwoman on the block to some key people identified by Kuljeet, and to other vendors who knew pockets of people they could reach. If a crowd was to come to Dhaulapur, then Ludhiana had to be explored as well.

Chaura Bazaar was one of the oldest markets in the city, the daily business transactions in these crowded streets ran into crores. With both sides of the street heavily encroached there was hardly any space to walk. Raahat wailed constantly about the cold and the crowd.

People thronged the market on both sides as wares were displayed in heaps. From bags to clothes to accessories, the market seemed flooded.

'Who is worried about Shani here?' Wondered Raahat, looking at people walk around in a hurry, haggling and going about their business.

'Traders! I know, they believe Shani stalls business. That is my audience.' Rajjo waved her hand around.

Raahat rolled his eyes.

'I want to leave some fliers with the shopkeepers in Pindi street – it's one of the largest drug markets.'

'I want to go there first!' His eyes shone wide with excitement.

'Well I doubt anyone in the drug market gives two hoots about Shani or Vishnu!'

'Drug as in the medicine market, Raahat' Rajjo emphasized. 'Then a few stops in Purana Bazaar and Ghaas Mandi!'

'What?'

'The hosiery market in Purana Bazaar and the cycle market in Gill Road.'

'Can we go to the cycle place first, pick up the cycle and then cycle to wherever we have to go?'

Ignoring his surliness, Rajjo marched on.

The blue was leaden and grey even though it was only half past two. The chill in the air increased and the low hanging smog almost touched the rooftops of the crammed shops huddled together, adding to the gloom in the crowded lane.

After finishing their rounds, having had a quick lunch of oily puris at a roadside stall, Rajjo was ready with her list of the Shani temples that were to be visited.

Raahat muttered for the n'th time.

'Hanging out around the Shani temples is not going to work.'

'If I am offering them to solve the Shani Dasha, and they come here, they will come to the Dhalipur ashram when we announce it. In my opinion people go to any extent to appease Shani and get good fortune.'

'First fix my Shani then! How do I get rid of my pimples and get more girls and become rich?' asked Raahat.

'Shani is not your problem! You head is in between your legs and that is your problem. Get your head sorted first and all your problems will disappear!'

Raahat ignored her barbs making mickey faces. He loved riling Rajjo.

The duo alighted from their rickshaw as they halted in front of a big temple in one of the marketplaces.

'You carry on… I'll wait by the roadside,' a sulky Raahat pulled his cap lower to cover his ears against the biting cold.

Rajjo glared at him as he fell behind. She went inside the temple to look for the head priest. The moment she saw his potbelly and tobacco-stained lips, Rajjo knew his faith did not lie in the colourful adorned deities displayed around the marble temple. It was in the coloured paper she carried with the face of a Mahatma. The question was how much.

Cautiously she approached him and made her offer. The old priest took his time assessing the situation.

'So who fixes the Shani again?' he asked in his high-pitched voice.

'I do…' Rajjo looked at him squarely.

He laughed. One could see some more ugly teeth on display. His dirty saffron robes were stinking as well.

'So you want me to tell all my priests to tell our patrons to go to you and get their Shani Dasha fixed? If they go to you, why the hell will they come here? What do we eat?' He pointed at his ample belly that clearly needed no nourishment.

'I am here only once a year, and I will send them back to your temple…'

'But I don't want more people! I am happy with what I have.'

'What if there is an option of earning a lot more…'

Rajjo deliberately left the rest hanging in the air.

'You know this will be associated with the ashram. There will be a lot more.'

'Well if Shani is merciful, that shall also come.' the priest left it in the air, his mind furiously ticking.

'Then Shani Devta is merciful now, you should not reject his offer of plenty.'

The priest stared at the young woman.

He mumbled something as she nodded.

Raahat stepped forward and handed him a bundle of flyers they had got printed from a devotee's shop for free.

The priest read it and laughed.

'Good try…but many people won't bite. People are not that foolish, madam.'

Rajjo thanked him once again, ignoring his cynicism and exited the temple. Just as they were about to leave, Raahat ran into the temple, took off his shoes, went to the Shani deity and paid his respect. Rajjo was waiting for him with an annoyed expression.

As soon as Raahat joined her Rajjo asked him with an amused look on her face, 'What was that?'

'What if he takes offence and my Shani goes for a toss? Where will I go! Bloody! We have to be careful!'

'As long as there are people like you, I am going to be prosperous!'

Rajjo rolled her eyes as they moved on to the next temple.

They entered another busy temple thronged by devotees with plates of sweets and offerings in their hands to give to the deity inside, while they ignored the hungry destitute beggars waiting outside for some grace and food. On their way out Rajjo pointed at the poverty-stricken figures begging for alms. 'Not many of them get much, because the Gods sitting inside draped in silken robes eat up all the offerings. I think instead of waiting outside they should ask the gods sitting inside if I can take your robes, your laddoos and your jewellery?' Rajjo muttered as she handed a coin to a man huddled in a dirty old blanket. The dark old man with peppered curls and unkempt hair guffawed. He kept the penny Rajjo offered and laughed with his head thrown back. He mocked her pitifully. Rajjo, confused and awkward, scuttled away, unable to bear the laughter of a beggar man on the dusty side road.

Rajjo and Raahat covered over twenty temples, big or small, with a fairly good success rate. They came to the last one. Raahat was delighted that the two days were coming to an end.

After a wait of a good two hours, the head priest of this very revered Shani mandir had agreed to meet them. Rajjo and Raahat sat on the littered marble floor. A barricade of steel demarcated the patrons and devotees standing in a line to visit the deities like they were queuing up to catch a bus. A priest wearing saffron robes sat next to the deity like a watchman, accepting the offerings and tapping the patrons after stamping their forehead with a mark. It was a never-ending procedure he repeated as the serpentine queue grew. The ringing of the bell hanging in front of the deity never stopped. One after the other people rang it loudly to seek divine blessings. The money was put in a box kept in front of the deity. The whole process repeated in Rajjo's head like a well-rehearsed logarithm.

Just then the much-awaited head priest arrived and took a seat. Rajjo was taken aback to see the small thin wiry man as the head priest. He was bald and had no hair on his face or torso. He wore a saffron lungi and seemed that he was here to suffer Rajjo's request like he knew he was not going to like it.

Rajjo cleared her throat and gave her a rehearsed proposal, certain that he would bite, but the thin wiry Pandit just stared at her.

'I won't because I don't believe you can…'

'Can what…'

'Help people improve their Shani Dasha!'

'You believe that our lives suffer because the planet Shani is not working well in our astrological charts?'

'I believe life becomes better with faith…'

Rajjo stared at him, taken aback and then she tried again.

'It's all in us. There is no divinity we need'.

The man stared at the fiery young woman and muttered.

'A wise man has said, if we are not stupid or insincere when we say that the good or ill of man lies within his own will, and that all besides is nothing to us, why are we still troubled?'

This was the first time he had smiled at Rajjo and Rajjo instantly liked him. His face was creased in wrinkles.

'You can be the main counsel in this… I will come to you again to persuade you.' Rajjo pressed harder.

The learned man laughed at Rajjo.

'My name is Narendra Tyagi and I have been here twenty-five years. I will be here for the next twenty-five years, God-willing, so you can come as many times as you want, my doors will always be open.'

Narendra Tyagi's statement left Raahat and Rajjo staring at him.

'He sounded like Amitabh Bachchan in a dhoti, and what diet does he eat, if he is going to live for the next twenty-five years!' muttered Raahat, chomping at some offerings he had received from the other priest.

'Shut up… I like him.'

'Because he is a nutcase and you like your kind!'

'You are five years younger than me, behave.'

Raahat relented for exactly five minutes and started riling Rajjo again.

'So where are we going next? You said we can have a sumptuous meal after this.'

'We are going to my husband's house and he will give us a meal.'

Raahat was stumped and without any further questions he trailed Rajjo as she hailed a rickshaw and climbed in resolutely.

'So when was the last time you saw him…'

As the rickshaw neared her crowded lane, Raahat asked tentatively.

'When I was half dead, beaten and raped by his politician friend, he saw me to the gate.'

Raahat's face twitched.

'Then why are we going there?'

'To make him pay. He owes me one.'

'How can you strike a deal with a monster?'

'He is nothing to me – hatred towards him is useless. I don't have time for that.' .

As the rickshaw pulled outside, Rajjo saw the familiar gate, only with a fresh coat of paint. The mango tree looked shriveled up, the house seemed the same. However, there was a cheapness about the place now. It was a thoroughfare. Lots of scooters were parked in a haphazard manner outside the house. Bright yellow hoardings stuck on gate and walls of the house announced in blue coluor: 'Hari Om' Cables. Seth-ji had realized his dream; he owned a cable TV business. She could see a garish dish and other equipment protruding from the terrace.

Rajjo looked at Raahat who decided to stay put in the rickshaw.

'I can come unless you…'

'No need…'

As Rajjo resolutely walked through the familiar gate Raahat stood outside with the rickshaw puller and pulled out a cigarette.

It had been twenty minutes now, but there was no sign of Rajjo.

Just when he was mulling over the idea of going inside, Rajjo walked out with a look on her face that was difficult to read. Raahat asked her twice, but she did not respond and sat in the rickshaw. They were headed back to the ashram.

After a deep breath she muttered, 'A high-profile local politician to visit my first congregation. A guaranteed crowd of five hundred people, a medium stature local singer, an advertisement in the local papers that they would be attending Guru Maa Durga for 'Shani Tod' Darshan at Dhalipur Ashram Hari Naam… and full cable TV coverage for the entire sermon, that's what the bastard agreed to give me.'

Raahat screamed with joy. The rickshaw puller stopped on the side road, wondering if someone had burst a blood vessel.

Rajjo had a smile of triumph.

'You blackmailed him with what...'

'He can't afford a scandal. His friend, that monster, is a big minister now, and he is getting a big ticket next year finally. I don't think he will live that long though.'

'What about Kesar? You told me there was a boy earlier on...'

'He is not there, I don't know where he is, the bloody hag would not tell...'

'Now I need two things from you, your drugged-out dealer who deals with foreigners and that smoking chimney Neeta Sahni! The reporter! '

But Raahat's mind was still reeling with all that Rajjo had told him.

'What did you blackmail him with?'

'The clinic that treated me, they filed my report. I told him to call and check. I would be in their records as a patient with enough details and pictures to slap a nasty legal case and destroy his minister friend's reputation. He also knew I am with Mehtaab now...I told him I was his mistress, and that this was a courtesy call, and that the next one would be from Mehtaab himself.'

'He will check with the clinic?'

'Yes, he will, he will check on everything I said. He is an old shark. But I am sure he will not be disappointed, he will get enough information and more to take the threat seriously.'

Rajjo chuckled as she saw the shrivelled old Seth-ji staring back at her. His hawkish eyes alert and calculating. A young girl sat next to him serving tea. Some great old aunt sat on the springy couch with her dentures in a steel bowl of water right next to her. The smell of cold and must, stale and old sat in the house. The first floor had a lot of activity going on, that was where the cable TV set-up was. Rajjo shivered again, glad that she was not there anymore. While she walked out with a deal, she could see the mango tree was infested with worms. The bark was weak and bled in places.

With one last look at the board, Rajjo bid adieu to her past, she was never going to visit this place again.

As the rickshaw whizzed through the narrow crowded lanes, both Raahat and Rajjo were lost in thought. Quietly, both boarded a bus back to the ashram. With a hint of excitement, Raahat enquired,

'What would I be when you become Guru Maa Durga? Baapu-ji Raahat?'

'Shut up, you will go back to college and then we will decide what to do with you.'

'No, I am eloping with Asha then… I don't want to study…'

'We shall see…'

Rajjo stared out of the window with a calm look and a smile. It was a matter of time.

'How are you getting Neeta Sahni?' Raahat asked.

'Get me the papers of the bogus land deal Mehtaab closed last month… I will give her news with the proof and she will cover my event.'

Raahat almost jumped up in his seat with a squeal, drawing some lazy glances from tired fellow passengers. The bus groaned and howled and screeched and wailed all through the journey, throwing its passengers mid-air with every bump.

As Raahat settled in his seat, and the bus hit a bump, and all were thrown out of the seats in symphony, and all settled back yet again, Rajjo leaned in and and repeated what she's said.

'Get me the papers of the bogus land deal Mehtaab closed last month… I will give her news with the proof and she will cover my event.'

'Are you crazy? Mehtaab will bury us alive!'

'Only if he knows… You better do it smartly… In fact you just point out the file to me and I will do the needful. You won't get into trouble' Rajjo placed her hand on his arm in a comforting gesture.

'No…,' Raahat said, shaking his head, already living the horrors that could follow once Mehtaab discovered their act.

'OK, I will figure it by myself.' Rajjo patted his hand yet again.

Raahat stared at Rajjo.

'Slow down…'

Rajjo responded with a smile.

'Fine! I will do it! Women!' Raahat rolled his eyes already wondering how was he going to get to the Xerox machine.

The bus turned a sharp corner and finally stopped with a jerk right outside a bus stop. A deluge of people awaited the arrival of the bus.

Before the driver could stop, Passengers made a dive for the doors in the hope of getting a seat. They waged a war against each other and those who could nudge, push, surge ahead through arms, bodies and legs were able to sit on the hard seat.

The bus instantly filled up. Amidst the ruckus she heard Raahat scream into her ear yet again.

'Did you call your hero this week…?'

It pinched her, the question he asked. Like a snowflake accidentally caught in her eye.

'I have stopped calling him.' She heard her voice come out in a hoarse whisper.

'Why will the files be in this ashram?' Raahat screamed his next question while a woman tried to squeeze in and sit with them smiling at Raahat to be an obedient boy and adjust. Her huge bag of vegetables bore into his leg and her sweat mingled with some floral powder. He turned to Rajjo again and nudged her about the files.

Rajjo sighed and confessed. 'Arjan has them, I saw them on his table…but I don't know where he has stored them.'

Raahat was impressed with Rajjo's detailing. It was beginning to seep in that Rajjo was going to have a good shot at this, their very own Godwoman. The thought made him smile. A sense of pride and victory lifted him, only to be smothered by the heavy old woman leaning on him as the bus took a sharp turn towards the left.

Rajjo turned to stare out of the bus window. That would make the crowd, the dust and the people go away. Every little window in the bus was a little getaway to a fantasy land that zipped by.

There was silence in her head as the bus made its way through a rickety road in the middle of some fields. She could see green patches stretched out on both sides. And then she heard herself say it aloud.

'We have two months. We have announced First March.'

Rajjo continued to stare out of the window, inhaling the smell of the soil and vegetation. She had an urge to run back to her village and meet her family.

She wanted to sit in the village courtyard and watch the cow with kind eyes and tinkling bells around its neck walk round and round. Fuschia-coloured memories whispered in Rajjo's ears.

## 20 February 1993

Kuljeet was breaking out in a sweat in the middle of the night. She was plagued by her devotion and affection. She needed to tell Rani Maa but she wanted to protect Rajjo. She had read her prayer books many times to find an answer, but it eluded her. Her decision flew like a flippant sparrow all around the tree, while the hunter sat patiently as the sun went down from dawn to dusk. But the sparrow would not sit on a branch long enough for him to catch her. Kuljeet felt the suffocation the guilt, the restlessness of the hunter, but she was also the hunted. She approached her quiet friend Arjan after a prayer session with her predicament.

As they slurped on the hot sweet tea in silence, mulling over the problem, Arjan finally asked her, 'Would you sleep better if you told Rani Ma?'

Kuljeet sipped her tea, as she did not know the answer.

'The day and the sun shall pass away, the moon and the night shall pass away: the hundreds and thousands of stars shall disappear – he alone is permanent. This state of angst will pass away too. The questions, worries and remorse will pass away too. Nothing is going to remain. All you need to answer is will you be able to sleep with the name of Lord in your heart if you tell her or will you be able to sleep and wander in the dreamlands, if you don't?'

Kuljeet thought about it for a while and decided to go and tell Rani Ma. But before she walked away she looked at Arjan, and with fear on her face she whispered, 'She will hate me. Rajjo will hate me.'

Arjan laughed. 'No she won't. She will understand, because she would have done the same, go tell her. Tell Rani Maa and ease your burden.'

Kuljeet gingerly entered the room to find Rani Maa meditating. Kuljeet cleared her throat.

'I have to tell you something.'

Rani Maa did not respond. Like she was having a silent conversation with the dust devils whirling around the room. She stood there for almost five minutes while Rani Maa sat in her meditative pose, her eyes shut in concentration. Kuljeet knew the woman had heard.

'Finally you are ready to talk…' Muttered Rani Ma. She had just come back from a gathering. There was a red dot on her head. She wore a pristine white sari with pink and gold borders. How pretty a vision she made, thought Kuljeet. She could also forgive Rajjo and let her go. Maybe she will find some kindness for the girl.

'Rajjo is going to have her own sermon. She is trying for it, I don't know how successful she is going to be…and she and Mehtaab.'

'I suspected,' Rani Maa cut her in a stern voice.

Kuljeet was relieved. Rani Maa was not going to react.

'But I did not know about the sermon, I did not. Throw her out. First thing tonight.'

'Tonight?'

'I mean she will be out in the morning. It shall be done.' Kuljeet muttered. The burden she carried was no less. It had merely shifted from her left shoulder to the right one. It was like a clever monkey with brown eyes. It was not ready to leave yet.

'Send for Mehtaab and the others. I want to meet them all… and all those who she was friends with, either remove them or send them to remote ashrams, I don't want any of her influence around me.'

Rani Maa stared into Kuljeet's eyes. 'Are you with me?'

Kuljeet knew that was a very loaded question. The answer was instant. The monkey sat on her left shoulder, scratching his armpit, grinning from ear to ear. He had taken a chunk of her flesh and he loved the taste of it.

Feebly, Kuljeet nodded and left the room.

Kuljeet immediately sought Rajjo out to inform her she could stay the night, but had to leave first thing. Rajjo, just back from a long journey, slumped on the bed. It took her a minute to take in the turn of events as she looked at Kuljeet. Some pain lurked in her eyes, but then she smiled at Kuljeet.

'Rani Maa has given the orders and she is meeting Mehtaab. Mehtaab is returning late from a dinner meeting. Rani Maa has taken sleeping pills and retired for the night.' Kuljeet had not said much but the warning was there, loud and clear. She scurried out of Rajjo's room. Rajjo's sweet smile and pained eyes followed her as she limped across the dark cold corridor.

The monkey leaped on her shoulder, left to right, right to left and laughed all the way to her room.

Rajjo, nervous, filled with dread, sat on the gate once again to wait for Mehtaab to return. It was a clear dark night. She could see the twinkling stars. It was all set. She had to get to Mehtaab. Kuljeet had done what she had to.

Rajjo came out of her reverie with a start as sharp headlights shone into her eyes. The car finally came to a stop and Mehtaab was delighted to see Rajjo waiting for him.

They entered the room together as Rajjo told him about her plan. Mehtaab drank scotch and heard her out in detail. His hand held hers and then he dragged it under the table.

His eyes were glazed. He had not heard Rajjo out. Slowly he pushed her face down as well and closed his eyes.

Rajjo thought of the river again. All she had to do was drown and reach the bottom of it. Her soul wet, but her heart still beating.

Rajjo exited his room as he was tying his pyjamas. She wanted to rinse her mouth a million times over. Before she could exit, Mehtaab stopped her. She could smell alcohol and something else on him.

'Get some food and come back, I am not done yet.'

Back in the kitchen Rajjo set up a plate. She had rinsed her mouth many times over. When she entered the room, she could see Mehtaab lying naked on the bed, his hand caressing himself. He called out to Rajjo and asked her to undress.

Rajjo did so as Mehtaab devoured her naked curves, her satiny skin, the swell of her breast, the rounds of her hips. His hand roamed all over as he turned her around and mounted her, as a master would mount a horse. She screamed in pain but Mehtaab was in a race. They stood leaning on the table, with Mehtaab's prayer books, pamphlets, prayer beads strewn around as he rode her like a driven horse.

While she moved under him, she vowed she was never again going to sleep with a man she did not love.

With a grunt Mehtaab disengaged, gulped some water, lit a cigarette and covered himself with a sheet.

Rajjo stood naked, some warm liquid flowing down her thighs. She bled.

'I want to hold my own sermon. You know I can handle the stage.'

The thick warm liquid trickled from her thighs and spilled further down.

'It's a good idea, let's talk more tomorrow.' Mehtaab rubbed his eyes wearily.

'She is going with Kumar, you would not have any option if Rani Maa leaves. Don't put all your eggs in one basket. Build another Rani Maa, and I can pull in the crowd. Give me a chance and I will show you.'

By now the trickling liquid was on the white floor. She had spilt her blood for this, she had paid for this with her flesh. Rajjo put on her clothes, soiled and crumpled, and walked out. The floor smeared with a crimson trail.

Rajjo went to her room and washed herself with water repeatedly. She came out to find Arjan waiting for her at her door. He had a calm expression on his face. His eyes took in Rajjo's plight and it seemed he read her untold ordeal.

'You are leaving tomorrow, I hear...'

Rajjo was unable to speak, she was unable to sit, she was unable to lie down. Arjan's discerning look had taken in the bruises both seen and unseen.

He sat down on her cot and she slid in beside him. She was happy to have him next to her; just breathing and sitting there. It was a tough night, and Rajjo survived it because he was sitting there giving her strength.

Rajjo was still unsure if Mehtaab was going to stand up for her. Would she end up on the roads again or was this going to fall into place?

That night, as she shared her plans with Arjan, she felt suffocated. The room was not large enough to contain her anxiety.

'Why do you want this so badly? Who are you trying to prove a point to?'

'Nobody.'

'You hate the concept of God, you disbelieve in it, yet you will spend your entire life, proving him wrong – that's a form of love and devotion.'

Arjan smiled.

'Will you come and see me?'

Arjan looked at her and then gently touched her face.

'Yes, someday I will, when you need me to.'

Her destiny was going to unfurl in a few hours.

She sat there on the cot, next to Arjan, waiting for dawn to bring in the verdict. She needed the Dhaliwal Ashram as the venue for her plans. If Mehtaab said no, it was all over before it began.

As the first ray of dawn gently brushed the horizon, Arjan whispered to Rajjo, like that was a parting gift to a dear friend. '*The birds in the beautiful trees fly around in all the four directions. The more they fly around, the more they suffer, they burn and cry out in pain. Without the name of the lord, they do not find his Mansion, they do not find his Ambrosial fruit. Seek him. Don't turn away.*'

On those words the beautiful clear dawn gently tiptoed in through Rajjo's window.

Rajjo's bags were packed. Her little red diary was tucked inside the blue suitcase Kuljeet had left for her at dawn outside her door. She made tea for everyone, hoping it was not for the last time.

Kuljeet popped into the kitchen to say she was sending for a rickshaw. Gurbaksha was fetching it and Rani Maa had asked three times already if she had been removed from the premises. 'Gurbaksha said he will take his time to find the rickshaw…' she added with finality. Her voice was hoarse, her eyes puffy and red-rimmed. Kuljeet was troubled.

'Where is Mehtaab?' Rajjo asked in a panic-stricken voice.

'He is still sleeping,' Asha chipped in, glad to see Rajjo being thrown out. She picked up a glass of tea and walked out of the kitchen haughtily.

Rajjo went to the langar house, where the lunch bell was. She rang it loudly, loud enough for the heavens to fall down. Rani Maa and all the ashram people gathered in the compound. She wanted Mehtaab to wake up by hook or by crook. The bell rang all the way to the afterworlds. If the gods were sleeping they would wake from their slumber and so would the serpents buried in the fires below. If this won't work she was going to run into his room and physically shake him.

'Just bidding adieu to all…'

Rajjo looked at everyone one by one.

'And a thank you...'

The faces gathered in the compound, a mix of pity, ridicule and fear. Rajjo made for a frantic image, ringing the bell like it was a cry for her salvation. The sighs, insinuations and hushed tones about her affairs had seeped through the thin walls of the compound and reached everyone within.

Rajjo was thinking on her feet when to her delight she saw a sleepy Mehtaab walking out of his room.

He was clearly annoyed at the commotion. Taking in the scenario, he told Rajjo to meet him in the conference room with Arjan Singh and asked Rani Maa to follow him.

Kuljeet served them tea as Rani Maa hurled abuses at Mehtaab.

Mehtaab heard her out, as if waiting for a wave to ebb.

Kuljeet limped around with food and beverage and was not considered a presence in the room. She wished they at least acknowledged her as an entity by telling her to leave the room. But to them she only existed, like the mirror on the wall or the painting of the forest.

Rani Maa abused Rajjo and accused her of many things. Finally, she lit a cigarette and Mehtaab knew she was ready to talk.

'She cannot have a sermon in the same town as me. Send her to the hills and set her up there. She is your whore so set her up there. Don't pollute my ashram.'

A nerve ticked. Mehtaab was clearly controlling his urge not be goaded into an altercation.

'Let her start off with one small sermon and immediately after she will be sent away,' promised Mehtaab in a placatory voice.

'It's good for the business. For the people, for the sangat! When you are busy with other things, she can be a stop-gap arrangement!'

Rani Maa gave a hesitant nod and turned away. She wanted to be left alone. She was playing it smart. She was an old fox. She had assessed that fighting to get rid of Rajjo was useless. She still was not strong enough to go on without Mehtaab. She was going to replace him. Kuljeet knew she was buying time.

Mehtaab, relieved to have contained a full-blown altercation, stepped out.

Rani Maa moved to the phone and then she paused. She looked at Kuljeet and stubbed the cigarette.

'Can I have the room to myself, please? Get me some tea and put some poison in it. '

The only time when Kuljeet wanted to stay in the room like a dead painting on the wall she was asked to leave.

Kuljeet carried the good news to Rajjo but she also warned her; Rani Maa was going to get rid of Mehtaab soon. He had underestimated her power.

Rajjo shuddered at the thought.

'It all depends on what I do with the first sermon…'

'I am sure you will say what the people want to hear,' Kuljeet encouraged her.

'Screw that… All I need is to get the people in there and then all I need is to get them to come back. But if I have big numbers for the first sermon, Rani Maa will be on a weak wicket. Mehtaab will be able to sell me as a better idea…'

'What are you doing? What are you doing… you are thinking this through?' Kuljeet was gasping for breath. Things moved around her like a blizzard. The monkey was back again, jumping on her shoulder from right to left.

Sleepy Raahat stood in a corner, biting his nails. He had gone completely quiet since the night before. The gravity of the situation ate away his insides.

'I need people I can trust. Will you two come with me?'

Arjan smiled and shook his head.

Rajjo looked at Kuljeet hopefully.

'You will need to find your people. You need them now.'

In the afternoon, Durga was packed off to a small ashram nearby. However, the sermon in Dhaliwal was granted.

Bidding her friends adieu, Rajjo set off, knowing only too well that she needed to bring in a crowd in her first sermon, or else she was not going to make it. Raahat had been allowed to accompany her as Rani Maa wanted him out as well. Raahat was elated. Kuljeet saw them off with a heavy heart and Arjan with a prayer.

'Asha told me to stay back and ask for forgiveness, as you were not going to make it as Rani Maa was having a sermon the same day as you!' Raahat whispered to Rajjo as they travelled in the rickety scooter.

'We kick her ass, we upstage her.'

'You are out of your mind. You are going to take on Rani Maa alone? With me – a seventeen-year-old pimply associate in love with Asha who is thirty-one years and twelve-days old!?'

'Yes!'

They spent the rest of the trip in silence, eating the dust and the road, mud and the wind, hope and despair all the way to a small nondescript ashram that was their destination.

## March 1993

With a light drizzle and gentle breeze, March had announced its arrival. It was four a.m. as Rajjo walked through the fields. She'd not slept a wink the whole night. Finally, giving up on sleep, Rajjo took a bath chanting the verses of Lord Shani. Not that she believed in them, but she wanted the people to believe that she believed in them.

She walked through the fields with her hair falling to her waist, dripping wet. Her body glistened with oil. The drizzle sprayed her body, coming through the clouds, connecting her to the vaults of heaven. Wind whispered in her ears. Today was the day when she was going to cross over from Rajjo to Guru Maa Durga.

As she walked through the luxurious green meadows, bathed in the salmon pre-dawn light, she chanted the verses as loudly as she could for there was no one in the vicinity to hear her, to see her angst or her faults. She had to perform in front of an audience today.

She continued the walk towards the small Shani temple situated on the far side of the fields. She walked barefoot, crossing the lush golden farmland of wheat.

As she reached the little temple, dawn broke. Diaphanous rays pierced the tangerine sky. Flocks of bird flew overhead. The smell of the meadows was overwhelming, reminding Rajjo of her carefree days with her sisters. She wanted to bury herself in the fields right here, but before that she had to go back and don the mantle of Durga today.

She finally reached the fiery black deity of Lord Shani and stared at it for the longest time. It was bigger than the one she had in her village back home. She gawked at a little mud structure in which sat the deity of Lord Shani, till the sky was a bright blue, the birds had settled in, and sweat glistened on her skin. It was time to head back.

She walked back through the plantation towards the ashram. She walked past a towering cardboard image of herself but as her avatar of Guru Maa Durga, clad in a satin black sari. Reams of shiny black fabric encased her body. Black the colour of Shani. She had submerged herself in his shadow.

They had taken a month to arrive at this look. She had perfected it in every way like an actor would, for the role of his life. She had eaten Durga, breathed Durga, insisted everyone call her Durga and now, today, she would become Guru Maa Durga.

She walked past the compound with a glazed look in her eye and shut the door. It was hours before she had to leave this room as Guru Maa Durga. She deliberately skipped looking at her picture in the newspaper. She flipped it around to read the little article under her photograph.

*Guru Maa Durga was born in a village near Gurdaspur. As a child she was drawn to the teachings of Hindu traditions, spent most of her time in the Maa Kali temple and Shani Mandir as her entire family was a devout. At a young age, Guru Maa Durga was introduced to the world of spiritual practice in the famous Ashram Shraddha Swami, with influences of the Godwoman Rani Ma. Under her tutelage she honed her spiritual learning and dedicated her life to the Lord Shani. Her first public sermon itself has attracted politicians and actors and many prominent people as the fame of her grace and blessings spreads far and wide.*

Rajjo read the little article three four times and carefully cut it out. She placed it in her cupboard. She was never going to lose it.

Rajjo stared in the mirror. She was Durga now. She wore a black sari with a thick red border. The colours and fabric draped her like a snakeskin. Rajjo smeared her face with carefully applied foundation. Lined her eyes with thick raven-coloured kohl, her eyes shining with a dangerous lustre. Thin string of Tulsi beads sheathed her neck and hands. Bit by bit as she wore her hair and make-up, bit by bit she fabricated a new shell to step into. Something she was going to live in for the rest of her life.

She opened the little box of red vermilion and put a flaming mark on her forehead that would be her trademark for years. She had learnt the mantra that was going to be her voice for the future, the appeasement of Lord Shani. She perfected every syllable, every note. She had to utter it with the courage of a lioness; otherwise they were going to see through it all.

She piled her wayward stubborn curls in a tight bun that sat like a crown. And then with white talcum she laced her hair to give her age. She had perfected the art of application over and over on Raahat's hair. She had prepared relentlessly. And now it was show time. Remembering the verse again, she muttered it under her breath.

Finally she glanced at her picture in the newspaper. The image staring back at her in the mirror was an exact replica. A wave of nausea threatened to take over. Her hands trembled. She was not going to lose her nerves and her mind to the jeering and howling in her head. Her deaf ear sat silent. It could be the silence of a storm. She was going to close her eyes and hide into a cave till they called out to her.

Seconds, minutes ticked by. She just sat there with her eyes shut. She heard the door open.

What if no one had turned up?

The fear was there to bite her again.

What if they hated her? Booed her off the stage?

She shut her eyes tighter.

She was getting lost in a subaqueous dark cave. She scraped through blinding darkness. It was difficult to breathe in the black that engulfed her. Black the colour of Shani took over her entire being and trapped her in a cave. Just when she was going to pass out breathless, smothered by the Cimmerian shade, something streamed in through tired cracks in a wall; a moonbeam. She was brought abruptly back to her surrounding with a voice calling out her name.

A pale Raahat cleared his throat.

Rajjo knew she had to get out of the cave and face the lights.

Raahat stood there with a strange expression. Rajjo was unsure how to read his expression. Was it despair at an empty hall? Was it elation at a packed congregation? Just then the cobalt-coloured silence percolated through the open door. The same one she heard in her deaf ear moments ago.

No noise meant no crowd. She had to go out and see the emptiness herself.

She moved past Raahat who stood there agape. The howling silence drowning her, she was ready to go under.

Rani Maa was all ready for her sermon when Sukhmani barged in with the morning papers. Sukhmani wanted to throw up as soon as she had read the fine print. She had seen the picture, the pose, the get-up. She prayed with all her heart to the almighty that Durga should be a miserable failure. She had woken up at the crack of dawn, taken a bath and sat with a prayer book. Convinced in her plea to God that a vicious woman like Durga was never going to succeed.

She threw the paper on the table in front of Rani Ma. She spewed venom, a woman so beautiful with flawless skin and angelic eyes could scare a demon with her spite.

'You made her Chhoti Maa Durga, now meet Guru Maa Durga. Your nemesis!'

Sukhmani's defeat was bearable as it was manifold on Rani Ma. Rani Maa simply stared at the picture as her eyes read every word written in black print.

'Your tutelage! I should be the one if at all to be there!'

Sukhmani stormed out. Rani Maa stood unmoving, not breathing, just taking in the papery image of Durga. Like the newspaper had brought Durga and her audacity in front of her and she wanted to stare it down, make it dissappear, and crush it under her feet.

The paper created a ripple in the compound. Even God was forgotten by his devotees for a minute as Kuljeet, Gurbaksha, Arjan, Mehtaab all saw the half-page ad on Guru Maa Durga. She wore a black sari with a thick red border. A circle of red vermilion shone on her forehead. She looked older.

She looked divine. Thought Kuljeet.

She looked captivating. Thought Arjan.

She looked determined. Thought Gurbaksha.

What the fuck, she was really something! Thought Mehtaab, as he immediately left the compound to see what this girl had managed to do and how! In her very first congregation!

His heart was beating fast, like he was about to win a jackpot.

The words were etched in his mind.

The small font that announced, 'Live Telecast on Hari Om cable of Guru Maa Durga's sermon on public demand!'

She was not just reaching to a few hundreds, she was knocking at doors of thousands and inviting herself into their houses. It was a brilliant stroke to get the local cable TV coverage, but how the heck had she managed that?

Mehtaab had taken her for a driven ambitious girl, but he had not expected at such a scale.

He was salivating at the prospect. Rajjo had opened the floodgates of opportunities in his mind already. But he had to see if she could actually pull it off.

He could see another car follow close behind. It was Rani' Ma's. A thought struck him; the stupid woman was going to leave her sermon to check out Durga! To his relief he could only see Kuljeet and Arjan in the car. Perhaps she had sent them to take a look and report back to her. Mehtaab sped off. The sermon was scheduled to start in another half an hour. If he took the shortcut he would easily make it on time. Just then a question rang in his head like an out of tune bell, annoying and eating at him, how did she get that surly journo to write the article? That Neeta! He had to get into the thick of it all.

As they alighted from the car at the venue, Kuljeet could see the elaborate preparations. In the capacity for 2000, almost 5000 people were crammed in. There were foreigners, there was a camera crew, the singer was being mobbed, head priests were in attendance. And there was that reporter Neeta Sahni covering the event and reporting it all!

*'Shani Tod!'* Neeta spoke into the camera. 'The new emerging Godwoman, Guru Maa Durga, has taken the sleepy village near Dhalipur by storm. The devotees are flocking to her as she is said to be

the one and only mantra to fix your errant Shani if it's not in the right position. She will bless you… She will guide you. She will reshape your destiny. Is she one of the many false gurus or is this the real deal? The crowd tells a story, see for yourself…'

The camera panned the teeming crowds, the bedecked tent, the banners and the stage. The crowd was transfixed as Durga entered the stage captivating one and all, commanding attention and submission.

The cameras took in the swelling crowd as Durga addressed them.

'*How rare are those who actually know his grace. The worshipper of Bhagauti practises self-discipline, Yogi speaks of liberation, the ascetic is absorbed in ascetism. The men of silence observe silence. The sanyasis follow celibacy. Pandits recite vedas, householders assert their faith in family life. The naked renunciates, the wearer of patched coats, the magicians, those who bathe in holy places of pilgrimage – all say they have found the lord!*

Rajjo drew energy from the warm stove, her mother's words, her mother's faith and surged ahead.

*But alas! So untrue for he alone is the devotee whom the lord has united with himself! And here in this house, with this way, you become a true devotee! That's the path we embark on!* '

There was applause. The congregation instantly connected to her voice, her eyes, her emotions, her presence. She engulfed the entire assemblage; she carried each and every soul with her. She had the charisma to ride it all by herself and it was as clear as the light of the day!

The raw power emanating from her sermon could not be a make-believe practised pitch. Kuljeet refused to believe that. She hoped she had drawn something from deep inside of her and found her faith in that. In the same breath, Kuljeet prayed for her God to forgive her mistakes.

Kuljeet was drawn into her speech again, like the rest who simply stood listening. Tired souls showered with a bird song after a long season of barren winter.

'*Someone wise has written: True instruction is this – to learn to wish that each thing should come to pass as it does. And how does it come to pass?*

*As the disposer has disposed it; he has disposed there should be summer and there should be winter, and plenty and dearth, and vice and virtue, and all such opposites of the harmony of the whole. Now my question is why can't we have more of the summer, and be thankful of plenty and be merciful of virtues – if he is a dispenser, we please him with our souls and leave the winters behind. If Lord Shani is the boon giver, we make him show mercy...'*

Sukhmani and Gurbaksha joined in to see the spectacle for themselves. As the sermon unfolded, Kuljeet muttered to Arjan.

'She is going far. Hope she has a happy journey.'

Arjan did not look too happy as he saw the woman unite the five thousand souls. She gave them breath to breathe, and sound to hear, made them think and ponder, made them wise and foolish at the same time. He sighed as he tightened his hold on the prayer book he carried. His calm voice with a touch of a quiver added, 'One who acts in anger acts with pain and one who acts in outrage acts with pleasure... Hers will be a path of pleasure, till the outrage burns her out, hope there is something left for us to pick up from the remains.'

Arjan Singh with that prophecy walked away from Rajjo and he knew it would be for a long time.

Mehtaab stood there smiling, watching the huge crowds. Guru Maa Durga was shepherding them through the peaks and valleys of life. The cameras taped her sermon hungrily and Mehtaab knew it in his gut; the star of the God business had arrived.

The question was, where was she going from here?

# DURGA

# 1

WIND as old as time whispered in Rajjo's ear. She was in Benaras on the eve of another winter. Located on the banks of Ganga, this town had pulled Rajjo towards it every year for the last five years. What she loved about the ghats of Benaras was how divinity washed down into the dirty Ganga, year after year, assuring her that she was on the right path. Though the Kashi–Vishvanath stood tall despite invasions, faith was fading fast here.

Sparkling dawn lighting up the ghats like antique jewels gave her solace. Rajjo forgot her turmoil and lack of faith, forgot her amassment of wealth, forgot the fraudulent cases her enemies had slapped on her over the years, forgot the monster of an empire she had created in the name of the Lord, forgot the gargantuan assemblage that gathered at various places to catch a glimpse of her, forgot the haste and the endless schedules she needed to keep, forgot her followers who were nothing but a sea of nameless faces.

When the first ray of the rising sun breathed life into the ghats, she successfully escaped the hum of her chartered flights and the buzz of her plush Rolls Royce and the perpetual consultations of her family members about running her empire. She had lost track of who was doing what. She was just driven by one need, to increase the mass. That was the only incentive cemented in her head and she had almost forgotten why increasing the mass was important to begin with.

One of her favourite moments while visiting the ghats was hiring a boat and a nondescript boatman who would take her for a quiet ride, paddling along the river, crossing the ghats dotted with ash-smeared sadhus and pilgrims who were praying, performing their morning ritual pooja to the rising sun. She was one with the surroundings. The mass that needed to be fed constantly with her sweat and her soul was a far cry from here. Sitting in the boat, swaying with the river, Rajjo was closer to the railway tracks back in the village that was now a distant memory.

Rajjo had been here for two days already. She was staying in one of the exclusive hotels known for hosting dignitaries and for their assurance of privacy and comfort, not to mention that it had the best view of the ghats. With her face partly screened behind a pastel scarf, her presence in the vicinity was known to few. Wearing the traditional Indian robes, Rajjo still made an arresting image with her waist-length curls and smoky skin drawing appreciative and confused glances. Some struggled with the familiarity of the face but most were unable to place this alluring waif-like figure as the formidable and powerful Godwoman Durga. However, Rajjo loved that anonymity the place offered her. It empowered her.

For the last two days she had watched the glittering evening arati at the Dashwamedha Ghat and walked around the streets of Benaras, where the aged whispered secrets into her ear and chanted mantras. The old were driven by their belief that dying on the ghats of Ganga would assure attainment of freedom and salvation, and thronged the rickety hotels. So that's what it was all about – Rajjo whispered back to the wind. The chanting enveloped her as she walked on the narrow streets of Benaras.

Rajjo walked quickly through the cramped streets. She was late for an appointment. Her heart fluttered, her pulse quickened as she approached her destination. Usually she never took meetings while she was here, as she liked getting lost on the ghats. But this meeting was going to be different. He was going to be here – Harsh Vardhan Singh.

Harsh Vardhan was the handsome face of his party poster and was pegged to be a decisive player in the next general election. Rajjo knew a win was assured with a merger; it was as clear and certain as the endless blue sky but she need not tell the party that. Her mind took her back to the time when she had first met Harsh at the ashram and had been completely smitten by the handsome stranger, foolishly waiting for him to come back to her. Rajjo had stopped making those calls to Delhi long back. She had resolutely moved on. But there was a lingering memory that clung on and refused to be scraped out like everything else in her past. It lingered in the deep dark crevices of her soul. Rajjo caught herself thinking of him now and then, yearning to meet him, romanticizing the time they spent together, and this indulgence angered her. Wanting to slay this memory forever, Rajjo had agreed to take this meeting with Harsh Vardhan. She assured herself after this meeting she could stop looking back and yearn for something she perhaps never had. She wanted to get rid of the spice of crushed grass under their bodies and the gentle ripple of the rivulet warbling a love song, flowing next to them, as they tasted each other. Before she could delve deeper into that memory, Rajjo shrugged it off.

It helped her cause that the almighty and powerful Harsh Vardhan, who had swept her off her feet the last time they had met and never looked back, was now meeting her for a favour. He wanted the Durga trust with its mammoth following to be an ally of his party. Him and his party members wanted to share the mass Rajjo had nursed and collected over the years.

She had this strange sense of elation at the feeling that she was the owner of something he wanted so badly.

She stood at the Manikarnika Ghat with her plainclothes security discreetly scattered behind. This was her favourite spot where she could see the entire city of Benaras along with the Ganges.

She sensed him before she could hear the shuffling of the footsteps. She knew two pair of feet had stepped closer. They were the awaited guests and one of them was him. Despite her resolve to stay unaffected, her neck tingled with a strange sensation. She could smell his aftershave. It was carried by the wind along with the smell of the wood and spice. Rajjo calmed her mind. She chose to take in the entire cityscape in silence as the guest greeted her and waited for her response. She recognized the voice! It was Prem Nath. He was Harsh's uncle and the middleman, a wiry thing dressed in expensive suits, shoes lined with extra soles and thick heels to look taller. Clearly, his small frame was a letdown for his big ambition. Prem Nath usually negotiated with Rajjo or the trust for favours on behalf of the party.

Rajjo was quiet as she took in the sight of the ghats from this high point and let Prem Nath continue his customary greetings. They waited for her to turn and acknowledge them, but Rajjo wanted a few more seconds to herself. She noticed that every inch of the ghat was covered with piles of wood.

Did he know about all those calls she made and all those hours she waited for him? It made her laugh.

She heard Prem Nath say in his calm business voice, 'We have come to seal and formalize our association in this pious place and to extend our thanks to the Durga trust for supporting the TRP party in the election next year. We can finalize the details with Karam-ji or Rano-ji, once you officially give your blessing. Harsh-ji personally wanted to meet you to start the alliance.' Rajjo wondered why *he* did not say a word, why he did not step forward.

She turned to face them but the moment she faced him disappointed her. Nothing happened in those seconds that passed by as they stood facing each other. She was waiting to see something – a flicker of emotion, recognition. Nothing. He just stood there, without a hurry in the world, as if nothing was going to shake him up.

'No,' she heard herself croak.

There was an awkward silence.

And it was then their eyes met for a longer time. It was then that Rajjo's heart skipped a beat. Slowly it dawned on her that he was not a phantom. Unfortunately, her memory had not done justice to him. Age had carved grooves and lines on his face that were etched in Rajjo's heart already. His piercing ebony gaze forced Rajjo to hold her own. She dare look down, she dare look away. He smiled at Rajjo, with amusement lurking in his eyes. 'We have met – a long time back.' Rajjo challenged him before he could push her in a corner.

He nodded assuredly. 'Of course we have…'

He was not upset, neither embarrassed. He was not anything. He met her like a stranger. Rajjo wanted to push him down from the ghat, so he could drown in the belly of the Ganga and learn some humility on his way back up!

'Sorry to have wasted your time…' She turned away from him before she could physically push him away.

For the first time in years she wondered what she wore. She hoped the saffron mark on her forehead was not smudged. Little did she know that her lithe form clad in the muslin white sari made her seem like an ethereal being.

'I think we shall stay back and persuade you…' she heard him say in a husky tone.

Rajjo turned to look at him, as he stepped forward, closer to where she stood. She could feel the heat trickle through the soft muslin cloth she wore. He was challenging her. He knew all along what she was doing. He was playing with her. Rajjo turned away from him, staring at the ghats.

'A lot has changed since we last met.' His thick voice hung in the air as Rajjo digested what was said. Their silence was interrupted as the temple bells rang in a chorus, giving Rajjo the respite she wanted.

'They say the fire at the Manikarnika ghat, the pyres have never stopped burning.' Her statement hung between them, challenging him.

'And they say it is not going to stop in the future either.' He stated in a baritone, with an intensity that matched hers. His voice took her in the past as they sat by the river and he touched her lightly for the first time. She shivered once more.

Meeting him was not a good idea. She was a girl smitten by a stranger then, but now she was a Godwoman with millions of people following her, millions of destinies commanded by her empire and a mass that followed the gesture of her hand.

'The continuous burning of pyre is proof enough that creation and destruction is a continuous process.' Rajjo clutched her sari against the ruthless wind and stepped down, turning her back to the visitors. She was ready to leave.

'Thank you for your time,' Prem Nath muttered to Rajjo's departing back.

As she walked away with a purposeful stride, her hip swaying in arrogance and beauty, she heard his voice follow her. 'We are still hopeful, Rajjo-ji.'

She continued to walk towards the ghats with that swagger. Rajjo had a sudden urge to descend hundreds of stairs and sit by the river, her feet dangling in the water. Almost suspended. She felt light-headed. Perhaps it was the heat.

It was a good thing she refused their proposal for she knew one thing from the way she reacted to Harsh. She had to keep away from him.

Prem Nath had left two hours ago but Harsh had decided to stay for another day. This morning, he had come to the serene ghats to clear his head and remind himself that Rajjo was a Godwoman, who could add much to the party's influence. She had a mass following that could strengthen the party's fortunes and they would be successfully perceived as a 'Hindutva' party. He had to make her comply or win her acquiescence. But was that the only reason he'd stayed back? The niggling thought chewed at him.

His security detail indicated that Rajjo was still around the Manikarnika ghats.

Harsh could not believe that the naïve chit of a girl with wide, doe eyes who called him so often, who wore her heart on her sleeve had become this Godwoman. He had no pious thoughts when he'd seen her clad in that muslin sari. Her waist-length hair whispered secrets in the passing wind. He was yet to feel a more luscious mane than hers.

He was married. A soft whisper hushed the imagery. He reminded himself that he was just going to stay here and pursue her for the benefit of the party leadership. If he convinced her to endorse the party, Harsh's grumbling father would be more than happy for a while and stop complaining about Harsh's lack of appetite and ambition in the political arena.

He was almost about to give up his hunt for Rajjo when he saw her sitting by herself on a ghat. Harsh knew her hotel was nearby and his hunch was correct. She had come out to enjoy the morning sun at the steps. Their eyes locked briefly as she sipped on her warm cup of tea. Harsh greeted her with a nod and sat on the steps. As he sat on the cold stone, he cursed himself. Perhaps he should have gone closer and sat next to her, exchanged a greeting at least! As time ticked by, Harsh gazed at Rajjo from a distance. He sat on the cold stone still warming under the morning sun, drowning in a river of desire. A similar vivid and haunting memory violently drew Harsh in.

Harsh, a fourteen year-old boy, was in love with a woman he could not have, his thirty year old aunt. Aishwarya was his mother's cousin and had come to stay with them after her husband had half burnt her face. She sought in their house and Harsh felt a strange pull towards her as he watched her furtively from behind the pillar. He would watch for hours as people sympathized with her, but her hazel eyes only ate up the floor. The wrathful swarthy burn marks claimed half her face but to Harsh they only made the other half of her face even more divine. She rarely looked up and never responded to sympathy. As his distant admiration and empathy increased, there came a point where Harsh wanted the wind to stop caressing her face as it passed through the marble courtyard. People sensed the young boy's melancholic infatuation towards the unfortunate woman and sent him to boarding school to finish his education soon after.

As years went by and Harsh came back for his twentieth birthday, she was still there in the room by the window, overlooking the backyard in one forgotten corner of the house. Thankfully her window faced the giant banyan tree in the backyard. Her ashen eyes were still empty and sad. She looked at him after he greeted her and responded to his 'How have you been? With one word and a dazzling smile she said, 'Ugly'.

That was the moment when the banyan swayed in the pre-monsoon winds and he knew he was in love with this broken exquisite woman. Soon after, one afternoon, with the wind pregnant with the impending monsoon, they made love, tender beautiful love.

He made her feel beautiful. Through the long spell of monsoon they made love only to part in the autumn. Their passion-filled cries had resounded from the concrete walls as they lay naked in the courtyard, and that was the last he saw of her. That was the first and last time Harsh was in love. Ever since he felt like he was an outsider living on the inside, trying to recreate that monsoon he spent making love to the woman he loved. Lying in her arms, easing her pain bit by bit and making her whole again. Everything else ceased to exist. He had gone through the rest of his life, politics and marriage with little interest.

But now at this moment he felt alive once more. Because of this Godwoman, who was a mystery to the world! He had stayed away from her when she was young and impressionable. He had withdrawn into a shell as news of his aunt's fatal illness had reached him. He met his aunt again one last time, just a day before his wedding. He was lost in the quagmire of his entangled relationships but the strange pull towards Rajjo was always there. And then he had to stay away, despite a strong desire to reach out, as she wore the mantle of the formidable Godwoman. Outlandish rumours about her made her more enchanting to Harsh but some instinct of self-preservation had kept him away from her all this while.

However, now that he had met her, the time they had spent apart did not matter. What mattered was that he had to connect with her. He urgently needed to know if her lips tasted like fresh lilies on a graveyard, violent and beautiful.

He came back to the present as she stared at him with an amused look, unabashed. He was not going to look away either. Today she wore another sari with a crimson blouse. She wore a saffron dot on her forehead. She seemed like a tender bride, married to an old groom. A bride who wanted to hide her fresh untouched beauty and look timeworn. He took in her curves, he was happy to just look.

Harsh smiled at her, gazing into her molten eyes, as she stood up and walked towards him purposefully. Harsh was confused, was he supposed to greet her? Before he could sort his confusion out she went past him and started descending the stairs that led to the waters. He just sat there and saw her graceful figure going down. He saw the beautiful feet take one step after the other, as her body went into the water one step at a time. Suddenly she turned to look back at Harsh. The water reached her calves, and then her waist. Harsh, without thinking, followed her. His strong desire wrenched him towards her, like the moon to the waves.

The water was up till her neck. She faced him now, with both of them in neckdeep water, only their eyes talking. Harsh knew she remembered every moment they spent by the river in the village and she blamed him for forgetting. Time stopped, the Ganga swirled around them in a dance of passion, the temple bells rejoiced this moment and then it was gone.

She started walking out of the water and Harsh stopped breathing. He wanted to stare at her. Her sari clung to her like a second skin. She stood there and let the sun play with her skin and body. It caressed her curves, it made Harsh struggle to breathe. His throat was parched.

'Do you usually reject people's requests on whim or do you give them a thought?' Harsh managed to croak. In response, she simply walked away – as Harsh stared at the curve of her back and the roundness of her hip. He wanted to steal her away and wipe every drop of water clinging to her body. He turned away from the bewitching form.

It was time for him to leave the ghats, or he knew he was going to die here.

He saw her standing in a hidden corner. A spot was reserved for her at the evening arti. She wore loose pants in beige colour and a white kurta. Her hair looked freshly washed; she had left it loose. Like a dawn petal, there was not a hint of makeup on her scrubbed face. Harsh gaped at her profile while she was engrossed in the arti that was going to start any minute.

Despite himself, Harsh went and stood next to her. She did not move. She stared on. Standing side by side, Harsh took in the massive crowd that had gathered to catch a glimpse of the arti on this winter evening. Some stood on the ghat steps, many perched on the rooftops and some negotiated with the boatowners. Perhaps he could take Rajjo in a boat and make her see the ghats. The thought made him smile.

The arti was elaborately carried out on seven wooden platforms. Seven young priests clad in silk off-white clothing performed the pooja.

Despite the spectacle unfolding in front of him, Harsh could not get the beguiling image of her draped in wet clothes out of his mind. She was taking over his senses. He needed to leave soon. Getting involved was going to be dangerous. She was not the sweet naïve girl he had kissed long time back. But the longer he stayed, the urge to taste her lips increased.

Harsh dragged his thoughts away from her to look at the young priests perform the pooja in a completely synchronized fashion almost like it had been choreographed to perfection.

He could hear the chanting of hymns and prayers. He reminded himself that she was a dangerous and a powerful woman now who was being wooed by political parties for support. She was shrewd and cunning. She was ruthless. Suddenly she leaned towards him and whispered, 'Politician…'

Her one word jolted his senses. The way she said it, made him feel that she knew. She knew how he hated being one. He was at the cusp of taking over the party reigns and it felt like the noose around his neck tightening. He was never going to be ready. He wanted to be an artist. He wanted to fly.

He replied back in a gruff tone, 'Godwoman.'

The urge to turn her in his arms and ravage her was overwhelming.

He was going to stop this nonsense and leave right away. He promised himself he was going to drink her in for another five minutes and then he was gone.

She came closer to him as the arti reached its crescendo. The ringing of the bells almost made time stop for him once again, or was it her gaze?

'You stayed for the arti? Are you a devout or a voyeur?'

Rajjo challenged him in a hushed tone. Harsh could smell jasmine and cinnamon on her. She compelled him to lean closer.

'None,' he whispered back in her ear.

The priests picked up multi-tiered pots decorated with hundreds of lamps and moved them in a circular motion. A synchronized frenzy of lanterns and chants flooded his senses. The feverish movement around him echoed in the pulsating heat inside. The cosmic dance of union became one with the ringing of bells in the temple. He wanted to hold her in his arms and worship her. He tightened his fists, lest he reached out.

'You are here for salvation then,' mocked Rajjo.

'They say here in Manikarnika ghat, Lord Shiva roams and utters the tarak mantra in the ear of the newly departed soul which releases him from the cycle of birth and death.' Harsh knew if she drowned him now he won't be able to surface again. His instinct prodded him to win the duel she lured him to.

'Oh that's why you stayed back?' she scoffed yet again.

'Maybe...,' he smiled back.

She chuckled. Harsh wanted to hear her laughter over and over.

'What's funny?'

'Nothing and then perhaps everything,' she whispered back and before Harsh could respond – she was already lost in the crowd. One minute he could almost touch her and the next she was gone. In her wake she left a void. Harsh knew, it was too late for him.

The moment she had agreed to meet him for a walk, Rajjo knew she was plunging downhill. There was no control. However, after ages she could feel the thumping rush of blood in her veins, she felt alive, how could that be wrong?

They were negotiating the labyrinth of small narrow lanes and bylanes in silence. They had reached a place called Godowlia. The opening of the lane was merely three to four feet and in some places it narrowed down to allow only a foot. His arm circled around her in a protective gesture. They never exchanged a word through the walk. Buildings crowded the narrow lanes that were devoid of sunlight for years. It felt surreal as his hand stayed on her waist and they walked in the shadowy afternoon. She could feel his skin, the heat of his touch on her waist. With his hand snaking around her, Rajjo smelled a wilted rose. It was beautiful. It was tragic. It was compelling.

Given the festive season, the alleys were cramped with people, yet they were the only two people in the world. The indescribable fervour and euphoria of the streets seeped in. The mingling crowds were a distant haze as all she could remember was the brown slippers and the beige kurta he wore over his scrubbed jeans.

He had stayed back to convince her to support their party, and not a word was said about work. Rajjo liked that. Perhaps he was playing her, perhaps he knew not to talk about it...perhaps he felt the same way she did.

The shopkeepers and policemen, scattered to show lost tourists the way, smiled at them. Rajjo felt the rose-coloured glasses slip on her nose. She almost chuckled aloud as she imagined herself guiding lost souls, hungry souls, pained souls, empty souls. She had seen them all. And here she was, heart filled with a spring, eyes seeking colours, and her soul craving for more. She was scared to guide her own soul. Perhaps it was worse than all of them put together! Rajjo smiled at the irony as she spotted yet another spire of a temple towering over the lanes. Every ten to twenty feet there was a temple, with innumerable shivlingas being worshipped in every corner of this complex matrix of gallies. Surprisingly, Harsh stopped at one such corner and paid his respect, his eyes shut in devotion.

Rajjo stayed put at a respectable distance. He looked at her and took in her rigid stance. After he finished praying, he said nothing but to Rajjo it seemed that Harsh knew her ugly secret. She was petrified yet happy that he knew, without being told. Perhaps that's how they connected. Words were an inconvenience.

He matched her step and whispered, 'Since the Godwoman won't worship God, what would she like to do in this holy place?'

Rajjo smiled and whispered back, 'Try the street food!'

Surrounded by the small shops serving Indian street food from Ragda patti, to sev puri, to various fried items, Harsh blurted. 'I am sorry I was unable to return your calls.' Rajjo felt the spicy gravy travel all the way down to her belly and she decided to turn away and look for another savory to try.

Resuming their walk they approached another temple. 'You can come in, you don't necessarily have to pay your respects.' He was challenging her again. She smothered the anger that rose like a hot molten volcano.

'It's just business for me... nothing personal. I sell his name in the market, I make profit.' Rajjo carefully kept her tone devoid of any emotion.

Harsh smiled. 'I always suspected you were a hoax, but having met you, I think you may just be for real.'

Rajjo wanted to argue some more, but he just moved inside the bright orange-coloured temple. The colour was almost taking over her senses. The orange was like a halo of divinity cloaking the visitors. After entering the gates, patrons were ringing three huge bells announcing their arrival and asking the deities for permission to enter the temple.

Rajjo just stood in a corner, taking in the ambience and refusing to think beyond this orange-coloured experience. Perhaps the colour of passion was orange, as it filled her up with joy.

After walking a few hours upstream towards the outskirts of the city, Rajjo found herself sitting in the boat with Harsh, as the afternoon was receding in the shadows. She wanted to hold it back. She wanted the afternoon to linger forever. She had taken the boat ride along the Ganges before, but sitting across from Harsh and taking in the old sites was surreal. Neither of them spoke, but they were clearly drinking each other in. The past few hours of the day were building up to this moment. Rajjo could almost smell his urge to reach out and touch her. As they travelled on the water with the boatman ferrying them along, a sea of people flashed in her brain. A mass bowed in reverence. Hundreds gathered for salvation, thousands looking at her for answers. She had to be careful. She was that painted deity who was accepted by the masses, fit for worship. She dare not change that image.

A string of warnings rang in her head and the decision was made. After the boat ride she had to say goodbye and walk away from this. She had built an empire and she was going to protect it. They passed the huge old buildings along the riverside and many familiar sights of the busy old city, but Harsh was drinking in her beauty and Rajjo was memorizing him. She knew she had to walk away after the boat ride.

'Let's meet for dinner. I want to spend some more time with you, Rajjo.' She heard him say at last. The boatman continued rowing the boat, the Ganga continued flowing, the chanting of the bells in the distant temples continued to ring, the sea of people stared at Durga with a questioning look.

She turned away to look at the old building and fortresses dotting the city line. A few old people stood in the balcony enjoying a hot cup of tea and taking in the sights of the city.

The question hung between them.

Harsh clearly wanted to go ahead in this. The question was did Rajjo have the courage to take this journey with him?

'I thought of you and us for months. I got to know about the calls you made but it was too late. And then you emerged as a Godwoman. Unreal. Unapproachable. Nothing like the girl I met and shared something with in the past. I wanted to protect that and did not reach out to the Godwoman till I finally gave in to destiny and met you again.'

'You know many old people come and stay in Benaras preparing for their final departure. Many places here are sort of retirement homes, for old people to reserve their seat in heaven – they say it's guaranteed if you die here.' She laughed and looked at Harsh who was staring at her with uncloaked passion and yearning. He was waiting for an answer.

'I want to leave, but I cannot. I am unable to leave this place, Rajjo.' There was admission in his voice. His vulnerability was taking her breath away, it was making her choke. She wanted him to be arrogant and dismissive.

'It's strange that death is part of a daily routine in this place...,' she heard herself say, not ready yet to face her desire.

There was immense sadness in his voice as he looked at her.

The water lulled her senses. She wanted to drown in the belly of the river, she did not want to send him away, but her choice was made.

'Perhaps it's the place. It feels I will have the most beautiful death if I was to die right here next to you.'

Rajjo turned away. She could smell the wilted rose again, it was overtaking her senses and she shut her eyes to run away from it all.

'But if you look beyond death, here is still a place of hope and colour.' She heard him say.

Rajjo turned to him and stared him in the eye as she asked him, 'What are you looking for here?'

'Finding myself...' There was a long silence and then she heard him say, 'I am leaving.'

The boat ride was almost over.

'When do you leave?' she whispered.

'In an hour from now,' he whispered back.

The last lap was covered in silence.

Rajjo stood on the terrace of the hotel and looked at the old city below. She could see the cremation workers and boatmen busy carrying bodies to and fro. The business of death flourished here. There was a silence in her soul. Harsh had left an hour ago. The evening arti was about to start soon but Rajjo did not have the heart to go to the ghats today, so she chose this quiet and secluded place to nurse her wounds. She was angry at Harsh for leaving. She was incomplete. She was restless.

She focused her attention on the bustling activity below.

Harsh just stood at the ghat watching the cremation workers throwing half-burnt bodies in the Ganges once the families left after finishing the rituals. Scavengers dashed to grab possessions and money kept with the body as part of the cremation ritual. The remains of the ashes, decayed flowers, plastic and half-burnt wood pervaded his senses. Nothing made sense in his life anymore. It was pointless as he stood watching the end of a journey; his political career, his marriage, and the ashes in the Ganga. If anything made sense to him it was being with Rajjo right now. He felt tied down. He wanted to be free. He wanted to escape from this life.

Harsh was a disappointment to his father for his lack of ambition in politics. He frowned at the idea of Harsh pursuing a career in art. Harsh wanted to travel, he wanted to live and explore life. He was married but his wife was disappointed with him for not giving her a child.

Finally Harsh had come to terms with his meaningless existence and decided to take a plunge in politics, to make his father happy and make his wife happy, but then he met Rajjo. Nothing was going to be the same again. He was waiting to meet her again. Every experience, every joy, every sorrow, every encounter in his life was preparing him to meet *her*.

She made him come alive and now as he faced death, he knew he was not ready to die just yet. He was going to convince her to at least let him stay one more day. One more glance, one more promise to meet.

Hurrying, he turned towards her hotel. He crossed barbers dotted along the road, under the shade of umbrellas, shaving heads, hands moving in a practiced dance. Unaware of the turmoil he carried inside his heart. He hurried along as her beautiful face beckoned him. What if she said harsh words and threw him out, what if she laughed at him?

He was already near the Ganges, he was ready to drown anytime. He would seek Shiva and beg him to chant the mantra in his ear to free him from the circle of life and death. The list of possibilities to a man drunk on love were endless.

Rajjo's gaze took in the expanse of palaces, temples and terraces, connected by an endless chain of stone steps that spread out in front of her along the waterfront. Ganga, the elixir of life, that brings purity to the living and salvation to the dead almost mocked her. She had come alive after meeting him on the banks of Ganga and she had sent him away, right here.

She stared at the water, taking in all its ugly sights and divine purity. Ashes of the dead, emissions from open drains, remains from religious rites, and promises of salvation.

The ghats were getting ready for the evening arti, the fervour had picked up, the sun was receding somewhere in the sky and that's when Rajjo's heartbeat quickened. She knew before she turned around that he was here, standing right behind her.

The priests took their positions and the lanterns were lit, the bugles and trumpets started blowing in the gentle breeze as he looked at her, and she at him.

They both walked towards each other till he took her lips softly at first and then they merged into each other. Struggling with the clothes, tasting each other, making up for lost time. They found each other, as the bells of the arti rang through the sky and drowned her cries of passion. He took her right there, under the twilight sky. His mouth devoured hers, his hands caressed her skin, cupped her breasts, circled her tiny waist. He worshipped every inch of her. Rajjo moaned. She could hear the Ganga flow beneath them, marking their union. She had found salvation as he cried his release and came inside her.

Hours later, tangled in each others arms, bodies entwined, they gazed into each other's eyes, drowning, till the ringing of the last bell died down and the ghats fell silent. The beautiful silence invaded her senses. She felt complete.

Perhaps it was the epilogue she had been seeking all her life.

# 2

## 'Government issues notice to Godwoman Durga'

THE headline in the paper stared at Kesar and made him uncomfortable. Wearing khaki pants and a crisp blue shirt, he sat patiently in the crowded train, absorbed by the sounds and smells. Now in his twenties, Kesar still looked like a teenager, thin, scrawny with a hesitant demeanour. As the train chugged away, Kesar tried hard not to be bothered by the newspaper headline.

A co-passenger, poring through the paper opposite him, made it a little more difficult to avoid the screaming headline. '*Godwoman Durga in yet another scandal?*' Kesar looked out of the window at the blurring landscape, a bit of green, a blob of brown, a patch of yellow. The open window was a blessing and he strained his neck to see the train winding through hills, valleys and forests. His butt ached from being squeezed, six of them sitting on a bench meant for three. He was scared to even cross his legs, lest the seat on which half his butt sat was also taken by the squashed man sitting next to him, waiting to spill out a bit more.

The passenger sitting opposite him shuffled the paper and the headlines were in his face again. Kesar willed himself to think of something else. The more he thought about the headline, the more he wanted to jump off the train and run back, his trip seeming increasingly pointless.

As the train stopped at another junction, Kesar bought a cup of tea and some local bread from the window next to his seat. He wanted to walk on the junction to stretch his legs, but he dared not. As he sipped tea from the earthern pot, he took in the vendors hawking foodstuff on the station. He remembered his few train journeys where he would step out to suck at the juicy oranges from the Nagpur, or taste the delicious *pethas* in Agra. The cries of the chaiwallahs, the wiry porters in their red shirts, the vendors and fellow travellers rushing by, everything had fascinated him back then. He never really noticed the dust, the flies, the stinking toilets or the sweaty crowds. They were just beautiful, perfect train journeys he underwent.

As the train started to pull away from the junction and gained speed, Kesar's fears came to haunt him yet again. But a tiny hope kept him going. Perhaps it would turn out very smoothly. At best Durga would remember him, hug him, wish him all the best and sign the papers. At worst she would not recognize him, feed him to the dogs and perhaps sign the paper he wanted her to sign. Kesar replayed the entire scenario over and over in his head, till the thought became an ache beginning to pound on his forehead like a hammer. He reminded himself that he was now handling the entire cable business of Rajjo's husband who had died without an heir. If Rajjo was to give him a no objection certificate, he would be able to expand the cable TV business and take it to the next level. He had a neatly typed letter; it had taken him a week and a cheap lawyer to get the wording right. The letter was tucked away in his pocket.

Just then a tea seller's welcome cry of 'Chai, garam chai' coming down the aisle broke his reverie. He reminded himself firmly that he was a grown man running a business, with the hope of doing better in life. He needed to make this trip, even if every cell in his body shrieked that he should turn around and go back home.

Just then he heard the fat man, the one reading the paper and hogging most of the berth opposite him speak out, 'These godmen and godwomen forget leading saintly lives. She needs bullet-proof enclosures, SUVs, personal swimming pools! In her case they say she has an empty one which is filled with milk and has a bath with it!' The other passengers were immediately interested in his rambling. Some were not too happy with his statement, a few nodded in empathy and one guy sitting three seats away, with a slightly balding head and a reasonable belly, immediately spoke up, 'Only the blind who cannot see her true grace fall for the media-written crap.' The others turned to acknowledge this feisty voice. The fat guy gave the puny guy a once over and dismissed him, 'Ya, we see her true grace for personal luxury – lavish lifestyle, holiday homes, swimming pools, foreign accounts, home theatre – and god knows what else?'

Kesar could smell a fight in the train compartment already.

'You have visited her house? Made an inventory?' The puny guy was clearly not ready to back off.

'I haven't but my sister-in-law's friend has. She has even visited that one of her Satlok Ashram near Barwala. The ashram is spread over twelve acres of land.'

Kesar's brain immediately screamed, *He was headed to the same Satlok Ashram to meet her today! Was it an omen?* He quickly buried the thought lest this man would see what he was thinking. He focused on his nasal sarcastic remarks, 'Your Durga is believed to have been living in a five-storey house in one part of the ashram complex. The building is also a home for her entire family! The whole building has luxury fittings from granite tiles, marble flooring, fancy grills, well-equipped bathrooms with modern fittings, split air-conditioners, flat-screen TVs and even massage beds. The personal rooms were big ones that I saw myself in a magazine last month!'

The man with the briefcase was not willing to back off.

'God knows why you are keeping stock of all her electronics especially flat screen TVs, like given a chance you would steal it!'

There was a little snicker from the audience. The puny guy had claws. The other passengers were settling down, a clear indication they were all set to enjoy the argument, a welcome entertainment during the long journey. Getting bolder by the minute as the fat guy decided to let the catty remark go, the devotee decided to press his luck further and drive his point home.

'She has the blessing of Goddess Durga. She was named after the goddess at birth. And her followers also live in the same grace. Her blessing can fight the mightiest impediments that even Lord Shani can't!' He reminded Kesar of a well-trained parrot.

The fat guy scowled, 'If you are living in the grace, why is your skinny ass occupying a berth? You should be flying a jet plane! Like she does. Why is your Shani making you work like a dog and travel in crowded compartments?'

The crowd chuckled once more, waiting for the puny guy to take his shot.

'She has a Facebook app, live darshan – she has more than ten million followers. Right now as we talk some twenty people have joined her grace.' The puny fellow commented haughtily.

The fat guy rubbed his cheek lazily, 'Right now as we speak some twenty people have also farted on this train.'

A hoot of laughter ran through the train carriage. Kesar was growing tense. The more he heard, the more his letter weighed on him. 'Doubtful money sources, nexus with politicians, all kinds of scandals, rackets; you name it, your Godwoman is involved! Live darshan on Facebook, my foot!'

'Have you watched television lately? The fourth eye of Maa Durga will be watching you from every channel!' A lady spoke up. She was clearly not amused and also a devotee. The puny guy was vindicated. There was a look exchanged, a complete understanding between them.

'Because of her fourth eye in forty channels – her turnover is in crores! And the money is going from your pockets! I can see that big hole in your head from where the money is coming out!' The fat guy pushed his point home. There was a guffaw. The woman continued her rant.

'She is watching you, you know. She knows. And she will punish you.' Saying that, the woman pressed a button on her phone and one could hear the Godwoman's voice spill through the carriage.

Kesar did not want to believe this, but the amused laughter actually trickled away in the train compartment. Even the fat guy seemed to tone down a bit.

The puny guy also decided to play his live darshan on the phone. Strangely, no one objected. Kesar could hear the chants of '*Jai Jai Durge*' in the bogey. Clearly the Godwoman had won. Was it faith or fear? Kesar was almost in two minds to jump off the train, but the train moved on, the wheels turned endlessly and Kesar knew he was not going to get off the train till he reached his destination.

The main office was in a crowded building. A huge potrait of Maa Durga hung over the teeming office. As Kesar crossed a large hall to walk towards the ticket window, he saw hundreds of mattresses and quilts stacked in the huge hall, perhaps used for lodging by her followers.

Kesar waited his turn to get his slip for the transportation he ewas to avail that would take him for the Godwoman's darshan. A lot of families, noisy wives, quiet husbands, ill-mannered children, lost elders queued up. Kesar, along with his letter, was one of them. Once his turn came at the ticket window, the administrator asked him in a bored voice, 'Will you be staying the night?' Kesar shook his head in the negative. The fee was calculated. He had to shell out two hundred rupees to enter the premises. The queue was long. Another two hundred for a subsidized family meal that was available at the darshan ground itself. The pamphlet shoved in his hand boasted of a tie-up with burger joints and fast-food centres. Another three hundred and twenty rupees for the special sermon – the rate card said two hundred and fifty for the special arti and special audience with Chhoti Ma. An all-inclusive package of seven hundred per person was also available. Kesar stared at the pamphlet with a glazed expression and did not want any of the packages. The irritated guy at the ticket window dismissed him and beckoned to the next customer.

Kesar settled into the van packed with families. Personal vehicles were not allowed and a fancy advertisement playing out on a small screen in the van engaged them. Durga was addressing them here as well. The audio-visual captured the teachings of the Godwoman.

The smoky smell trapped in the leathery seats of the Innova suffocated Kesar. Minutes after he rolled down the windows, the smell of cigarettes from the old leathery seats stayed with him. He was trying to find Rajjo's face in this Godwoman, but the closer he got to her, the harder it became.

Kesar closed his eyes and waited to reach the destination. The car trailed on for another twenty minutes, and hit the outskirts of the city before nearing the ashram. The complex had a twenty-feet wall all around for security. A public address system was constantly churning out promotions and messages across the ashram.

As the van entered the compound, the atmosphere was scenic yet charged. Lush green vegetation, trees and plants soothed the eyes. The compound milled with people and twinkling fairy lights lit up every tree branch. Birthday greetings for Guru Maa Durga fluttered in the slight breeze. Her lifesize cut-outs stared at every devotee. Kesar felt he was being watched by Rajjo every step of the way. He was a non-believer. He was guilty. But he appreciated the business model. He hoped she read the appreciation in his head in case she had the powers they claimed she did.

As he got off and stretched his legs, he was ushered inside the foyer. Sepia flashes of Rajjo smiling, Kesar running after her in the market street barefoot, a battered Rajjo leaving him and going away rose unexpectedly and left him rooted to the spot.

A variety of prayers and chants brought him back to the present. They blared from various corners. Booths were set up for registration and payment. Someone slapped a yellow VIP band on his wrist and then looked at his slip, angrily switching the band to a green colour – normal entry. People wearing black uniforms and with walky talkies managed the crowd as they escorted some important-looking guests and whisked them through security.

Just then he saw a woman cross the foyer. Kesar recognized the familiar face instantly. Neeta Shahani. She was from the inner circle of Durga Maa and had made quite a fortune with her association. He would watch them closely while monitoring the cable TV coverage. Perhaps by watching them he would know more about Rajjo. Kesar knew about all her aides by heart. She was in charge of running the TV channel business but lately the rumour mills suggested she had distanced herself from the inner circle. She was strictly looking at the business side of things.

Kesar worried about Rajjo not recognizing him, or not being happy to see him come for a favour. A sense of foreboding rose in him yet again, should he meet her unabashed like this? Should he wait for a more appropriate time?

Kesar came back to the present as he was ushered into a dark amphitheatre. He was taken in by the elaborate stage set up with professional lighting, music and other technical apparatus. A huge stage, lit up like a jewel amidst a sea of people, made him pause. Different levels of seating made the view clear from all corners. A mammoth assemblage sat there, waiting in anticipation. He had just made it in time as a woman in a black sari – Kesar recognized her as *Chhoti Ma*a – addressed the crowd and told them to prepare to greet their Guru Maa who was going to deliver them from all the worries and impediments of life.

Kesar remembered this woman on stage as Rano, Rajjo's sister, who had come to take Rajjo away when she was battered. Kesar remembered the face, he remembered that time – the heat was rising up, the grass had dried up and Rajjo's wounds kept him awake. That was the time Rano had come to visit her sister and she had refused to go with her.

A roar of devotion, appreciation and excitement ran through the packed amphitheatre. The roar was so loud and powerful that it almost carried Kesar along with it. He had no time to pause or breathe. It was all happening too fast! He felt he was one of them. He wanted a piece of her too!

Holographic images of Rajjo in all shapes and sizes appeared on the stage. Lord Shani, her symbol, sat at the centre of it all with his giant image forming the backdrop motif of the entire auditorium. The lights were cleverly used to conjure the image of Lord Shani that would come and go in between the sermons and proceedings.

As the crescendo built up, the lights dimmed and what followed took his breath away. She appeared in an extravagant balloon-type structure, as if she was floating in the air and descending from the heavens. Her entry had the desired effect as the gathering went into a frenzy. Dressed in more than usually heavy bridal jewellery and nuptial finery, Durga Maa sent the crowds wild. As the balloon approached the stage, the bottom panel opened with fireworks and Guru Maa was seen sitting with a trident in her hand, almost as if she was Goddess Durga herself. The devotees bowed in devotion as the balloon – masterfully guided – settled as her throne in the middle of the stage.

Each soul in this maidan believed they would attain salvation right here, with this woman sitting in a balloon on the stage.

As Durga settled on stage, the –much-awaited sermon began.

Kesar left without meeting her, she was perhaps not the same woman he knew. His paper with the NOC application for taking over 'Maa Cable'– *Rurki Chowk* – lay crumpled on the floor, trampled on by the devotees who were in a frenzy to catch a better glimpse of their Godwoman.

Kuljeet sat patiently in Rajjo's room waiting for her sermon to finish. This was the second time Kuljeet was visiting her after Rajjo had donned the mantle of a Godwoman. Kuljeet stared at the large TV screen that ran the live telecast on Durga's channel. Life had come a long way. The naïve girl, taking refuge in the ashram, was light years away from this woman who ate up the TV screen with her sheer presence and left you spellbound.

A hassled-looking man barged in and wheeled out a rack of clothes hurriedly from the room, politely nodding at Kuljeet. It was a fairly big room with mirror and lights. One corner was filled with racks with saris and robes. Another contained a pile of books, primarily of the literary kind and pamphlets about the Durga foundation.

The door opened again and a chubby man in his late twenties ambled in. She recognized the round face covered with an unkempt beard, clad in sparkling white and starched kurta pyjama that barely contained his ample stomach. She recalled seeing him on the news channels when he was charged with murder and alleged rape. This was Rajjo's youngest sibling, her brother Sheru. His tobacco-stained teeth smiled at her. In return Kuljeet glared at him. She did not want to engage with Sheru at any level. Gluttony was writ large on his face. To Kuljeet's relief Sheru scuttled out. She was distracted by a flurry of movement through the open door. A few performers were running with harmoniums and tablas. Maybe some performance was planned.

She turned her attention to the imposing wall with a built-in glass case displaying herbal products from the Durga trust. The bottles lined the shelf-like soldiers, proudly wearing the Durga trust symbol. Herbal pills for male sexual disorder, an energy boosting muesli, a maha mantra DVD for wish fulfilment, pills to combat female infertility, acne products, oils, skin and hair care products, pills for relief from joint pains, arthritis, even shaving foams! There was another bottle sitting on the shelf with a white guy wincing in pain on the cover. There were cures for weight-loss, obesity, and constipation on the shelf as well. Kuljeet was amused to see that shampoos for dandruff and hair growth were also manufactured by the Durga trust. The last shelf made Kuljeet wonder how many people bought it and if it really helped. The products confidently offered remedies for cataracts, cancers, cervical problems and tumors. By now Kuljeet wanted to collect all these items and try them one by one. Rajjo's meteoric rise in the last fifteen years could be seen packaged in these bottles on the shelf.

As time ticked by and Kuljeet waited in the room that smelt of roses and jasmine, her uneasiness grew in leaps and bounds. She wondered how she was supposed to tell Rajjo that she had a premonition. Kuljeet had watched Rajjo brave many a scandal, media reports and attacks against her empire from a distance. But this time it was different. This time there was evil riding on the storm that was brewing. It had every intention of uprooting Rajjo and tossing her on the shore like a wasted corpse. For Kuljeet, Rajjo was still the lost girl who she met over a decade ago, whom she wanted to protect, whatever her sins.

Perhaps, her judgement day had arrived too soon.

Just then the door opened yet again and the stunningly beautiful Rajjo, decked up like a bride, walked in eagerly and hugged Kuljeet tightly. Her amber eyes had become deeper, her riot of glistening curls longer. Her face had a maturity that made her beautiful and a wildness that made her dangerous. She was still a wild flower in the forest.

Rajjo's excitement and happiness was evident in the glitter of her eye as she fussed over Kuljeet. Even though she was not expressive, Kuljeet knew how much it meant to Rajjo for her to come and visit her.

Kuljeet nodded at her companion Devi, who stood at a safe distance, not wanting to intrude. She had the build of a man, but her eyes had the softness of a woman. Her face had strong lines – sharp and firm, complete with a man's cleft and a strong jaw, but her beautiful silky hair fell in soft waves framing the strong face. Compassion for Rajjo mirrored on her face. Kuljeet was relieved to know if need be this woman would jump into the fire for Rajjo. It comforted her that Rajjo had such a loyal aide around.

As they settled on the couch again, Kuljeet chided her. 'You were right, Rajjo. Running the God business with corporate finesse is indeed a loss-proof proposition! It's a money spinner!' Rajjo laughed at the teasing. Hearing her tinkling laughter, Kuljeet wanted to delay her chat further but the urge to let the beast out strangled Kuljeet. She wanted to delay her talk as much as possible, but the tormented look in her eye gave her away to Rajjo. As Rajjo looked at Kuljeet closely, her smile vanished.

Kuljeet took a deep breath and waded right in. 'I am scared for you.' Those were the only words that Kuljeet could manage to utter.

Rajjo felt a strange fear. But without hesitation she stated in a clear voice. 'I am in love with him.' Kuljeet saw the tearing pain lurking in her eyes.

'I won't tell you what to do. You remember Rani Ma. What was her undoing? Don't think it was you, Rajjo. '

The statement hung between them. Kuljeet could see the confusion and battle Rajjo was fighting. It was Rajjo's choice. Kuljeet knew she wouldn't be able to help her any further. It was time to leave. Kuljeet had a long journey back home through the eucalyptus groves.

'I don't know what to do? What is important?' she whispered to her friend.

Kuljeet heard herself say, 'First, the baby loves mother's milk; second, he learns of his mother and father; third, his brothers, sisters and aunts; fourth, the love of play awakens. Fifth, he runs after food and drink; sixth, in his sexual desire, he does not respect social customs. Seventh, he gathers wealth and dwells in his house; eighth, he becomes angry, and his body is consumed. Ninth, he turns grey, and his breath becomes laboured; tenth, he is cremated, and turns to ashes. His companions send him off, crying out. He came and he went, and now, even his name has died. After he left, food was offered on the leaves, and birds were called to come and eat.'

She looked at Rajjo, her words washing over her. 'I am not saying this, it's written in the holy books. That's the cycle of life. Do what you need to do – remember in the end the birds are called to come and eat the rice balls. That's how it ends.'

Leaving her beloved Rajjo rooted to the spot, Kuljeet made her way out. Her heart sang for Rajjo was in love, and her soul wept for the love was going to be her atonement.

Rano had finished an entire pack of cigarettes, yet the momentary relief she seeked eluded her. There were too many troubles piling up and she felt like she was drowning. The herbal medicine business was incurring losses despite good sales. Someone was fudging the accounts and that made her blood boil. It was not the swindled amount that angered her but the fact that someone had the nerve to cheat them from the money they rightfully deserved. Rano was on medication for anxiety and she had been steadily increasing her dosage in the last few months since Rajjo had decided to switch roles from a successful Godwoman with a turnover in crores to a pining lover of a married man whose father-in-law happened to be the only guy who could screw them. She felt like a sitting duck. The guy was a ruthless politician who doted on his daughter Upasana, Rajjo's lover boy's wife.

Despite warnings, threats and a lot of cajoling, it was clear that Rajjo was in no mood to listen. Rano had witnessed her disastrous taste in men since they were in pig-tails. That reminded Rano of the days back in the village when they were still growing up and the world was theirs to conquer. She remembered Rajjo's hasty lover by the railway tracks and piles of hay baking in the sun.

She lit another smoke, fingers quivering with anger and irritation. She took in a deep breath and sensed a silent shadow cross the door. She knew from the faint rustle and the odd smell of dried spices that it was Rajjo's trusted confidante Devi. She hovered around in nooks and corners she should not be. Devi reminded Rano of a slithery black blood-sucking leech. She'd stuck on to Rajjo and it was impossible to get her off Rajjo's skin. Like it was impossible to get any information out of Devi about Rajjo.

In the recent past Rano had tried to cajole Devi to share Rajjo's thoughts, her moods, and lately her schedules as she arranged secret rendezvouses with her lover, but Rano realized soon enough that even if they had to pull Devi's teeth out one by one, she would not give away anything about Rajjo. She was a wall of nothingness. The only thing that made her human was her very obvious devotion to Rajjo. Dressed mostly in white salwar kameez, she was a strange masculine–feminine mix. Rano wondered if she was a man in the robes of a woman. Those piercing black eyes took in everything. Sometimes Rano felt they bore into her too close. She was an odd one all right.

But Devi was the least of her worries right now.

To her relief, Karam looking handsome with his unshaved grizzly face and his trademark white kurta over jeans sauntered in. She was expecting him almost thirty minutes ago. Karam knew her well enough not to ask what the problem was as he sat down on the couch with a sigh. Rano puffed away in silence. As expected, Rano took off before she could finish her last smoke. 'We have bloody invested in the 150-acre facility near Pune, set up a four-pronged distribution channel, and marketed all the products under the Durga trust. We have invested in medical centres all over the country – 1067 fucking chikitsalayas – this was her pet project, and now the turnover is nose-diving, not to mention the media, and political parties are baying for her blood and she just sits there and fucking broods!'

Karam knew Rano was in one of her moods. One large part of the wall was taken by Rano's cutout where she wore a plain white sari and a painted halo in hues of gold. She had an angelic smile on her face but Karam knew what she looked like when she was spewing venom with the same celestial smile. It made him chuckle. Rano continued agitatedly, 'What gets me is that she is just not bothered anymore! You know what that means?'

Rano wanted a reaction from this handsome man sitting on her couch, unruffled and faintly amused. Rano felt the habitual indignant drone starting at the base of her neck, taking over her entire brain within seconds. Pulsating like a living beast, it claimed her body and senses.

'We will figure something out,' Karam muttered in a soothing tone.

Rano hissed angrily, 'For a year we have been fielding that bloody Pujari. He holds that political party in his fist. You know if they win the election next year what happens? If they win the election and we are not in line with them, they will grind us to the ground. The lands, the settlements, the investments! Am I the only one who has a bloody brain here?!'

Rano's voice bordered on hysteria.

Karam held out a glass of water. Rano's ranting increased. 'Why can't Rajjo see it? How can she be so blind? Why is she refusing an alliance with them? Pujari's PVP party is our salvation and they are handing it to us on a plate!'

'She has other things on her mind, she is going through a lot.'

Envy like a snake uncoiled in her heart. He was always taking Rajjo's side, since they were running in the fields or chasing the fireflies by the railway tracks, he was always looking out for her.

Rano wanted to smash something or someone. 'Or why can't you say she is fucking the brains out of that Harsh Wardhan and in return for a party alliance Rajjo will have to stop fucking him because the party belongs to Pujari and Pujari's fucking daughter is Harsh's fucking wife! Rajjo's affair with Harsh Wardhan is a ticking timebomb! '

Karam's face was pale for a second and Rano knew she had hit her mark.

'Since when was *fucking* more important than Godly business?'

'Since we started running it! Can you please calm down?' Karam waited for Rano to reign in her temper.

'And she is not doing this deliberately, she is helpless. Understand her.'

Rano turned to look at Karam. She wanted to twist a knife in his heart.

She still had the same longing for him that she did decades back and Karam still had the same yearning he had for Rajjo.

However, over the years Rano had mastered the art of quelling that envious serpent that uncoiled in her throat time and again when she saw Karam pining for her sister.

But Rano knew she had other serious problems to focus on. If this was not contained, it could very well mean the beginning of the end of everything they had worked towards all their life. She could hear the hooting of the train they had left far behind in the village; she could hear the wheels turning and inhale the smoke rising from the engine, the piercing whistle of the incoming train was keeping her awake in the nights. If the business fell apart they were all going to go back to that village, and Rano would die before she would let that happen!

Karam smoked pot under the starlit sky. His head throbbed. He could hear the lake's stillness, and the sweet smelling flowers reminded him of Rajjo. He could sense the pale petals nestled quietly in the dark green leaves, spreading their fragrance. It was comforting to have this scent around him, just like the knowledge of being near Rajjo.

He knew about the torrid love affair and the very latest rendezvous Rajjo had had with Harsh, and it broke his heart all over again. The day she came back for him in the village, to tell him that she needed him, he had stopped looking at her with lovestruck eyes. But he knew she was never going to be his. Was that enough for Karam?

She stood there in a mango-coloured sari, an expensive leather bag dangling from her arm. She smelt of a different world. He could not smell the village in her. She was on a different path. She waited for his answer.

He was done with the cycles of battling the harsh winter, burning the crops to start a new one, harvesting, storing and selling. Despite the hard backbreaking work Karam did to forget Rajjo, everything reminded him of her! Every monsoon. Every cloud. Every raindrop. She loved rain! The only way he was going to stop pining for her and yearning for her was if he could be around her.

Her voice washed over him once again. 'I promise you, you will have more money than you know what to do with and we will be rich. I need you to work with me.' With an overcast sky behind her, Rajjo stood tall and proud staring at Karam. He could hear the storm around him and he could see it in her eyes. Those beautiful brown eyes that reflected the green of the fields, and the blue of the sky.

'What are you doing?' he asked in a gruff voice, careful not to be too excited just yet. She'd pointed towards the Shani deity residing on the filthy side road with an old tired man offering some fresh flowers and replacing the old shriveled ones. 'Nothing much! Just selling him.'

Karam was stumped as she uttered the words. He'd worshipped this diety day in and day out. Despite the Saturdays he devoted to him, he had not given Karam what he wanted the most. It was easy to give him up. As she turned around to walk away, Karam was one with the sway of her hip. Karam had taken all of one second to decide the next course of his life. There was no other answer for Karam than to follow Rajjo. He simply nodded and walked out of the fields to follow her. Karam's father still covered in a sodden crumpled scarf, feet soiled in mud, his hands holding a sickle, called out to Karam but Karam took off his robes. He was glad to get rid of the sweaty afternoon smell.

He followed her through the fields and the muddy roads, the milk man's house and the rivulet, he bid adieu to the old mango tree at the end of the village with a faded red kite fluttering in the wind from last winter. Old and tired, it still blew in the wind, tied to the branch. They were destined to be together, the branch and the kite, till one of them decided to let go. Just like Karam had decided to let go of his family and everything he knew and loved in this world to follow this woman.

It was over a decade and now here he was: he had comfort, luxury, expensive cars, women and the only thing he did not have now was Rajjo.

A sound alerted him to Rano who was standing behind him. Her beautiful face softened by the light, the love for him glistening on her eyelash. 'I've heard from confirmed sources they are coming to power next. They have secured alliances from other parties. You know which way the wind is blowing. They will finish us if we do not stop Rajjo and Harsh. Pujari will do anything for his daughter. Harsh's TRP party is merging into PVP officially. They have all the control. The political might of his wife Upasana Wardhan and Harsh's family will crush everything we have built over the years.' Her voice trembled with fear. There was a silence accentuated by a ripple on the lake. Rano looked at Karam closely.' Doesn't that bother you? Don't you think we need to do something about it?

Rano had come here with a mission and it was very rare that she failed to get what she wanted. She'd waited a long time for this and the time was finally here. She came very close to Karam and whispered in his ear. 'She loves him...' Her whisper wrenched his gut. 'He will destroy her. Are you ready to stand by and watch her getting destroyed?' She stepped closer and Karam felt the weight of her desire. He wondered what would Rajjo want, to be happily destroyed in her love or be saved without it? Rano stared at him. There was a moment of complete understanding. Rano slowly took of her clothes. Her naked body bathed in the moonlight. She stood in front of him. She knew she was standing in for her sister, but she wanted him regardless.

He finally touched her. He could smell the jasmine on her breast, between her thighs and he wanted more of her, he wanted more of Rajjo as he captured Rano's breast in his mouth and thrust into her over and over again, taking Rajjo's name in his heart.

As they lay naked side by side, Rano felt a strange sense of accomplishment.

'I am not sure what she would want, Rano, give me time to think. I don't know what we should do.' The chirping of the crickets in the sooty dark night completed their silence.

'Sometimes I wish we could go back to the village when we were growing up and that things would be the same.' Rano sighed as she looked at the calm serene lake and smelt the jasmine drifting in the air.

'Things are the same, nothing much has changed, just that we are on the other side of the tracks,' Karam sighed.

'And I would not want to go back there at any cost, Karam!' There was a steely edge to Rano's voice. The decision sat between them. Rajjo sat between them. Rano remembered her as a fierce warrior of a sister with a relentless spirit and Karam remembered her beautiful soft face under the moonlight as she spoke about her love to Karam, her first love. They both fiercely wanted to protect her.

'Heard Saroj tai has decided to go back…' Karam said in a gruff voice. Rano waited for more to come – Karam was still undecided, it seemed. With a sigh, Rano let it go for now but knew they were going to have to decide soon. 'It's better as she won't be able to see what is about to unfurl.' Karam gave her a puzzled look. Taking another deep breath and inhaling a bit of Karam, Rano muttered, 'You need to take over Sheru's role as well. In the next few months he will be fading out of the system.'

'Does Rajjo know?' Rano nodded. Rano stood facing him to take her leave, but she stepped forward and hugged him instead. They both held on to each other, drawing comfort and strength. The love and longing had bound them together in a way; both were suffering from unrequited love. Rano shut her eyes to capture his breath on her cheek. He was kissing her again – he had become hard. Rano pressed her full breasts against him, his heart next to hers, his hand on her hips. She wanted time to stand still and lose its way. She could hear the lake whispering sweet nothings and the leaves quietly rustling. A sweet smile sat on her lips. She hoped one day there would be more.

As Karam lay spent on the grass for a second time and Rano savoured each moment she had snatched with him, Karam asked her in a small broken voice, 'Where in Ahmedabad do they meet?' His pained question destroyed the moment, a violent feeling attacked her body. It was dark, perhaps purple, it was blinding. It made Rano choke. Rano resisted it but with years it had only grown stronger. As they were two decades ago, she could not battle the urge to inflict the pain he had given her. The stench of her own failing and her wanting doused her.

'Three days, they were holed up in Pal Bhavan. It's a quaint old bungalow hidden in a crowded lane. The terrace at full moon seems to invite lovers and angels. It is beautiful.' Rano wanted to stop but she could not. Every word she said burnt him and despite herself she enjoyed it. It doused the burns she felt herself. She was ashamed. She was helpless. She was in love as she looked at the ravaged handsome face of the man holding her in his arms in a moonlit night, by a silver lake under a beautiful tree soaked in the scent of jasmine. She whispered to him almost ominously, 'It's time to save Rajjo from her own self.'

# 3

RAJJO was ready in her silks and satin. Her face was painted with gold and silver. Crimson marked her forehead. She was ready to meet her devotees as the Godwoman. Her mind constantly wavered and struggled to focus on the people present in the room. She had not answered Harsh's question. It whispered in her ear yet again, 'Can they be together?' A delicate moth fluttered on the wall, mocking her. She was still unaware that silken threads of love were weaving a spell.

The indecisiveness numbed her as she sat in her room listening to her brother Sheru and others describe his expansion plan. 'I think it's a bloody good business plan and we should back this construction guy. He is designing it in a way that the sprawling campus will have three kinds of flats for the elderly. Category I, Ganga, the biggest in size will be available for Rs 21 lakh; Yamuna is for Rs 11 lakh and Saraswati for Rs 5.5 lakh. Any person of the age of fifty and above can apply for these flats. One can start living there once the payment is made. If the person dies, the spouse gets to use the accommodation. But once the spouse dies, the flat goes back to the trust and is re-allotted. These flats have ACs, reverse osmosis water purifiers, geysers, and pipeline gas connections. It's a money-making machine – we don't sell any estate, just rent it out and given the bad polluted air in India, oldies are not going to live long.' Sheru waited excitedly for his sister's response. Rano and Karam stood there disapproving. This was another one of Sheru's schemes to swindle people and the trust. Not to mention his excitement over his tenants dying soon, if only he could reign in his thoughts of profit and appear sombre. But Rano had to admit it could work well.

As they waited for her response, Rajjo wanted the wind to howl in agony. The pale brown moth arrested her yet again with a gentle flutter. It knew she felt thunderous inside. Harsh had whispered the honey-dripped promise of starting a life together. She hated him for giving her that option. She was trapped in her robes of a Godwoman, woven with her sweat and blood. Sewn with her desire. The robe was her skin, how does one peel their skin and still breathe.

It was clear that Rajjo was not going to respond to Sheru's business proposition right away. The silence stretched on as Devi smiled. She was the only one who knew what Rajjo's heart battled with. Devi towered over her protectively. Her face painted with heavy makeup, always prepared in case of a public performance. Apart from Rajjo, the other thing Devi loved was the camera on her face. She thrived on seeing a fleeting glimpse of her arm, her face, or her hands, on the TV. Her bright red lips and green-rimmed eyes popped out of the screen but even Rajjo could not talk her out of it.

As the silence in the room stretched into eternity, Sheru's face fell. Rano opened the soundproof door and said, 'It's time to get back on stage.' Devotees could be heard chanting Jai Jai Durge. Sheru was left standing, without a definite answer and not too happy as Rajjo and her coterie moved towards the stage. The devotees and volunteers bowed reverantly as Rajjo crossed them, wearing her black and red robes. Her beautifully painted face hid her agony. Rajjo wanted to scream and cry, but she continued to bless them with a smile. The moth fluttered somewhere around her shoulder. It carried the innocence of a lamb and the venom of a thousand snakebites. Just when she stepped from the darkness into the spotlight, it bit her and flew away.

She stood on the stage, bathed in light, thousands of devotees chanting her name. To her horror she did not feel the usual throbbing of her heart. The adulation did not make her come alive anymore.

She desperately hunted for the feeling that she belonged here, but all in vain. Rajjo wanted to burn the stage and rip the curtains. The rotating image of Lord Shani, the chants, the spiritual experience overwhelmed her. Her devotees chanting and cheering left her breathless. Thousands of them gathered in the arena, and seemed to threaten her like they would pounce on her any minute. They would swarm over her till she was unable to breathe. She could feel the panic in her heart. She wanted some space to breathe. She wanted her own piece of clear blue sky she could hold in her palm and hope.

For the very first time, Rajjo decided to leave the stage without addressing her devotees.

A shocked audience saw her abrupt departure and the hurried attempt of Chhoti Maa to address the masses.

Rajjo headed back to her room, followed by her shocked coterie. Rano hurried towards them after managing the on-stage activities. A thunderous expression was on her face as she gave Karam a knowing look.

'What happened, Rajjo?' Rano's tone was accusatory. Rajjo continued to walk like a woman possessed. She needed the sanctuary of her room.

Devi scuttled behind Rajjo, wanting to block out the shock and disapproval.

Rajjo headed for the whiskey bottle kept in the hidden cabinet and downed the drink in three neat gulps. Rano hissed in Rajjo's ear, clearly unhappy. 'The VIP darshan is pending.' Rajjo wanted to run away to be in his arms, the only place where she could breathe.

The nimble-footed moth was back in the room. It settled on the delicate petal-shaped lamp on the wall. It reminded her of a time in the recent past where he left her in the middle of an unfinished fight, an unfinished kiss. She was yearning to give him some love but he had to leave because his wife had called him. It never bothered her before but now it tore her apart. When was she ever going to be the priority for Harsh? And he had the same answer – when they started a life together.

The walls were closing in. The moth fluttered again and flew out to sit on the windowsill. Rajjo wanted to capture it in a glass jar and watch it suffer like she suffered. Why had he given her that simple option; to elope from the life she had created? She envied and hated his wife who slept in his arms night after night. The moth whispered, '*It could be you.*'

She wanted to smash something. She hated his wife and empathized with her in the same breath. She was breathing deeply, trying to quell her raging emotion. Her bloodshot eyes, beads of sweat on her forehead and neck, alarmed the others. The room spinned around her, Devi's hand was the only thing that kept her from collapsing. She struggled to breathe. She had everything around her that money could buy yet she seemed little better than a beggar. The giant motif of Lord Shani looked down at her with disdain and she drank some more, spilling liquor on her sari with unsteady hands. Rano immediately called for some people to take care of the spilt liquor. In her business-like tone, she took charge swiftly.

'You need to be touched up… That sari has to be cleaned, Rajjo. I need you to be ready in ten minutes.' She turned to Devi. 'Get her ready.' Devi lowered her eyes awaiting her mistress's consent. 'Did you hear me, Rajjo?'

Rajjo focused her mind and breath on Rano. She could hear her loud and clear once more as she nodded. Devi muttered to Rano, 'I will get her ready now.'

Rajjo brushed her bodice and turned towards the mirror. She was ready to be prepped up. The sash was puffed up. Hurried hands sprayed hair and makeup on her. She was ready to face it all once again.

The door opened and Rajjo's old and frail mother Saroj walked in with a deep motherly concern, snow-white hair, aged face, beautiful tired eyes. She saw her daughter looking tired, exhausted and troubled. Devi moved swiftly to offer her a chair and offered some fruits and water to the old woman. But she wanted none of that. All she wanted was to wipe out the grief from her daughter's face.

Saroj and Devi exchanged a knowing look; Rajjo at the helm of such a big empire carrying a bleeding heart. Saroj hoped it was not going to bleed to death. She hoped her daughter would find her way before she was completely lost. As the drumming of the AC and the soothing chant filled the room, Saroj placed her tired hand on her daughter in a comforting manner. 'What is the point of all this wealth and riches? You need to have the real thing. If you don't have faith, you are barren. If you find your faith, they say the fire does not burn it, and the wind does not blow it away; thieves cannot get near it. Accumulate the wealth of the Lord's name; that wealth does not go anywhere.' Her words echoed in the room.

Rano rolled her eyes. All they needed in this drama was her mother mouthing lines from the holy book to dissuade Rajjo from continuing the business and find faith. Mother had definitely gone senile and she had become worse than their feisty grandmother. She needed to get her out for now!

'The temperature, it's too hot…I want the AC on.' Rajjo muttered in response to her mother. She took deep breaths as the others shivered in the cold blast.

Saroj was panicking for her daugher, 'Rajjo, it's never too late. Just leave all this and go get some rest. You have done enough for the day. Everyone should go home now!'

'Leave the room, mother, we will come and see you later.' Rano instructed her mother – her tone did not invite a discussion. Saroj faded into the shadows. She looked at her daughter sitting in front of the mirror. A TV channel played her sermon in the background. Rajjo as Maa Durga. She was telling people about the Lord. There was a pitiful expression on her face.

Saroj stood up and gathered her old chiffon dupatta. She was on her way out and 'You know I told this Durga Maa all those things when we used to sit in our courtyard in our village. I had a parrot called Totu. I thought all my children heard the message of God, but I forgot he only chooses to be heard by those who he wants…,' her tired voice trailed off.

Devi opened the door gently for the old lady to leave. A faint trail of moths and the passage of time moved with her. She smelt of the cold winter nights in the village around the warm fire. Rajjo could smell the firewood on her skin. As she disappeared through the open door, a giant roar from the sea of devotees on the TV screen claimed her attention. It was like Rajjo held their pulse in her hand and made them act like puppets. She was moving the strings and performing a beautiful magic trick, commanding a sea of people.

She opened the windows. A familiar smell invaded her senses, the smell of saffron, mixed in milk, soothing her soul. Her mother's soft hand on her head as she lay under the stars on her cot in the summer months. Kesar's beautiful face bathed in tears, running towards her in the crowded market place. Rajjo wanted to run away in her past or run towards her future. She was trapped in her now; she was trapped in the sea of devotees, in an image, in her robes. She was trapped in the mirror that stared back at her decked-up like a Godwoman. She was trapped in the TV screens. She yearned for the old mango tree bordering her village. She'd heard the mangoes only got sweeter with each passing summer.

Harsh was appalled and amused at the same time as Rajjo descended from a balloon. As usual she looked breathtaking to him, familiar, with each and every line etched on her face as she spilled on his huge TV screen. The door opened suddenly before he could have his fill of her. Not quick enough to break his train of thought and switch to a sports channel, he knew his beautiful wife noticed Rajjo's close up on the TV screen before she turned her delicate shoulder clad in a fashionable white muslin slip.

The strong rumours of their affair weighed heavily on him as he tried to switch the channel nonchalantly. The rumours like wild weed spread in every unwanted corner, in the press, hushed inner circles, his own drawing room, but not once had his wife Upasana brought it up. Her perfectly arched brow on her milky white skin did not waver as she heard rumours floating around, low hanging nebulous clouds waiting to burst any minute.

Her silence on this topic both intrigued and irritated him. Over a period of time, he was sure about one thing; that his wife was a strange creature. She was quick to learn and slow to speak – truly a lethal combination. Her beautiful face looked at him through the dressing mirror. She was a wintry snow princess, with a lustrous pale skin, peaches and cream complexion. The media loved her poise, her hesitant fame as she posed with those strong features, a hooked nose and drooping baby eyes. They were a shade of brown, soft and vulnerable. If you saw her cross the street, her natural rose-coloured lips and angelic soft cocoa eyes arrested you.

The first time he met her, he wanted to protect the porcelain beauty, a helpless waif braving a storm. His attraction to her vulnerability was like a moth to a flame.

But with time he realized, this beautiful dove with the air of a tragic broken wing had mysteries woven around her that he still unravelled. Buried in a corner was an astuteness she chose not to wear. The helpless demeanour served her well to further her end. An heiress to a huge empire, the only daughter to one of the biggest political parties, she was groomed to find a good useful husband and strengthen the father's empire and political ambition. She moulded herself to play that part beautifully. Or maybe he looked for pathetic reasons to run away from her into Rajjo's arms, he was not sure. He stoked these conspiracy theories against his angelic wife to feed his guilt.

He took in her beautiful scented body and a sudden rush of long passionate nights spent with her blinded him. It cleared away shortly leaving a sad wilted fragrance, for although the initial year of lust brought them together, it never moved towards love. Many other things filled his time and soul but a part of him was still stuck under his wife's pillow. It slept under the curve of her cheek. He felt her vulnerability, he wanted to protect her, he wanted to punish himself, or then he wanted to blame her. In seven years of marriage he was still unable to understand her smile. He'd seldom seen her break out into a spontaneous laughter. Her face was always a mask of pleasantness with her smile pasted on. She braved every situation, issue, turmoil, rumours and celebration with the same smile. The winter she lost her mother, the summer her sister delivered a baby girl, the autumn she ran a cat under her Mercedes while she was reveresing the car out of the driveway or the spring when the first paper published a hush-hush rumour hinting that the stunning Godwoman was in an illicit relationship with the political heir – she had braved it all.

With time he suspected there was a sliver of steel that ran in that spine. And then there was a soft innocent denial. He was torn between his own theories about her.

Harsh remembered the first media report in the paper. He cursed the sun for climbing up into the sky and the reporter snooping into their bedroom! He had prepared his defence and hoped to find lies that will hold his marriage and buy him some time, but all she did after reading the report twice was to calmly finish her breakfast of papaya, pomegranate, eggs and orange juice.

After she finished reading, she instructed the help to dispose off all the newspapers piled up in the store, including the one on the table. 'A lot of trash is piling up lately,' was all she said to him. At that moment Harsh felt he was the trash she referred to.

The squeal from the television set brought him back to the room. His gaze met hers again. She sat in front of the mirror, applying moisturizer to her ivory smooth skin. Her hands moved in measured circular strokes. Her thick lush mane sat perfectly around her shoulders, cut in the familiar layered pattern, always fallling in the same way. He wondered if she stuck it there. A perfect doll, she never had a bad hair day. He wanted to see her with messed up hair, burning in anger or crying out in passion. But he was disappointed on that count.

The initial years of marriage were marked with passionate lovemaking and frantic coupling and made him realize that she never lost control. She somehow had the genie in the bottle. The lid was tightly shut even when she screamed her release, panting in the throes of an orgasm. Be the angle of her head falling, or the arch of her back, her creamy naked legs circling his waist, she was a perfect lover but her perfection made him lose interest over a period of time.

Or was it something else? A guilty voice whispered.

Harsh buried the voice and reclaimed his theory.

She made a little sound as she turned on the low stool, to take off her lacy robes, dressed only in a singlet, her full breast and cleavage revealed, she stared at him with a question. Harsh felt no stirring or rush of blood, just a complete stillness as he prepared to erupt and explode inside Rajjo.

Their eyes locked as they shared a moment, a tension rose inside him. He dreaded this pregnant silence – usually it was followed by a statement or a question.

'I want to visit her, this Durga Maa,' she removed her bra as two beautiful breasts spilled out. He felt a stirring, an animalistic reaction to her body. She slipped over a scrap of satin, leaving nothing much to the imagination.

Harsh was knocked out at her request and the assault on his senses. This was the last thing he'd expected. Harsh knew he had to stay calm and breathe. He was not ready to discuss this with her yet. It was a matter of time that she explored the rumours.

'Since when did you start believing in Godmen types?' He teased her, switching channels yet again.

She laughed at his playful question. He knew it was strained. There was something he could not put a finger on.

'Since you started following them.'

Harsh gave a dry laugh. The noose tightened around his neck. She suspected something, someone must have told her about the secret rendezvous. He was ready with a denial but she never asked him the question. He had always dreaded the moment his wife asked him about the affair. He had practised and rehearsed several answers and excuses, for could not take the risk of admitting his relationship unless he had a future with Rajjo. But Rajjo had made it clear there was none.

He needed to keep the peace at home for now. The wheels needed to churn, the engine needed to move on. A lot was riding on the merger between Upasana's and his father. He was a pawn playing his part. He was ready to rebel only if he found a just cause. He cringed at his cowardice but he was ready to live with it for now.

'Why do you want to go to her?'

'They say if anyone has a problem in life, or Lord Shani is not favourable – seeking her blessings can remove those impediments and you can get what you desire. So many people swear by her power. She has helped millions. They believe her…'

Harsh smiled, 'And what is it that you desire?'

She stared at him longer than usual. Like she orchestrated this entire conversation to come to this point and savoured this moment – her honeyed-eyes trapping him.

'I want to pray to her for a son. I want to ask her for you to impregnate me with a baby.'

That was the second time in the last two minutes he found himself at a loss for words. The noise of a monitor beeping a flatline perhaps was all he heard. Was it his affair, or his non-compliance to give an heir? Did she really want to see Rajjo about a son? Harsh was unable to wrap his head around this.

He realized she was sitting next to him, very close. She smelt of daises, soft and beautiful. From somewhere in the quagmire of guilt, panic and confusion he found his voice.

'I ve told you, Sana, I don't want to have a child till I have figured out what I want in life.'

'What does that have to do with anything? Give me a child to keep myself busy when you are too busy doing things that occupy you…'

Harsh wanted to gently open her head and take a sneak peek of what really went on in there. Her tone laced with suggestion, he was unable to comprehend. Why would she always play games? Or then she was just making an innocent statement. Harsh turned away from her. He was not ready to delve into any of it. Upasana, sensing her husband's hesitance, moved away gracefully.

Harsh sensed Upasana's patience. It weighed on him, growing heavier by the day. She waited for him to come to her, to make love to her, to impregnate her. They had not made love for the past six months, as she did not want to be on the pill anymore.

She was not going to let him enter her if he was not ready to impregnate her. It sounded brutal, but just. She was going to wait patiently for him to be ready. It suited Harsh as he only burned for Rajjo.

The clock was ticking and Harsh had a lot to lose. He was going to run the PVP party that was all set to win the election next year. His political ambition was his to make or destroy. For now he just wanted to be.

He looked at his wife who had gone back to the mirror. She was rubbing the cream on her cheeks again. Her soft brown eyes were empty. Like they were just gazing out of the window at a bunch of daisies – with no hint of a strenuous conflict. She was either a goddess or a witch, perhaps a bit of both. Ironically, he was the only one who did not know.

Upasana, just eight years old, sat all by herself. It was a special day as she laboriously decorated her room to welcome her new baby sister who was arriving from the hospital with her mother. She was going to get another playmate and she wanted to impress her. It had to be a girl as she hated boys and they were not as excited about dolls and other stuff. As per her wish, the servants had fixed twinkling fairy lights in her room – they sparkled as she opened the windows that brought in beautiful sunlight. The mango tree in front of her room happily greeted her. She could see the huge green gate and the long driveway where the car would appear later today carrying her mother and her newborn sister from the hospital.

She arranged her dolls perfectly, taking up the entire bed. They all sat waiting for the festivities to start. Just then her cousin peeped in through the door, and marvelled at the sight. 'It's so beautiful! I wish I could have my room done like this.'

Upasana preened as she brushed off some imaginary dirt from the sheet.

'The baby should be here any minute now. Grandma told me two hours back it was on its way. I am going to bring her right here as soon as they come.'

'What if it's a boy?'

'It's a girl,' she said in a defiant manner.

Just then, little cousin pointed, making a face, 'Pigeon shit! Your little sister will run away!' She giggled. Upasana turned to see the offending mark on her pristine white wall. She liked to keep the windows open. Perhaps the pigeons came in through the widows, and hid behind the curtains.

'But I wish the birds visited my room,' squealed the little girl in delight.

Something dark and beastly boiled inside. She asked her cousin to leave the room. She sat there all by herself, wondering where the nest was. She remembered two summers back her grandmother had got the curtain rods cleaned and one nest was hiding behind the curtain rod as an open ventilator sat right next to it.

She howled. The servants came in running. She pointed towards the curtain beam. 'There is a nest…'

Hurriedly, one servant climbed a chair and reached out. The fluttering of wings, some disturbance – and there it was, the startled pigeon. With tired eyes, hefty and bulky, it refused to fly away. The servant clapped and shooed and forced her to fly out of the window and settle on the mango tree right outside the window, as she was reluctant to fly futher away.

The servant dug out three eggs from the corner, holding them carefully in his hands. Upasana marvelled at the shape, the texture, and the delicate shade of the eggs, the colour of pearls her mother wore.

The pigeon watched her with a stillness like it was frozen. It watched the little girl walk towards the window and climb to the windowsill. She dangled her delicate arm in the air, her palm carrying her precious eggs. It forgot to blink, move or twitch.

In that stillness she dropped the first warm and perfect egg to the ground and it cracked. She felt the bird looking at her, pleadingly. Her little heart fluttered with pity but she was taught better. The pigeon moved a bit closer to her, hoping that the little girl would have mercy and spare the rest of the eggs.

She let go of the second egg, watching it fall two floors down and shatter on the same spot as the earlier one. And then she dropped the third one.

The only thing she heard was the silence and the gentle rustling of leaves.

The gardener limped towards the broken eggs and looked up at her. Upasana screamed, 'Don't clean it!'

As expected, the pigeon flew down, to where the broken eggs lay. Splattered on the floor in a mess, a colour of yellow liquid on red baked bricks. The pigeon hobbled around, walked around, flapped the wings. She could feel its pain.

A tear escaped her eye as she saw the pigeon and her broken eggs from her window. She believed in balance, she believed in justice, however tough it may be.

Her little cousin came and stood next to her at the window. Just then the gates opened and a gleaming car drove in.

The little girl whispered in Upasana's ear. 'Your grandmom is crying. It was a dead baby.'

'It was a boy?' Upasana whispered back, as her cousin nodded.

Upasana went back to staring at the pigeon hovering around the eggs.

Finally it flew away and disappeared into the foliage of the mango tree and the eggs were swept away. It was her secret, apart from the mango tree no one knew about it. Upasana smiled and shut the window firmly on the dark rustling tree.

# 4

THE hum of the powerful air conditioning in her Rolls Royce soothed her. Rajjo tried to calm herself repeatedly as her car swished through the lanes of Ahmedabad. The eagerness, the anxiety, the feverish desire made her impatient. She wanted to fly out of the window and be next to him. It was almost one month and twenty-eight days since she had seen him last. She brought the large brown hand mirror to her face and inspected herself yet again. Clad in a black hijaab, her entire body hidden behind the cloak, her eyes stared into the mirror like a stranger. Devi gaily pointed to the crowds, from the front seat. The crowds mingled outside shops selling kites and spools of kite thread, *manja,* laced with ground glass and bound by adhesive. The enthusiastic *manja* makers were dyeing kite strings with bright colours and ground glass. Customers were checking if the *manja* was sturdy enough to outlast the opponent in the kite fight!

'It is the day when the sun starts to travel northwards, marking the decline of winter. The days become longer and the skies clearer, the breeze becomes cooler. Devi could feel the anticipation and joy mounting in her mistress's voice.

Rajjo wanted to laugh and celebrate this festival with hundreds of people outside in the street. She could feel him tasting her and she shivered. She was going to see him in less than an hour. She wanted the time to run. 'Uttarayan marks the awakening of the gods from their deep slumber.' She sighed.

'The kings and Nawabs had nothing better to do and they decided to fight with kites to entertain themselves.' Devi jabbered playfully, happy to see Rajjo in a talkative mood.

Suddenly Rajjo saw a flash of Kesar; the vulnerable nine year old, telling her not to leave him and go, running after her in the crowded market street. His little heart breaking into pieces. She had not gone back for him. But she knew one day she will. Kesar loved kites. He never flew them in the skies, he kept them like precious postcards, marking the summers as he grew up. His mother wanted him to save the kites for someday when he grew up. She wondered if Kesar flew those kites now.

'They take it very seriously!' she heard Devi say. 'Months before the festival, homes turn into kite-producing factories, and all the family members start making kites. We should introduce this as a meditation technique in the ashram. Shani kites…,' she laughed at her own joke as Devi added dryly, 'And then all your siblings will swoop in to manage that factory.' Rajjo heard the bitterness in her voice. Devi having spent the last ten years by Rajjo's side had earned the right to be bitter for her.

'Its hard work, Devi,' Rajjo added in a placating tone. 'Kite-making is hard work. The glue is stirred for a long time, paper and glue is cut and then stuck. Strings are coated with rice and glass powder. This simple thing also draws blood. It's important to them.' Devi gave Rajjo a look.

'We made kites back home in our village. Sheru loved to fly them.'

The simple days came rushing back and the Rolls Royce stopped like an arrogant bird at the entrance of a small bylane. Rajjo was supposed to walk and get lost in the crowd where he would be waiting in a nondescript house.

'I will be in the hotel. The guards are going to be a foot behind you in plainclothes. Kripa and Shailesh are on duty.' Rajjo nodded as Devi sped away after giving the instructions. Rajjo adjusted her burkha, covered her face, clutched her little purse. She was ready to get lost in the crowd, as she proceeded to meet her lover.

His trademark khadi kurta, leather chappals, overgrown beard, a low slung cap, he stood in the shadows and waited. Harsh Wardhan wanted to chuckle at the thought of waiting for his girlfriend in disguise. His trusted guardsmen watched the streets. He could not wait to take her in his arms.

His wife had to attend to some urgent family business in London so Harsh had seized the opportunity and immediately planned to see Rajjo. She was around Gujarat and this was the closest and fastest rendezvous away from prying eyes that they could manage. An old peeling picture of Rajjo stared at him, stuck on the stained wall of a grocery seller's store across the narrow lane. He could feel his heart racing as he thought of her with him. Was it her eyes, her soul, her body or was it destiny that always had Harsh in knots. Despite a wife and marriage of five years, he waited to see her like an adoloscent waiting for a glimpse of his first love.

Things were already getting tougher, with the latest party merger between PVP and his own party. They were slated to win the elections next year. His father and uncles expected him to appease the in-laws enough for a smooth merger and a distribution of portfolios within the party. He was supposed to don the mantle anytime soon. Doused in the stink of political ambition, they had made this alliance revolting for Harsh, but how was he to tell them it was making it difficult for him to breathe, let alone live? He just wanted to to travel, explore each day, or perhaps be a student of literature. He wanted to take off from the world. A gypsy at heart, he dreamt of living in a world far away woven in the hues of a perfect delicate rainbow. He waited to break free and overthrow the mantle of his lineage that bound him in chains and party positions. The pressure of coupling with his wife to produce an heir, the noose of vice president to the PVP party tightening around his neck. The only time he could breathe was in the arms of his beloved Rajjo. Now his life was all about waiting to live a stolen moment with his Rajjo.

Dusk gave way to night as he waited. The sky was dotted with multiple kites, and a few moments later it was cloaked in darkness.

She was supposed to walk around for forty minutes and then reach here but it was little over an hour – Harsh was beginning to worry. Thankfully she crossed him. He smelt her before he saw her. She continued to lead and he fell in line. His heart singing, he followed her. The house was just a few blocks away. She knew the address. It had a narrow green wooden door that opened into the street. She went through. Harsh followed, latching the door behind. A cursory glance assured him the guards were in place, they were not followed. Finally they were alone.

The interior was dark and lit up with lamps, lending an old-world charm to the place. He called out to her, his voice echoed. She did not answer. He made his way to the living room, lights and shadows playing hide and seek in dreamy corners of the charming house. He tumbled upon her discarded hijaab and followed the seductive trail of clothes; her saree, her petticoat, her blouse, her delicate lace panties and her bra was the last thing he picked up. Where the train ended, he saw her delicate foot, toe nails painted the colour of vibrant poppy fields. She stood like a flower, naked and ethereal at the doorway. Her full breast ached for his touch. She was even more beautiful than the last time he left her. Unable to speak, he went to her and tried to kiss her as she turned away.

'You cancelled on my birthday…' the husky voice wrenched his heart.

His mouth ached to feel her, he tried to kiss her again, but Rajjo turned her face away as she stood at the door. Harsh devoured the rest of her as she stood there suspended between pain and pleasure. She gasped and moaned, as Harsh tasted every bit of her; she was going to melt away standing right there and so was he. Before they could lose themselves, he filled her up with a thrust as she stood – backed up to the wall. Harsh lost himself in her softness. Time stretched and paused, ran forward and came back in a circle till he cried his release. This was it, his literature, his poetry, his freedom. With Rajjo he was the Harsh running in the fields barefoot, the wind caressing his face.

The colours of bougainvillea, sweet and alluring. With Rajjo the rain tasted syrupy.

'Sorry,' he muttered as he picked her up and tried to kiss her. She evaded him once more. She was a fiery childwoman in his arms, he knew she would not allow him to have her soul till he repented not meeting her till the last breath.

The blissful two days passed in a haze for Rajjo. Another night arrived with illuminated box kites strung on a line adorning the dark sky, celebrating love. Harsh stood on the terrace of the old house staring up at the sky, smoking his favourite brand of cigarette. 'These are called Tukkals,' he pointed to the kites in the sky adding the touch of splendour.

The days were filled with lovemaking, eating traditional food, the delicious *undhiyo* aroma of vegetables and the succulent taste of sesame balls and *chikki*. Rajjo loved the taste of the food mingled with the sweat smell of her beloved. One more day until both went back to their respective worlds! Rajjo to her Gods and him to his political party and wife. She hated the Gods even more. She wanted more than a secret rendezvous. Harsh circled her in his arms and whispered again, 'Sorry to miss your birthday. Upasana was sick.'

'And me?' muttered Rajjo. She still refused to let him kiss her. Depriving him as he deprived her. She knew it would kill him to not kiss her but she was going to make him feel the pain she felt. 'You know she desperately wants a baby and my continued resistance is taking a toll on her health now.' Rajjo looked away. Tears pricked somewhere just behind her eyes and threatened to spill over. The thought of Harsh making a family with another woman crushed her soul.

'And no matter how much I beg you, you don't want to come away with me. You are destroying all three of us…' Harsh tried to stop not wanting to ruin the moment. But it was too late. Rajjo turned away. 'So for that you will sleep with her and give her a baby?'

'I am not having a baby with her…I haven't touched her in a long time.' Frustration was creeping in. Rajjo, not reassured, this time moved away. Every time both of them wanted a bit more. No one told them love was a hungry beast that had to be fed constantly. Until you throw in your heart, your eyes, your soul it is not satiated. Rajjo was reminded of the fact that he shared a bed with another woman. He was a kiss away. An unbearable ache accosted her.

The last day was spent in strained silence. Harsh wanted to change the charged atmosphere and step out. Thankfully they had word that it was safe to go without the hijaab up to the market square. Rajjo piled up her hair, lined her eyes with kohl, draped a scarf mirroring the colour of the sky and made an effort to enjoy this stolen day with her beloved.

Harsh stared at the beautiful Rajjo, her familiar beauty settling around his heart, 'I want to visit the small temple outside the market area. It's a durga temple…mother said to give offerings…' Rajjo smiled knowingly. 'It's not just your mother, you too.' Unlike her, Harsh was a believer. 'Of course we'll go. And I want to buy a kite.' Harsh smiled at her excitement.

They walked along the trails lazily. His cap on his head. A regular nondescript tourist couple, the guards had done a recce of the area many times over to allow them this freedom. They waited for the old kite seller as they handed him the spindle they'd bought. The *manja* maker on the roadside got busy preparing it. He ran his padded fingers expertly and they stood and watched. That was the moment Rajjo knew she wanted more. She had the world, fame and riches, she had given up God, and the only thing she wanted was love. She could hear the shrieking of the train on the railway tracks in the village back home. She was a little girl telling her sisters she wanted to grow up and elope. A few young boys sat by the handle and spun it slowly to ensure that the sun wrapped around the thread evenly. Rajjo watched the thread baking in the sun while Harsh went into the small temple across the road, disappointed that Rajjo had not accompanied him. He was forever trying for her to make peace with her Lord, 'You will thank me for introducing him back into your life,' Harsh winked at her. She rolled her eyes as a loving blush sat on her cheek. 'I do that for a living – I don't believe in any of this. I sell him for a living. If I find faith in him, I will starve!' Harsh smiled at his stubborn fool. 'There is no point reasoning with a rock. Faith finds you when you are ready to receive it.'

'I DON'T need it. Haven't you heard I sell deliverance to his devotees?' Her arrogance was evident in every word, as she shot back with a smile. Harsh bowed his head mockingly as Rajjo laughed. She threw her head back and arched her neck. Her laughter rang in his ear and he never wanted it to stop. Still drinking in her laughter, he disappeared inside the hustling bustling temple.

Rajjo decided to spin the wheel with the young boy. He reminded her of Kesar. The late afternoon sun was warm, seeping in, thawing her back and drying the *manja* as they headed to an adjoining outlet to select colourful kites. Walking along the streets it looked like gaudy dollops placed outside to entice the passersby.

Harsh crossed the road, smiling at her, turning the spindle. She was complete and happy. The sun, the wheel and Harsh where all that she needed to feel fulfilled, yet there was a giant gorge inside that refused to fill up. Purple-hued bile came rushing back inside and ate up the sun in seconds. The well-being she felt a minute ago was gone as it dawned on her that tonight was the last night with Harsh before a long separation.

They were in the old city, where a sea of people flew kites from their rooftops in celebration. Waves of rainbow-coloured kites stretched across the blue sky. Rajjo had her kite in the sky as well. Their eyes met as they tugged at their respective kites soaring in the air, passion quivering between them. She was finally going to give him the kiss. He stared at her with an answering dark hunger and passion. The sky changed colour, like a tailor layering one beautiful satin after another on an underskirt. Just then, Harsh's guard came rushing up on the terrace with a phone and a feeling of dread took over. It was his wife, Upasana.

His face hardened, he turned away from Durga's keen gaze. A vehement feeling took over, she wanted to scream and cry, all she did was let go of the string, her kite disengaged, unanchored just floated in the sky. They exchanged one last look.

'I will be in the room, I have to leave within the hour.' He turned away from Rajjo and left her standing like that, much like the kite floating aimlessly in the sea of kites up above.

'Good bye. You go, I will stay. We were supposed to stay another day. I want to fly another kite,' Rajjo heard herself say out aloud with a defiant look on her face. He held her gaze for the longest time and then stepped forward to hold her close one last time. He kissed her forehead, with a long wanting sigh, he whispered, 'Till later…' A yawning grief sat in her heart as she looked at the colourful sky and wept in agony, staring at her colourful kite still trying to make way in the sky and fading away from her sight. Eventually it was a floating speck in the sky and then it was gone, swallowed by the giant blue expanse.

Standing alone on the beautiful terrace where they say angels sat on a full moon night, Rajjo was beginning to feel the rage within. His absence was unbearable to her. She tried to calm her heart with the beautiful moments of togetherness. Soon his voice took over her mind. Her feet started moving in a circular fashion, revolving from right to left around the heart. She remembered that beautiful day when she spotted a rose outside her window, the dawn was special. Harsh surprised her with a trip – he wanted her to experience something – the Sufi dervishes. The place and time had a silken gauze over it, what she remembered clearly were the dervishes in their wide skirts moving in circular motions, they were spinning their body in repetitive circles. Symbolic imitation of the planets in the solar system.

Rajjo was spinning faster, wanting to get closer to the moment when he was beside her. He sat holding her hand, wanting her soul to drink in the nectar, to abandon the egos and personal desires through music, reaching closer to all creation. She had laughed at him again, dismissing his sincere efforts to warm up her cold heart. But now as she moved in a circular motion, she was closer to him. His voice echoed in her ear. She could feel the semazen's camel hair hat sitting on her head, representing the tombstone of ego, and the wide white skirt swirling around her in a circular motion – her ego's shroud. Her arms now open as she whirled, one hand pointing to the ground, the other pointing to the skies, ready to receive god's beneficience, embracing all humanity with love. She wanted to stop but the whirling had taken over her mind and body. She was not in control anymore. 'Semazen conveys God's spiritual gift to those who are witnessing the Sema, the customary dance performance through which the performers, the semazens, reach the source of all perfection – and send the message that human being is created from love in order to love.' Harsh whispers echoed in her head till there was nothing else but a beautiful white light blinding her eyes. There was no earth beneath, there was no sky above, as she was suspended from a fathomless place. Bathed in silvery moonlight she was floating far away, closer to the mango trees in her village, unable to stop herself until a hand held her tight and dragged her all the way back to the terrace. Icy cold water numbed her senses, till the whirling stopped, the chaos within calmed. Devi's soothing whispers brought her back into her mind and her senses. A crackling noise erupted in her dead ear. The silence was broken in her deaf ear after a decade. She tried to whisper into Devi's ear as she passed out. 'The terrace with kites and twinkling lights invites angels and lovers on a full moon night.'

# 5

RAJJO stood at the highest level of the Mantap Hall from where she could reach out and gather fistful of clouds from the sky. She was waiting for the sermon and other formalities to get over so she could retire for the day. Lately her days seemed to drag on endlessly.

For once she wanted to believe in her own abilities. It was ironic, she had earned her power by selling a promise to her thousands of devotees that she could remove impediments by Lord Shani through her divine guidance. But when it came to her own life it was a losing battle. Soon after, Rajjo could hear the chanting of Sanskrit shlokas. It was a sign that they were expecting her on stage. As Rajjo climbed down the circular stairs, her face didn't give away any of the tension she was feeling. She was getting into the skin of Durga.

The lights were dimmed in the main hall, so the devotees could soak in the spiritual experience. Rajjo made her way to a smaller room. She sat there in her characteristic black robes without any makeup. Her mind wavered, a thought flashed, she did not want to do this session today. Her stomach churned. The static in her dead ear left an aftertaste of stale garlic on her tongue. A mass of resentment floated around. Quick to read her own bodily reaction, Rajjo knew her visitor or seeker was no ordinary person. Perhaps she should send them away. Curiosity trumped over caution as Rajjo readied to meet her patron.

Upasana was summoned into the small intimate room. The lighting was deliberately low, incense and flowers adorned the Gods placed in one corner. In the middle of the room sat Rajjo, focusing on her breath. A few of her coterie members sat on a couch placed unobtrusively next to a wall. Upasana counted five people sitting in the background and a devotee sitting in front of Durga. She squeezed herself in the room and found a low stool to sit on. She was quiet as a mouse, lest she disturb the concentration in the room. Upasana wanted to chuckle aloud. She bit her lip. These untimely chuckles besieged her when she was nervous or a little excited. Unlikely places like a funeral meeting was also a place where this affliction hit her. With an effort she bit her lip harder and thought of painful things in her life to get rid of that urge to laugh. It all seemed like a theatrical mini set as if she was in a role-play. Upasana focused back to her immediate surroundings and forced herself to look at Rajjo.

The moment their eyes met, Upasana knew that Rajjo had recognized her, her game face on. As the two women continued to exchange looks, the daggers were drawn but she was not going to back out now. Rajjo extended her arm as a challenge for Upasana to come and sit on the stool in front of her. Upasana, without wavering, accepted the challenge. Rajjo was holding her hand like a doctor checked a patient's pulse. Upasana wanted to chuckle yet again. This was one of her better ideas and she thrived to see the drama she had created. She was alive and throbbing in the middle of it all. 'Your biggest fear?' she heard Rajjo ask in a clear timbre. 'I am scared of water amongst many other things.' Upasana whispered, her voice shook just a little bit, surprised she was telling the truth. Perhaps she wanted to test the Godwoman along with the other things she had come here for.

Rajjo's liquid gold eyes met her silvery gaze. 'Breathe for me, focus on the breath, see it, feel it, let it fill you, take God's name, you are in his care, you are in safe hands and now with that faith you walk down a long circular staircase.' Her voice washed over her in gentle waves. She could suck you in. Upasana had to give her that. What was she doing? Everyone in the semi-lit room was under her spell, yet somehow Upasana knew she was in control.

Rajjo's voice flooded the room, 'Start opening the doors you see, take the name of Lord, hold my hand and open the doors… Stop testing and start trusting.' Immediately Upasana cleared her head and followed her husky voice. It was too late to back out now. The cat had the mouse by the neck.

Rajjo put her hands on either side of Upasana's head. The force of her energy was warming her up. Upasana noticed Rajjo's beautiful skin and piercing eyes. Did he caress her skin for long lazy afternoons? Upasana hated her straight, sharp, slender nose. It was the nose she had always wanted. Rajjo dropped her hands and continued to chant the name of Lord at regular intervals. It was calming. Upasana closed her eyes, and muttered in Rajjo's ear, 'Leave my husband and let us live happily.'

Alarmed, Rajjo opened her eyes. Defiant, Upasana challenged her. Rajjo closed her eyes yet again and repeated the instructions, lulling them into a calm state. Taking them to a warm day, birds chirping, making them sit in a sunflower field. As they enjoyed the bird song and Upasana felt the yellow petals melt in her hand, Rajjo whispered in her ear, 'Who are you?'

Upasana was climbing down a circular staircase, the light fading away to dampness and darkness. She crossed snow-clad mountains and dried-up rivers. She wanted to scream and run back, but she could not stop herself from sliding further down till she stopped on a familiar face. It was a lady with sad droopy eyes who spoke in a peculiar child-like voice. Her voice reverberated in the room, a strange texture, 'I am a willowy young woman in a homespun skirt. It is America in the eighteen-fifties, Midwest – Prairies. I am wearing a bonnet with a satin ribbon beneath my chin. Blood red. The bonnet makes me happy. A rivulet is running next to me as I look at it, the cool beautiful water gushes past me. And I see him, my face recoils with fear. And then I am old, in mourning. Wearing a black dress, everyone is sad beside me, but my heart is singing like it would sing in spring after a cold long winter. A tall window let in a faded sunlight that fell on the coffin. It was my husband's coffin and I wanted to sing with happiness. I was filled with hope. The terror was leaving me and disappearing out of the tall pale window.'

'You killed your violent husband with a poisonous herb and you got away!' Rajjo whispered into her ear.

Upasana wanted to tear something apart and get out of this scene, her whole body in flames while someone was stripping her soul naked. Rajjo had played her. She opened her eyes with a jerk. Rajjo smiled at her calmly and stated, 'You live with him, your husband. He has issues with you, in God's name you are a good couple, you have to forgive him some and he has to forgive a lot! Meditate on this chant. You need his forgiveness in this lifetime and he needs yours. The Shani mantra will remove the impediments you may face in reaching your goal.'

'There is another woman. Will you give me a chant to remove this other woman who has this terrible hold on my husband? She is sucking out my life, our love, our child, who we want but because of her we cannot have. You think Lord Shani will forgive her for snatching someone's husband?' Upasana dared Rajjo to respond. Before Rajjo could retort, Upasana continued in a menacing tone…

'I have thoughts sometimes to kill him even today. I can't explain the violence I feel towards him. But perhaps I should wait and watch what this woman will do next. Perhaps there is a lot I can do which I am not doing. I need your help to sort this out' She bowed and folded her hands in front of Rajjo mockingly. Rajjo wanted to run and hide. She wanted shelter from these accusations. She may have guided her to her past, but this woman could burn her future. She wanted to trap her, but Upasana had cornered her. Who was the cat amongst the pigeons?

'Let it pass…It will all work out for the best,' whispered Rajjo in a shaky voice.

'I will remember your kind, calm and clear voice. I will carry it in my heart. I believe you are a woman too and you completely understand my plight, like you are a part of it.' Rajjo turned her face away.

Upasana knew coming here was the best decision she had taken in a long long time. It felt great. It felt like she had chewed her up and spat her out in her own little religious room. With a victorious smile she took her leave, leaving behind a guilt that smelt like an expensive perfume, a scent that entered every nook and corner and every crease in Rajjo's room, her mouth and her soul.

Rajjo was travelling between her ashrams around the Gujarat belt. This was the third she had visited in the last two month. This was 36 km southwest of Ahmedabad, near a village.

The ashram sat behind zealously guarded perimeter walls, was a green oasis of peepul, neem and banyan trees growing around the main building. The walls of the buildings were adorned with larger-than-life images of Durga and excerpts from her teaching. The symbolism of Lord Shani could be seen with his idol placed in the middle of the reception areas, bedecked with oil and flowers. Nearby, the Sabarmati river quietly flowed, passing the godly ashram and devotees sitting around in meditation.

Rajjo travelled from one ashram to the other looking for peace of mind. Nothing made sense anymore. Something had changed the night she saw angels and lovers under the starlit sky and her heart moved in cosmic circles. The pirouettes she took wound her up in silken threads of love. The beautiful gardens did not soothe her. The chanting millions did not drown her sorrow. Her empire was not enough to hold her back from meeting Harsh. After her meeting with Upasana, Rajjo knew the wise thing was to walk away, but then who said she was wise. Wisdom came at a price and Rajjo was not ready to pay.

A tumultuous year had passed by and strangely Rajjo was feeling more detached than ever. She took a calming breath and forced the beautiful surroundings to lull her senses. The deer and elephants spotted in the flowering foilage spread over 65 acres mocked her. The winding footpaths, peaceful lake and beautiful buildings left her feeling barren. Her days were spent agonizing over Harsh and their secret meetings. She yearned for him every minute he spent away from her. She tortured herself about every minute he spent with his wife.

To keep her mind sane, she had started to do menial jobs in the ashram. Karam and Rano were finding it extremely difficult to explain her erratic behaviour to the media or her devotees. They were not going to hold fort in Rajjo's absence for long. Rajjo walked on eggshells and it was going to fall apart as the clock ticked on. She felt the churning was starting inside her heart once again.

As she casually walked barefoot by the calm lake, the calm and deep waters made her shiver. Rajjo knew that many sinister secrets and strategies were mushrooming in the lofty gardens of her empire. She knew they were dripping from the mango trees along with the luscious fruit and lurked behind the flames of candles and incense sticks that lit up the ashram in the evenings. She could smell them in the air. Her siblings and family was carrying them in their hearts. No one could be trusted. With this empire that fed hundreds, many lifes were at stake and they were not going to let go of Rajjo so easily.

Recently, Rajjo found out that her own brother, Sheru, had been in touch with Upasana the whole of last year. They told her Upasana visited his ashram twice a month. What cure did she seek? She was a wronged, meek housewife in the background and that only made Rajjo more uncomfortable. Ever since Upasana had visited her in the ashram, Rajjo had been in a state of discomfort.

All she was left with was her acute faithlessness, her longing and this empire that was eating away at her like a termite. She longed to go back under that starlit sky once more, and disappear in the swirls of the wide white skirts of the dervishes.

Rajjo woke up early in anticipation. She looked forward to an afternoon with Harsh today by the lake. There was a secluded spot and she was going to pack lunch for both of them. Harsh often met her there and they made love under the cloudy sky, with the smell of jasmine and the silent lake watching them with a smile. She loved that spot. She had called Devi and informed her about the meeting. She had also instructed her to pack a picnic basket for her. They were going to have a light lunch of sandwiches and the leftovers would be fed to the birds after their lazy lovemaking. Perhaps she could pack some champagne instead of wine.

Rajjo stepped out in her little courtyard where she had personally supervised a rose garden. The perfume and lovely fragrance of roses sweetened the leaf buds of the flowering plants. Peacocks and white-feathered birds adorned her little garden. She sat beneath the shade of the banyan tree and created a flowery fantasy about the afternoon that was to come. Bathed and oiled in scents, draped in red silk, kohl in her eyes, moist rose-tinted lips, Rajjo waited for Harsh.

Hurried footsteps alerted her to Karam's arrival. Devi hid behind them in the shadows like she did not want to be seen. Rajjo loved that about her. Her need to be invisible, Devi saw and heard the most.

Karam had a strange look on his face and Rajjo did not want to hear what he was about to say to her. Before she could cover her ears Karam spat out, 'Harsh is not meeting you today as he was supposed to. He is in Delhi. You met him last week.' Karam spoke slowly like he was talking to a child. A dreadful feeling rose in her lungs, or was it bile? It happened to her again. How could she be so wrong? She was convinced it was the day and time they had fixed to meet. Devi stepped out from the shadows with a phone in hand. Harsh was on the line. She stuck the phone to her ear. Harsh spoke to her in a soothing voice. Telling her he was in Delhi, they would meet soon and his heart was beating for her. He continued to talk, like a mother singing a lullaby, soothing her, telling her about his day.

Rajjo knew they were all worried for her. The rose scent and the spidery web were disappearing, and bitter dark dread was filling her up. She was getting blurred in the head. Something told her this was not the first time. She could hear it in Harsh's soothing notes, she could see it in Karam's compassionate gaze and she could see it in Devi's shadow.

'Bring me the picnic basket.' Rajjo ordered Devi, as she stood up after returning the phone. Devi was ready with it nevertheless. If Rajjo asked her for something, Devi would get it, be it the moon, the stars or a piece of her flesh. Rajjo took the basket and walked out barefoot. She was going to sit by the lake and feed the bread crumbs to the birds, she was going to drink a bit and she was going to lie down on the grass for a while. She was going to swallow the green of the grass, the blue of the water and the yellow of the temple flowers. She wanted to run away from who she was, just for an afternoon. No one stopped her as she disappeared in the luscious gardens.

Karam saw her disappear into the trees, wearing a silken robe – the red silk like a beautiful stroke of paint against the brown and green of trees. She was drowning, and perhaps it was time to save Rajjo from her own self, before it was too late.

Rajjo stood on the terrace of her complex. It was the second Saturday of the month. Thousands of devotees gathered in the ground in front of her for a darshan. Rajjo had come out for the darshan after four months.

She had not been meeting Harsh. Rajjo had called off their relationship two months ago, in response to her sanity being threatened.

The crowds were swelling. Rano and Karam stood next to her like proud parents. Devi stood a step behind. Devi saw the smug faces of the two people standing next to Rajjo and knew they had no idea that the storm was coming. Only she knew, and that gave her joy. The two thought this adulation would soothe Rajjo's breaking heart. Rajjo was always energized and drunk on the power of her devotees for days after such congregations. But this time, Devi could see she was unmoved, but perhaps the two could not. The devotees started chanting. As the chanting grew louder, a wolf's howl echoed in her deaf ear relentlessly. Rajjo looked for cover as if under attack by the chorus. Rajjo moved aside to sit inside the shaded area, away from the direct adulation.

Rano approached her with a diary for the day. 'Purshottam and party are here for the meeting. They will help against the allegations for land allotment.'

Karam continued, 'Upasana's father is behind it, they have started taking action even before they have come to power.' Rano gave him a warning glance.

'Well, and some good news, the five-campus university plan is approved. We can have 55 schools from pre-primary to high schools across the country. Also, along with Durga channel, we have the permissions to float another one, Maa Durga and all our products and services will benefit from it. This afternoon we can go over everything and in the evening Karam has the update on the luxury resort. In fact, you can visit it next month yourself.' Rano was giving her toys to play with.

Devi chuckled. The dance they were performing had no audience.

Karam stepped forward, 'The resort is a perfect marriage of spirituality and luxury. The zen environment with bamboo trees, water bodies, peacocks, Buddha busts, mood lighting also packs in everything that a luxury holiday would comprise: swimming pool, cottages and great food.'

Rajjo could hear the chanting on the speakers, the voices were drowning her. She was up in flames. She was burning. It was time for her to save her soul or to perish. She wanted a way out, perhaps there was none. Perhaps this was the destiny she had to follow. She had risen from the ashes and created this mammoth beast, she had it in her power to soar to new heights. She was not going to quit. She was not going to melt. She was going to unlove and detangle her soul from him. The swirls of the cosmic cycle, trapped her, made her forget her hatred and her business, her maya and her faithlessness. Like a chant she repeated over and over, this was the only truth, she seeked nothing more.

Rajjo sat in the Radha Gardens, with parrots and other birds nesting in the thick foliage of banyan trees, her mother oiling her hair. A tradition she cherished as a child. The garden was replete with a pair of elephants, a pair of geese, some rabbits and the exotic birds that were her mother's favourite. She chuckled like a child as beautiful birds flew over the lake. The tress swayed to the Sanskrit chanting from the temple gopuram. It was a course started by Rano where kids were trained in temple rituals. Rajjo did not understand any of it but it did make for good business and more money. Life had come a long way. She felt a searing pain as Saroj's sweet fingers touched her scalp. What ached her mother's heart, she wondered?

Saroj's heart still ached as she thought of her five children sitting around her, eating and bickering, enjoying the monsoons, sharing stories in the winter. How time had changed and here they were. She wanted to gather all five of them – Rano, Rajjo, Rikki, Reet and Sheru – take them back in time and huddle next to them. She heard Rajjo talk and her reverie was broken as her hand gently rubbed oil in her daughter's luscious hair. She found her voice and hoped her daughter heard her.

'Too much of anything is bad. It is a curse. Wrap up this empire before it eats you up.'

Saroj had seen the wealth come in, she had seen the family getting rich, and she had seen what it had done to of each one of them. She was worried the first time her daughter had come back to the village in a big glistening car and said she was here to take them all away. She was selling God and she had made a fortune. Saroj should have stopped her then but perhaps it was too late.

The empire her children nurtured had grown now and it held them in its shackles. She arrogantly looked at a mother defeated. She drove her children as slaves, making them forget the simple joys of calling out the weather, rolling in the hay or sitting around the courtyard waiting for the first monsoon shower. Saroj hated the Durga trust with a vengeance and if Saroj could give it a human form she would gouge the eyes out of it.

'I am not the only one eating from it. It has become Rano's dream. Reet's husband runs the factories, Rikki's father-in-law is expanding the manufacturing unit, Sheru, as you know, is doing a lot more than he is supposed to and that is going to stop. There are many who have toiled long and hard…' Rajjo said in a voice laced with an emotion that was hard to describe.

'In God's name you fleece them, in God's name your people commit crime, I worry for you... When his wrath comes.' Saroj's voice shook again with fear for her child.

'He has already done what he could and forgotten me, there is nothing to worry,' Rajjo cut Saroj's statement midway with a touch of vehemence. Saroj sighed as she pointed out to her daughter, 'You sit under this shade, sleep in silk and satin, bathe in milk and oil, and you think he has forgotten you? He is keeping you very much in his sight and you should be afraid of the day when he does forget you!'

'I sell him in the market place.' Scoffed Rajjo. 'Because he allows you…you are doing good for people, Rajjo, they believe you, and through you him!'

'I sell him! It's a sham.' Saroj smiled at her daughter's ignorance. Time was going to whisper in her ear what the others could not. The mother and daughter sat there without talking. Both defeated in their own way. Saroj's heart ached for her daughter yet again. She was always the troubled one. And then like a mother and daughter sharing a beautiful secret, Saroj whispered in her daughters ear,'Does he make you happy?' Rajjo looked at her as tears glistened in her eyes. 'Very'. Saroj sighed, 'So that's where you begin and that's where you end.'

Rajjo looked at her with fear, 'He belongs to another woman.' Saroj looked at her daughter and whispered, 'He belongs to her whose laughter sings in his heart.' A joy rose in Rajjo's stomach. Soothing her. Only a mother could take her demons away and fill her up with a warm well-being. But it was a forbidden dream. If she chose that over her present, she was going to bleed. It was best left this way, caught between a dream and a wish. One day they would meet under the starlit sky on a boat that danced on orange waters in Benaras. On the other side. She hoped it was enough to get through this lifetime.

Just then an agitated rustle broke the peace and tranquility of the moment. It was not the wind, but a furious Rano. Rajjo stared at her angry sister. Her pale skin coloured with some extreme emotion. Anger made her look even more flushed and beautiful. Age had already stolen a lot from her face and Rajjo wanted to hide her sister's beauty in a little wooden box and take it far away with her. Where time was unable to touch it. Rano had always been the emotional one. As a young sibling, she would move heaven and earth to be with Rajjo and makes things go her way. She was the one who had toiled night and day on Rajjo's thoughts and ideas and given them the shape of this spiritual empire. 'You need to meet Harsh and you need to tell his family to back off! We can't have anything to do with him anymore; they are slapping cases on us left right and centre! Don't let it spin out of control, Rajjo!'

At the mention of Harsh's name, Rajjo's cheeks flushed. Rano wanted to scream. He had a hold on her and Rano suspected they were secretly meeting. Rajjo had taken a decision to walk away from Harsh, but perhaps that was not enough. There had to be an end to all this, one way or the other. Rano was furious. She just wanted her sister back as a whole person. Whenever she came back from a rendezvous, she could see she had lost a little bit more of her to him. Rano struggled to keep Rajjo close. She wanted to gather all of her in a fist and never open it again. Link their little trusting hands together and run through familiar lanes in the village.

Rajjo, not perturbed with the outbursts, focused on the chanting that washed over her. 'Sit here and get a massage. Remember how we ran in the dusty streets. Ran from the fields, from our father, from the bridge, I ran from home, from my husband. I am not running away from this. I will deal with it.'

Rano knew when Rajjo returned to that part of their life that she could not push her further. It was time to back down now and return to it later. Rano flopped herself next to where her mother sat, oiling Rajjo's hair. A few peacocks crossed in front of them, as if deep in conversation with each other, ignoring the mother-daughter trio. No one spoke for a minute as the mother sighed.

'When I sat in that courtyard with Totu and all five of you, I read out the verses of the lord, so that some of it would always stays within you. I see you all today, so different yet so alike, the words were the same to you all, the house was the same. I wonder how you become strangers to each other on the way.' Her woes met with silence as she spoke again. 'I want to go back to my village. My house, I don't want to live here anymore' Saroj picked up her bottle of oil and the light cane mattress she favoured and walked away from the paradise her daughters had built by selling her lord in the market place. She walked quietly through the foliage. A silent tear clung on her soft wrinkled cheek, she wanted to go back to her village and see one last spring before she died peacefully.

# 6

RAJJO'S plush Jaguar ate up the miles. They crossed Ahmadnagar. Another 35 kilometres and she would be at her destination. The rendezvous she had arranged with Harsh at her sister's and family's insistence troubled and excited her at the same time. She had chosen the pious town of Shani Shingnapur for this meeting, the village famous for its popular temple of Shani, the God of Saturn. Durga paying obesience to Lord Shani, her benefactor, it was a natural and beautiful cloak to hide her desires. Sent on an errand to convince Harsh that his family had to stop the viscious attacks on her empire, Rajjo's heart beat like a child – excited to run free in the meadows and eat the forbidden sweet hidden in his little fist.

Rajjo was meeting Harsh, it all came back, the floodgates of love, desire and wanting opened yet again and this time they coloured her in the hues of a beautiful morning. She knew her love for Harsh was beyond that of two bodies or hearts. She ran away as far as she could, and here she was, running towards him without any fear, without any consequence. The arguments she had built for months, the chains she bound her heart in for days, the fears she nurtured to quieten her heart beat if they sang his name, the fortress she built to keep him out crumbled in a heap. All it took was a quiet breath with his name on it.

With a sigh she quietened her mind and brought herself back to the present. The merger of Harsh's party and Upasana's father's party had been successful. Harsh was set to take over the reigns of the joint alliance, trumping his very able cousins. But since then they had been chasing the Durga trust with a vengeance. The road continued to take her towards her destination, her body moving to a rhythm of darkness and light inside the car, the leaves casting shadows through the magical windows as the sleep fairies kissed her eyelids.

She woke up with a start.

For the first time, so many people knew that she was meeting him and waited for an outcome. It was not a hidden lovers' meet anymore, it was a business meeting. As the road disappeared, Rajjo's unrest grew. She willed her mind to imagine the place she was about to reach, the mysterious location she had chosen. A piece of folklore came to her rescue, to amuse and entertain her, something about a shepherd who touched the stone with a rod and the stone started bleeding, the midnight black stone spilt a deep red liquid. Soon the village gathered around to watch the miracle and by nightfall Lord Shanishwara had made an appearance in a local's dream, telling him that the most unique black-looking stone was indeed his own form. The village asked if he could build a temple for him, he just replied that there was no need for a temple, as his roof was the entire sky and he preferred to be under the open sky. He then asked the village to come and do the customary pooja every Saturday, and promised in return the whole hamlet would have no fear of dacoits or burglars or thieves.

Rajjo chuckled. She mocked the lore in her head but she could not mock the fear or faith that made this village almost crime-free. Due to the fear of Lord Shani, none of the structures, be it dwelling houses, huts, shops, etc., situated within the one-kilometre radius of this Lord Shani temple, have doors or locks. To this day, no doors for any houses, shops or temples mar the free-flowing spirit of the hamlet.

Fear not faith drove the masses.

By now nausea was building up inside, the constant movement of the car adding to her discomfort. The trinket hanging on the rearview mirror caught her attention. A little angel carrying a dagger in its hand, pointed towards Rajjo. She could feel a searing pain in her heart till she cried for the driver to stop the car.

As she stepped out to look at the clear blue sky, she could see an ominous cloud cross a hill and suddenly a raven shot out of the cloud. The shriek of the raven pierced her deaf ear. Ravens always carried a message from her ancestors? What was she trying to shout out? A pulsating headache began. The strange thing was there were no smells around. Just before a storm, the smells disappear.

As she sat back in the car, a nursery rhyme started playing in her head:

A single magpie – One for sorrow, two for joy, three for a girl, four for a boy.

She laughed until the laughter died in her throat; she spotted a single lone magpie on the bonnet of her car. She was going mad. Where did the rhyme come from? Why were the winds putting it in her head?

As the car resumed its rhythm, Rajjo forced herself to focus on the future, the village, the deity, Harsh. By now, Rajjo knew it was no accident she picked this place. She did not believe in God, religion or faith, but she definitely respected this voice inside that guided her through many a disaster, warned her of impending calamaties and she was sure now that she was heading into one. The question was, what was the message? She had to evaluate everything in her mind before it was too late.

As the car cruised forward to tackle the narrow twisting road, Rajjo spotted a cloud, the same cloud she left behind at the last stop. Its shadow, menacing and dark, loomed overhead as the car slowed down near a curve. From someplace beyond the curve, a giant eagle flapped mighty wings and soared towards the cloud, its beak a deathly clasp for the dead rat it carried. She wondered how it trapped its prey. How the rat was blind to the swooping shadow that came its way. She suddenly remembered the persuasion. People were telling her to meet him one last time to talk to his wife because they were hurting each other. Was she being blind too? Unable to read the swooping shadows? Was it the expressionless face of her brother, the sad Karam, or the restless Rano? Was she being paranoid?

Rajjo glugged down a bottle of water boiled with a tinge of tulsi to heal the burns inside. She settled back in her seat as the lore played out in her head again. The villagers' voices reached her from the temple, 'Some who have tried to steal have died vomiting blood within minutes of their act and before they could cross the boundary. Many others are said to have received varied punishments such as being ill for many days, suffering from mental imbalance, etc.'

As the thought flashed in her mind, Rajjo knew what it all meant. The discomfort, the premonition, the dark shadows, Rajjo was gasping for breath. Someone was going to try to steal from her the thing that most important to her. She needed to stop it. She barked at the driver to turn around and tried calling his number. As expected, her battery was dead. Sweat trickled down her face, for it was clear she was the prey, they walked into a trap, but the worse part was the hunters had summoned enough forces above and beyond the human realm to cheat them. How were they to fight that?

His BMW reached the tarmac, his chopper was ready and waiting and polished to a gleam, ready to carry him into the skies to his beloved. Rajjo and him had mutually decided to part ways, but this time when they met, he knew they were never going to be apart. He'd agreed to her request to move on, he knew the distance would bring them together forever.

Harsh expected the sudden and urgent call by Rajjo – she wanted to meet. After so many ups and downs, deciding to put the relationship to rest, they were still craving to be together. Excitement to meet her outweighed the high stakes, his political career and his marriage many times over. This was pure throbbing emotion, he never felt so alive – she made him reckless and childlike – that's what he craved for all his life.

The phone stuck to his ear, it was Upasana on the line, refusing to hang up. It seemed she was in one of her neurotic modes. Upasana had tried her level best to dissuade him from the trip, and now she was making sure he spoke to her till he climbed the chopper. Perhaps her woman's instinct had alerted her that he was going to meet Rajjo. She thought he had an important meeting to attend, but as she waved him off he saw something cross her face. An anger crimson in colour mingled with the carefully applied blush in her cheek. The rage reigned in her mouth, meeting her coral lipstick as she told him, 'Don't go for this meeting. Please stay with me.' But Harsh unable to stop himself, moonlight threads guiding his feet all the way to Rajjo. 'Call me when you reach Pune,' she said after a while, the black clouds reflected in her brow. She looked beautiful and dangerous to him. It was his own fear and guilt reflecting on her angelic face.

*She touched her lips and pressed her fingers to his.* One for sorrow, two for joy, three for a girl, four for a boy.'

He turned to see a single magpie hopping in the garden, the sunlight fading on her wing as late afternoon made way for the evening sky.

He drove out of the house, her face arresting him and once again she was like a lost dove with a broken wing as she waved at him long after he was gone.

Soon after she had called on his cell. 'Don't hang up. I want to talk,' and there was silence. Guilt sat on his shoulder as he indulged her. 'Describe the sky,' he heard her ask. The glistening gleaming chopper invited him. He just wanted to get the phone off his ear and take off into the skies. He looked up at the evening sky. Dotted with perfect white clouds against the giant blue. To complete the picture he spotted a raven flying across. The raven suddenly reminded him of his Rajjo. She always wanted to feed them. She would make rice balls and leave them outside. She would look at the sky, open her arms and invite the ravens to come and eat. Harsh was beginning to like ravens, even more so when he learnt they were messengers of the dead.

'I like Ravens,' he said into the phone after a short silence. She said, 'They are bad omens.' He said, 'Their croaking call and diets of carrion have given them a reputation. They could be just lost souls.' There was an odd pause and she said, 'Apollo sent a white raven, or crow in some versions to spy on his lover, Coronis. When the raven brought back the news that Coronis has been unfaithful to him, Apollo scorched the raven in his fury, turning the animal's feathers black. That's why all ravens are black today.' There was a deathly silence. Harsh was more than suspicious if he heard something in his wife's voice. There was nothing he could do about it. He was unable to stop himself or turn around. He decided after this meeting he was going to tell her the truth. She deserved to know that he was in love with another woman. In fact, he wanted to tell her right away. There was never a better time. 'I want to confess something. I am really sorry, really very sorry, but I need to tell you.' She cut him midway. She knew what the confession was and she was not ready for it. Perhaps it was for the best and she deserved to know in person and not on a phone call. Harsh controlled his urge to come clean.

He heard Upasana's voice again, 'How is the weather?' he cheerfully squashed the guilt inside, for now he was going to humour her and the first thing after he returned he would tell her the truth. Having made a decision, he felt lighter than the magpie hopping on the aircraft. 'It's going to be a beautiful clear evening and night. Perhaps not great for those early plants that are far ahead of the season with this record warm March. But with this clear dry air, it will be perfect to view another sunset.'

Upasana heard him out quietly and then he heard her saying – 'In a short while, we'll see the crescent moon right next to Venus – high in the evening sky – as high as it will ever get. Tonight it will shine the most beautiful of them all. Watch it and remember me.'

There was something odd about her voice, 'The evening sky can be a time machine, a magical place, an omen, a prophecy...do you see anything else.' Harsh had rarely heard her talk like this. There was an odd feeling settling inside his heart. An ache? A fear? Was it anxiety? Rajjo always told him the universe knows. It will whisper to your body. Your instinct will try and tell you in any possible manner it can. It will use your body, it will use the skies, the birds, the animals, it will try and warn you.

'Magpies,' he said into the phone. There was a pause on the other side, and then she said, 'See carefully how many are there.'

'You and your magpies!' Harsh chuckled. He heard her throaty voice break into a sing-song jingle, 'One for sorrow, two for joy, three for a girl, four for a boy, five for silver, six for gold, seven for a secret never to be told.'

Harsh laughed, her desperate voice pleaded 'Can you please cancel your meeting for my sake and come back?'

Harsh hesitated as the metallic bird started churning its wheels for the departure. It was too late for him to turn back. He climbed the chopper as the pilot greeted him.

'I want to be on the phone till you take off and the signal goes.' Harsh was uncomfortable with that request but if Upasana was adamant there was nothing he could do. The rumbling of the giant machine made it impossible to talk further. As the machine took off just about touching the low hanging clouds, a giant explosion filled up the firmament.

The ravens, the magpies and the skies, all stopped to witness it in silence.

# 7

THE hospital corridor was stuffy and the air had an undertone of bleach. The magnolia walls were scraped in places from hundreds of trolleys that had bumped into them. The pictures on the walls, benign prints of uplifting scenes, promised a better tomorrow. Above the double doors were large blue plastic signs announcing the areas of the hospital they opened into. Rajjo always found hospitals creepy – big, sterile, labyrinthine structures where people often went to die. But she had now been here for over three months, since the fatal crash that had swallowed Harsh in its lethal jaws and spat him out half dead.

Her suite was on floor no. 5, the same floor as the ICU where Harsh lay oscillating between life and death, but not once had she gone to see him. She'd heard from Devi that Upasana was by his side, day in and day out. Devi was her eyes and ears as she shut herself in the suite, away from the prying eyes and burdensome world, and would tell her about the stream of visitors who came to see him, the doctors, the nurses and their tantrums. Nothing missed Devi and nothing was left out in her relay to Rajjo. She described the tinkle of the nurse's laughter as she flirted with the handsome doctor, the look in Upasana's eye as she conferred with Harsh's parents and the defeated doctors, the colour of the pastries the ward boys ate as the patient in room number eight was discharged. In return Devi loved having Rajjo all to herself.

The hospital suite, her home for the last three months, was packed with amenities – access to a landscaped terrace, plush bathrooms, separate TVs with multiple channels, fridge, Wi-Fi facility, direct dialling, two-way nurse call system, personal safe and manymore facilities for total comfort. Rajjo did not make use of any of it. She was happy to sit by her window and welcome the sunrise and hold its hand all the way to the sunset. One beautiful afternoon, as a pale yellow butterfly hopped on a white lilly whispering a secret and the clouds came a little low to hear it, she laughed. It was a perfect day in summer. She told herself over and over again this was no time to die. The bouganvillea and the bluebells were blooming on the terrace gardens. The skies painted a beautiful tangerine. This was no place to die yet. She could smell it in the divine milky cloud that passed by. Harsh was not going to die. No matter what the doctors, the nurses or the shadows on the wall prophesied.

As the afternoon came and went, Karam and Rano made a customary visit and left without exchanging a word. Rajjo refused to interact with anyone; she enjoyed the quietude, it kept her sane. Devi hovered around organizing things for Rajjo – another meal, another bath, another new doctor flown in to study Harsh's condition, another night and Rajjo would find herself alone staring out of the window again. The terrace was so familiar now, that she could outline every tree, every flower and every bud, giving it a name. Bathed in silvery moonlight it was more seductive in the night, and she imagined walking hand in hand with Harsh, kissing under the canopy of trees, making love behind the rose bush. It was just a matter of time.

The clock struck midnight and Rajjo ran down the corridor to the nurse on duty. 'Is he awake yet?' the nurse, Mary, a motherly figure, nearing fifty, shook her head sympathetically. She went to the church every Sunday and lately she had included Rajjo in her prayers. Every morning she lit an incense stick on Jesus and Mother Mary's photo stuck on her bedroom cabinet. She offered them yellow marigolds. Every week she bought a new bunch and stored it in her fridge. Night after night the beautiful girl came to her, asking the same question and night after night Mary had the same response. She had, in fact wanted to change her rota as her heart broke every time she said no to this woman. It was clear that the Godwoman was losing her head. Sometimes she would talk. 'He was coming to see me, you know. I called him. He left everything for me.' Mary dare not breathe out to anyone the revered godmother had gone senile in love with the political dynamo of the country, who lay half dead in the hospital. Jesus and Mother Mary were the only things that kept her mouth shut and kept her going.

But this one time Rajjo asked one more thing, after which Mary decided to leave her duty station and not come back ever.

Rajjo leaned on the counter and whispered, her eyes dancing bright like an excited child up to a trick, her disheveled curls framing the innocence on her face, 'There is a woman crying, huddled down the corridor and a man appearing on the second floor before bursting into flames and decapitated shadows wandering through the halls at night. What happened here?' The scared Mary took a step back. 'Perhaps it was an execution hall a long time back?' Mary was rooted to the spot. Was she playing games with her – was it public knowledge that years and years ago there was a military hospital here, and then a burial ground before this swanky hospital was constructed. It was a well-kept secret she knew since she worked here for the last twenty years. It was time to take a break from this floor, or perhaps from this hospital. Before Mary could turn away Rajjo added, 'You know why you keep putting on weight on that belly of yours lately? Because you can't stomach your guilt! Let it go. You made a mistake and you have been forgiven. He says he knew.' Rajjo walked back to the room with her dreamy eyes.

Mary's heart was in her mouth and she had a flash of her dying husband on the hospital bed. He had looked at her with so much love as he squeezed her hand. All Mary could think about was that one night when she slept with his brother who was visiting them. The carefree younger brother with youth and dimples, charm and cigarettes, who she knew from college. They could have been college sweethearts but he went away and she married the elder brother instead. And many years later, as Mary and her husband battled through a quagmire in their relationship, he had came along one night. Wine on his breath, love on his sleeve, Mary succumbed with an aching heart. She guarded the secret as a dragon would a gold treasure, and even at her husband's deathbed she would not let it out. It ate her insides, it ate her heart, and she wished she had told him before he died. Rajjo's whisperes echoed in her ear, 'He says he knew, he whispered it in my dead ear.'

Mary stared at Rajjo who quietly turned the corridor. No one saw Mary in the hospital again. They said when she left the hospital her laughter rang all the way till the parking lot. And her tears soaked her uniform. She was at peace.

Rajjo stood on the terrace wearing a hospital gown. Rano and Karam were still enduring her silence as another month passed by. They asked her how long she wanted to be in limbo? But Rajjo knew she was waiting for something. She was waiting for a word, a direction. She was gearing up for a journey. She had kept her mother away from the hospital. Perhaps she needed to see her. The restlessness inside was growing. The churning of change had begun.

She had to be patient. She could see the days slip away into nights and weeks into months in Devi's eyes but she was in waiting. Her routine was the same, long walks in the hospital compound and one question to the floor nurse on duty. Room No. 10 – did the patient wake up yet?

The nurse was Mary's replacement, younger and beautiful with sad eyes. Her name was Sitara. She smiled the same way and shook her head. It seemed she was certain he was never going to.

Rajjo stared out of the window looking listless, when Rano announced the doctor who just entered the room. The quiet doctor who entered with Rajjo – stepped forward as Rano gave him a look. It was his turn to try. Before he could say anything, Rajjo looked him in the eye, 'You know of a sobbing young girl who stays here? Many people have seen her but are scared to say. We are becoming friends now. She stays in suite No. 9. Why have you locked it?'

'We are going to reopen it soon.' The doctor was clearly flustered.

'Exactly 4.30 in the morning she stands at the foot of the bed, crying,' Rajjo looked at the doctor and his team in a disapproving manner.

'It is nothing, there is some renovation work. There is no young girl here.' As the doctor said it, the nurse behind shifted in discomfort.

'Mary told me that the nurses felt nausea or sensed someone following them even after they've left.' Rajjo countered. 'Your official report says that the nurses are horrified as the suite has been shut after the girl died in the suite a year ago. Inexplicable feelings of sadness, unease and sudden drops in temperature have also been reported in that room.'

The doctor clarified, 'You know how the nurses have an overactive imagination – they hold on to a story to amuse themselves.'

Rajjo smiled at him, disbelieving. She had cornered him.

'What are you trying to say?' The doctor stood his ground firmly.

Rajjo looked at him with manic eyes and whispered, 'She crawls on the walls and she plays with the others, she will get me some information and she will whisper it in my dead ear, in return she asked me to tell her parents she will find a way back. Can you deliver the message to her parents?'

Everyone in the room was rooted to the spot with fear. Including Rano. Rajjo was beyond saving perhaps.

It was 2 a.m. when Rajjo ran down the corridor. The hospital staff sprung into action to control her. Devi ran behind Rajjo to stop her. 'The girl woke me up! She came and told me he is going to leave if I don't stop him! She should stop them!' As she tried to go across the corridor to Harsh's room, Upasana came out, looking immaculate and beautiful in her sorrow. She wore a pink suit, and looked like a pale rose bud in winter. But her face mirrored her tiredness.

She knew about Rajjo staying in the hospital and she had let her stay in the vicinity as Harsh battled for life. She had to share the suffering of waiting for him to die. Each episode of Rajjo's senile behavior gladdened her heart. It was poetic justice. And here she stood, disheveled, maniacal – a mere shadow of the beauty she once was. Her face shriveled up in sorrow. Upasana looked her in the eye and compassionately broke the news, 'The doctors are advising to pull the plug. Time is running out. You can come and see him once, you can come and say your good byes to him.'

Upasana allowing Rajjo to see Harsh was her last victory and Rajjo would have happily accepted defeat had she not known there was still hope. He could be saved. Ignoring Upasana Rajjo made a beeline for the nurse. 'Did the patient wake up?' the awkward nurse shook her head yet again. Rajjo turned to both off them and muttered with a strange conviction, 'He will.'

Upasana rejoiced in her turmoil. Her pain acutely lessened as she saw Rajjo suffer. 'I think of him, I hope and pine for him day and night: is there any saint who may bring him near me?' By now her sleepy companion Devi stood behind her, nudging her gently to move. Rajjo would have none of it. Despite herself Upasana whispered with pity and hatred, compassion and sympathy, 'You are the Godwoman. You should not be begging for his life in these corridors… What will your devotees think? What happened to your faith that you sell in your shops with ointments and balms?'

Rajjo was beyond all that. Rajjo knew it was time. She was waiting here in the antiseptic walls and corridors to pass the time, till she knew the way. Ironically it came from the woman who hated her guts.

Looking at Upasana squarely in the eye, Rajjo found her mother's voice from her village mingling with her own resolve, 'The lord himself makes the demons pursue saints and he himself saves them. I am overflowing with sins and demerits. I have no virtues at all. I abandoned the ambrosial nectar. I drank poison instead.'

She could smell the wet mud in her courtyard. She could hear Totu imitate the call of the bangle-seller outside the house and she could feel her mother's love enveloping the house. She remembered her mother's faith that kept them safe. She remembered the village. It was time to move on. It was written on the walls, the shadows had whispered. His precious life sat in the palm of her hand. It was time to fight destiny and bring her beloved back.

# 8

IT was post five and visiting hours were over for the imambara. Built by the Nawab of Awadh, Asaf-ud-dowhala in 1784, the building was a magnificient piece of architecture. Karam waited in the empty halls of the Bara Imambara and Rano moved around reliving the history while Rajjo had her meeting. She could almost imagine the nimble nautch girls gracefully dancing in the jasmine-scented courtyards. Although visitors were not allowed at this hour they had managed a private audience as Rajjo wanted to meet Kuljeet and Arjan here. Rano plonked herself on a ledge. Tired and exhausted. The last few months had taken a toll on her.

'They say the construction of this took fourteen years.' She looked at her handsome friend with peppered hair and crinkled eyes. It had been tough on him too. Perhaps it was Rajjo's state that ate Karam up or perhaps his guilt. The nagging thought refused to leave her head. Perhaps she could have stopped things escalating to this. What if Rajjo's mistrust for her and Karam was not baseless? Not wanting to wallow in this thought, Rano turned away from Karam, impatient and restless. She was certainly in no mood to talk or admire any architecture. All she needed was to know Rajjo's exchange with Arjan and Kuljeet. Warning bells were ringing in Rano's head the moment Rajjo expressed her desire to meet them, after getting out of the hospital. Rajjo was not in her senses completely and she wondered what the idiots filled her head up with.

It did not help matters as Rano had the feeling Rajjo suspected their hand behind Harsh's crash. Both of them felt the weight of Rajjo's suspicion but never discussed it.

'Don't worry. Devi is there with her.' Karam tried to soothe the worry lines knotted around her brow.

It didn't help, as Devi troubled her the most. She stayed close to Rajjo like a shadow, while Rano sat here, an outsider, wondering what her sister was thinking. It made her violently angry. But she had to control her fury. She needed a calm head to see this through. A lot was at stake. She was going to fight Rajjo till the last breath to save what they built together. How she secretly wished that Harsh had died and they could have carried on with their lives!

'You know the Nawab started as a fat drunkard who was gifting away territories to the British.' Karam read out from his phone. 'Just googled his history, he used to laugh with no apparent reason, would abuse others and expected to be abused in return.' He chuckled. It irritated Rano no end.

'He had immense respect for people who used filthy language and the more obscene the language, the more he was pleased. He was juvenile, unambitious and would drink with his servants.' Karam was back to his favourite past time. Pretending that all was well.

Rano snapped, 'I am not interested in some retarded story. You think they will allow us to smoke in here... What the hell is taking Rajjo so long with those fools? I am telling you I have never taken to that Kuljeet. And I have never liked that man's nose. Arjan. It's always up in the air.' Karam chuckled at her outburst.

Trying to take her attention away from her obsession, Karam pointed to the large arched room they were in, 'You sit in the world's largest arched room without any pillars and rant about people and complain? Forget your worldly woes. Can you picture the Nawab holding his public hearings here?'

Rano looked at Karam in the eye and before she could control herself, she spat out, 'Isn't it ironic, standing in this place, it feels like *we* are in a public hearing. Rajjo is losing her marbles and you are getting kicks from discussing some nawab of Awadh?'

Karam chose to ignore the barb. 'At least I am not wasting my time sulking or throwing a hissing fit!' He scrolled his phone some more like the answers to all his mysteries would appear on his screen.

'So did you have anything to do with it? Or is it stupid of me to ask?' Rano blurted out the question that had been stuck in her throat for the last three months. Karam clenched his jaw. He refused to take Rano's bait. She was bitter, she was angry and she was disillusioned.

Karam went back to his screen, silent and sullen. Rano realized Karam was not going to rise to the bait or answer the question. She prodded further. She wanted to shake him and make him realize the desperation of the situation they were in. Either he was a damn good actor or he genuinely had nothing to do with it. But then a nasty voice whispered in her ear that a scorned jealous lover was capable of anything. She was capable of anything back then when she was in love with Karam who preferred her sister over her. She leaned closer to Karam, wanting to press further. 'Let me tell you something more about the place. The acoustics here too are astonishing. A whisper against one wall can be picked up beyond several turns and twists of the corridors. Always suspicious of political and military conspiracies, this was how the rulers of Lucknow guarded against disloyalty on the part of the keepers of the imambara.' Karam was no fool.

'Devi told Rajjo how you met Sheru and discussed "options" to solve the Harsh situation months before the accident. How you dangled a carrot to Sheru, that he will get a bigger share in the pie. How you encouraged his association with Harsh's wife Upasana all these months secretly! Rajjo knows. The whispers have reached her ear loud and clear. The acoustics of a conspiracy against your loved ones will also astonish you. How fast they reach their ears.'

Rano could feel the rage building inside her. She felt betrayed by Karam. 'Why didn't you tell me earlier? I was just trying to protect her! Of course you did not tell me all this. It was convenient for you that she suspected me!'

Karam stared at her with a deadpan expression. 'Are you trying to say something? Hint at something?' Rano smirked, ' I am not hinting, I am asking.'

'And what makes you think I was involved in Harsh's accident?'

Rano sat defeated. She had to clear this mess out before it was too late. She was not going to fight Karam anymore. It would have been nice to have him by her side rather than having him as an enemy.

She sat in the imambara and smelt the trees. Autumn was upon them. Change was here again. Rano inhaled sharply. She could smell the vegetable dye on her sari. It was earthy and cool. It was time to stop playing games and just talk.

'I am scared for Rajjo. We remember Anarkali for her tragic love story. She was buried alive in a wall as a punishment for her relationship with the Mughal prince Salim. She died of suffocation. I don't want Rajjo to be buried in that wall. That's all I wanted, but I am not responsible for Harsh's accident.'

Karam was quiet for a moment and he gently replied.

'Have you ever thought what might have happened had Anarkali found a way to escape from the stone prison she was kept in as punishment?'

Rano smiled ironically, 'She was doomed to haunt the pleasure garden as it slowly filled with tombs and weeds and ruins as time eroded away the glory of the Mughals. Karam, we have built those gardens as well. We have an empire to run. I want her in flesh and blood. Not a haunting shadow.' Then she added in a dreamy voice, 'You know, back then in the village, when the fires were lit in the courtyards for everyone to sit around and share stories... When I was waiting for my little sister to come in to the world... even before she was born my grandmother whispered in my ear that I had to look after her. How do I sit back and let this happen to her?'

Karam shuffled in his seat. Rano turned to him once more. The colour of red fiery autumn leaves smouldering in her eyes. 'I want to know how this happened. I want to know if you played any role in what happened. I don't want any secrets between us.'

'You think I would do anything to harm Rajjo?' Karam looked away, uncomfortable with that scorching gaze.

'They used to sing it a lot back in the day. Do you remember that song? Every Sunday we would run to the village headman's house – his living room filled with families who came to watch the Sunday movie on Doordarshan on the old television set. I still remember the cold big hall, peeling green paint on the wall, the imposing wooden dining table. The cold floor we sat on. You remember? You used to come too. Not to watch the movie but to watch Rajjo. One particular song caught my fancy and Mother explained to me why the man was pitifully crying. He was pleading to all. Lovestruck he cried out to the world to destroy a mosque or tear down a temple, but never to break someone's heart as that is where God lives. But perhaps that's where the devil lives too?' Rano was too close to the truth. Karam wanted to breathe steadily and quell his ire.

'Yes, I still love her very much, but the empire is yours to lose not mine.' Karam stood defiant. 'How many Mughal dynasties have bloodied thrones, with their kith and kin killing for power? I always suspected you and so does she.' Rano seethed with anger. She never knew Karam would harbour such a deep violent suspicion that she would plot against her sister. That he would gather evidence of her plotting. There was no time for pretences anymore. 'Whatever you may be implying, just know this and know this well. The PVP party is in a huddle. There was a rumour that the wife was going to take over. But once she takes over, God only knows what is going to happen. We need to secure our interests. We need to share secrets, if any. Winter is coming, and a dark one at that.'

❦

The day started on a beautiful note as Rajjo sat under a mango tree, on a bench bordering the lawns of the old Residency, listening to the drone of bees and the harsh cawing of crows. She enjoyed the crowded market street, old houses and traffic chaos right outside this peaceful haven. The narrow lanes of Aminabad bazaar in old Lucknow danced with colour and movement. Popular Bollywood film music blared out from small food kiosks. Flower sellers heaped marigold and jasmine garlands, and fruit and vegetable stalls were piled high with ripened produce. Cows ambled through the crowds, unhindered with an air of self-importance. The kaleidoscope of a busy bazaar was the beautiful change she needed to wash out the sterile hospital from her skin. To sit under the sheltering tree with sunlight throwing dancing specks of light through the leaves, where dust devils whirled briefly in the warm breeze, and the air carried the scent of marigold flowers was what her soul needed.

She was glad they had come to Lucknow for the meeting as Arjan and Kuljeet were stationed in a ashram around here for a month. This place smelt of the overripe fruit sold in the streets. It smelt of the delicious kebabs and saffron of the Awadhi biryanis. She knew life was going to change after meeting with her old friends and she wanted to enjoy and relish each and every moment of the day. As she waited for them she enjoyed the historical building with sculptured domes and minarets. The imambara. The complex included a mosque, the bhulbhulaiya (a labyrinth) and baoli (a step well with running water). Rajjo found the space almost lyrical as she walked around aimlessly. The only sound that followed her was Devi's tinkling bangles. Devi wore a sari and anklet and was walking right behind her. It made her feel safe. She enjoyed the freedom to move around the decluttered halls as she approached her rendezvous point with Arjan and Kuljeet.

Devi's voice echoed, 'They say this is the world's largest unsupported structure! God knows what those people knew back then. I think they had help from the gods. The Devas. They came from another planet!' Rajjo enjoyed Devi's mindless chatter as she walked through the building. 'You know, I heard a guide telling a tourist about a mile-long hidden passageway that led to a location near the Gomti river!'

Rajjo hoped for a hidden passage like that to escape her own life. 'There were other passages from this place that were rumoured to lead to Faizabad, Allahabad and Delhi,' Devi said.

They were supposed to meet near the bhulbhulaiya. She spotted Arjan standing there in his blue robes and next to him, sat Kuljeet, hunched forward. 'I'll come back.' Rajjo left Devi standing there and walked towards her friends.

Arjan, a few years older since she had last seen him, smiled at her. His face lit up as he saw Rajjo approaching. It was a handsome face. His tall frame was leaner than she remembered and his hair peppered with white. As she approached them a fragrance of a distant secure and warm memory filled her. It was the smell of incense sticks that doused the village temples and small shops in the mornings. As they crossed the streets wearing uniform and lugging their school bags, the incense smell hung around welcoming a new day in the village.

They met like long-lost friends with deep hugs and sat in a companionable silence for a while. There was no hurry to ask any questions. Rajjo just wanted to be with them. They walked around the maze and Arjan pointed out gently. 'You chose a place of faith.' Rajjo did not question it or deny it. The trio continued walking through the imambara in silence.

'The roof is made of rice husk. It is the only structure where the sponsor and architect are both buried. It was built in the time of famine. So the masses built it up in the day and the noblemen brought it down at night, to create more employment. Famine continued for over a decade and the construction of the building continued for this time.'

'Awadhis are too proud of taking alms,' muttered Kuljeet.

'Yes. It was a food-for-work arrangement. He employed thousands of people to work day and night. Around one-fourth of the work done during the day was demolished at night against payment. There was always the scope of work for the people. It is also said that before distributing muskmelons amongst the poor, Asaf-ud-Daula used to get jewels inserted into them.'

The general banter soothed her as she walked along. But it was only a matter of time where her turmoil came back in her head and in her eyes. Harsh was battling for his life, the shadow whispered in her ear, 'Only you can find his breath,' where should she start looking?

'Like I said – you chose a place of faith, Rajjo.' Arjan looked at her and smiled. Rajjo smiled back, and continued walking. She led them into the maze without thinking. She knew they would give her all the time she needed. For now, she just needed to be around them, hear their voices. Soak in the place.

They entered the maze, a labyrinth of hundreds of narrow stairway passages, some of which had dead-ends, some ended at precipitous drops while others lead to entrance or exit points. 'The bhulbhulaiya was constructed to confuse any intruder,' muttered Kuljeet as they walked along. The guide had mentioned it was a three-storeyed structure surrounded with almost five hundred doorless galleries, where one can roam endlessly for hours, adding to its mystery. There were strategically built hollows in the corridors.

The narrow lanes of the labyrinth strangely did not make them feel as if they were lost as Rajjo guided them through.

The trio stood at one of the exits, taking in the quiet evening. The gentle breeze brushed their sweat-laden skin, cooling it. It was an echoing silence. Finally Arjan turned towards Rajjo, 'It's ironic that we walk through this maze. It's meant to make people forget their way.' Rajjo smiled. 'He is dying. It's whispered in my ear, only I can find his hidden breath, where do I look?' she looked at Arjan with despair. Arjan smiled at her and said, 'You cannot find his breath in the dark devious hands of your empire. Nor in the time you played with fire, when you sold him in anger. Find your way back. Go back to before you started your journey as a Godwoman, when the raindrops on your skin warmed with hope and faith.'

She remembered the window from which she had thrown the deity out. She remembered the smell on her skin of that man who had raped her through the night. She remembered the cold tap and the water dripping on the bathroom floor as she sat there, half dead. She remembered sitting in the bus and leaving her village far behind. There was nothing more to be said here. To go back in time she would relive the horrors she left behind, open the wounds, tear the scabs and let the blood ooze out, till there was nothing left to cover and hide.

As they stood at the five-storeyed stepwell, formerly a royal bath, Arjan tossed a coin inside the well. Rajjo waited to hear the clink of the coin hitting the shallow bottom, but to her surprise, it never happened. 'Only the first two storeys of the baoli are above water, the remaining three remain permanently under water. It was constructed around a large well that was initially dug as a reservoir for storing water for construction work near the imambara. It turned out to be a perennial source of water, being connected underground with the river flowing nearby.'

Kuljeet sighed, 'This baoli is magical. They say a secret treasure's map and key was thrown into this well.' Tightlipped Kuljeet knew all along that Rajjo had chosen love as her penance. The time was here.

Rajjo sat on the warm stone bench and imagined this place with people living in the rooms surrounded by the minaret and the baoli. A guard keeping watch at the entry gateway, in case an intruder entered the baoli and his reflection alerted him. She could smell the women frying curry and mustard leaves, preparing lavish meals in the kitchens back then. Her reverie was broken by Arjan's calm voice when he said, 'The water in the well appears green and covered with algae, yet when a coin is dropped it can be seen for quite sometime, going deep into the well and vanishing.' Rajjo looked at the still water carpeted in a hue of green. 'You have been drowning ever since you started your path of revenge. You flourished and prospered like the algae.'

'You think he went because of all that I have done? You think God made me pay for my actions?' Rajjo wrenched the question out from her gut. Since the accident she was burning with the question – these two were the only ones who could douse her fire. Kuljeet looked at her friend lovingly and whispered in her ear.

*'The wicked shaaktas, the faithless cynics, do not know the Taste of the Lord's Sublime Essence. The thorn of egotism is embedded deep within them. The more they walk away, the deeper it pierces them, and the more they suffer in pain, until finally, the Messenger of Death smashes his club against their heads.'*

'So he did this to teach me a lesson? Your God?'

Kuljeet looked at her little girl with compassion-filled eyes 'He is not looking down from the heavens Rajjo, it is within you. You can bring his breath back, you can let him die, you can repent, you can rejoice, it's all within. It is fathomless, if you slip beyond a point there is no returning back.' They knew Rajjo had to shed her Godwoman's robes if she wanted to have a shot at living again.

'You ll find his breath when you find your faith,' Arjan sighed

'I don't know where to find faith?' She looked at them, helpless.

'Perhaps the same place where you lost it?' And that was the point when she heard it. Rajjo was sure she heard the coin hit the bottom. She heard the clink. It was time for change. She could feel the post monsoon air, dry, cool and dense. The winds spilling from the Himalayas were going to reach here soon. The leaves were beginning to dry out in her village. It was time to destroy what flourished to start a new beginning. It was time for autumn to set in her life. She was ready, for her beloved to be whole and hearty, she was going to find his breath, even if it was hidden in the heart of a mountain or the bottom of a deep black sea.

# 9

RAJJO sat in her courtyard looking at the clear blue sky. It was familiar. She was back in the village again where everything was as dusty and old as she'd left it. Only a new bunch of children, different faces but familiar smiles. They ran down the railway tracks or played in the river with the buffaloes. They chased the tractors filled with hay. They stood with a wide cloth under a mango tree, shaking the branches, waiting for the fruit to fall in the cloth. They squealed in delight as the branches ruffled and made a noise. Rajjo smiled as she passed them by. She could see her siblings in them. She could smell the mangoes they ate soaked in buckets of water in the courtyard.

The farmers toiled hard in the fields. As she walked the length and breath of her village she stared at familiar faces staring back at her. The tired woman was the little girl who walked with them to the school every morning – Lalli. Now she had a broken tooth, dark baked skin and five children. She worked with her brood in the fields along with her husband. She had married her next-door neighbour. It all came rushing back to Rajjo.

After eating the dust in the familiar streets, smelling the ripened fields, tasting the mangoes, revisiting the stories each familiar face wove in her head she was ready to go home to her mother.

On her way back she whispered a release for the pale red kite stuck on the old tree, trapped and straining to break free.

Saroj prepared a simple meal and waited for her daughter. The house had few new amenities that Saroj allowed, like a geyser and a television set. A generator that was grudgingly allowed to sit there. She had refused a car altogether, and a lady to help her out was also shot down by Saroj. Thankfully, her distant cousin's help had come to stay with Saroj, as she had no place to stay after the cousin passed away.

Saroj firmly kept her world seperate from the empire. She made her own rules and boundaries and no one was allowed to cross them.

Older and quieter than usual, Saroj was not surprised to see Rajjo at her doorstep. It was almost like she was waiting for her to come home. As Rajjo settled on the small dining table to enjoy the meal, Saroj complained,'I told you, I don't need that ugly thing sitting in my courtyard. It annoys me.' Saroj referred to the generator sitting in the courtyard like an eye soar.

'Use it.' Rajjo smiled.

'When I die, you can switch that monster on.' Rajjo chuckled at the comment by her hard-nosed parent.

At nightfall, mother and daughter sat on the cot under the stars. Just like old days. Saroj sighed as she told her daughter proudly, 'Your grandmother was a stubborn fool. I never wanted to name you Durga but she had a dream. Apparently a goddess came and blessed her in the dream and asked her to name her granddaughter after her. I never believed that old bat!' Saroj sipped her warm cup of tea remembering the old wrinkled woman. 'You know she was so happy the day you were born. She named you Durga, she sang and danced all day, she distributed sweets and the next morning she died. Like she was just waiting to be a pain in my neck and so she died after creating a ruckus. That woman loved two things, to rile me up and drama!'

Rajjo smiled again. She wished she knew her grandmother. Despite her complaints Rajjo could sense the warmth in Saroj's tone as she spoke about the senile old lady. Like she missed her.

She had heard stories about her grandmother from her sisters. It was like old days, them sitting in the courtyard, a slight chill in the air, exchanging tales and lores and myths and secrets. Life was rich and beautiful then. Only they couldn't see it, it was all covered under a muddy gauze.

She could hear the crickets in the night. A gust of cold wind made her pull the cover a bit closer. It seemed like Rajjo was in a time warp. She was far away from the maddening crowd, from her devotees, from her worries. She wished she could bring Harsh here to see the village she grew up in, sit in the courtyard and share stories of her grandmother.

'She said, you'll see Saroj, this girl will make a name for herself in the world, she will show them the way. I thought she had gone mad. But she was stubborn. I guess you take after her.' Saroj sipped the hot tea again.

Rajjo remembered her mother saying this to her very often. When she called the weather or predicted a mishap in the village, Saroj was quick to pull her up.

'That's why I was never your favourite?' Rajjo teased. 'You loved me all right but you loved the others more. Reet, Rikki, Rano and Sheru…' Saroj looked at her daughter and smiled.

'I may have not given you all my love, but you always had my maximum attention. I have never told anyone this but you are right. My firstborn, Reet, was the closest to my heart, because I'd almost lost her. And then many of you came along, each one precious to me, but Reet made my heart stop.' Saroj confessed. They chatted like old friends. Rajjo was happy her mother spoke from her heart. She felt special, for the first time. Saroj chose her out of all the daughters to confide in her, share her secrets. It warmed her belly.

'God is punishing me. He has taken him away. Harsh is battling for his life.' Rajjo cried in pain.

'Ask for mercy. He is always merciful.' Saroj placed her wiry old comforting hand on hers.

'If he gives Harsh back to me – I will destroy everything I have made dishonestly in God's name.'

'Tell him that. He is listening.' Saroj pointed to the dark clouds gathered above the courtyard, they had choked the twinkling stars and the moon.

Rajjo stared at her old mother. She had a slight hunch now, silvery hair, eyes that were rimmed with grey. She was becoming a shadow of her old self, but her faith was steadfast. She did not waver. She was certain he would hear Rajjo.

'And what if he does not listen.' Rajjo whispered fearfully.

'He will. You just need to ask for forgiveness. He is waiting.'

Rajjo sat slumped on the cot.

'When your sister was born, the first year was tough. The village doctor said she wouldn't live another month. I didn't throw God out of my life, I just asked him to give me her life, and in return I made a promise, whatever he may throw my way, I will never doubt his faith. Reet started recovering the next day. I never gave up on him as promised. He tests you.'

Rajjo knew why she was here. She finally knew where to find his breath.

Saroj looked at her troubled daughter,' I worried for you then and I worry for you now. I am holding on to see you find your way. I have said good byes to the others. I sit here in the courtyard night after night waiting to say my good byes to you. I knew you would come home sooner or later. I wanted to be here when the time came. I cheat death every month. It creeps up with a cold or a sneeze. It sits on my doorstep and I shoo it away. I was waiting for you.' Her eyes glistened with unshed tears.

Rajjo was quiet. Her throat clogged with emotion and tears. The crickets got louder. Finally composing herself she opened her heart. 'I have to walk away from it all.' Rajjo looked into her mother's compassionate eyes.

'No. You should run away from it all. Burn it all.' Saroj muttered with a smile.

'It won't be that easy. I have nurtured my empire with my sweat and blood. It is a living thing – it is flesh and blood. If I need to end it, I need to finish myself.'

Saroj looked at her daughter strangely. She understood what her daughter was saying. She didn't want to accept it yet.

Saroj looked up at the dark sky. She could smell the clouds gathering in the courtyard. Rajjo continued. 'I am going to pay for my sins. That's what you wanted.'

'No. I want you to repent. Not to punish yourself,' Saroj said teary eyed. But she was not going to weaken. She had to be brave for Rajjo.

On that comforting note, Rajjo closed her eyes. She was going to have a sound sleep. She was going to rest as tomorrow she had a long journey ahead of her.

'Perhaps it will rain tonight'. Saroj muttered, eyeing the thick mass of black hovering over the terrace.

'No,' muttered Rajjo and closed her eyes.

Saroj shut her eyes as well. She was happy to see her daughter asleep. She counted the stars and looked for her Totu. She could feel him flying around in the courtyard. She whispered to him as a tear escaped her eye, 'She is home now.' She prayed to her lord to show mercy on her daughter. But Saroj knew a treacherous path awaited her daughter. Atonement was ruthless.

Saroj was ready to leave her village once and for all. She wanted to wake up her daughter and tell her that all she wanted was to be scattered in the fields right outside the house so she could spend her summers playing under the mango tree and winters around the giant pot used for community cooking at the village temple. So she could sit by the fire and tell stories to her children in the courtyard or she could feed Totu near the cage. So she could weep next to the cot where her husband lay, never to wake up again. So she could smile at the little hands of her son, etched out in the wet cement. She had guarded the imprints forever.

But she knew. She had to see her daughter through. She had to wait some more. She could see Totu standing on the offending generator nodding his head and shaking it vigrously. It seems he was trying to tell her something, He pointed towards Rajjo. Saroj put a protective hand around her daughter.

She was going to fight with him if need be, but he had to forgive her. She shivered in fear for Rajjo. She looked over her sleeping daughter tenderly and took out her prayer beads. The dry winds made her cough, the long winter settled in her bones. She prayed for her strength.

Two days after she went back to the Shani diety and made her vow, to give up her empire in exchange for Harsh's life, she finally got the news she awaited. He was not dead, he was showing signs of recovery. She stood in the fields for a long time, staring at the diety, offering it oil and flowers. She chanted the Shani Mantra loud and clear, ringing the small bell in her hand. The wind howled around her but she stood there ringing the temple bell in her left hand, grateful that God had accepted her vow. Harsh was recovering.

She shared the news with Saroj who hugged her daughter tight. She cooked brown rice in sweet jaggery and distributed it around the village.

Rajjo knew it was time to pay her respects to the goddess and figure out her way forward. She was going to visit every shrine of the goddess Durga she could in the following months, till Harsh walked out from the hospital.

But Rajjo knew getting rid of her robes was not going to be easy. Durga Maa, the Godwoman, was entwined in her soul, how could she kill her when Rajjo was alive? How would she give up her vast treasures when so many sat on the gates guarding it? The moment they got a whiff of this, they would unleash the dragons. They would kill Rajjo and keep Durga Maa alive, they would give up their lives, but they would not let the trust die. Rajjo knew she had a dangerous and mammoth task. She had to stop the giant wheels of the Durga trust that churned business worth crores.

As she sat in the courtyard, packing her bags with a frown on her face, her mother whispered in her ear, 'He has heard you, he will show you the way forward.' Saroj hugged her daughter. She wanted to dance under the clear blue sky.

Rajjo prepared to start her journey. Her first stop was the Vaishno Devi temple in Jammu. She was ready to climb mountains, bow down in caves, face the winter and bear the blisters. She was ready to have faith. She believed in the devotion and the purity of purpose. It was her cleansing.

Rajjo was at five thousand feet, sixty km north of Jammu, a sacred spot somewhere in Trikuta hills, in the cave, paying obeisance to the goddess at the Vaishno Devi shrine. She had walked for thirteen kilometres to reach the shrine of Goddess Kali, Saraswati and Lakshmi. She had heard every legend of the sacred place. She climbed the difficult terrain with hundreds of other devotees, bearing the harsh winter. She pondered over the legend of Vaishno Devi, a devotee of Lord Vishnu who ran into the cave where she was chased by the tantric Bhairon Nath, where she assumed the form of Goddess Kali and cut off his head. The head fell on the spot where the Bhairon temple is now located. Rajjo prayed that her faithlessness would fall at the same spot where Bhairon's head fell. She prayed she was able to slay her empire, without killing the faith of millions. One way to finish the empire was to confess. Tell the truth about her business. But what about the devotees who lived by her name?

Her next stop was Sharda Mata temple also located somewhere in the hills.

She had heard they were seeing some recovery and the expert doctors were flying down from overseas to tend to Harsh.

As she climbed the 1063 steps to the top of the temple, she understood the hardships she went through in her life, made friends with the fate that made her suffer. With each step towards the shrine she understood the devotion and love she received from her followers, understood her own folly, understood her own ego, understood the faith behind her faithlessness. It was not in the surrounding deities – it was all within her soul.

She could see many old and handicapped being ferried on the ropeway system burning with a need to meet their maker and pay obeisance. The legend of the two brothers, Alha and Udal, stayed with her for a few days. She wanted to meet Alha who came to the temple every morning at 4 a.m., according to the local legend, to perform the pooja. She wanted to ask him why he wanted to stay in the hearts of these people and remind them of his faith. Alha penanced for twelve years and got the blessing of the goddess here. She also heard another lore, where forty years back, people residing near the temple had started getting blood stains on their clothes at night. As terror engulfed the area, the temple priest had a dream in which Maha Kali asked him to build a temple. The villagers pooled in and the Maa Maha Kali Murti was established on the right of the Shri Mata temple.

The priest may have lied about the dream and conned the villagers into building the temple, much like what she had done, but the faith was real. She could touch it, she could feel it, it was as gentle as a lake, it was as deep as an ocean, it was as blue as the sky and it was as salty as the wind. Faith.

A bird whispered in her ear, '*She had to kill the business but she had to keep the faith alive.*'

It had been a couple of months and Rajjo heard Harsh was being shifted to a normal room. He was asking for her. Her followers were asking for her, Rano was pleading for her to come back, but Rajjo knew she was not going to return until she had some answers, until she was ready to finish her journey. She knew there was something more to find in the Tara Devi temple, situated on a hill-top in Himachal, surrounded by lush green devdar trees, green forests and meadows. She searched for the answers; how to keep the faith alive in her devotees while she payed for her sins. She searched for answers on the hilltops of Indrakiladri mountains, on the banks of river Krishna and in front of the the self-manifested deity of Goddess Kanaka Durga in Vijaywada.

Her next stop was Chamundi Hills at Mysore in Karnataka. She finally found the missing link and the answer in the Shiva temple, as Rajjo was tying a thread in the branches of a tree in the Mansa Devi temple in Haridwar. It was a beautiful temple located on the top of a hill, the Bilwa Parbat on the Sivalik hills, the mountain chain of the Himalayas. The temple was said to have emerged from the mind of Lord Shiva. She hoped once her wish was fulfilled she would come back to untie the thread, but she also knew she might never return. On her journey for thanksgiving, she had found her road to freedom, while she offered coconut, fruits, flowers and incense sticks to the goddess.

Having found a ray of hope, Rajjo reached the narrow caves of the Adhar Temple in the Mount Abu region, as she climbed the 365 stairs, she deliberated on each step she was going to take hereafter. Each step had to be measured and counted because this was her last chance.

If she faltered now, there was no second chance.

She stood at sixteen hundred feet on a hilltop at Maa Bamleshwari Temple in Chhattisgarh. By now she was sure how she was going to leave it all behind. As she looked down at the valley, she smiled. The sound of the temple bells echoed around her. The chanting of the priests filled her up. She was ready for her last stop.

At her last stop, the Tara Tarini temple, she covered her forehead in red vermilion, to mark the start of her journey. The red on her forehead was symbolic of the sacrifices needed to carry her through this path.

She was ready to bleed.

# 10

THE news of Harsh's recovery spread. Rajjo patiently waited for her turn to meet him, wandering in her small ashrams, keeping a low profile. She had withdrawn from public life on the pretext of ill health. She knew time was not her friend. She also knew she had to wait for the right moment before she planned her meeting with Harsh. It had to be at the time when the vultures slept for they moved in flocks, soaring over the habitation, waiting for a chance to swoop in, waiting for the carcass. She was not going to give them an opportunity to strike again. The nameless faceless vultures who bred in her backyard.

After months of deliberation, the time was finally here for the meeting she had awaited. She had planned the meeting in Orchha, a quaint town in Madhya Pradesh. It was some hundred and twenty minutes from Gwalior. She was staying in the Jahangir Mahal that overlooked the river. It was a three-storeyed structure built in the Indo-Islamic style, with hundred rooms, several courtyards, hanging balconies, porches and domes. The moment she entered from the elaborate and traditional gateway with the front walls lined with turquoise tiles, the sight of the magical palace with windows and airy balconies, she knew this was where they would meet for the last time.

Wearing a white muslin shirt and loose pants, her face covered with a pale scarf, Rajjo was blending in as a tourist in the forgotten town. A number of beautiful temples, big and small, were built around the banks of the serene Betwa river that flowed through the town from the crimson light of dawn to dusky twilight. She wanted to have her last meeting with her lover in this magical place. She had to tell him about her vow. She had made a deal with God.

*'If he spared Harsh, she was going to forsake her empire – the ill-gotten empire she had acquired selling his name. Now she had to surrender her own self'.*

Her voice echoed in her head, as she sat watching her reflection in the beautiful waters. Her long dark curls falling below her waist hid her face from the curious onlooker.

She wanted to see the images of the future mirrored in the magical river, but she could see none for now. She had a vow to keep.

She had another day before she met him. As she waited for him to arrive, Rajjo soaked in the little town. This mystical place where spirituality permeated every street corner wove a spell of well being. She liked the colourful bazaars, the saffron-clad men playing the tambura – making her experience musical, as she walked back after attending the evening arti at the temple. Post her evening tryst with God, as she waded through the crowds – gunshots pierced the sky. They were coming from the temple, marking the gun salute for the diety. As always, there were legends around the temple, as always, some lord had visited the queen in a dream asking her to build a temple.

Rajjo did not scoff at the lores anymore. They were not real for her even now, but the faith of the devotees visiting this shrine and believing in the lore was real enough.

As she walked back to her room in Jahangir Mahal, she could see the distant outlines of the Ram Raja and Chaturbhuj temples bathed in moonlight. She stood on her balcony, another pre-monsoon night with a full moon hanging in the sky. Rajjo felt the air and knew a mango shower was not far behind. Her heart warmed at the thought that Harsh would be in her arms in less than ten hours from now.

Harsh was staying in another hotel nearby, the Sheesh Mahal, a grand, medieval palace from the sixteenth century. Rajjo sat in his room, waiting. Beautiful pictures adorned the walls, with sophisticated art work and handicrafts.

She was nervous to see him after so long, after his illness. For her things had changed in many ways, but she did not know how he would feel. Devi, staying in a hotel nearby, had informed her that he had checked into the hotel and then stepped out for a long walk.

Rajjo, unable to sit in her room and wait, sat in his room and waited for him to come back. Wearing a long pale blue kurta and loose white bottoms, she ran her hand through her glistening curls and checked the perfect rosy bow of her lips in the little mirror. Her hands shivered as her heart was beating in her mouth. She sensed him before she saw him as the key turned in the lock and the door opened.

He entered the room as they stared at each other. He had marks and lines on his face post the accident. Lines and scars across his cheek and forehead enhanced his handsome look. Knowing him, Rajjo suspected he was going to enjoy his dramatic appearance. It made him look more appealing and dangerous.

He walked towards her and simply hugged her. For as long as she could remember they stayed locked in an embrace. Rajjo lost count of the minutes and hours. She could smell his sweet sweat. They kissed each other for a long long time. She was back on the terrace under a starlit sky, where lovers and angels sat.

Finally he took her by the hand towards the bathroom and led her under the shower

Rajjo knew that more than talking, they needed to feel each other. He removed his clothes – and Rajjo did the same. They stood facing each other, naked and bare, vulnerable. His body was scarred badly too. But for Rajjo it was sheer perfection.

Harsh's eyes drank in her beauty, her body even more beautiful than he remembered. Her swollen breasts, her flat stomach, her curves ached for his touch. He wanted to worship her body like a slave. He sponged her very slowly and very gently, around her breasts, between her legs and all around her lovely back. With the water still running he began to kiss her and explore the inside of her mouth with his tongue. She responded in a way he couldn't remember her ever doing before. Like both of them had lived and matured during their long separation. As soon as his tongue poked between the lips of her flower she arched her back and moaned. He needed to taste all of her. It was a beautiful desperation. She held onto him tightly as he pounded her. He was desperate to come inside of her after such a long time. For a while he just kept pumping into her and she continued to cling to him, digging her teeth into his shoulder, her entire being in a cosmic whirl, the familiar chaos and then the white light as they both cried out together. The water caressed them, their bodies entwined under the sharp spray.

A gunshot pierced the sky, a temple bell followed. The gun salute at the temple had begun. It reverberated through the night as the light faded away and Harsh took Rajjo many times over to feed his famished soul.

One moon later, they were on the streets exploring the city. In the evening the dramatic sound and light show lit the fortresses of Raj, Sheesh and Jahangir mahals, the courtyard was now an open bazaar selling anything from sweets to knickknacks. Hand in hand they passed the cows being worshipped and fed.

That night, as they lay side by side, he took her hand and whispered that he'd rather die than live without her even for a day. As Rajjo lay in his arms she heard his breath, sometimes shallow, sometimes long, sometimes at peace, sometimes disturbed. She lay awake and listened to his breathing in the dark night. Till she heard the thunder outside. Monsoon was announcing its arrival. The sudden mango shower drenched the temples on the riverside and the jasmine-laden courtyards. She wanted to breathe in this shower forever, as she felt the most complete in her life at this moment. She soaked in the tender raindrops till she'd filled her soul with the smell of the pre-monsoon shower. She wanted to remember the scent of crusty dry earth absorbing the grey water. She thanked the heavens for the mango shower that would help her douse the burning flames of her pyre.

Rajjo took in the beautiful dawn. The leaves glistened after the night shower. Standing from the terrace of the Jahangir Mahal, she could see the monuments of Orchha framed against the dawn with the mist gently hovering over them. Beyond the terrace of the Raj Mahal stood the towering Chaturbhuj temple with the Ram Raj Mandir adjacent to it. And in the distant horizon, lay the Laxmi Narayan temple, hardly visible in the mist.

The vultures distracted her as her eyes scanned the remaining montage of monuments, all wrapped in a hazy sheet of white, orange and yellow. It was a sparkling new beginning. Surrounded by Mughal structures, ornamental paintings, intricate trelliswork, lores of romance and loyalty, it seemed that both of them had stepped back in time, into a beautiful era of abundance and romance. It was a town where the walls whispered stories, where paintings revealed a promise, where tales of romance, and mysticism echoed from every monument and breathed life into the ancient mahals and mandirs. It was a perfect place to script the end of her love story.

Harsh came and stood behind her softly, linking his arms around her. 'You see that beautiful minaret? It's the Praveen mahal. The guide had a fascinating story about her. How Akbar wanted this beautiful poetess and musician Rai Praveen in his harem against the wishes of the Bundelkhand king. But the witty courtesan spoke her way out of Akbar's heart and went back to Orchha.' Harsh whispered teasingly as he kissed her neck and inhaled her scent. 'If someone was to woo you and take you away from me, you better remember the devotion of the princess!'

Rajjo whispered back, 'You know what she said to Akbar, that she was not fit for him as only a royal servant or a crow or a dog will like to eat something that has already been tasted and polluted by another.'

Harsh smiled and kissed her some more, 'You smell of rain…'

Rajjo took a deep breath. It was time to start the conversation.

'You know my mother's sister-in-law got married in this village. They said when any local boy got married here, the first offering was made to Lala Hardaul.'

'Why?'

'Lala Hardaul is the dead prince, who is still alive here. He had to sacrifice his life to prove the purity of his love for his sister-in-law...' she looked into Harsh's eyes. She could see the beautiful sky mirrored in them.

As they walked by the river, hand in hand, Rajjo marvelled at the beauty of the mysterious town.

'How did you find this place?' Harsh sighed, watching the sunset framed behind a temple dome. 'Orchha means hidden. Sometimes the most beautiful things are best hidden, be it romance or poetry. Only the ones who really seek find this beauty.'

Harsh looked at her enthusiastic face, she wore a plain white cotton suit and her dupatta was dyed in fiery colours of red and orange. It shone like fire in the twilight. She looked like a warrior princess with her shiny curls around her face. Suddenly she turned her beautiful face, the river flowing behind her – the setting sun kissing her face. The beauty of this entire town, carrying the hidden legacy of medieval India settled around Rajjo.

'I came here because of the dead prince who is still alive'.

'I want to just look at you some more, I don't want to know about the dead prince.' He tucked a curl behind her ear softly. Rajjo continued, 'He was King Jujhar Singh's step-brother. The king's real brother, Pahad Singh, wanted the throne and falsely framed the Rani and her brother-in-law Hardaul for having an affair. The king immediately ordered Hardaul's death, to be sentenced by the Rani herself. Jhujjar ordered his wife to poison Hardaul to prove her innocence, and Hardaul willingly accepted it.'

Harsh was looking at Rajjo very carefully. His heart was beating profusely. He knew something was approaching and he had no way to stop it. The feeling had not left him since he saw her standing in his room yesterday. Her eyes cloaked in sadness, a hesitant smile on her face. He knew something was coming.

He turned his gaze away from hers. Once again the overhanging balconies and huge decorous gateways of the temples loomed large in the setting sun.

Rajjo's voice stirred him from his reverie, 'The story doesn't end here. When Jhujjar's niece was getting married, his sister asked the king to help, who sarcastically asked her to seek the dead Hardaul. The dead prince apparently attended the wedding and served the guests. The local woman exclaimed that even today it is believed that Lala Hardaul attends weddings he is invited to and most locals leave an invitation card for him and seek his blessings as well. A small temple close by has made the prince into a God, claiming that he is still alive.'

Harsh looked away, watching the sun sit on the riverbed in the horizon. He turned back to look at Rajjo as she spelled it out for him, 'In his death he found what he was looking for. He was a folktale, he was an enigma, he served at his sister's wedding, he was somewhere between dead and alive. He was never fully dead, he was never fully alive.'

A sense of forboding engulfed Harsh. She was trying to tell him something. Her husky voice whispered in his ear, 'He became the dead prince who is still alive. These people live somewhere in the legends of the dead prince.'

'What do you want from me?' Harsh stared into her beautiful eyes, a hint of panic lacing his voice.

Rajjo took a deep breath and looked him in the eye, boldly.

'You have to let me go.'

The river had eaten the sun, a dark veil descended on the riverbank. The twinkling lights adorned the domes and came alive. Perhaps the sun was resting in the riverbed. What if it decided to stay there and never come up? What if the riverbanks were cursed in darkness forever?

'I made a vow, if you were to live, I would give up my life, my riches, my faithlessness. I would destroy Guru Maa Durga. He granted my wish and now it is my turn to fulfil my promise.'

Harsh wanted to scream, but he could not find his voice. He brought her face very close, holding her tight – hurting her with his grip. 'So you can give up everything, dissolve the empire.'

Rajjo knew this was the difficult part. A sharp piercing gunshot echoed in the evening sky. Followed by the temple bell. Rajjo could feel the bullet tearing her heart. 'It won't happen as long as I am alive, they will keep selling his name through the Durga trust, even if I retire I will be Guru Maa Durga for them, in this lifetime. If I need to keep my promise, I need to finish her. As long as I am alive, she will live on too.'

Harsh was stunned into silence. A storm raged in his heart. The chants of the priest, the sound of the temple bells and evening prayer faded out, until he could hear no sound at all.

'Guru Maa Durga has to die to pay for the sins of her devotees. That's the only way I can kill my empire and keep the faith alive. Faith lives in the legends of Lala Hardaul. Faith will live on through Guru Maa Durga's lore as well. '

Harsh turned around, rage and anger evident on his face, and walked off. He left her standing by the bank of the river, her scarf bathed in the colour of blood. Rajjo whispered into the wind. 'I'll meet you on the other side.' But Harsh was long gone. All she had was a dark violent river by her side and the ringing of the temple bells.

# 11

UPASANA had been glued to the TV for the last seventy-two hours. Durga and her legion of followers had become the talk of the town with the media providing an extensive, if not blow-by-blow account of the seige of her ashram in Barsala town in Madhya Pradesh. Social media had exploded with the news. Her Facebook page with millions of followers and the Youtube channels were all talking about her announcement of self-immolation. Her following had doubled after the announcement.

The police and the government had made their stance clear of not allowing the self-immolation bid. But the Godwoman in her last sermon had announced that it was time for her to pay her devotees back for their faith and devotion towards her and the lord. So with all the trust they had put in her, she was going to self-immolate to pay for their sins and dissolve the Durga trust. It would only function as a charitable organization. The businesses and ashrams were going to shut down.

For their deliverance she was going to go up in flames. That was her ultimate goal and aim to serve her devotees. Not only that, she had gone missing as the police wanted to call her in for questioning and preventive detention. Her disciples were not allowing the police to enter the main ashram where she was supposedly hiding for the time being.

The reporter was reporting how more than two hundred people were injured in violent clashes at the self-styled Godwoman Durga Maa's ashram in Barsala as police lobbed teargas and used batons to disperse hundreds of stone-throwing supporters who vowed to prevent them from entering the premises. Violence mounted as supporters of Durga refused to heed to repeated announcements by the police over loudspeakers to allow them to enter the premises. The Barsala police had set a 2 p.m. deadline on Thursday for Durga's followers to vacate the ashram. Thousands of followers who were inside the ashram had begun to vacate the premises by late Wednesday morning.

The ashram management claimed that she was not inside the complex. After the violence outside the ashram, the police slapped sedition charges on her under Sections 121 (waging or attempting to wage war, or abetting waging of war, against the Government of India, 121A (conspiring to commit certain offences against the state). During Tuesday's crackdown, her disciples also attacked several journalists reporting the standoff. According to news reports, around twelve followers, including women and children, tried to self-immolate themselves on Monday to protest the government's stand of not letting the Godwoman publically immolate herself, forcing her to go into hiding.

Unconfirmed sources were also reporting that the Godwoman had managed to flee from the ashram and disappear. Security forces dragged several people standing guard at the ashram gates to the local bus stop and railway station. Finally, towards the end of the day, the police managed to breach the wall of the ashram and remove around four thousand devotees from inside.

Upasana had not left the TV screen even for a minute. She was glued to her phone. Inquiring, asking for detailed reports, she was like a scavenger for any bit of information on Rajjo that they were not showing on news reports yet. She was trying to solve the puzzle in her head. She knew there was more to this.

Upasana switched the channel as another news reporter with a bright red lipstick and immaculate hairstyle looked into the camera and reported, 'As the police tried to enter the ashram where Durga Maa is reportedly hiding, Durga's followers fought pitched battles by lobbing petrol bombs. Her supporters challenged the police to come near the property by pouring diesel on their bodies and burnt an effigy of the chief minister and the prime minister to mark the protest. A lot of followers living abroad were adding to the pressure against the government, especially questioning the need for the arrest warrant against the Godwoman. The key aides of the Godwoman were also absconding and the extended family members handling the trust are claiming to not know her whereabouts. The Chhoti Maa, sister and director of the trust are absconding.'

Upasana switched the channel again, her heart singing. If this was true, her husband would be free from Rajjo's shackles forever.

Another reporter flooded the TV screen. 'Police have so far failed to gather information regarding the whereabouts of the controversial Godwoman in connection with the case.'

Upasana switched the TV off. She opened the windows and took a deep breath. It was a clear day. The evening was perfect, a pale moon hung in the sky already as if waiting for the sun to dissolve and the night to take over. After ages a small smile crept over her face. The moon was beautiful. The moon was impatient to hang in the sky. Its pale benevolence was just a façade. It commanded a key place in mythology and in time. They said strange things happened when the moon was full. Perhaps Rajjo had succumbed to a lunar episode. Upasana smiled at the moon; it was the most beautiful moon she had ever seen in the wide blue sky.

Harsh stood on the terrace of a hotel in Pune. His phone was switched off. After continuous babble for the last four days he wanted some silence. The roof-top terrace had an infinity pool on the other side but thankfully it was empty at this hour. A panorama of tiled roofs lay beneath him. Harsh could barely breathe. He was losing all sense of place and time. The lively street running through the back of the hotel, the tooting of horns, the hum of traffic reminded him that he was still in the same place. The only difference was Rajjo was gone.

She had decided to keep her promise. Despite innumerable attempts, threats and pleading, Rajjo had chosen this path for him. The news reports hounded him as the entire country had erupted in a heated debate over her announcement of self-immolation. His head ached with everything he had to process. He looked down at the city and felt he was floating above it. The infinity pool gave a false sense of comfort. A glass room placed on the far end of the terrace with beautiful expensive plants and flowers offered a sweet haven. It was a good place to hide. He just wanted to sit here and think about Rajjo. Rajjo was on the run from the authorities, hiding in deep dark places as the law of the land had banished her. It made his blood boil but he was helpless and defeated. Rajjo was going to burn. Rajjo was going through all this because of him. And all she had asked of him in return was to let her go.

He could go with her too. But was he ready to go?

She had begged him to stay on and live the life he was supposed to lead. She wanted him to lead the party to victory and fulfil his family's dream. But Harsh had adamantly told her if she left him he would come after her. He knew he was limiting her options and putting pressure on her but he was unable to let go. And now she was gone.

He looked around and saw a beautiful summer day. The flowers bloomed, the trees flourished, the birds nested and the eagles soared high above with a watchful eye. Everything in the world and nature went about their business but Rajjo was gone. He even wondered how the sky was still stuck in place. But it was. It gave him marginal solace to think that it was his choice to stay in the world and continue with his life or he could slip out. Silently. He could find a road to freedom.

They had discussed the option together but Rajjo had warned him of the consequence. He knew Rajjo ideally wanted him to let her go and move on with his life, make a mark with his political career.

Harsh could hear the TV anchor's voice ringing in his ear. Rajjo's picture splashed across the TV set reminded him of her smile as she bid him adieu from her balcony. The hotel looked magical against the setting sun. Her blood-red dupatta flying in the air, like it was trying to break free, like it wanted to follow him. Like it wanted to cover the sky.

He was not ready to let her go. He just prayed she reached where she wanted to reach; there were many people baying for her blood.

The decision was made for him. He had to let her know somehow. He was coming after her. He stared at the pale moon already visible in the evening sky. It just hung there waiting for darkness to come. He felt he was hanging in there like the moon, hoping and waiting to be blanketed in the darkness. His desperation to be with Rajjo was utter and complete.

A battered jeep drove on the pot-holed road. Tyagi had an upset stomach and to add to his discomfort he was put on VIP duty, not any good VIP, Bollywood celebrity or TV personality. The VIP duty was for that absconding Godwoman.

As the battered jeep slowly climbed the steep slope, threatening to give way, Tyagi manouvered the jeep. He was supposed to pick up his team from the main chowk in less than ten minutes. The Godwoman had been missing for the last two weeks after threatening to self-immolate. Tyagi wanted to laugh but with his gurgling stomach, he did not want to attempt it. It was a hoax like everything else! She had made her money, and now she was bored! Or was this just to be back in the headlines?

Her followers, since the self-immolation announcement, had grown in leaps and bounds. Half of his family offered their prayers to Guru Maa Durga. His own house had more pictures of the black sari-clad Godwoman than his own dead mother! The thought of his dead mother reminded him of her advice for a bad stomach. Curd was the cure. Perhaps he should look for some curd on the way. Not that they were going to find the Godwoman hiding here in this godforsaken place. His bet was she was in Greece, cooling her heels in a bikini!

Just then his phone rang and Tyagi's wife screeched, 'I hear Guru Maa was spotted in the town. Swear on your dead mother, you will call me the moment you know everything!'

'Why? Will you jump and the fire with her? If you promise, I will call you right away.' Of course the phone line went dead shortly after, and Tyagi cruised on, ignoring the woman on the side road with the backpack, clutching a package in her hand, looking lost and worried, slipping into the shadows.

Footsteps echoed in a long dark solitary stretch of road as the lonely figure walked briskly, her head covered against the cold night. Her breath came out in short bursts of smoke, her specs sliding down her nose. Her nervous cold fingers clutched at her backpack time and again, as if she carried on something precious in her hands. Her heart thudded in short sharp bursts like a church bell ringing on a clear afternoon. Rajjo was in Manali and somehow she had to reach the undisclosed location in two days, where Devi would be waiting for her. She knew she was being followed and tracked in every manner possible. All sorts of people from her family to her enemies to her lover were hunting her down. All she had to do was not get caught and reach her pyre. Almost like a beloved meeting her lover against all odds. She hurriedly walked through the roads in Manali, her brain racing, to decide her next route. Tall shadows of the deodars and pines loomed menacingly over her. Rajjo shivered. One false step and it was all over. Her final destination lay in the lap of beautiful Manali.

Manali, known as the land of the Gods, was named after the Hindu lawgiver Manu. Manu the sage stepped off his ark in Manali to recreate human life after a great flood deluged the world.

The old Manali village even had an ancient temple devoted to Sage Manu. Her destination was this temple.

A suspicious jeep crossed her path, as if the driver was hunting for his quarry. Rajjo stepped in the shadows once more. The very thought of what was in store in the near future gave her the shivers. Unable to breathe, she sat in the quiet dark corner and let the shivers pass. She could see the headlights of the jeep again. Suddenly a thought came to her head: *It was all going to work out… it was all going to be OK…* She told herself over and over again.

Devi was supposed to get in touch with Kesar and Raahat. She hoped they were going to deliver what they needed to. Even though she had not seen them for ages, the bonds were strong enough for her to trust their loyalty. The threads she had woven with Kesar and Raahat were going to stand the test of time.

She went back to the small hotel she had checked into for the day and sat by the window looking at the fireflies playing hide and seek in the darkness till sheer exhaustion made her sleep. She woke up to the first ray of the sun, her hands still clutching the package carrying her camera. Taking stock of her surroundings, Rajjo was ready to face another day in the chilly hill station. She had to wait for the signal that it was clear for her to move out towards the undisclosed location.

Many were looking for her, hunting her down. A massive empire, the future of the trust, her destiny and the faith of millions was at stake. When a giant tree is readying for the fall, the birds flee, the squirrels scamper, the angered snakes coil around the trunk, hissing, wanting to hold on – suffocating it into submission. She could see the signs of her future in the sky; a myriad hue of colours from bloodshot crimson to hazy gold to hopeful turquoise to serene white. The skies were a prophecy of things to come. Many would be looking at it once Durga was to go up in flames.

It was imperative she reach her destination without getting caught. To do that she had to be on the move constantly, she had to blend in. Staying in one hotel room was not advisable at all because she had got word that Rano and a few others knew she was in Manali. They would be moving heaven and earth to hunt her down.

Rajjo changed her SIM card in her cheap phone yet again, burning the one she had used for the last few hours and neatly disposing of the ashes. She was meticulous about her actions. It was imperative to be alert and cautious. This was her only chance to stay alive and die the way she wanted.

Rajjo walked through the day following the local tourist guide the hotel had arranged for her and the other two families who were on vacation. Today she wore glasses, hair tied in a neat plait. She had stuck on bushy eyebrows and false braces as a part of her disguise. In the mirror she felt like another person already. Now she just had to believe that, and no one would be able to spot her. She would cloak herself with the mist of the dawn and the shadows of the twilight. As Rajjo faded away from the image in the mirror, even she could not recognize herself. She reminded herself to be cautious as the eye of the enemy was sharp and shrewd.

The tour in the dilapidated mini-bus lasted a full day and Rajjo was glad for the distraction. Moreover, she could sit the whole time without talking. It was also a good place to hide in case someone was looking for her.

They made their first stop at a picturesque location. She stood at the top of a valley to take in the beautiful view. She could hear the guide's voice. 'Manali, a hill station at the altitude of 6726 ft in the Beas river valley.' She drowned out the voice of the guide to listen to the valley. Did they have a message for her? It was quiet and serene. It was at peace. Rajjo smiled as she returned to her seat in the bus by the window.

Dark shadows loomed ahead as the sun was beginning to set in the orchards. Rajjo inhaled the scent of the apple trees and it went all the way to her belly, sharp and tangy. She remembered her mother smearing a delicious-looking apple jam on her bread and telling Rajjo how the first apple orchards were planted by the Britishers – who learnt it from her own great grandfather! The branches looked as if they would collapse under the weight of the fruits. The smell of the tangy jam on the soft bread made her mouth water. Rajjo sat on the roadside again, sipping some hot tea. She knew she was not going to see her village or her mother ever again. Rajjo could still remember the bell ringing in the temple behind ominously, with a deafening intensity – '*They will come after you. Listen to your instinct...reach where you have to.*' Kuljeet's husky voice warned Rajjo.

Her followers had cried in pain but supported their Godmother's decision, but the gatekeepers of her empire, the vultures, were not going to let her go. She sensed a bullet could come through the window anytime and pierce her. Paranoia was building in her. The face of the saffron parties who wanted Durga to continue as their benefactors hounded her. The industrialists thriving on products endorsed by Durga, politicians, builders – there were many and more who would rather kill Durga and operate on her behalf than have her self-immolate and dissolve her empire.

The next morning Rajjo was back for another tourist excursion, dodging vehicles hunting for her. It was not safe to be on the roads. It was 7 a.m. as Rajjo stood with Danny at the bus stop to catch a bus to Sona llah. Danny was waiting for two more hikers, who turned out to be two guys from Eastern Europe. They briefly introduced themselves and were happy to stay together, lost in each other not making much effort with Danny or Rajjo. Rajjo noticed the strange buzz cut on their heads, some geometric figures drawn into their hair with a razor. Rajjo wanted to chuckle aloud but nothing escaped her tightly pursed lips! The little party stood waiting for the bus to take them to the starting point of the hike.

As they alighted it was clear they had to walk another seven kilometres along a former road to where the actual trail to Dhundi and Beas Kund started. On the way it seemed the only people living in tents were farmers and their massive black cows. As they walked further ahead, a magical water body took her breath away, like two rivers merging with each other – two water bodies becoming one – just like Rajjo had become one with Durga's legacy.

Rajjo sat at the corner tea stall and sipped her piping hot tea laced with ginger as Danny chatted with the woman running the small tea stall. The woman too lived in a small tent nearby, which she called home, with her two children and the most basic amenities. Rajjo heaved a sigh of relief, sipping the hot tea as the drizzle hit their face with a gentle caress. As they walked further ahead, yellow flowers burst forth like a carpet to the right, and a powerful gurgling river to the left soothed the cacophony of thoughts in her head. Crossing the stream a couple of times was tricky and exhilarating. Big hops from rock to rock over icy cold mountain water made her forget the bigger worries plaguing her mind.

She wanted to capture every little detail in her head, for this was the last trip of her life. It had a spiritual rhythm. A couple of hours passed, the clean crisp air washed away the tiredness and anxiety of the near future. Sunny day, blue sky and occassional white clouds. The European guys stopped now and then to take pictures and capture on their cameras whatever they could. It was just the four of them and a stray dog that trotted beside them through the trek who had decided to accompany them mid way. A little further ahead they could see locals and some men in military uniform building a wooden bridge. Out of breath, they sat by the stream on a warm boulder as Danny passed some snacks around, oily and fried, but very welcome. The yellow flowers swayed in the breeze, lulling the senses and that was when it hit Rajjo yet again. She was very close to her destination and little further away Devi awaited her, with a ready pyre.

The landscape was breathtaking as they trudged on, a backdrop of well-defined snow-capped peaks. The Beas River meandered through on either side of the road. They crossed an old temple nestled on a little hill surrounded by pine and deodars. Rajjo bowed her head in reverance as the bus neared its next stop. Her heart sang like a bird. She had almost reached her resting place.

# 12

UPASANA had been waiting for this day forever. Her satin robe whispered around her ankles. He was ready to make love. He was ready to have a child. He was ready to come back home to her. Icy cold fingers clasped her heart time and again. Her instinct whispered sharply, *make this count.* She was determined to get his seed in her womb this time.

Her body bathed in the soft yellow hue from the lamp above, naked and hungry. She stood facing Harsh. He was fully clothed. He stood staring with a detached passion. Upasana knew it was a man's reaction to a naked body. He was not seeing her. The cold fingers and the voice screamed again – *it does not matter.* She had to move past this question, she had to have him inside her. He discarded his clothes in an automatic manner, like he would do before stepping into a hurried shower. She shut her eyes and mind to all these thoughts. The urgency of the cold fingers and the voice claimed her.

She turned her back to him, as he grabbed her from the waist, penetrating her from behind. Upasana let her chest fall completely forward, holding herself on a lower stand like a chair, low table or cushions. '*This position allows the sperm to better access the cervix.*' A gravelly voice popped up in her head and she tried to block it out. It was a roughened voice of the cold fingers. It belonged to an old lady.

She tried to fight the voice; that was not the reason why she had chosen to have sex with him in this position. The voice laughed aloud – old woman's cackle. It was not why she led him to this spot. He pumped into her, making her moan. She wanted to drown out the old woman's voice with her moans and his grunting. It was true that she had pored over these babymaking articles for hours, but was this old woman her own self? Her own soul?

She shivered in distress. The old woman breathed into her ear.

'This is a version well suited to women who have a tipped uterus.' She kneeled on her fours as Harsh continued penetration from behind. The raucous voice came in her left ear, 'Like the union of the wolf, this position allows the sperm to better access the cervix.' She moaned louder, wanting to shut it out completely.

'The woman sits on the edge of a high piece of furniture and supports herself with her arms behind her. He stands in front while she wraps her legs around him'. She could see a gnarled face, a wide toothless smile, a gluttonous gaze. She shut her eyes. She continued in the same position. The old lady was above his shoulder now, moving with the thumping as Harsh pumped on.

Gleefully she added '*If you were hoping for a boy, you would allow deep penetration in this position. Since you are hoping for a girl though, you will be charged with maintaining shallow penetration during sex. It's generally thought that positions where the man is standing up helps to conceive a boy!*' Upasana could feel it was time. She disengaged the last minute, surprising him and herself. The old woman cackled again. Was she playing a game? She leaned against the wall with her legs slightly spread, facing Harsh. She was in control and she knew he was not. He grabbed her from the thighs and lifted her up, pushing her back into the wall, then thrusting away till he cried his release.'

It was done. The cold fingers loosened their grip from her heart. The old woman disappeared from the window behind the pale pink curtains.

Upasana's heart sang after the coupling, she had what she wanted. She knew she was pregnant. As she woke up with a yawn and stretched herself on the satin sheets she saw him sitting on the couch, all dressed, his suitcase placed next to him. Without him uttering a word Upasana knew he was going to leave her. The recent turn of events clamoured in her brain. Rajjo was dead. The news was doing the rounds already. The video of her self-immolation had been circulated far and wide and debated on every news channel until there was nothing more to be said.

The only logical end and conclusion was ashes to ashes.

Upasana was confident that in his grief Harsh was going to seek her and then be hers. But perhaps she had missed out on something. Her mind raced ahead. Everything was going as per the plan. Harsh was ready to take on his party post, her father was happy with the way things had panned out and she was impregnated by him the night before. So where was the problem?

He was looking at her with a smile. Upasana knew she was not going to like what was coming. She wanted to stop him from talking. She had the same acute sensation before any unpleasant incident occurred in her life. The same needles and pins she felt in her hands and legs before her father gathered her in his arms and broke the news that her mother had succumbed to her illness in the hospital and she was no more.

She heard him say out the nursery rhyme – slowly and deliberately. *One for Sorrow, Two for Joy, three for Girl and four for Boy, five for Silver, six for Gold, seven for a secret never to be told.*

He looked at her accusingly.

'I like the seven part. What about you?'

Upasana knew that he knew. It was all over.

There was a silence between them. There was nothing more to be said. She was not going to stop him, she was not going to ask him questions.

'I knew it before last night.' Harsh looked her in the eye and challenged her with his statement.

A revulsion rose in Upasana. He was fucking her last night knowing that she had tried to get him killed. Upasana wanted to tear at the walls but she just sat on her bed in a heap. He was in control all this while, and he had let her think that she was leading him on. *That son of a bitch!*

Just then she heard his warning tone, 'I gave you your heart's desire, we had unprotected sex, twice, it may lead to a pregnancy. I did that for you. If you come after me, I will not leave you either. I will go after every little scheme that you have hatched in that pretty head of yours all these years and I will expose them.'

Upasana could smell the defeat. She spat at him. 'She is dead, you hear me? That bitch is dead! I don't care where you go because you won't be able to reach her!' There was bitterness and desolation in her voice.'

Harsh gave her a pitiful smile. 'Perhaps I can still reach her, who knows?' Upasana knew she had never loved or hated a man more than she did this man, her husband.' So you will leave your career your family and go where? To the mountains, or cover your body in ash and hide in a cave?'

'Don't worry about me. You can take over the party as a grieving daughter-in-law. My father would love to have the mother of his grandchild take over the party. You are the touch of drama the family needs. You can take over as the wronged woman. You can be the mother of my child, you can keep my name – if you wish – but your punishment is you cannot have me.'

Upasana reached out to slap him as he grabbed her arm tightly and came very close to her ear, his breath on his cheek, like a lover's caress.

'And your atonement is you won't come after me. If you look too close, I will rip you apart, bit by bit.'

She knew Harsh was a good man but she knew him well enough not to court his vengeance. She knew this time he truly planned to get away and this time he did not want anyone to find him.

'How did you know?'Upasana asked in a defeated manner.

Harsh just smiled back.

Something was creeping up her back like an ant and then it started annoying her, it became a spider as it crawled over her lungs and she spat it out, her worst niggling suspicion, 'Is she even dead?'

Harsh in his leather chappals, jeans, a white t-shirt, a mysterious smile – the smell of wood in monsoon, he was out of the door and he was gone. She ran after him, barefoot. 'Just one last thing. I love you in my own way… I will keep your name. I will have the baby and I hope you feel guilty and rot in hell.'

Upasana turned around – happy that she had the last word. She was still victorious. Her father had taught her time and again that victory was everything. She was going to live and die for it.

She saw her husband sit in the white car and drive out of their home and life.

All she heard was an old woman's cackle, lonely and bitter. She hung from the ceiling fan, looking down at her. She whispered from there – 'We won.'

Shivering like an addict denied his dose of heroine, Upasana opened her laptop and uploaded Durga's video again. She needed to see her burn one more time to breathe again.

The pyre burnt ferociously. The fires reached taller than the deodars in the forest behind. The angry flames were ready to eat her up. A faint smell of that ointment was nauseating. Her hair was wet. Her skin glistened with oil. She wore ornaments and trinkets. She wore a glistening red sari. She was a bride ready to meet her lover. The record button was switched on as the camera shook in Devi's hand. She was saying goodbye to her mistress. Just Devi and Rajjo, together, alone in the world.

A long look was exchanged between the two women. Complete trust, complete gratitude, complete harmony that can only be conveyed in a silence. Rajjo looked straight into the camera as she spoke to each and every one of her followers out there.

'*As you keep me so do I remain.*' There was a long pause. Devi mesmerized by Rajjo's beauty continued to capture her. Devi herself wore an identical red sari with a gold border. Dressed like a mirror image of her mistress, she wanted to invite Rajjo's fate upon her.

Kesar, hesitant and wide-eyed, stood there looking at the two women, not daring to breathe.

Devi pressed the record button and handed it to him. Kesar just stood there watching Rajjo talk through the camera, arrested by her gaze. Rajjo's warm smile passed through him, assuring him of better days when the mangoes ripened in the summer on the tree behind their house. She had reached out for him at this hour of need. He was ready to give his life. But for now Kesar was shivering and it was important he kept his hand steady even though his heart was in his mouth.

He focused on the words coming out of Rajjo's mouth. She was a goddess talking to her devotees in her enigmatic voice, her body bathed in oil, her flaming crimson sari draped around her, glistening like a snakeskin. She looked surreal as she spoke into the camera, talking to each and every one of the millions who were watching this video.

'On cold winter nights in our village, my mother would sit by the fire in our courtyard, with me and my siblings sitting around her. If we'd have a tough day she would close the holy book and then open it again, her eyes shut in faith and prayer her finger would hover on the pages, looking for an answer and would stop at a verse. She would read that aloud to us, and that was the message that carried salvation for us that day. One cold night she read this verse out to us and I think I saved it for this day.' Rajjo stared at the camera once again and as if in a trance, repeated the lines. Every word clung to her memory and glided effortlessly from her tongue:

*'The pandits recite the Vedas, the householders assert their faith in family life. The naked renunciates, the wearers of patched coats, the magicians, those who remain always awake, and those who bathe at the holy places of pilgrimage. The ascetics, the hermits, the sanyasis and those who are wise in their own mind: all say they have found the lord but he alone is a devotee, whom the lord has united with Himself!'*

She looked at the camera one last time as she doused herself in oil that consumed her from head to toe. It clung to her clothes, ornaments, face, hair and eyelashes. She kept pouring the silken liquid, the thick dark menacing oil till it filled up her pores. Till her body was ready to offer itself to the hungry flames.

*Abandoning all devices and contrivances, I have sought his sanctuary.*

She turned away from the camera and walked inside the circle of wood. The dramatic pyre created for her in the backdrop of the ancient temple. The wooden pyre was set on fire as the camera zoomed in. The act of Rajjo lighting herself with a matchstick – the sari engulfed in flames within seconds, was captured forever on film. The entire screen was taken over by the burst of fire from the pyre and the body till they became one. The final burst of fire engulfed the spot, rose up to the skies and rained down to the ground. It was yellow, all consuming, definitive, defining the end.

The last words Rajjo had muttered echoed in Kesar's head as the fire consumed her body:

*As God's pen has written on your forehead, so it shall be with your soul.*

A tear escaped his eye as he clicked his mouse and restarted the video clip – to take a look at it one last time before he was going to send it to a nondescript town – from where it was going to reach the entire world.

He reached the part where he saw Rajjo walk into the fire, and then he had to make his magic work. Two figures merged as one. He had worked round the clock for the last couple of days to amalgamate the video. Sitting in a sleepy locality in Seattle, listening to the thunderous rain, Raahat bid adieu to a friend he loved and missed.

His pregnant wife with a sweet smile and a toddler with golden locks and blue eyes glued to her hip looked at him curiously.

'Are you all right? You have been holed up here all day…'

Raahat turned the screen to an angle to shield it from curious eyes.

'Just owed something to a friend that I need to finish. Just give me a couple of hours.'

Raahat could sense the whirlwind of emotion inside him.

She gave him a peck on his cheek and whispered, 'We are right here,' her words like music in the thunderstorm that raged outside.

He could smell the fear of running away from a riot, the relief of finding Rajjo, the comfort of falling in love at the ashram, the stubbornness of following his own path and leaving the religious faction to come to America for a better life, the bittersweet good bye and the parting gift his friend had given him – a life in America. She had done it for him with a sense of betrayal but a deep commitment. She was the only family he had. He wished her peace and happiness. He wished for a chance to say goodbye.

A video played out on the computer. A reporter's face came alive as the picture of a beautiful Godwoman floated on the screen. 'A thirty-four-year-old Godwoman immolated herself in a live camera recording, in the presence of a small-time cable operator Kesar Kishori and a constable at a temple in the outskirts of Manali after claiming that she was taking 'samadhi' for people's welfare. The video she left for her devotees has gone viral and sent the devotees and followers in a frenzy… However, claims that the video was tampered with have drowned in the overwhelming frenzy of her devotees.'

Rano and Karam stared at the video, watching Rajjo was engulfed in flames. 'As the body of Durga Maa was consumed by fire, two witnesses sat on the ground near the pyre and were seen holding their palms together in reverence.

'The question remains what happens to the huge empire that she has left behind. Some initial reports indicate that the assets will be managed by a trust for charitable causes. None of her family members have been given the reigns, but a young cable operator who was with the Godwoman when she threw herself in the pyre will be taking over the trust. The police have taken the cable operator for further questioning.'

Harsh was numb and excited at the same time. He was on his way to freedom. He was heading for Manali. He wanted to visit the place where Rajjo had bid adieu to the world, to her family, to her devotees and to him.

As he crossed many cities in his car, he could see giant posters of Durga covering the cityscapes. Her devotees hailed her as the goddess who took all their sins. Perhaps in her death she found the ultimate love and devotion.

To Harsh, her skin was radiant, her eyes shining and her smile captivating. Every poster he crossed seemed to reach out to him. Rajjo was in his soul and his breath as he reached the outskirts of Manali.

At the foothill of the mountains, the car started turning around the curves of the hills. His eyes wet with tears, he could see her beautiful face. He remembered her dupatta flying in the wind, crimson against the setting sun. She was sad as she saw him leave. He could feel the kiss by the rivulet, her sweet soft lips offering more than taking. He could smell the kites as they made love in Ahmednagar. The sum of his life was the stolen moments he spent with Rajjo. He could almost touch the red fabric that brushed against her face softly as she bid adieu to him against the rising sun. She whispered the story of that legend the whole night, telling Harsh about letting her go away to fulfill her vow. He held on to her tightly and wept. He begged her to change her mind but she was adamant. Now she was gone and the only way to be with her was to go after her.

As he approached the temple ruins, Harsh took a deep breath and instructed the driver to stop the car on the side of the road. He stepped out and smelt the sharp tangy air. He was in the vicinity where Rajjo had passed from this world to the other about four weeks back. Harsh breathed in long and hard, as he believed she was still in the air, in the mountains and in the water around. All he had to do was become one with her.

Harsh had taken the wheel and instructed the driver to wait by the roadside. Confused by the strange request the driver complied. He knew better than to ask questions or resist. He had a job to keep. The worried driver looked at the car dangerously racing away up the hill. He eyed the burning tyres as the car sped off. His master was behaving strangely. He had even thrown his cell phone in a bin. The new phone kit on the backseat of a car also hinted at him buying a new instrument but he did not want to poke his nose too much into his employer's idiosyncracies. However, today his actions seemed more ominous than his usually erratic demands. He knew it was not a good idea to let him drive off. After a brief moment of hesitation, he ran after the squealing tyres as the car took another dangerous and sharp turn.

He took out his cell phone and called 'Madam' on his phone. He had never called her before, only received her manager's calls or taken her calls twice. His palms were sweaty with anxiety as he heard the bell ring. The shrill phone bell rang in his head and shortly after he heard her pick up the phone. An irritated voice barked into the phone. He could hear the tyres squealing. Up, up and up, till he heard a deafening crash.

Rano was in her village ever since Rajjo's disappearance. She felt betrayed and abandoned by her sister. As the days passed and nights wore on, alcohol doused her senses and her pain subsided she realized how desperate she was to hold on to her sister. She had sent people to hunt Rajjo down, to get her back before anyone else got to her. But it was all in vain.

She'd parked herself in the village in her old house and begged her old mother to not reveal her daughter's whereabouts. Saroj was glued to her prayer beads. Rano knew it in her bones that Saroj knew. Finally after repeated attempts Saroj looked at Rano with disdain and said – 'Let her be, she does not need saving.'

Rano was shocked to realize her mother supported Rajjo in her act of suicide. But a tiny wriggling voice said perhaps she was supporting Rajjo's attempt at freedom. Rano played and replayed the video over and over on her laptop, witnessing her self-immolation like million others. It left her numb, it made her cry, it made her sing, it made her howl like a child.

Karam had been on the move ever since Rajjo had disappeared, in a desperate attempt to stop her. Long after her self-immolation video had hit the channels, Karam still refused to give up. While Karam hunted her down Rano prepared to let go. Rano went back into the fields, the fields sparkled golden, the railway tracks as vivid as she remembered. She befriended a grasshopper perched next to her as she sat watching the trains come and go. She sat on their favourite spot day in and day out remembering her time spent with her sister.

She visited the tracks every day to relive the monsoons, the winters, and the little games they played. She was learning to say goodbye to her favourite sister. A part of her was gone forever.

Just when she'd given up hope, she'd heard about the car crash and Harsh's sudden death. It was like a sapling growing in a desert. The bad news had shocked her but also ignited a hope. There was hope that her sister still lived on with her lover.

If that were true, she did not want to catch her or haul her back, she only wanted a sliver of hope that she found her lover and eloped with him like she always wanted. Or perhaps Harsh was truly dead. But Rano lived on in hope, that somewhere in this realm she was breathing, watching the setting sun and remembering the games they played in the village together. She rememberd Rajjo stating emphatically by the railway tracks. 'I will elope from the world.' She had truly done that.

And now, finally, Rano was tired of life. Rajjo had entrusted the task of running the trust to her and the young man Kesar. Rajjo left enough for them to manage and keep busy. She watched a kite floating in the sky without a tether and the kids running barefoot, gleefully trying to catch the thread. The crazy, spirited kite, reminded her of Rajjo. It escaped all attempts to be captured, disappearing into the clouds, leaving behind sadness and a promise. Rano stood and watched the pale red kite disappear in the blue empyrean. They had watched many a kite pass away, hand in hand. Wearing overused frocks, Rano and Rajjo had stood together looking up at the wide blue expanse. Sisters who knew they were there for each other. Rano could jump the highest to catch the thread and go for the kite because Rajjo was two steps behind her. She remembered the pride on her face when Rajjo would snatch the kite and run away. They would meet at the sweet shop as always. They were a team. They trusted each other. But in her last days she looked at her sister with a jaundiced eye. Their eyes never met in the same wide-eyed trust. It pricked her heart, it made her bleed. If only she could hold her hand one last time.

Rano sat next to her old ailing mother who stared on with empty eyes. She finally looked at her daughter Rano and smiled. They were one in their grief, they were one in accepting destiny and they were one in letting her go.

'She called out the weather, she was always right. If she was here tonight she would tell me to gather the clothes and cut the fields, tomorrow it will rain. The heavens will open and the skies will fall.'

On that ominous note Saroj closed her tired eyes. Rano sat in her courtyard hearing the crickets. She heard someone come in through the front door. She knew Karam was back. Harsh's news had brought him back. Karam sat next to her with a sigh. Rano took in the beard of grief and despair on his face. He had aged. Rano offered him the glass of tea she nursed. Karam sipped the tea and sighed like a traveller who was home after a long journey. 'She may be alive after all. Devi is nowhere to be found. There is no way to ascertain that the woman who died was Rajjo.'

'Devi,' smiled Rano.

'She wants to be dead. Leave her be.' That was Rano's final decision and it was evident in her tone.

Karam knew it was the end of the road. Either the stream was going to perish, eaten up by the rocks and mud or find a way to reach the sea and become one with it. He was not going to perish. They sat huddled together drawing comfort from each other.

He held her hand and she settled back. They sat together like comrades, hand in hand. Tired and defeated. 'This was her favourite part when she called the weather...The singing.'

Rano broke into a beautiful song she sang with Rajjo as the clouds gathered. It was an old folk song that described the smell of the mud and the cry of the bangle-seller crossing the street. She could hear Rajjo screaming and running out of the house to the river, wanting to warn people about the broken bridge. Rajjo coloured all her memories. She had no need to look for her outside.

And now all she had was a tired companion. Soon they would have to pick up the pieces and start walking again, hand in hand. Rajjo drew them apart and now Rajjo brought them together again. Rano sensed another salty tear trickle down her cheek. She bid a final adieu to her sister as the raindrops fell in the courtyard. It warmed her soul. It seemed Rajjo was visiting her.

She just stood there getting soaked to the bone with a smile. Karam sat there watching, the raindrops fall. He could hear her laugh in the pitter-patter of the drops. It warmed their hearts as the rain poured from the vaults of heaven. Rajjo was never going to leave them, she was in the raindrops, she was in the wind, she was in the scent of the jasmine, she was in the red kites floating in the sky and she was going to remain as long as the raindrops filled up the seas, for eternity.

Somewhere far away was a man who rowed a boat along the ghats of the Ganga, the evening sun colouring the river orange. The man and the woman sat staring at each other with so much love that it made his heart sing. After ages his throat opened to let the rusty musical notes out, the song he sang for his first love. He sang for the coral river, he sang for the birds, he sang for the two sanguine souls, he sang for the clouds. He sang until the raindrops washed away the tiredness in his soul and filled it with the colour of love.

# ACKNOWLEDGEMENTS

I would like to express my gratitude to the people who saw me through this book; to all those who provided support, talked things over, read, wrote, offered comments, assisted in the editing, proofreading and design.

I would like to thank Amrita Chowdhury; my editor, Charlotte Merritt; and, the entire team at HarperCollins for enabling me to publish this book.

I want to thank my family – Mom, Prakash and Bons, who supported and encouraged me to finish this book.

And my sister Harman, who listens to all my stories with a smile. The good, the bad and the ugly.